BEAUTY OF A CRIMSON SOUL

BOOK ONE

MONICA SHANTEL

BEAUTY OF A CRIMSON SOUL

FEATHERS & FLAMES
BOOK ONE

MONICA SHANTEL

Beauty of a Crimson Soul

Cover art courtesy of author

ISBN 978-1-960696-99-1 (Paperback) 978-1-960696-10-6 (Hardcover)

Second Edition

To all the good girls who've been told following the rules makes them boring.

"Angel"
Monica Shantel
3/14/21

PORTAL TO HELL

SPOTIFY
FEATHERS & FLAMES
PLAYLIST

MONICA SHANTEL

A DEAD THERAPIST

PROLOGUE: GOLD
AYDEN

F ar too large, proud, and entirely not my style. Why were we here again?

"What do you think? Is this the one?" Arabella glanced at me.

With a shake of my head, I said, "I'm deciding university is not for me. What was your plan with this? Take me out of state and change my mind?"

She shrugged. "You don't want to work at the bakery. I figured maybe you wanted some options. You're an adult now, Ayden. You have to make these decisions about your future."

"And who told you? Esme? Mum? Dad? It's all bullshit."

Arabella released a sigh and faced me. "If not this, then why not the bakery? The real bullshit here is you acting like you're too good for us."

"Maybe I am." I jutted my chin, crossing my arms over my chest.

"Screw you." Her eyes watered as she turned on her heel. "I hope this loneliness satisfies you." She disappeared beyond the horizon as I scowled at the building.

University? Who in their right mind would *choose* school?

Just as I thought those words, a blonde girl in a skirt hurried past me, her heels clicking along the pavement. She appeared to be in awe of the school, much less worried about what others thought. She seemed young, too young to even be here. Certainly not university age.

Yet here she was.

"This is the one!" She squealed as she looked over at two adults—who I assumed were her parents.

Her mother smiled and looked up at the large structure. "Are you sure? It's a bit away from home."

The girl shook her head. "Nonsense. It's where I need to be to complete my studies someday. This will be the one. I just feel it in my gut." Her lips curved up, something so deep and genuine that nobody would be able to steal that kind of joy from her.

How did she find happiness here?

Snickering, I walked away from the building and shoved my hands into my pockets. What was I going to do with my life now? I'd disowned my family, and I skipped out on university. Maybe a job would do me good. But which one?

The bell dinged as I entered the shop. A woman emerged from the back room and smiled. "May I help you?"

"I was looking for a job. Possibly."

"Possibly?" She cocked an eyebrow.

I shook my head. "For sure."

"And what brings you to my shop?" She wipes her hands on a towel.

Clocks of all sizes lined the wall. Every colour, every style. Some had numbers, while others had none at all. "What do you think a clock means?"

The owner furrowed her brows. "Excuse me?"

"A clock. Everything has to mean something, doesn't it? Fire. The creatures at the bottom of the ocean. What does a clock mean?"

As she approached a clock in the wall, she pulled it off and laid it face down on the counter. She changed the batteries before looking over at me. "They represent life and death. Nothing lasts forever, does it? It could change at any given time, and that is why we have to cherish those precious moments." She placed the clock back in its spot. "Now, are you really looking for a job or are you just figuring things out?"

A ding echoed as a man in all black entered the shop. With a gun raised, he pointed it at both the owner and I. "You, down on the ground!"

Without questioning him, I lay down and put my hands out for him to see. He proceeded to point at the owner and ask for the money. She narrowed her eyes at him. "And do what, comply? Be left with nothing? I worked my ass off for this business. I'm not handing it over to some entitled prick."

"Put the damn money in the bag!" he yelled, shoving the gun in her face. "I won't ask again."

I swallowed. "Just listen to him. You can make more money down the road but if you lose your life, you won't have a business."

She gave me a pitiful look. "That's not something I can do."

The robber grabbed a fistful of her hair and pulled her from around the counter, forcing her onto her knees. "Wrong move." He pressed the barrel against her temple and pulled the trigger.

Blood splattered the wall of clocks and her body thudded to the floor. He grabbed the keys from her lanyard and opened up the register, shoving money inside.

As he walked to the door, he turned to look back at me. I kept my hands in plain sight, but he approached anyway and grabbed me by my jacket, yanking me up onto my feet. "You've seen too much."

"No, I swear I haven't."

Sirens blared in the distance. I didn't have much time to plead my case.

"I'll go with you if it makes you feel better. I won't say a word." I straightened my clothes.

He scanned my expression for a moment before grunting. "Say anything and I'll be coming for you next." He hurried out of the door and disappeared around the alley corner.

I was left in silence with a corpse at my feet.

Police showed up and entered the building, pointing guns at me. I put my hands up but without a real alibi, I was going to be the suspect here.

I peeked at the corners of the shop only to be disappointed. No cameras. No proof that I wasn't part of this crime. How long would it be before they realised I wasn't him and the real culprit was out there on the run? How long would it be before they realised that no eighteen-year-old could pull this off and vanish?

Right. I didn't vanish though, and I should have. I should have gone with him. Americans took pride in their justice system with the *innocent until proven guilty* mantra.

The man behind me pulled my arms back and cuffed my wrists. Was this better than working at a bakery?

Maybe, or maybe not.

INCARNATION

NINE MONTHS AGO...

*D*eath is the easiest end to a miserable beginning. That was what I thought nine months ago, before I was brutally murdered—my soul ripped from its vessel. What I did not anticipate was the level of difficulty the afterlife weaved together. Between love, heartbreak, and hopelessness, even Heaven appeared like Hell when humans were permitted to mingle with the angels. Humans continued to turn lives upside down and I would never believe otherwise.

The loudest laugh erupted from Selene's throat, pushing away the silence. Anything and everything caused her to lengthen her lifespan by widening her arteries with giggles.

Blood pooled around the actor in the movie. That was what Selene found to be so funny. According to her, the effects were far more cheesy than realistic, and to some degree, I agreed.

With a smile on my lips, I gave her a look. "You have quite a laugh. It wasn't even that funny." Yet, a piece of me was content when she laughed at what I had said.

"I laughed because I thought it was funny. Shaming people for what they laugh at is not cool," she said.

I shrugged, watching her every move. "I know. I guess my humor just doesn't align with yours." My eyes landed on her chips as she snacked on some. She was so free being herself. I'd tried to be myself and yet, I never felt unrestrained. I was constricted by the rules.

People judged me, casting me out of their groups. I wished I could change my personality, but that effort took more time than I had.

"Tell me about that boy who was staring at you," Selene said as she turned her head my way.

Furrowing my eyebrows, I shook my head. "Boy? Where?"

Another laugh. "The one by the far table in the cafe. He seemed really cute."

I searched my brain for this memory before it popped up. "Oh, I think you're talking about Sam. I don't know. I think he's just being a creep. He would never want to date Eliana Wilson." It wasn't that I was insecure, but it weighed more on the fact that I was not eye candy for the average college guy.

"Stop it. I hate when you talk like that. If he likes you, you can't help that." She wiggled her index finger in my direction. She had such a pure *soul*. She sat up as her phone pinged. Reading the message, her smile grew wide. "He wants to hang out. I'll see you soon!" She rushed out of the room as I laughed to myself. Nothing could compare to the feeling of being alone. *Yet, now I spent every day without a soul by my side.*

I suppressed that emotion. I was not going to allow jealousy to eat me alive. I wanted to be everything she was, but I couldn't be. I desired her presence to keep me company, but that void would never be sewn back together. There was nothing interesting about me according to the human population.

I sat on my bed, the ache growing in my chest. The movie continued to play and more people bled out until they were no more.

Who ever survived a horror movie?

A knock echoed throughout the dorm hours later. I answered the door. "Yes?" It was her boyfriend, Liam, the very man she left me to go hang with instead.

"Something happened." His face reflected a deep torment that I could not begin to process. "Something bad happened to her."

I followed him out of the building, taking in my surroundings. Outside the college was a parking lot with small buildings surrounding it, all for the students, but beyond that was a road sandwiched between fields. He led me to one of the fields, and I recognized her brown hair immediately. "No. Liam, tell me this isn't true." I covered my mouth, praying it was a stupid prank.

He walked closer to her body. "I just went to go get us some drinks. We were going to have a winter picnic." His stares showed me an emotionless void, one where he couldn't comprehend that this was our reality. "It sounds so stupid now that I think about it. When I came back to finish our date, someone had killed her. I didn't know who else to turn to," his voice croaked.

I shook my head as the anger and sorrow controlled my mind. They began to cloud all logic. "Tell me this is a sick joke. Please, tell me." I glanced at him, tears threatening to fall.

"I can't tell you that because it's true." His eyes began to water. I had never seen him cry but there was a first for everything.

I let the waterfalls go free and my cheeks warmed up as the liquid rolled down my face. I stared at the cause of this pain—the lifeless body sprawled across the frozen ground. Selene was gone now, and I had to live with that.

Blood soaked into the frost, tainting the grass beneath.

I didn't want to see her anymore. I turned my eyes in a different direction, letting my own tears blur the sight before me. I didn't want to believe it, but it was true. Someone killed Selene. How could they?

"She was so sweet and happy. She didn't hurt anyone. Whoever did this is pure evil, someone who doesn't deserve to see the light of day again."

"I don't know. I don't know why anyone would do this to her." He came over to me, putting his hand on my shoulder.

The cold air could not harm me. I felt nothing as it rushed against my bare legs, reminding me of who I lost. I wiped my cheeks, as my glasses shielded my eyes from my hands. "I'm going back to the dorm." I looked at her once more. "I can't believe this is her body. She deserved better." I turned away from her.

"I'm going to call the police," Liam said in a whisper, his eyes still glued to the hollow shell of Selene now without a soul. Although, I could not be certain that it was gone just yet. Nobody but God knew how long it took for a soul to exit the vessel after death.

I faced him, saying, "Let me say goodbye. Let me just have a chance in case her soul hasn't left her body or is somewhere nearby." I scanned the area in case I caught a glimpse of her fighting to come back to us. It wouldn't do any good since her throat had been sliced open.

Kneeling down next to her, I said in a quiet voice, "I am so sorry. I didn't mean for this to happen to you. I would have saved you. I could have helped you. I should've protected you."

She didn't respond.

I sighed to myself, looking away from her pale frame. That was all she was demeaned to. Her body had been a vessel for her soul before it could pass on into the next life. I could only hope I would see her again someday.

Liam returned, putting his phone into his pocket. "I called the police." I nodded in response.

I studied the scenery, taking note of the season's mood.

The earth was frigid. Everything dead, including her. The trees had lost their warmth, leaves rotting into the ground. The field was a muted green with a white cover as the frost had coated every strand. The white flakes began to fall as if mourning for our loss today. Fog poured in from every direction, claiming the air as its home.

Trees stood far and few, their dozens of arms reaching out for help as the snow threatened to hide them from existence. They looked almost *human*, withering away until the next season came.

Unique flakes began to stick to the earth, taking ownership of the weather. Within minutes, a thin sheet of white ruled the town, not ready to give up now.

The air was thin and dry with just a hint of liquid as the snow began to hydrate in its own form. My own breath formed before me, forming a cloud in front of my lips with every exhale I made. The temperature gradually dropped one degree, dying with us after our own loss.

Winter was on our side, and it didn't come to harm or hurt, but rather to comfort us. It wanted to let everyone know that Selene meant something. She mattered, and this cold evening was not going to let anybody forget.

As I stepped back at the sight of flashing red and blue lights, my toe pressed against the fresh snow, making a soft cry for assurance. It was letting me know that it was here for me, here to feel my pain and regrets.

I shoved my hands in my pockets as the snow tried to stick to her body, doing its best to wash away the blood. The gesture was thoughtful, but it was not going to work. Snowflakes were just too weak.

The police approached us, peeking around our figures to see the dead body. Selene would live on in my heart and I was going to make sure of that.

Liam came over, answering questions and telling them his story.

He knew I was in no state to talk. Eventually, I would have to tell the police the same thing. However, a few more minutes to understand the situation couldn't hurt.

I walked back to my dorm after answering whatever they wanted to know. Now noticing the color—or lack of—of my legs, I walked inside, locking my door. They were colorless with a mixture of purple and blue, begging me to bring them back to life. I fell onto my bed, hugging my pillow and giving a good squeeze.

Shaking my head, I put the pillow against my face. I screamed into it and let it eat my frustrations. I could not even begin to fathom the idea that she was lost in the puzzle of her own murder.

I got off my bed and swiped a pencil off my nightstand. I snapped it into two, yelling out in anger. The anger was aimed at me for letting her go. A storm brewed within me as I played a scene of her begging for mercy and being given a death certificate.

I couldn't even allow the idea that cops would take pictures of her body to fill my brain with evil thoughts. I didn't want her to be another unsolved murder in their files that went forgotten. I shouldn't have allowed her to be on display forever as a victim, being remembered only in a state of horror. She should not have been famous for being slaughtered.

I paced back and forth, wondering if this was going to be negotiable. Maybe I could get her back. I'd sacrifice myself instead.

"God, what if I take her place? She had so much to live for. She had it going for her. I have nothing. I have a future of maybe being successful, but what good is that if she would have a future of getting married and raising better people for this world? Work with me, please. I think making money doesn't come close to making this world a better place, not as much as it would if she were to raise amazing humans who could be a part of the change," I begged.

I folded my arms, looking up at the ceiling. "Can you hear me? Please. I swear, I will do anything. I just want her to have her life back. Please, let her have her life."

I did this all day long. I was praying and requesting that we switch places. That was all I desired. *I had never predicted that He would take me up on this offer. Sometimes He did consider bargains.*

I lay on my stomach in bed, my hair unbrushed. Pajamas enveloped me and I didn't bother to fix the shorts riding up my butt. I pulled the covers over me, covering my ears as the alarm rang for me to get up and go to class. I refused. I denied.

My mind drifted off in the color of the walls. Blue. It was blue just like the pain I felt. Blue—the color of sadness. It was exactly how I viewed the world.

Beep. Beep. Beep.

How did anyone go on like this? I didn't want to continue without her. I couldn't. Selene had been everything to me. She had helped me with anything that I ever needed a guide to. She was charming and kind, and she was worth more than the world itself. Why her?

Beep. Beep. Beep.

I'd remembered all those times that she taught me what the abbreviations meant when students used them. She taught me how to be social. She was my friend and yet I had let her heart stop within seconds.

Beep. Beep. Beep.

Depression devoured my happiness, crushing it with the weight that laid on my shoulders. It kept me pinned to this bed, not letting me go. *Desolation* kept me hostage in this box.

The tears started again, soon turning into sobs. Nothing about this was fair. I could not begin to explain the burden in my head. It forced down every bit of me, crumbling my inner being. Life would never return to normal with a piece of my heart consumed by agony.

Beep. Beep. Beep.

I had gone my whole life without someone to love. I loved her like a sister who didn't need to return the favor and yet she did. She had been my mentor to surviving college. She kept the bullies away. She made me feel like I was worth more than just my thoughts.

Selene never even got a thank you. I didn't get to say goodbye. She vanished in the blink of an eye. We never truly knew what it was like to lose someone, and we never realized how short life was until it was too late. We all had limited time with the people we cared most about.

Beep. Beep. Beep.

A few months were all I was given with her. She taught me so many things that nobody else had wanted to tell me. She enlightened me about how to make friends.

My heart ached for her to come back, but she never was coming back. I begged God to assist me in trading places with her, but He didn't listen. She got the worse end of the stick and I couldn't even fix it.

The alarm still yelled in my ear, blaming me for the entire situation. My anger rose from the depths and I slammed my hand onto the button that shut it up. If I could bring her back again, I would do whatever it took.

However, I was helpless.

I folded the last of her used laundry and took extra care of her possessions. I smelled her shirt, not daring to wash the scent of her out of her own clothes. They were hers and not mine to mess with.

Putting them in a plastic bin, I sealed the lid. Her bed was made this morning with every corner in the perfect position. I had been sleeping in her bed for comfort every night since. She would always be my best friend and the sister I never got.

I walked over to the window and watched life move forward outside these walls. The snow had melted again, but I knew it would return in a few days. A repeat of last year. And the year before.

The room made not a single peep when I turned around to observe the deserted half of her side. I grabbed some bobby pins to pin the strands that hung from my bun in an uncontrolled environment.

Today was a new day.

Selene had been like a sister to me, the other half I'd been missing my entire life, but I had to begin to move on. I would take what she taught me and use it, making sure she knew she was still with me somehow.

I put on my heels, tightening the straps of the buckles. I straightened my posture and studied myself in the mirror to ensure everything was in place. I fixed the collar of my shirt, folding it down nicely.

A knock echoed through my door and I wondered who would bother coming for me. Not a single soul cared about how I was doing.

As I answered it, surprise dominated my expression at the sight of Liam. "What are you doing here?"

Furrowed brows. Tight mouth. "I've been thinking about what happened to Selene. I want to figure out who murdered her, and I need you to help me."

I would have been an abominable friend if I'd told him no.

EPIPHANY

If humans told people that they didn't deal with death and the consequences of Hell after the last heart would beat within a body, they were liars. They had no idea what happened in a place they had never visited. But I knew.

I kept a lookout while Liam studied the crime scene. My eyes scanned every area surrounding us, confirming nobody suspected a thing. "How is this going to help? She's dead. We need to try this in a different way and become a genius like the one kid on that show."

The area of her murder was blocked off with police tape until they got what they needed. The police had started their investigation as we started our own. Both of us had to be careful as to how we went about this. If we were caught snooping, the cops would have a chat and kick us off the team. I was not about to lose my opportunity to have justice served for the most important person who was once in my life.

"Technically, I'm the sexy agent who puts himself in the scene." He gave me a slight smirk.

I cleared my throat, noticing how still and quiet it was. It amazed me that this place stopped for her. Nothing but respect was given for

Selene's passing.

"I'm not much of a detective. I'm using most of my knowledge from the show." I scrunched my face while in thought. "Wait, this is an open field. Could someone not have seen her? Could they not have heard her screams? The school is right over there." I pointed to the building a mile away.

I tilted my head, getting immediate chills all down my body. Today was just as cold as the dead but the *fog* was missing.

"We can go around and ask people if they'd seen anyone." He nodded and stood from kneeling on the ground.

I sighed a bit. "Well, we have to go about this the right way. We aren't actual detectives or FBI. We are kids. If people start questioning, the police will notice and we will be kicked out of our own investigation." That was the last thing I wanted.

"Why don't you want the police to solve her murder?" he asked out of curiosity.

I turned to face him, hands balled up in my cardigan pockets. "Because it makes her famous. She doesn't deserve to be famous for something like this. Her murdered pictures should not be out for everyone to see. I don't want people to hear her name and say, *the girl who was murdered like this?* I want her image to be kept pure for who she was and not for who she ended up as. I don't trust the police to know her like I did."

He came over and gave me the most awkward hug I had ever experienced. "That's a valid explanation. You care about her. We don't have to let the police mess up our investigation. We'll do this ourselves. How hard can it be? Agents are humans, too, and if they can solve a murder, so can we."

I nodded, my chin hitting his shoulder. "Thank you."

He began to walk back to the campus to ask anyone if they saw anything.

I spun on my heel, but something caught my eye. I walked over to the empty spot where her body had lay, as close as I could get without crossing the caution tape. Images flashed through my mind, haunting me with the last portrayal of Selene Miller.

Her throat slashed, showing us a sliver of the inside of her neck. Blood stained her skin, clothes, and the earth hugging her figure.

The metallic smell of her crimson filled the air with its horrifying scent. Her skin pure white, no longer a tan complexion. Her glass eyes had watched the world go on without her. As hard as I tried, I could never erase this memory from my mind.

Moving on from the crime scene, I followed him into the cafeteria. This was *quite* the location to interrogate students. This area resembled a food court at a mall with multiple restaurants lined up so students could pick what they were in the mood for. I was in disposition for justice.

I waited a few feet away from Liam as he asked others what they might have known about Selene's killer or her murder.

He approached me when he had enough answers to report something worth mentioning.

I asked, "Why hasn't the campus done anything about her murder? What is going on in the office?"

"Well, from my knowledge, college isn't exactly reliable. They are never concerned with their students feeling safe. We have a lot more work to do."

We headed back to my dorm. Her empty bed was a constant reminder of who I was missing in my life.

I took a few steps towards mine and grabbed my computer, turning it on. If the police had leaked any new information to the public, it made our crime-solving that much easier to guide us.

I looked over at Liam, noticing the tears in his eyes. I had forgotten about his pain while dealing with my own. "I'm so sorry. I wish I could say it was going to get better."

He wiped his cheeks, refusing to show any misery. "I'm fine. I'm doing great."

I put my computer down and gave him my full attention. He deserved that much. We both had lost someone special a few days ago. "No, you're not. I know how much it hurts me to deal with this and I can only imagine it hurts you the same. You were together for a long time. You were happy and I knew she was falling in love with you. You can't pretend you're fine. I'm a woman and we know that fine doesn't mean fine. It's okay to show your pain. Nobody expects you to be a rock. You're human and we all hurt." I put my hand over the top of his. I didn't want him to bottle up his sorrow. "Men are allowed to have emotions. There is no universal law against it. It's just a stupid standard that other men teach you. You don't owe them your obedience."

Liam laid his head against my shoulder. "I wish it were that easy, Eliana, but it's not. When you grow up believing something, it takes a lot more than one conversation to make you believe otherwise."

A drawled-out breath left my lips and I bothered not to say another word about it. I was not about to argue with the only other person who understood what I was going through. "Why did this have to happen to her? Why does anything have to happen like this? Death sucks. Loss sucks."

He patted my other shoulder in a gentle gesture to comfort me, but it didn't work well.

I set my laptop back in my lap. "Okay, so the police mention some suspects in custody but won't name who. They say they know that this kind of killer is out for blood and vengeance for whatever reason people kill for. He wants to kill because he's sick." I let out a low groan. This was going to be much harder than I anticipated. The information was so vague and yet so common. It could be anybody at this point in the search.

"How are we supposed to find someone who doesn't want to be found?" he asked.

I shook my head, shrugging a little. "I don't know. We must try. I won't let her murderer get away. He will pay for taking Selene's life. He will just end up killing more people if he isn't caught. If he does…" I couldn't finish my sentence. If he had killed Selene, *I* could be next.

"We won't let him kill anyone else. He has a pattern which we can find if we study him as the FBI would. We know how to find a serial killer. It's the least we can do for Selene." He grabbed hold of my shoulders, forcing me to face him. The thing keeping me locked on this scrutiny was the love Selene taught that I had within me.

I nodded as I rubbed my eyes underneath my glasses. I fixed them again and took my heels off. "You can go figure out some more clues if you'd like. I'll stay here and finish the research." We both had forgotten one key to tracking a serial killer. We needed to study all their victims and as far as I knew, Selene was his only victim thus far.

Liam left me to my own thoughts. The cold rushed to my shoulders and I wondered if I would ever be embraced by warmth again. Being so close to *death*, I craved love. The one person who gave me that had left so suddenly, and now I was alone. Liam was the only friend I had, and he wasn't even mine to call friend. He was Selene's boyfriend.

I explored more on the killings around this area, seeing if any more had connections to any that might have been off campus. If he had killed others, we could find a signature.

It just didn't make much sense to me how this guy had killed our own student and nobody cared. The faculty could care less about our safety.

My eyes landed on her side of the room. "I wish you were here." I lay back against the bed, staring at the screen of my laptop for too long. I needed a break from the blue light.

Mine was expressed through red, black, and white but hers showcased her colorful character. Minimalism was advocated for by the lack of decorations. I never chose to embellish my dull personality. I didn't need my room to look pretty and distract me from my homework, or in this situation, take my attention away from this case.

She had a lot of aesthetic things on her side, including plants, jewelry on its adorable handmade organizer, some antique wall clocks, a little shelf with books, and more. I had books on my side, too, but those were for educational purposes. A few were fun little reads because I did wish to escape this world every now and then through solving mysteries.

It was the only reason I felt qualified enough to solve her murder. I never thought I would have to do such a thing, but it was all I could do to pay her last respects.

My mind wandered to how Liam was doing with the clues. I wasn't sure how much better he was doing than I was, but it had to be a step up compared to my attempts. I was getting nowhere. I was far too busy reminiscing over Selene.

Memories ran rampant through my head, ones about all those times she showed me where the cool kids would hang out around campus. I yearned for the way she laughed at my dumb jokes that were never even meant to be funny. I ached for when she would tell me about her and Liam going on a date. I longed for her to talk to me again. I was utterly solo in life. *The same could be said now that my soul had vacated my body. Selene was nowhere to be found up here.*

I wanted to get her back, but I knew it wouldn't happen. I'd tried to bargain with God, but He didn't negotiate with me. I was determined to just find her killer instead and put him away forever. He warranted being locked up because nobody else deserved the destiny of demise. Nobody earned it to begin with.

Soft hums passed through my lips as I aimed to keep myself sane through this whole process. I pondered what we would be doing if she were still here. We would be watching movies and laughing at the stupid decisions people made.

Sitting up from the scenes in my head, I let out a loud sigh. I couldn't do this on an empty stomach.

I grabbed my heels and put them on, getting up and venturing over to the cafeteria building. My decisions were split between multiple shops, my brain rejecting any choices. What was I in the mood to eat? Nothing. I wasn't craving anything, but my stomach sure was. I knew I had to feed it or my brain power would begin to weaken.

My final verdict was pizza with a salad. The salad was there to even out the poor option of greasy cheese and pepperoni.

I took a bite, taking an entire pepperoni along the way. I observed the students, studying their behavior. Everyone became a suspect in this crime, and I would need to remember to take precautions with every person I conversed with. Nobody was trustworthy.

I watched one girl toss away a half-eaten sub sandwich. I couldn't comprehend the waste of food. It was disgusting that people could waste good meals when children starved. Were they not appreciative? No, they never understood how privileged they were.

That didn't make her a killer, though.

My eyes caught a boy who looked around and picked his nose when he thought nobody was watching. He had no manners, and his high school behaviors carried with him into college.

I turned my attention to a couple. I didn't suspect this would be a Bonnie and Clyde type of kill. This was done by an individual. The toughest part would be discovering who that human being was. My guess on the gender was male. Most serial killers were men, and they desired that power over others.

I finished my pizza and salad when I gave up on watching booger-eaters and food-wasters. I made sure to enjoy every bite of my lunch to make up for the wasted subway in the trash. The crunch of the lettuce blended with the croutons, filling my ears with a pleasant sound.

Chewing crunchy foods had always been pleasant, if it was done by me and not anyone else.

Misophonia was something I certainly struggled with.

Liam found me in the corner and came over. "Okay, I have some information now."

"What did you find?" I threw away my empty paper plates when all food resided inside my stomach.

We were stuck in a rut with this case and I was clawing to get out.

"It turns out some of their suspects all have something in common. They're well-known people. They are all male, probably around their late thirties. They're all potential losers who have no friends or girlfriends." He nodded as he concluded his findings. That ruled me out, being female and all. I didn't want to be a suspect.

I nodded and scanned the room. "All right, so we just have to look for a male who is nothing but an outcast like I am, the male version of Eliana Wilson." A nervous laugh escaped my lips. "Easy enough."

PARABLE

How so much bloodshed painted my life, yet I found my way into the light was beyond my comprehension. Did I belong here? Justin never thought so. He had despised me. Darkness engulfing our lives did not decide where we ended up when our last breath passed our lips. I knew this to be true because I flew where angels laughed.

Snow fell from the skies, mourning the emotions blanketing everyone who knew Selene. I couldn't think of a time when I hadn't seen a white winter and experienced sorrow. It would always remind me of when she left too soon.

Her funeral was in a few days, after Christmas would be over. Her parents did not want to taint the holiday with the death of their daughter but that was too late for me. This celebration was poisoned with bad memories no matter which direction I went.

I couldn't seem to stop thinking about her. It just felt so wrong without her by my side. This wasn't home anymore. I missed laughing with her. She made me see the joy in life. It all had felt so natural around her.

This room was lonely now, even if I was still *alive*. I longed for the morning when I had to wake her up for school. I wanted her to tell me about the drama that she got involved in. I wished to listen to her go on about things she felt passionate about, things that made her whole world worth living.

But she was not here anymore...

Selene had been home to me; she was where I lived. I was homesick for her, and just her alone. I was a stranger in this room. I was an intruder who did not belong, disrespecting the depths of friendship she left behind.

She had been everything this universe needed and more. She was my best friend, sister, and mentor. She made me feel like I mattered to this world. She made this a home that would now forever be empty and broken. The hollowness swallowed me up, threatening to take my place. I would be nothing without her existence.

She was always the life of this dorm. She brought that energy everywhere she went. I was not at home without her bringing that vibe. For a few minutes, I'd forgotten what it was like to have her around. This would have been my first Christmas with someone who wanted to be near me. Now my home was torn apart. Nothing was right. Everything in this room felt like the empty box abandoned in grandma's basement. Selene was *never* coming home again. Despite that reminder, the memories flooded like a dam giving way.

"Elli, you have to do it like this." She groaned and pulled her hair back, showing me how to properly French braid my own hair.

I smiled a bit, coming up with excuses on the spot. "Can't you just do my hair? I like it when you do. Gives me chills."

Our eyes met through the mirror in front of us. "You'll never learn if I do it for you. I won't always be around." She hadn't known how true that statement was at the time. Unfortunately for me, I could not French braid without her to this day.

"Why do you call me Elli?" I tried to grab my hair the way she did

hers, but I was causing a tangled mess.

"Why not? I think everyone deserves a nickname. It makes them feel closer and more involved in the relationship." She shrugged as she watched me screw up my hair. She let out a sigh. "Let me do it."

I smiled and let go of the strands. I just didn't like doing my own hair. I enjoyed the feeling of someone doing it for me. That was why I always threw it up in a bun. I never knew how to do anything else.

She stood behind me, brushing through my hair. She began to braid it, humming between us both. "Liam is amazing. Last night he took us out to a beautiful restaurant. When someone spilled wine on my dress, he didn't go crazy like the other dates in my past. A man who can control his temper is a keeper." Her reflection in the glass smiled at me.

I returned the smile. "I'm glad you found your true love story."

"You'll find one, too. Any man who doesn't want you is crazy. You might be quiet, but the quiet ones also have so much to say. He will love to hear what you have to think about everything." She finished the braid, keeping it together with a ponytail. "Beautiful." If only she had been correct about him *wanting to listen to my thoughts...*

I watched her as I touched it. "When we leave this dorm, will we stay in touch?"

She came to the side of me and sat. "Of course. Elli, you're my friend. I will always be there for you. Everyone needs support. Everyone needs a shoulder to cry on." And now I had none.

My eyes were directed at the ceiling while tears poured down my cheeks. "Come back, Selene. I need support. I need a shoulder to cry on." A sob broke out of my chest.

I heard a knock on the door. I wiped my pain in a hurry as I answered it. Liam noticed my state despite my attempt to hide it. Puffy eyes took more time to get rid of. "Oh, I'm sorry. I didn't mean to come at a bad time," he said.

I shook my head, dismissing his apology. "It's fine. I just wish she would come back is all."

"Do you wanna talk about it? I miss her too." He came in and turned to face me, his question trailing off.

I closed the door behind him.

"It's just not fair!" I yelled. I sat on my bed, letting the sadness flow of its own free will once again. "She was my only friend. She meant everything to me. Tomorrow is Christmas and I was supposed to see her. I was meant to spend my first Christmas with her. I'd never had a real holiday and she was supposed to change that. She's not even here, and I don't know how else to feel except for angry. It's the worst holiday I've ever had."

He asked, "You've never had a good Christmas?"

"No." I didn't want to talk about that. It was not about me. I wanted to focus on getting justice for Selene. "I just miss her so much." I played with my skirt. "It feels so wrong with her gone."

He sat next to me and pulled me in, letting me cry on his shoulder. I had nobody else to comfort me and share my hurt.

I released more pain and tears, mourning for her life. It would be like this for the rest of my days on this earth. "I want her back. I want her to come back. If she doesn't come back, how am I supposed to have friends?"

"I'll be your friend," he said.

I pulled back and rubbed my eyes. "No... Someday you are going to get married and have a family. You're going to meet a beautiful woman. I don't want to get in the way of that." I stood from my bed and looked at the one on the other side of the small room, the bed that had not been touched by her in almost a week. "She used to sleep there. She stayed up late, texting. We would watch movies. We balanced each other out. She helped me live a little and I kept her in check so she wasn't missing important classes." I swallowed.

"She told me you would wake her up early." He chuckled a little.

I gave a short nod, eyes fixed on the blankets. "I did. I woke her up so early. I would wake her as soon as I could, making sure she wouldn't fall back asleep. She would do that a lot. She tried to go back to bed. She told me I was the only reason she even had good grades. She helped me socialize and I helped her with her schoolwork."

Liam stayed silent, allowing me to go on.

"That was how we met. We became roommates here. She used to ask me why I was quiet and if I had friends. When I told her that I was not the type to make friends, she called that bullshit. She said everyone needed a friend. She told me we could help each other out. That was when she came up with the system. She taught me to socialize and come out of my shell. I kept her in classes, guiding her through the academic part of college. She helped me survive the social aspect." I approached the window and stared into the iciness that infected the town.

Liam didn't say a word. I was grateful that he was listening. I just wanted someone to hear me. Without Selene, I needed someone to be open to me talking about how wonderful she was.

"I should go console her parents and let them know that I'm here and I'll remember Selene for the wonderful human she was. It's only right." I cleaned my eyes from sorrow and spun around to face the room. I put some heels on. "I'm going to go alone if you don't mind. You can start your list of suspects. We'll do better if we cover more ground."

With a nod, he got off my bed. "That sounds fair."

He left for his duties while I drove to her house. It was way out there so it was quite the trip. Every song that played seemed to recognize that Selene was gone. They all sang depressing lyrics in tune with her demise.

The trees flew by in a blur, ending up behind me. The road was long and barren of other drivers. With the snow out, I had to drive slower and turn on my headlights. I would never risk my life. I was not going to lose my common sense when it came to driving and give up on justice for Selene.

Justin didn't think the same way. Even being sick, he valued not even an ounce of what mattered. He craved self-gratification.

I arrived at her parents'. It was a large family home on the older side of the spectrum. A dark, ugly brown paint coated the outside. The house was still standing, refusing to give up its functionality as a home but it was beginning to wear down.

I walked up the front, wooden steps and took a deep breath before knocking on the door.

A woman answered it. "Yes?"

"Hello, are you Selene's mom?" I asked.

"Yes, who's asking? How did you know Selene?" She straightened her posture, opening the door a bit more. Red tinted the white of her eyes and her cheeks had been stained from the tears she shed for her one daughter.

"I was her roommate." I decided to correct myself, "I was her friend."

Worry took hold of her expression. "Oh, dear, come inside. You look like you're freezing." She waved me in and closed the door. She grabbed a blanket off the back of her couch and wrapped it around my shoulders. "Have a seat." She gestured to the sofa and I planted myself on it.

"Thank you. You have a lovely home." I looked around, admiring the little decor that was placed in a careful manner throughout the area.

"You're welcome here. Any friend of Selene's is a friend of ours." She smiled a little, but the despair was embedded deep within her eyes. "Would you like anything? Tea?"

"No, thank you. Water is just fine," I assured her.

"Who chooses water over tea?" she joked, laughing a bit and going to get me a glass of water.

I took a moment to take in my surroundings. I could see how Mrs. Miller was attempting to handle the loss of her baby.

The house was filled with a lot of antique items, expressing a different era of history. The aura of this home was beautiful and nostalgic, but also sorrowful. Without Selene, this house was not a complete home.

The staircase stood off to the side of the house, against the wall. Family pictures hung about, reminding everyone of who owned this home and who was related to who. The theme was of muted warm colors with gold to top it all off.

Her mother brought me my glass of water. "Oh! Let me get my husband." She left and brought back her husband. "This is Selene's father." I got off the couch to shake his hand before seating myself again. "She was friends with Selene," she said to him.

He turned to look at me. "Why is she here with us?"

The desolation washed over me like a wave. "She was my roommate and best friend. Ever since her death, I've been trying to figure out how life can go on without her. Your daughter was an amazing person." A few tears escaped my eyes.

They let me have a moment to recollect myself, but the sorrow clouded their eyes.

"She was murdered and I didn't stop it. I found her in the field outside the school after someone killed her." I closed my eyes, swallowing the lump. The silence closed in on us. It was all we heard for miles.

I heard the sobs rack through Mrs. Miller, and her husband had to gather a hold on her. She was too buried into the pain of loss to speak a coherent sentence.

Pulling the blanket around myself, I gripped it tighter. "I'm so sorry. I've spent the past few days grieving. We have been trying to get justice for her. Without her, I feel so alone. I just find it so hard to live without her by my side. Your daughter was incredible. I want you to know that." I lifted my eyes at them, wiping the tears as I sniffled.

Her mother continued to cry into her father's chest.

They deserved to know. "Selene was the only friend I had. She made me feel special. She was such an amazing person and I wanted you to know that you had raised such a beautiful daughter. She will not die in vain. I will make sure she gets justice and she the proper memorial. I promise." I closed my eyes once more, unable to see the hurt dwelling inside her parents. "She didn't deserve this. I can say that her life was well-lived. She will always be remembered."

"What do you mean you'll make sure she gets justice?" I opened my eyes at the sound of his voice. Her father faced me, but his eyes iced over that even fire couldn't melt.

I was not quite sure what he was getting at. "Liam and I have decided to do our own investigation. We knew Selene and we have a better chance to find her killer."

Her mother was able to catch herself after losing many tears. "How do you have the nerve to say you knew her? They are trained professionals and you need to let them do their job. I will not let some inexperienced kids mess this up and destroy our lives. Selene is our daughter and we trust them to find her killer."

I could understand their concern, thinking that we would be the stupid children screaming for the adults to lock away someone we thought did it. Her parents had been suffering in misery for quite some time and they never had a chance to say goodbye. The last thing they wanted to hear was about the two kids meddling in their daughter's murder case.

I swallowed my fear. "It's time for you to leave," Mr. Miller told me, "and if we hear about you trying to get involved, we will have you banned from this investigation and there will be a restraining order against you. Am I clear?"

I confirmed his request with a nod, standing from the couch. They turned against me in a matter of minutes. Grief was a force to be reckoned with and I couldn't do anything to make it better.

INCENSE

*H*ere, I stood, watching him waste away. Justin had noticed me and yet he never carried with him the family who loved him. He had abandoned them before I had a chance to meet the people who shaped who he was. Now, his lifeless body was all my fault.

My toes begged for socks—socks I did not wear. My heart had been numbed and frozen, so why did it matter if my toes followed suit? Walking through the school triggered a love so deep, it could never be erased. This was where I had first met Selene and forever here was where she would reside.

I took in the layout of my new room, setting my bags on the bed to the left of me. A deep breath was exhaled from my lungs and the nerves tingled at the thought of my roommate. I wasn't prepared for my junior year of college.

The beginning of every year proved difficult for me as I tried to make sure my roommates were tolerable. I didn't want to end up with someone I couldn't stand to be around.

Opening my suitcase, I searched through the items inside. I had brought only essentials and things I could fit into it. Those consisted of clothes and bathroom necessities. I didn't have much with me. I'd never had a lot of things.

I began to unpack the luggage and fold the clothing in a neat pile, laying them inside the drawer. Someone entered the dorm, her footsteps firm and solid. She must have been my roommate.

I turned around to greet whoever it was. A brunette girl stood in front of me, a prominent smile on her face. "Hi, I'm Selene. I'm assuming you're my new friend?"

I nodded a little, confused by her usage of the term friend, and I put my clothes down. "I'm Eliana. I won't bother you much. I am usually quiet, and I don't have any friends to come hang out with me. It's just me and my books."

She tilted her head, eyebrows knitted together. "You're a lone wolf?"

"Whatever that is, I'm it." I pointed at her, nodding again.

She laughed a little and set her stuff on the other bed. "Don't worry. We can be friends. I think it's a good idea to get along with the person you live with. Besides, everyone needs a friend. Without friends, how do we feel like we mean anything?" She shrugged.

I was a bit taken back by her words. I had never met someone like her before. Most people refused to make the effort to befriend me.

"So, Elli, do you mind if I call you that?" she asked. I shook my head and she went on, "I was thinking that maybe we could help each other out. You don't seem like the social type. I can help you with that. Is there anything you're good at that could help me?"

"I'm good with school, academics, and what other synonyms you can think of." I didn't know how to properly respond to her. She was really beginning to confuse me all the way down to my bones.

She nodded a lot, her head bobbing up and down. "Great! I suck, so we can help each other in those areas and be great friends. What should we do first, new roomie?" She smiled big.

This girl was so out there unlike any other roommates I'd had in *the past. How could someone like this exist? I would never answer that question. I would never be able to.*

"I'm not too sure. This is all new to me." I gestured to the room.

She came over and peeked at my stuff. "I think maybe we should go shopping. I have to get some new decorations and I could find out what your taste is. I can tell that you're an interesting person." She wouldn't think the same if she knew what I was doing now, investigating her murder myself.

I carried my bag with me at my side and walked around the school. I was trying to get myself on my feet, looking for any clues. I kept myself moving to distract myself from the reality that was.

The floor was covered with a dark, thin carpet to keep my heels silent. The walls were of a plain, white color, making it classic and uniform. Windows were at the end of the halls where the doors leading to the outside stood. Classrooms, bathrooms, and offices lined every hallway.

I looked at the picture of her that hung on the wall in the main hall. It was by itself, surrounded by flowers that were sitting in vases on a stand in front of her image. Everyone was remembering her name now. Everyone was giving her the proper memorial she deserved after a week of no respect.

The halls were empty since everyone was celebrating Christmas and hyping up their spirits. Classrooms were locked, quiet and empty like the joy in my heart. This holiday became unforgettable.

I made my way outside into the snow, wearing just a skirt but it had slipped my mind minutes before. I couldn't be bothered to wear something cozy.

Everyone was busy with their families, honoring the season of giving and joy. I had nothing to give. It was stolen from me and not an ounce of kindness was left in sight. Bliss was nowhere within my reach.

Christmas was a time of love for all. It brought people peace and cheer. I had none of that. I never thought it was wrong for these people to celebrate the season, but I refused to be merry with them. This time of year brought painful memories and thoughts once left behind.

I couldn't see the pretty lights, the excitement of a white Christmas, or getting presents. I did not understand hot chocolate, a cozy fire, or family. None of that registered with my brain, reminding me that I truly had nothing in this world.

Printing my footsteps in the snow, I ventured through the fields and my skin chilled from the frigid powder. My gaze landed on a couple from afar who were kissing and exchanging some gifts. I could not even comprehend romance. I was an outcast for being far too different, for never having had a boyfriend or a kiss in my direction. I would never belong anywhere and with Selene gone, the universe would make sure of that.

I stopped as I felt a lump beneath my shoe, taking a step back. I picked it up from the ground and admired the small piece of jewelry. Rushing back to my memory was a necklace I'd bought for Selene. I had planned to give it to her as a present, but I no longer had that chance. I wanted to go back in time and reverse this. I was stuck within the pits of despair as her body would rot under the earth.

I never knew what it was like to love Christmas as much as everyone else had. They had families and friends. They had reasons to acknowledge the holiday. I didn't have any of that, therefore, I didn't like Christmas. It was a cold, brutal holiday. It reminded me of what I could not have.

Arriving back to my dorm, I turned on the little heater. I sat down and put my frozen toes in front of it. The combination of heat against icy skin was wonderful. It was thawing itself, promising me the warmth I craved.

A moment in which Selene shared her love for Christmas came to my mind. It had been her favorite holiday and she was so excited about the event. It was unfortunate that she didn't make it in time to see her happiest season of the year.

She begged me to celebrate with her even though I was never a fan. I needed the push to try something new. I needed to face my fears and stop being afraid of letting people in. She showed me that even if it were rare, people could still love me.

I sighed as I picked up the little box that hid under my pillow. I opened it up, rubbing the gold chain between my fingers. I took it from its box and walked over to her side of the room where I laid it on her nightstand. I sat on her bed, letting out another sigh, one that was much louder this time.

"Merry Christmas, Selene. I know it isn't much, but I didn't know how to do this gift thing. I've been alone one too many times. I hope you like it anyway." I smiled a bit as I smoothed my hand over the comforter.

"I know you didn't get me anything but that's okay. I just wanted to give back to the one person who made me feel so special. I tried so hard to get the right gift. This Christmas deal is a lot harder than I thought. Thank you for being so kind to me. Thank you for being my friend." I looked up at the ceiling, wondering if she could hear me on the other side of the fluffiest clouds.

I lay back on her bed, watching in case the ceiling decided to cave in if God changed His mind about that negotiation. "I didn't know if you liked gold or silver, but I thought gold would look pretty on you. I know that I am probably the only person allergic to silver. Let's face it, gold looks amazing on everyone." I laughed a bit, but no ounce of joy was laced within it.

I played with my fingers to distract myself from the sorrow. "It feels hollow without you here. I told your parents about you. They miss you, too. We all miss you. Nobody down here is going to forget you. We have a memorial dedicated to you. I'm trying to move on, but it takes a while. After all, you only died a week ago. It doesn't happen that fast. I just wonder what happens when I die. Will I have anyone to remember me? Probably not. With my only friend gone, I will be lost amongst the wind." I rubbed my thumb over the top of my hand.

"Will you get ready to see me again up there? Do you promise not to forget me while you find new friends in Heaven? I don't expect to see you soon, but with this killer on the loose..." I didn't finish my sentence because Selene never wished for me to think that way. "We're trying to get justice. I promise it will happen. I will not give up on you. I won't give up on future victims he plans to target." I took a deep breath.

I fixed my glasses. "Everyone is counting on me. They're all counting on me to stop him and bring you to justice. They need me to protect them and be the good guy. Do you think I can do that? Would I be the type of person who could save someone? I don't know. I never know if I could truly save anyone, but I try. I like helping others. It's the only thing that keeps me going. I wanted to help you do good in your classes, and I did. That must count for something," I whispered the last sentence.

Getting off her bed, I left to my side of the room. My feet couldn't make up their minds as I glanced back at her half.

I approached her bed and grabbed her pillow, fluffing it up as if she were still here. She wasn't. She was never coming back and I had to remind myself of that.

I looked out of the window, watching the snow engulf the town in its white, cold delicacy. Christmas was different without her here. It was all wrong. This night would forever be empty in the years to come because she was no longer with us.

She had been the sweetest human around and yet someone had a vendetta against her. Who would do this? Why would anyone want to hurt her in such a way? I never understood the human desire to kill, and I could never begin to comprehend such a vile thing. Every day since she'd gone, I had told myself just how evil humans could be, the lives they tore apart.

We were the real monsters of the world. We were the worst of them all. Some people believed in vampires, demons, and fallen angels. They were evil, and there was no denying the lack of compassion in such a creature. However, humans far surpassed those creatures. Humans had the choice and they chose evil. Humans knew right from wrong and they chose immorality over everything else. They delighted in such a thing and never felt remorse.

Whoever murdered her, he had felt not a single drop of shame as she suffered and choked, fighting for her own life. She'd been the closest person I ever had to a real friend.

I turned away from the window and scanned the darkened room. I wallowed in the black of the night because the light could not erase the pain. The moonlight nudged me to remember that no ounce of radiance was present during a tragedy like so.

The gleam of the moon reflected off objects within the room, conjuring up a small glow as if they were nightlights. It kept the room even just a little bit lit so the blackness didn't swallow me whole.

One last time, my eyes landed on the made bed on the other side of the room, judging my unkempt one. Even without her presence, I kept her side of the room clean. She deserved respect.

My phone pinged, letting me know that a new article on her had been posted. I opened it up to check out what new information could have been revealed. I could only hope it was new information and not just another news article repeating the same story. Too many news outlets would regurgitate what everyone already knew, just to try to jump on the bandwagon of relevance and success.

My eyebrows furrowed together in confusion as I watched a video on the profile they released of the suspect behind this wicked act. They painted him as a man in his early twenties, one who was loved and accepted by everyone surrounding him. This kind of guy was one who could get away with murder and nobody would ever guess him. Why had Liam told me a whole other story?

A knock came through my door and I opened it up to reveal *his* face. Letting him inside, a sigh escaped my lips. "I was just getting ready for bed."

He faced me, nodding while something devilish flashed inside his eyes. "Let me help you." Before I could question his command, he grabbed my arm and pulled my back against his chest. I swallowed as he brought a silver blade to my neck, the coldness threatening my warm skin. "You can sleep forever *just* like Selene."

In one swift motion, he sliced across my neck with a clean cut and the skin opened to let the dark red fluid spill onto everything in its path.

He squatted down, pushing hair away from my face. "You were too smart for this. I had to get rid of the enemy before you got rid of me."

I choked, unable to breathe or stop the blood as my hands flew up to try to keep it from leaving my body. The thick liquid spilled through my fingers, unfaltering, and within seconds, I dropped to the floor as the twilight swept me away.

My name would forever drift through the air with not a soul remembering who I was. There was no legacy I would be leaving behind. I'd be lost in the depths of whispers.

Nine months ago, that rung true. Standing and studying the body of Justin now, those words still saturated my soul. I lost my first charge and Selene was still nowhere to be found. Even in Heaven, my name was not even a whisper. If I couldn't save a charge, why was I here? God would never trust me with another human again.

ADVENT
PRESENT...

T he clock ticked with every passing second as the hands moved at different speeds. God spoke the words we all dreaded to hear, "Time of death—14:08."

As minutes passed, I was glued to the past that haunted my thoughts. Liam had betrayed me that winter, the one that took place just nine months before. He deceived both Selene and I. As easy as humans had made it seem, it was anything but. I was here with my own murder poisoning my mind. *Death is the easiest end to a miserable beginning.* That was if you didn't end up in Hell when your conclusion settled within in your mortal bones.

As I observed Justin's lifeless body, I pushed some strands of my own hair behind my ear. With my hands clasped together in front of me, I stood, keeping my lips together out of respect for the departed.

His body was in an odd position as if he were trying to make the pain go away while he had slept. His skin had no color, paler than any human's complexion while giving off a hint of a blue hue.

His eyes lacked every sign of warmth. His heart had given out on him too soon due to the cancer cells that had destroyed him from the inside out.

Matthew came over and placed a hand on my shoulder, peering into my eyes. "It couldn't have been prevented. He was too far gone. I'm sorry, Eliana."

I nodded a bit, not aiming to start any arguments. Was it my fault? He'd died of cancer, pancreatic to be more precise. It had progressed too rapidly to be treated. This man had many issues that included multiple different sources. I could change people, but I could *not* heal cancer.

We exited the room and I walked through the big, golden doors that led to the grandest room of them all. I waited patiently for my next task, and I was certain it wouldn't include people.

I'd never lost someone before him. I would strive to succeed, and I always did in the end. However, during this one instance, I did not win a soul. That soul was burning and rotting deep within the depths of the earth where fire scorched all that symbolized love, and now I was forced to live with that.

"You are going to go back down to earth to save this next human. This man is a tough one. His name is Ayden Dyer," God told me. Another emotion flickered in His eyes before disappearing. I couldn't quite grasp it in that short time.

"Father, I don't understand." I shook my head, hoping this new man did not have cancer as the previous one had.

"What is it that you don't understand, Miss Wilson?" He leaned forward, open to hearing what I had to say.

He would tell me the same thing Matthew did. It wasn't *my* fault. He had been too far gone. "Nothing. I'll focus my next goal on Mr. Dyer."

"Thank you." He smiled, and I left the big room where echoes filled the walls. Dreams, hope, and love resided all around us.

Ayden Dyer. I could only pray he was not in stage four cancer like Justin Smith.

The man I had been assigned lit his cigarette and inhaled as the embers of the fire burned up some of the stick. He exhaled it into the form of smoke, knowing that some of that smoke had stayed in his lungs instead, building up as black tar.

He repeated this process until it was just a butt of a cancer stick. He dropped it onto the road and crushed it into the rough asphalt with the bottom of his shoe, leaving the faintest imprint on the cigarette. Littering the street by leaving it behind him, I made a face at the scene. We had enough trash in this world.

Walking without a care in the world but with arrogance, Mr. Dyer came upon a bar and ordered the bartender to get him a cold beer. A brunette woman sat at his side, now giving him the attention he ever so craved.

Ayden was certainly no eyesore. His eyebrows were a masterpiece upon his brow bones. Even I could not deny such beauty. He didn't seem to smile often but he smirked to make up for the lack of happiness. His eyes were the most mesmerizing part about him—deep forest green—and held all his secrets, burying emotions he wished would never surface.

During this time of year, summer was beginning to transition into winter. Humans called this transformation autumn. Leaves would change colors, and you would be wearing a sweater in the morning but then walking in shorts by the middle of the day.

He was no stranger to the women that wanted him, but he never chased them. His ego was what drove him to let other women pursue him first.

The woman's eyes fluttered like a butterfly's wings as she put her hand on his arm. The two found their way out the door and into an alley to do things that were nobody else's business. I knew right away what kind of man he would be, and this was already proving to be a stubborn guardee. Reminding someone about the dangers of sex with strangers would be like trying to explain to a child why they shouldn't eat candy so often. When people found a guilty pleasure, they would never give it up until they saw the problem for themselves.

When they had finished with their five minutes of self-gratification, he returned to the main room of the bar. He paid for his beer and made his way outside to a red Mustang.

The buildings varied in height and size, but it looked like most cities on the west side of America. There were roads, stop lights, shops, and a downtown. It was a welcoming town to all new residents and visitors. Ayden was neither of those.

He walked with ease at a constant pace. Those long legs of his did him well in attracting the kind of woman who desired him. It guaranteed he had one thing going for him considering his hair was a shade too light. Dark hair seemed to be the preferred feature, and one he did not have. His light brown waves rolled across his scalp, enough for fingers to brush right through.

He got into his car and started the engine. He pulled out onto the main road and drove through downtown. I sat in the back, using the ability all angels were gifted to hide myself from the human eye. Nobody could see me and I had to keep it that way until it was time.

What he also didn't see was the huge black Dodge I'd seen coming that drove through the green light as Mr. Dyer ran the red light on his side. I could already assume Ayden was never very aware of other cars. He expected everyone else to be perfect drivers.

The large truck smashed right into the passenger's side of the red vehicle, totaling the car in half. The red car flipped once and landed back on its tires, while horns blared in every direction. I was completely unharmed, not a single scratch on my soul.

I could have warned him but that would do no good. It served no purpose to my presence. I knew ahead of time that he would survive this accident so I had no right to stop it. We did not change events. We changed *people*.

Not before long, the police and ambulance arrived. The driver in the black truck barely had a cut. The same could not be said for Ayden in the red car.

Ayden's car was smoking just like he would do every few hours of the day. Some people yelled vulgar words while others ran to check on Mr. Dyer. The man from the black truck was on the verge of having a panic attack over the whole situation. The woman who'd been in the car with him came to his side, comforting him and rubbing his arm. She had to reassure him that he did not see the guy run the red light. This was all *Ayden's* fault.

He nearly lost his life due to his reckless actions, and it would be easier to convince him he needed to change after a near-death experience caused by him.

Ayden could be thankful it was a hit from the passenger side and not his side. There was blood seeping out of him, right in the corner of his forehead. He was long gone into unconsciousness while they loaded him into the ambulance on a gurney before rushing him to the hospital.

As much as I had wanted to stay to make sure everyone here would be okay, they were not the ones I were guarding. Ayden was my priority. I had a duty to watch over him before anybody else.

Looking back at the man and woman who were okay, I let my eyes linger a bit too long on them. His gaze landed on me and I wasn't sure what was running through his mind. He could be trying to explain this by saying I saved Ayden, or I was taking him away to Heaven.

The third option was that I was just a figment of his imagination hyped on adrenaline. I turned and flew into the sky, leaving the mess behind me.

Upon arrival, they rushed him through multiple double-doors and took him in to check everything they could. He had a broken arm, and his forehead earned six stitches. It was safe to say his injuries were a miracle in that kind of accident. I believed in such miracles.

I thanked God that Ayden was knocked out during this time so he couldn't fight against the doctors. He was not very keen on receiving help as it showed in his file I had been handed before I had come down to earth.

He lay in the darkness of his mind for hours before he opened his eyes. The doctors had come to inform him of the news and couldn't seem to get in contact with any family since he'd never listed any emergency contacts. Ayden had no one by his side except me.

Even when they insisted that they could call someone for him, he said in an English accent, "I didn't list them for a reason. I'm an adult. Let me handle myself." Being from England was just one more reason he could charm women well. A lot of females were seduced by his thick words.

He groaned from the pain of the injuries. He was attempting to leave the hospital, but it didn't surprise me. The doctors asked him to stay but he could not be convinced. He was on a mission to vacate the premises.

And soon, considering the bill was not something he could afford. I understood the doctors' concern, but moreso understood why Ayden needed hurry out before they charged him an arm and a leg just to get a few more tests.

A shame, coming to America only to realize our system had been so broken. Less about compassion and more abound the greed. However, I knew enough to know where he came from, his system hadn't been much better. England wasn't known for its healthcare. No, that'd been Scotland.

Ayden finally checked himself out and made it back to his tiny apartment on foot. He wouldn't be getting his license or car back anytime soon.

His place wasn't homey, and it had very little in the space. It could have been a homeless man's bed if I hadn't known better.

Before sitting on the couch, he turned on his small TV, watching the news. It was probably one of the few channels he had. He didn't have money for cable since the man could barely hold a job. He didn't want to take orders from anyone, especially other men, and plenty of males ran the companies throughout *this* city.

He had no real friends, no family. He showed careless expressions and did not trust a single soul. What was his will to live without love?

His emotions were hidden deep down, never to be revealed to anyone, and not even himself. His pleasure came from making bad decisions and following through with despicable acts. Nobody should have smiled by doing wrong, and I vowed to change that about him.

Inside his mind, he didn't think the way people should have. He got off on the sins that tethered a soul to Hell. Without health in every area of his life, his mental stability was nowhere to be found. He was truly a hollow shell of a man.

Did a man like this even have good thoughts? What would it take to get those back into the light? Determination was my key to succeeding in this challenge.

I had memorized his file, so I knew everything there was to know about this man, such as where he came from and who his family was. I just wasn't given access to his childhood secrets or what went through his head on a day-to-day basis.

While he lived in America now, he had been raised in England until he was thirteen. He had moved here with his family around ten years ago to leave home and explore. The question that prodded my mind was which country was his favorite? On one hand, America had a justice system that let criminals get away with much more. However, England was still his home. Nobody could read his mind and surely, he would never tell.

The pain in his broken arm caused him to grit his teeth, the movement being far from pleasant.

He pushed himself up with his good arm and went to his room, slamming the door. He was trying to sleep off the pain and misery. I couldn't blame him for that. I decided not to follow him to his room just yet but soon enough I would need to get to know more about the man from the file. There were things I had to learn on my own that God would never tell me. Only through trust would these secrets be exposed, and Ayden would be a difficult man to gain that kind of trust from.

Like a snail, the night dragged on in utter silence. He had not come out of his room since. There weren't any pictures of anyone in his home, none hanging on the walls or standing on the tables. All the man had were essentially the clothes on his back and food in his stomach. He also had a phone when he needed to contact anyone he would pay to do his job.

Mr. Dyer lived a simplistic and minimal lifestyle. It wasn't because he didn't believe in things but because he had no money for anything else. All his money went to bills and food. If he couldn't afford it, he'd steal for it, and that was why I pitied him.

He came out only once to release his bladder and get a snack.

Walking into the kitchen, he went for that late-night treat, although you couldn't call it that since he was eating a full meal at three in the morning. I'd wondered how anyone got hungry at that time of night when they should've been sleeping.

He finished his food and tossed the paper plate and plastic cup into the sink. He went back to his room, and this time I decided to follow him in, hiding within his closet with the door cracked. He peeled the clothes off his body, leaving him in just boxer briefs. I unmasked myself, no longer invisible to the naked eye. It was due to my negligence that I believed I was safe inside his closet after he'd discarded his clothes outside of it.

He lay on his bed with his good arm behind his head. He stared up at the ceiling, almost like he was trying to see the stars. I was not one to judge what helped someone get to sleep at night.

"This has got to be one of your worst days yet. Bloody hell, you're talking to yourself, Ayden." He rolled his eyes and pulled the arm out to put it over his eyes instead.

His current home was a one-bedroom apartment, making it almost the size of a house's living room. Ayden's footsteps were heard loud and clear even without his boots as he got off his bed and walked away from it.

He headed straight into the closet, against my poor judgment. He'd given me no time to hide. "What the fuck? Who are you?" He stepped back.

I looked at him and stood from my spot. I had not been ready to meet him yet, but I couldn't rewind time. Things had a funny way of working themselves out in the end.

His eyes wide, a pocketknife in hand, he stepped forward. It wouldn't do him any good, nor protect him from me. I wasn't alive. I was not a *physical* form.

He stepped closer, pushing the knife into my abdomen. He stepped back in horror, not sure how to handle me now. It hadn't even touched me. It was a weapon and those could not hurt me in this world. His eyes gazed at the wings that hung on my back, the feathers as white as *snow*.

I cleared my throat, explaining my presence before he had a heart attack or went insane. "My apologies, Mr. Dyer. I'm your guardian angel."

He did not want to believe me at first as he rubbed his eyes and hoped he was hallucinating. When the brain was fogged up and exhausted, it could create anything. I was not *his* creation, however.

Coming back down to earth, he scoffed at my reason. "Guardian angel? Why the bloody hell would I get that?" He shoved the blade back into my soul, and when it failed to penetrate my skin, he closed the closet door to keep me trapped inside while he processed this.

I rested my head against the barrier, raising my volume as I said, "You were in a serious accident. Believe it or not, you were granted a second chance at life. Because of that, I am here to help you. I must help you be a better person." I refused to let my confidence falter. If I had learned anything at all, it was that courage got someone farther than one who lacked it.

His laugh was static and humorless as he denied everything I told him. "We? I don't want any part of this. I like who I am. I didn't agree to change, and part of changing is my permission. I didn't give consent." He held the door in place in case I tried to open it.

"You will, if you want to live that is." I kept my face neutral and words short, hiding the secret that I had been told about Ayden and I.

He chuckled in a dark tone. "Or you'll *kill* me?"

The door slid open in a second as he kept his eyes locked on me. To him, I represented danger. I came off as a threat.

"No, but he will. I am your guardian angel. I'm not just helping you change but I am protecting you from that fate." I gestured to the ground beneath us, referring to Hell and its tortured souls.

"Why do you care? We don't know each other." He eyed me warily.

"I care about everyone. I don't have to know you to value your life." I may have judged people once for things I didn't like about them, but I had learned to move past that. It'd been a learning process and now I could care about everyone despite their actions, with a few exceptions. Some people in this world were just too evil to love.

He narrowed his eyes as if I had killed his pet turtle. "Who's he? Who wants me dead?"

I shrugged in a nonchalant way. I was aiming to speak his language by not making it a bigger deal than it needed to be, despite what I presumed. "Lucifer, Satan, Death—we call him all those things but most of all, we call him wicked."

DISCIPLE

From the look in his eyes, I could see disbelief swirling around in them. "You say you're here to protect me from death? Why would I die? I don't deserve to die according to you."

Shaking my head, I said, "We all deserve to die for our poor choices throughout our lives. However, we were given the option to turn it around and go to paradise for eternity. You deserve to change and make it into Heaven. Use your second chance to make life worth living; be a soul that is full of never-ending joy. You almost died in that crash and it's not up to me whether your death is justified. I do know it would be right for you to try to get the ending that is very possible for you to achieve if you just give it a shot."

Ayden was not very keen on the idea of getting his life in check. It piqued my interest as to why he would want to continue down this path if he knew, without a doubt, what kind of ending he would earn himself with these choices he made every day. I had to guess that he was too prideful to admit he was in the wrong at all.

"Every time I say I don't want to change, you're just going to ignore that, aren't you?" He backed out of the closet and turned on his heel as he walked the other way.

I was slow to follow him out, keeping a distance. "It depends on how important your life is to you. I was sent here to help you and I don't want to fail. I wouldn't be okay with failing my job or you."

"You better learn to accept it really quick because I refuse to change and," he paused, "you say you come from Heaven, as in Heaven is real?" He stopped in his tracks and spun around to face me.

"That is correct; Heaven and Hell are very real and every human who has tried to tell you otherwise is a liar or someone who just doesn't want to believe they have to change." However, I was here to save souls and help people find true ecstasy, and I was not referring to the drug.

"Were you always an angel, or did you die and land the guardian angel job?" he asked, crossing his arms.

I gave him a genuine smile, despite my next words. "I cannot answer that. Any more questions?" If I revealed who I once was, that could lead us down the wrong path. I knew God told me it would happen, but I was fighting against my own fate. I would have to hide who I was to make sure Ayden and I were *just* a guardian angel and her charge.

"I have plenty, but the questions probably won't be answered. You seem to think this can work in a way that you can just keep important things to yourself but still manage to change someone who doesn't want to."

I answered with a simple, "Okay."

"Okay? Is that all you're going to say?" Exasperation was displayed on his face.

"Yes. Did you want me to say anything else? Please don't take this the wrong way, Ayden, but I must let you know that I have one job. I am not here for any other reason. I will succeed and I will make sure you become a better person. You are not supposed to know who I am or anything else about me. Do not expect me to tell you my name because it is no longer of importance. My name is a thing of the past. It was something given in my human life and there is where it will stay." None of what I said held to be true, but I had to make him believe so. I was given the responsibility to protect us both.

A smirk crept up on his face. "So, you were alive once. You're dead, and I wonder why; I wonder how. I also question if you're here to change me because maybe I remind you of your past-self. Maybe you were a bad girl who lost her own life due to her bad decisions and now you have to work on saving others so they don't end up like you. Am I right? Am I getting close?" He leaned towards me, getting a bit too into my personal bubble.

I let him have a small smile in return, shaking my head. "No, I'm here because I truly want to help. It has nothing to do with who I used to be." That was yet another lie. I was a lying angel, but it would pay off in the end, if I didn't lose my job first from hiding all the truths.

"Whatever you say, Angel. Do you care if I call you that? You shouldn't since you won't tell me your real name. I have to call you something. You don't want to know what other word I had in mind. Be glad I chose Angel." He winked at me before turning around and going into the kitchen. "I won't feed you. I can barely afford food for myself." He leaned his backside against the edge of the counter as he studied my movements.

"I don't eat. I do not use a bathroom or anything else for that matter. I am of no maintenance, so do not fret. I am here just for you."

"That's what I'm fretting about." He snickered while rolling his eyes. "If I understand this right, you're my stalker but I can't report you since you're dead. I didn't realize stalking was allowed in Heaven."

I picked up a plastic fork and inspected it. "I'm a guardian angel. There's a huge difference."

"It's the same thing," he said before facing the cabinets and grabbing himself some food.

Instead of arguing with him, I kept my mouth shut. He wouldn't understand it so there was no use in trying to explain rocket science to a dog.

He left the kitchen and took a seat on his couch, the crumbs of previous snacks spread out everywhere on the cushion. He brushed them onto the carpet to keep his spot tidy. "How do you suppose you're going to save me? I would love to hear a good joke come out of this misfortune."

"As you said, the first step is for you to want to change. I'll work on getting you to realize the error of your ways, then wanting to turn it around."

"I already realize the error of my ways. It just so happens I choose not to care."

"How have you not been arrested?" I asked.

For a moment, something did flicker in his expression. A smallest tug as the corner of his lip, the slightest narrow of his eyes. Because he had been arrested once, and I knew that. He didn't know I knew, but I had moreso been referring to present day.

He gave me a look, causing me to feel like an idiot. "Because drinking, smoking, and having sex isn't illegal. The women give consent. I'm of legal age so I can drink and smoke on my own accord. Any other questions? I have nothing to hide, unlike the perfect angel," the last four words dripped with venom as they passed through his lips.

Ignoring his insult, I opened my nonexistent brain to store this newfound information. "You're legally allowed to make bad choices, but I still have to know why you choose not to care."

"Why should I care? Because you do? Because I have a soul to save? Maybe I like doing what I do. I enjoy having sex. I enjoy getting drunk. The taste of beer grows on you. I also happen to be addicted to nicotine, so that's been solved. Why waste your money and pay for things when you can just take it instead? That is who I am. You like to be the good guy just as I like to be the bad guy." He pointed at me, then at himself, and with vague reasons, he painted the lifestyle he lived with pride.

"You know these things are bad for you. Smoking fills your lungs with tar, turning them black. Drinking kills your liver which filters your blood from the digestive tract before giving it to the rest of your body. Having sex with strangers creates a higher risk of getting STDs and having kids you may not know about. You deserve better, and everyone does. Maybe you had a bad childhood but that is no excuse to justify who you are today.

"A lot of people have rough days—even lives—but we're in control of how we handle it. How we react is our responsibility and only we can be held accountable for the result. Some people use their past to make them a better person and take down the bad guys to help cope with what happened to them. Some let it destroy who they could potentially be, and then they end up like you." If he took it as an insult, I would not feel guilty for it. No child wanted to grow up to live this life because it wasn't anyone's ideal future.

His eyebrows furrowed as he locked eyes with me. "You just said I deserve better, but we all deserve to die. How does that go together?"

This question caught me off guard, and I commended him in silence for picking up on my hypocrisy. He made the wrong decisions, but his intelligence was very present, whether he showed it or not.

"Humans are sinful by nature and sin brings death, so by that fact, humans deserve to die. However, humans are given the opportunity to do better for themselves, the world, and society. They deserve to do better for everything that can go wrong. We need humans to do better if humanity is going to continue," I finished the last sentence in a whisper.

Something in his eyes sparked emotion. "Thanks, Angel," his words rung with sarcasm.

A part of me wanted to slap the sense into him but I knew that was lawless. "I'm serious. You are a human and every human wants a happy ending, unless your mental state loves tragedy. You deserve *redemption*. You should want love and joy. You just must work on achieving it. It is possible. You do not deserve this misery you put yourself through day in and day out. I'm here to make sure you become the person you are meant to be. You will be thanking me for helping you find true bliss. Think of me as a therapist."

"A dead therapist, how thoughtful." He munched on some of his chips—or crisps as he would call them.

"We need to compromise on at least something. Can you give me anything to work with?" It was a long shot asking this question, but I had to try.

His demeanor changed in an instant, all sarcasm and humor fleeing his soul. "No, I didn't ask you to come and help me. I didn't ask you to *save* me. I want you to learn that I'm my own responsibility and nobody else's. I bloody chose my life. Let me be and stop trying to butt in and fix everything." His green eyes darkened with anger as he shoved more chips into his mouth.

My mind wandered to the possibilities of how I could get through to Mr. Dyer. I wasn't going to give up as he wished. I could handle being insulted and pushed away. I had to gain his trust and figure out his weak spot, building him back up into a better man. I would be there to comfort him, to understand him along the way. I'd keep offering my help until he accepted it at some point.

"All right, Ayden, I understand that you are on edge and I'll leave you be. Please consider it; I won't be leaving you until you're saved. I care about everyone, and that includes you. I'll be back tomorrow.

If you need me, call me and I'll be here. Angel works just fine. In the meantime, I'm going to go for a flight." I refused to let his temper control me. I would keep myself calm and collected. I understood that he was upset, and it was okay for him to feel bothered. I'd give him some space so he could process all of this on his own.

I took off through his window, flying above the variety of trees that spruced up the city. I landed in the forest and curled my toes against the dirt covering the floor. The location had been my go-to when it came to thinking about my goals. The scenery of the forest relaxed my mind and refreshed my ideas.

From my perspective, Ayden didn't care about anyone in his life, nor was he receiving it. I wanted to touch on the subject with him without making him go off like a missile.

I gazed off into the starry night sky, wondering how I could work with him. Ayden was a new one for me. I'd worked with troubled people before, but they were not this kind of disturbed. I'd worked with the occasional popular kid or the mean girl—the skeptic or the delusional. My job included everyone on either end of the spectrum, but they all had one thing in common that made it easy to get through to them. They craved love deep within their hearts.

Ayden didn't seem to want any of this. He was determined to keep his life the way it was. How did one talk sense into another who didn't wish for love?

There were many reasons as to why someone may have not wanted love in their life. Love could have reminded him of the bad things. It was possible that he believed love was too good to be true. Someone could also have taught him the wrong kind. They equated love to pain, or maybe even told him it was toxic. If this person taught him at a young age, he would've been impressionable enough to believe it as the truth.

My findings were beginning to clarify that I had to undo the brainwashing by a human, whether it be someone he knew or himself. His family was an option, but I didn't want to reopen old wounds, either. Patience was key to seeing the finish line.

Mr. Dyer was handsome without a doubt. His personality was what needed all the work. That attitude he owned turned many people away, and had I met him when I was alive, I'd walk the opposite direction with no questions asked. He lacked compassion and humanity and that had me quizzing myself whether he was a Fren or a Wisp. It has always been just the two.

There was a way to teach a man about love; you had to love him first. Based on what I was told, I'd end up doing it. However, I needed to find someone else who'd be willing to love a man like him. That would be nearly impossible to do.

Aside from that fact, I couldn't bring in other humans to do the job I was given. I'd build a friendship and love him as I had with Selene. The one difference was that Selene initiated our friendship, and we both were constructing it. In this situation, I was doing it by myself.

From here on out, I'd make the promise to be his friend, striving to destroy the feeling of being unwanted and unloved.

There was a single obstacle in the way that I had to avoid. *Romantic* love. This could be catastrophic for both of us if it bloomed during the platonic bond. If this was going to succeed, I had to make sure nothing went too far.

A beautiful array of colors lit up the sky as the sun rose above the horizon. They ranged from orange to pink, reminding every pair of eyes seeing it that this is what God created. Maybe they didn't see it that way, but I did. Despite that, they could still appreciate a sunrise, and I sympathized with those who didn't admire the artistry in life.

On bad days, I'd wallow in my sorrows. Jealousy would take hold of me as I lingered on the reality of those who stayed alive even if they hated it while I was forced to lose my own heartbeat. As quickly as the thoughts formed, they were erased because they were poisonous to every soul.

Before the bad apple festered inside of me, I would remind myself that I was here to help others enjoy what they had, using my own life as an example. I'd lost mine too soon, missing it every day. Now I had to teach others to appreciate theirs and the end goal was worth it. I gave people the boost to value their own lives again and that was all I asked for.

Not considering Justin, I hadn't failed yet and Ayden wasn't going to be the first one who caused that. I picked this job to serve and help other souls. That would not be taken away from me. Ayden was not given my permission to be the death of my joy—pun intended.

Tomorrow would be the day I began this journey with him. I was going to bring him and his emotions back to life. I'd be nothing if he ruined my reputation among the Virtues. He was a troubled man, no doubt, but a man I would most certainly mend back together.

I hummed as the morning progressed, letting the tune lift away the worries. If I wanted this to have a positive outcome, I had to focus on the pros. I denied the cons of failure to bury me six feet under. I suspected Ayden would find my puns lame and *half-baked*. It was unfortunate for him that I chose not to care about his thoughts on my sense of humor. Attachment to charges was forbidden, and that was my number one rule. I'd *always* be dedicated to it.

LUST

F our walls encased the moans from Ayden and his date. This simple act pleased his sexual needs as much as hers. On some occasions, they'd focus on each other. The other majority of the time, they were only in it for themselves because it wouldn't be meaningless sex if they were selfless. It was just sex in their eyes and nothing more.

Listening to the noises and being in a bad spot didn't begin to describe how this made me feel deep down. I wanted to rip my hair from their roots. My eardrums were trying to bury themselves within my head. If I had a chance, I would leave.

Two of the women in the past week had tried to screw Mr. Dyer over and I had been there to make sure they didn't succeed. One of the women had attempted to steal his money but I held the door shut from the other side so she couldn't leave. It woke Ayden from his slumber, and he caught her with his wallet. It came as no surprise when he didn't thank me for keeping her from escaping with his valuables.

It was still a work in progress, my ability to only show myself to people of my choosing. When the girl left, I kept myself masked. Once she was out of sight and out of mind, I revealed myself to Ayden and that was when he became aware of who was behind it all. His door had never been locked or jammed. I was just looking out for him and his possessions.

Another woman who had been in his pants this week tried to take his life. That was a more serious case and I was thankful I'd been here. As much as I despised listening to sexual encounters, my charge was still alive and that was my top priority.

It was after Ayden fell asleep that she had tried to kill him. With him so vulnerable, she put a knife to his neck. I hadn't come across a woman who killed her lovers, but it was never out of the question. This world was full of humans who were much more exposed to the shadows scaring them, demons possessing them, and fallen angels influencing them.

I was quick to pull the knife from her hand, and at that time, I was not careful or worried about her seeing me. When she noticed who I was, she booked it and never turned back. Nobody would be able to believe her anyway, because if she told them about me, she would be revealing her true intentions. She was a serial killer.

After those experiences, I vowed to be here for Ayden and protect him from the women he trusted to bring into his home. With my guesses, I had come to the conclusion that he never learned about stranger danger.

As soon as the gasps subsided, heaving breathing took its place. It wasn't too long before the bed squeaked, and belt buckles were put back on the pants. When each scene was over, all tension left my muscles. I'd been listening to all his good times for the last week. I hid in his closet each occasion, my one task to watch out for the bad women. On a good note, it wasn't the first time I'd heard two people going at it like rabbits. College dorms prepared one for situations like so.

I stayed in my spot until the man of the hour opened the door. It was safe to come out. "She's gone. You have serious restraint to listen to that all week."

Exiting the closet, I turned to face him. He hadn't told a lie when he said it was clear. There was no trace of her in his space. Ayden's main purpose for this didn't lay in the fact that he loved sex but rather because he wanted to prove he would never change.

He stopped in his tracks and looked back at me. "It's almost as if you have restraint because you're used to it." I was not new to this game of his. He was set on finding out who I was to screw with me. I'd entered his life and threw it all out of proportion and he was bent on revenge. Some days he lost. Today, he won. He assumed the right reason; I had been used to it. However, I would neither confirm nor deny his accusation. My human life had to stay where it was—buried in my grave.

"Why would you be used to it?" His determination didn't falter. "Did your parents have sex all the time? Maybe a sibling or a best friend did." A light bulb lit up in his head "You're a voyeur. Maybe that explains so much more about you in your previous life. You get pleasure from watching others, don't you?"

As he started walking again, I followed at a distance. That was the moment he realized I wasn't going to answer him. Before he could linger on that bit of information, I changed the subject, "A piece of you went with her. You're aware of that, right?"

"I know. We did just have sex and orgasm inside of each other. Well, I cummed in her." He gave me a smirk, causing my face to show an expression of discomfort.

He was so careless with it. Unaware how easy it was to get a woman pregnant. Condoms weren't entirely effective, and neither was birth control. In fact, many people didn't realize how often pregnancies occurred even with the protection. It was too easy to end up being the one or three percent.

"What I really mean is that when you have sex, you emotionally attach yourself to that person. It happens within the subconscious part of the brain. We, as creatures, are built like that. You can try to separate your emotions from sex but it's going to be hard to do. Aside from that, it's also not a good idea to try it. We were made for one person and sex is created for two people to connect on multiple levels and deepen that connection. You—"

His warm finger rested against my lips as he placed it there. "I did not ask for an abstinence lesson."

Giving a slight nod, I pressed my lips together and he took his finger back. He was a challenge, but I was taking baby steps with him. If I looked at it from afar, the end seemed impossible to achieve. With small goals along the way, it wasn't as overwhelming.

Ayden's eyes landed on me. "As you know, Halloween is coming up. That means I'm going to be going to a party. Parties bring about sex, drinking, and drugs. I advise you not to come, seeing as this is not your kind of scene. Are we clear?"

I nodded a tad. Another lie. A daring guardian angel I was today.

I wasn't too interested in Halloween, or a party, but I'd sneak in later on to keep my eye on him. At some point, Ayden would catch the hint that I was not to leave his side. Bad stuff could happen at such functions and I was his guardian angel after all. He needed me to keep him safe.

He went to his kitchen and put together a sloppy sandwich. His mannerisms got exposed in full glory as he practically shoved the sandwich down his throat. "Let me make you proper food." I began grabbing some ingredients from the fridge.

He faced me, mouth full of food, but he spoke regardless, "You cook, too? Did you die during the fifties?"

"I'm not going to answer that, and it's not cooking. I'm just making a sandwich." I turned my head to meet his gaze. "A real sandwich."

My first tactic in gaining his trust would be kindness. I'd be nice, showing him that he was a person of value. He was a bad boy after all, and if I was going to help him without knowing everything about him, I had to remind myself that the typical bad boy had a tragic past. Someone had been a part of his life and they were the root cause of his carelessness. It was my duty to reverse that, so I would be doing the opposite of what they did. *Kill them with kindness,* someone once said.

He snickered, finishing his snack. He had room for another, and I knew so because Mr. Dyer had the appetite of an alligator. "You are from the bloody fifties. I'd have guessed the seventies, but women weren't too eager to make a guy a sandwich in that decade."

A small smile formed on my face. He was talking to me without insults or questions. That was a good start.

I toasted the bread until it came out with a golden tan, then spread on some mayonnaise. I layered it with cheese, meat, lettuce, and tomato. Watching him enough led me to learn what he liked to eat. The difference between him and I was the tomato slice. Those fruit-vegetable hybrids had an odd taste to them, one I didn't quite savor.

I put his sandwich on a plate and slid it across the counter for him. His glands salivated while his eyes were glued to the food. He chose to give me his attention for just a moment. "This looks like a masterpiece. I don't normally eat this good." He picked it up and took big bites, not bothering to truly taste any of the flavors. Mayo spilled onto the sides of his lips, then all over his fingers. "This is the best I've ever tasted. If you can be my maid, that would be great." Nine times out of ten, he didn't eat something that took longer than a minute to make.

On the other hand, his apartment needed just as much work as the rest of him. A cleaner life was sure to motivate someone to want to get their act together. If it pushed us towards that, I supported his suggestions.

I glanced at his messy abode, responding with, "Sure."

The lunch in his hand had his heart and gaze. When he ate it all, he questioned for confirmation, "You'll be my maid?"

"That's what I said." Directing the topic elsewhere, I asked, "may I ask you a question?" I wanted to ask about his personal life, but I had to walk on ice here.

He shook his head. "I hate when you ask those."

Respecting his answer, I gathered the dishes instead. "I'll begin by tidying your apartment." It was backed by psychology that if his home life got cleaned up, it could drive him to want to purify his own life. Whichever angle I worked with, he'd become a righteous man.

He decided to relax on his couch and watch some TV. While he did that, I found what cleaning supplies I could and began cleaning the apartment. I had to work some magic with just rags, soap, and water but it was better than nothing at all.

Washing the paper and plastic dishes kept me occupied, along with scrubbing the counter. Being neat and organized was my thing. I was not telling a lie when I said I enjoyed fixing it up. I was a fixer with people, places, *and* things.

After hours of making his home look nice, I propped myself against a wall to take in another look. I had done well with limited chemicals and a lot of time. I was still just a guardian angel and not a genie. I was limited with how much fairy dust I could sprinkle.

I waited for Ayden to notice and say something, but I forgot you couldn't get appreciation out of him. His eyes met mine. "What?"

"Your apartment is clean." I gestured to the whole place he paid to live in. Mr. Dyer had some serious eyesight issues to not notice me doing his job for him.

He was welcome, by the way.

He scanned the space in a matter of seconds. "Wow, you actually cleaned. You really are a good little maid. Oh, I'm sorry. Did you say you were a *guardian angel*?" He shrugged off guilt and regret if he had felt it.

Taking a deep breath to control myself, I glanced at the ceiling. The insults couldn't have been gone for too long or something would have been wrong. It was unfortunate considering change did not work that fast.

I gave him a nod in response, not retaliating. It would have been like arguing with a brick wall.

I needed to fill my time with something entertaining. My job could be dull at times, and maybe it wasn't meant to be exciting, but a girl could dream. I was an angel and angels were guaranteed a gleeful afterlife.

Taking the cookbook with me, I made myself at home inside his closet. I'd learn a little about some recipes and which ingredients blended well.

To clarify, I wasn't a slave or Mr. Dyer's pet. I lived inside this clothing space to keep my eyes on the prize and not stray from the path. At the end of the day, the closet smelled just like him, and it was a putrid scent consisting of alcohol and cigarettes. Those things did not wash out of clothes so easily.

Over the next few days, I kept my word and looked after the health of his apartment. God knew he didn't put any effort into giving me a hand. When he'd get hungry, I would search through the lack of variety in his fridge and whip him up something better than bread.

I'd be lying if I said it wasn't amusing to take care of him.

At this moment, I used a cloth with water and lots of soap to clean the sides of the toilet. When one had a penis, there was logic nowhere to be found inside his brain that told a boy he had to aim *into* the bowl.

My eyebrows furrowed at the playing of sexual sounds. I feared Ayden brought home yet another woman but when I peeked out of the door, he was on the couch with his phone in hand. This was new and still not something I wished to witness.

His hand was in his pants while nude colors flashed across his screen. I'd never understood much about self-pleasure. I'd tried tickling myself as a kid and it did not have the same effect as someone else's touch. It had to work the same way with masturbation and yet somehow, people could achieve it. Just like sex, it felt just as wrong if I'd been asked.

As if on cue, I heard Ayden's response to that inside my head: *Nobody asked you. Nobody ever asked you.*

I pulled my head back in the bathroom, refusing to watch anymore. It was far more awkward to be present for masturbation than just sex. The one light at the end of the tunnel to this came from me being in a different room this time.

I looked into the mirror, peering at my invisible reflection. Being a spiritual form meant I didn't show up in reflective objects.

His groans grew louder with every passing minute.

Through the mirror, I saw the edges of the tub. Their orange tint needed to be transformed back into white and it was up to me to make that happen. I climbed into the shower and worked hard at the grime on the silicone trim.

My eyes went wide when the bathroom door opened, and Ayden strolled in. He was focused on getting something special, ignoring my presence right behind him. He got onto the floor and moved things around in the cabinet until he found what he was looking for. He used the counter to pull himself up. His phone laid on it, his head down. He squeezed lube on his palm and put his hand back down his pants.

His groans mixed with the moaning and gasping from his phone. *Porn.* Anyone could tell from a mile away that those noises pointed to porn.

I was horrified by the event before me. Was it in my contract to listen, to watch this? I'd signed up for a wild job title and I was ashamed about every bit of it.

The porn was fake, as imitated as the plastic surgery women got to accentuate their perfect face. Their gratification was slow to register if what came from their mouths was as anti-climactic as the act itself.

I slid down the wall in slow motion, covering my ears but the attempt was useless. These kinds of sounds made it through the walls of my hands and tainted my mind some more. I'd tried to block it out, but it was impossible to do.

In a normal setting, I wouldn't interrupt Ayden, but this was the one exception I'd make. Listening to him jack off was not going to continue if I was right behind him, just two feet away. Making it aware that I was a fighter had been my objective from the start, but that plan would dissolve today. I had some sanity to keep guarded. All the senses combined brought imagination to my life—imagination I did not desire.

I stood from inside the bath and pushed the curtain all the way against the wall. Ayden lifted his head and met my gaze through the mirror. A lump formed in my throat and I swallowed it, frozen in place. The scene had not been as traumatizing since every piece of clothing still covered his body. However, his porn was in full view and I caught a glimpse of two naked lesbians using objects on one another. Much to my surprise, I was astounded that Ayden was turned on by two women. It shouldn't have been as shocking as it was to me, but it didn't change that I'd never expected him to be into it.

It'd been even more disgusting to say the least.

He didn't say a word, whether it was because he wasn't sure what he could say or because he was upset with me for being in this room to begin with.

Still, I stood, not moving from my spot. My muscles gave up on working and I was unresponsive to this whole moment unfolding before me.

Ayden zipped up his jeans and fixed his belt. His cheeks had a pink tone and if I had the chance to giggle at his embarrassment, I would have. "I was just doing what every guy likes to do when he's not up for finding someone else." He left the bathroom in a hurry, abandoning me and my thoughts.

I'd never seen Ayden humiliated but there was a first time for everything. I found it adorable in my own way, adorable that Mr. Dyer did not enjoy masturbating in front of me. It also happened to display his human side. He'd been without any humanity for a long while.

I stayed in the same position for almost ten minutes before my body figured out how to operate.

Ending back up in his room, I headed for the closet, but my idea was put to a halt when he called out to me, "Angel, we should talk about what you saw."

Immobilization coursed through my veins due to his words. "You were touching yourself like a lot of people do, and there's nothing to talk about." Why would he want to have a conversation about his disgraceful hour? I was clearly out of the zone to want to discuss that bit of his day.

Not wanting to continue this further, I crawled into the closet and sunk into the opposite corner where peace and security wrapped me up in their embrace.

"It wasn't intentional!" he yelled through the door separating us.

My mind wandered back to the flashback just minutes earlier, replaying over and over again. I redirected my thoughts to a better place, a happier location. The more joyful and sweet things of the world were simple—kittens, puppies, flowers, and rainbows.

My idea failed. Images of cats and dogs licking their private areas rolled across my brain like a tumbleweed in the desert. It brought me straight back to the cursed incident that went down tonight.

I was forced to ask myself if I could fix the bad boy before he broke the angel.

 IDOLATRY

The Halloween decorations on the front of the house were minimal with skeletons here and there, and fake cobwebs strung about. A few eardrums would be busted tonight with the volume of the music. During this moment, I had to thank God I was dead because my eardrums would never burst. Booze and sweat hung in the air, creating a thick layer between each person despite their proximity.

The cigarette between Ayden's lips continued to burn as he entered the house. At this kind of party, he wasn't forced to keep his nicotine addiction under control.

Nobody acknowledged his presence. He walked through the crowd like a ghost, making his way to the kitchen where he took a bottle of beer. He grabbed a handful of pretzels and shoved them in his mouth, downing it all with the alcohol.

He didn't bother to dress up as anything specific but rather just Ayden Dyer. Almost everyone else had worn a costume in the spirit of celebration. Although, most of the women were those who took full advantage of this day. They wore sexy versions of the characters they portrayed. I was impressed by the few girls who went all out on the horror aspect of Halloween. A few didn't try at all, but those extra *Aydens* were few and far between.

Lights flashed in the main room, letting everyone know where the energy of this function was at. It was enough motivation for people to dance to their own rhythm while they mixed that with the beat of the music.

"Nice costume!" the guy behind me yelled. I glanced back at him and gave him a small smile, keeping my cool. This was far from being my scene, but I fitted right in. He proceeded to touch the feathers of my wings, causing me to shiver. "They feel so real. Whoever did this work was amazing." His laugh seemed out of touch with reality as he stumbled in another direction.

Over the next hour, compliments came at me from every person. They all took notice of my wings and admired them, despite the fact I did not follow any of their costume customs. Angels were not scary, sexy, or casual. I was dressed as the good of this world—a Virtue.

This scene reeked of alcohol, and had I been human, I'd be puking it up in the toilet at this time. The scent of cigarette smoke irritated my throat and caused me to cough it away. As much as I wanted to hide in a room without people or drugs, most of those places were occupied by horny adults. Despite Ayden's guess, I was not a voyeur.

A man bumped into me and I grabbed his arm before he crashed to the floor. His hair was all over but his eyes were red, revealing more than just secrets. "Are you all right?" I asked him, shouting over the music.

He gave me a small smile. "Thank you! What's your name?"

I shook my head, laughing in return. "Angel. It's not ideal but it'll do."

His hand covered mine, but his touch was gentle. "You're smart. Don't give out your real name here. Who knows who these people are and what they could do. I would hate to see something awful happen to you. You deserve to remember this night as something adventurous and not as a horrible memory. Watch out for Todd." He gestured to a guy with a red cup in his hand, talking to a girl. "His intentions are never good."

I glanced over at Todd and as soon as I turned to face this guy again, he was gone. As a woman who'd been in college once, I would always wish guys like Todd would be put away. The justice system wouldn't understand our pain. If Todd had money for a good lawyer, he'd be let off with probation at the worst.

Glancing at the clock, the time read 23:08, and Ayden was lingering somewhere in this house doing God knew what.

A girl sat beside me, and I decided to take my chance at saving a soul while I was at it. She was intent on listening to what I had to say, learning about the harm of this kind of lifestyle. It was refreshing to be the good guy, considering Ayden never saw me that way. He refused to save his soul. His cold shoulder was insulting, and I had to admit that it drove me nuts. I appreciated those who took the time to open their ears and accept help. I wanted to help people, and I didn't like the idea of not being able to do that. I was nothing without my job. Being a guardian angel made me whole.

"You deserve true love, romantic or otherwise. What you settle for is not good for you because you are worth so much more. You should set goals and pave a future you will be proud to tell your kids about," I finished saying with a smile on my face. People were more responsive to forgiving words.

She let out a breath of relief. "Wow, you're right. I deserve better than this. I am going to do better for myself." She stood on her own two feet and put the cup of beer down. "I'm going to go home and get a good night's rest for tomorrow's test. Thank you." She exited the house, keeping her wishes.

It eased my fears when she understood the importance of her own life. I hadn't lost my touch. Some people were easier to talk to than others. Ayden was one of the toughest.

"You followed me again! And you say you're not a stalker?" I closed my eyes, picturing Ayden right behind me with resentment displayed on his face.

Without twisting my body, I turned my head to look back at him. "I can't let you out of my sight. You should know by now I will follow you. I have to make sure you don't get yourself almost killed again." As dangerous as these parties could be for women, they were still just as menacing for men. When drugs and alcohol were involved, everyone was in trouble.

He shouted in frustration, running his hands through his hair. It wasn't the first time I'd seen him get angry, but his fury rained down on the *spirit* of Halloween.

Shaking his head, he crossed his arms and said, "You have no idea how much I despise you. Can you just bloody leave me alone?" As he stormed off, he finished his bottle of beer. I knew he was headed to get some more.

"You know Ayden? I didn't think he would ever talk to a girl like you. No offense, but you're not his type," said the guy to my left.

I faced him and smiled a little. "None taken. He does talk to me, but it comes out more in the form of insults. I like to think of myself as his therapist."

"He lives with his therapist? Dudeeeee." His laugh boomed in the sky.

"Excuse me." I left my spot, finding Ayden. His fifth beer was about to fill his stomach. I slowed to a stop, not knowing what to say. I'd let him have the first word.

He didn't look back at me as he spoke, for which I didn't blame him. "You are ruining every part of the life I chose to live. This is my party; these are my people. You come here and start helping these people turn their lives around for you. Everyone loves you. I don't get it; it doesn't make any sense. You are not lovable." He threw the bottle on the ground and shattered it into pieces.

After five whole beers, I had a right to assume he was no longer sober. His mind had been altered, and his emotions were not his to control.

I began understanding the source of his hatred during this situation. He wanted to fit in somewhere and I was ruining his acceptance. Here seemed to be the one place he felt loved. It tore my heart into pieces to know he felt loved by the people who were the most threatening to others and themselves. "I hear what you're saying. You despise my guts, and I am the opposite of you. All these people are just like you, and yet they want to be around me more than they do you. You want attention and love. You can't deny it. Your actions show what you're missing."

"Don't you pull that pity bullshit with me. I don't want any pity." He used his arms to mimic a gesture that told me to stop where I was going. "These people are changing now, and they shouldn't. How else will I have people to possibly have a beer with? These are people who know me and now I can't even talk to them because they're going to bloody preach to me just like you do." He pointed his finger at me.

"You're upset but maybe you should change along with them. We are not meant for this life." Before he could cut me off, I put my hand up to stop him. "Just let me talk, please. I'm only asking this once." I started to pace a bit, gathering my thoughts in an order that would make sense.

Ayden's eyes almost rolled back in his head with vexation. He was giving me a small window and I had to seize it fast.

I started with, "We are meant for so much more. We are complex human beings, Ayden. Well, you are, and I'm referring to all of you. Humans are made with an intelligent but complicated design with many layers. We have so many different purposes in life, but your lifestyle is not one of them. We can feel all these emotions. We can love, hate, and feel pain. We have a heart and brain that both work in mysterious ways. Everything works together in our body for us, for that one sole purpose. Eyes observe the environment around us. They are connected to our brains which then take those same images and translate it all for us. Did you even know that everything we look at starts out as a picture, upside down, with missing bits and pieces?

"Our brain takes that image and turns it into something that makes sense, right side up, filling in the puzzle. That's how humans work. We take things that don't make sense and connect in the pieces we can. To me, it makes sense that you are like this because someone in your childhood had used you. To you, it is perceived that I am just stealing all the love you never got because, in secret, you want that love for yourself. You want to see the image right side up. That is what I am here for, Ayden. I am here for you. I came to help you achieve what you need—a second chance. You require another opportunity." He craved love after all, and he could no longer hide it from me.

He shook his head, eyebrows shifted downward. "Wait a minute, go back. Are you telling me that—and I don't know what to assume—you were alive within the past year? You keep saying *we* as if you are human. You're supposed to be dead. You're a guardian angel."

"I just said it out of habit. It's not that big of a big deal." I cowered from his intense gaze.

He came closer, breathing in my face, the booze wafting up my nose. Maybe I couldn't feel pain, but my senses still worked. His mouth called for a whole pack of breath mints. "Angel, you died recently. You lost your life not that long ago and it shows."

"Why does that matter?"

That damned smirk was back on his lips.

Damned was not a curse word, the same way hell and ass were not when used in a different context. That was what I told myself to justify saying it.

He popped my personal bubble with his lack of distance in the middle of us. "It brings me one step closer to figuring out who you really are. Nobody refers to themselves as a human that much. Death stole your life within this past year and now I know. You're not used to not talking about yourself as a human along the rest of us. You're still getting used to this idea that you're dead. I am going to find out who you really are, soon enough. I will know what happened to you."

I backed away, putting a gap between us. "Why do you care to know about me? You don't even want me to be in your life."

"Because whether I want you or not, you will continue to stay. I think I have a right to know exactly who is going to be changing me. I deserve to know if you were just like I am, and if you now spend your days helping others just so you don't have to go to Hell." He kept his gaze fixed on me as if I were a prize to win.

"I wasn't at risk of going to Hell." This encounter made me uncomfortable but if I swallowed, he would know he had gotten into my soul.

"So, you were a good girl the whole time?" he questioned.

"I said too much. This isn't about me. Let's talk about you and veer away from the subject of who I may or may not have been once in a lifetime ago." I worked on keeping my words open-ended and vague. It was not my intention to tell any of my patients about my past life. That information didn't play an important role in this job.

He shook his finger at me. "I'm onto you, Angel. You will slip up. Your persistence to not fail with me will keep you here longer, as I refuse to change. We will be stuck together for a while and I'll have the advantage of being around when you give up more information as you seem to do. One thing I can confirm is you don't think before you say things."

"That is not true! I do think!" I smoothed the gown and looked at him. "I apologize for getting emotional. That was not appropriate."

His demeanor shifted. The waves rolled in as if his mind were the shore and the tide washed away all his frustrations. Instead, it left tranquility in its place.

Ayden admired my emotional state, using my eyes as the windows to my soul. He didn't need to see into my soul, though, because that was all I was now. "You remind me of a rose."

I was taken back by his statement, but I couldn't forget the alcohol in his system. It was discussing his thoughts without his permission. "I evoke a flower? How does that register?"

"Red roses symbolize love and romance." He nodded but his stare informed me he was off in a faraway land.

"I was never in love with someone and I've never experienced romance." His words were more puzzling than his personality but one's mind went to some strange locations when intoxicated.

"Okay, so white roses symbolize purity and innocence and that's what you are. You're an angel. Your name is Angel."

"Angel is the name you gave me," I corrected him and unveiled my disappointment at his pathetic attempt. "Must I help you out? I can see the gears turning but you have a hard time expressing what's going on up there." I moved my hand in a circular motion, fingers spread out, directed at his forehead. "What do I, an angel, have in common with a rose?" I tapped my chin.

Ayden watched me as if he were waiting to see if I could read his mind. He was beginning to stumble over his own feet.

"Petals. Petals are soft and fragile on a rose. They have many layers." I found it harder to compare myself to a rose. Did I not know who I was or was Ayden just so out of it that he was matching me with something so foreign?

He twirled his index finger and squinted his eyes. Failure corrupted me and he had to take over. "You're soft and fragile. You have many delicate layers and I'm peeling them back one by one. You show us your pretty side. You, along with roses, try to distract with the colors you carry so that I don't pull off your petals and expose your secrets. You're unpredictable. You have your gentle petals and your beautiful appearance, but beneath all that, you have thorns. You have a dark side, the side that can hurt someone if we strip you of the pure parts that protect us from the *danger* below."

As if my lips had been sewn shut, my eyes stayed fixed on him. I never guessed Ayden had a thought process that could work like that. By comparing me to a flower, he knew more about me now than when I let things about myself slip out on accident. That was what terrified me the most.

It was apparent that booze brought out the honest and buried thoughts of Mr. Dyer.

Triumph rested on his face, combined with a relaxed look upon seeing my reaction. Instead of teasing me about it, he dropped the subject and moved on. Beer did unusual things to a human. "Hell is real? Hell and Heaven are not just made up lies?" He folded his arms and caught onto a tree branch when his balance faltered.

"Yes, they are. What do you want me to say? They exist. There is an afterlife to this. I prove that. Can we go now? This party is not my thing." I waited at his side until he let me wrap his arm around my shoulders. He was in no condition to carry his own weight.

"Oh, but why? Everyone adores you. You're saving lives," he joked.

I shook my head and took a few steps until his feet fell in line with mine. "I am here for *you*. I keep telling you this, and you seem to refute it every time."

"Of course. Who would I be without my ability to ignore some angel who claims to care about me?" he whispered in my ear as I led us back into the crowd.

I steered him through the house and out the front door. The looks we earned were the same ones I wanted to let slip out of my mind. In their eyes, they saw Ayden leaving with his therapist. Sex was their best guess at what would happen to him tonight. I knew better than that.

I guided him through the streets of Salt Lake City, praying to God he would get his car back soon. If Mr. Dyer hadn't been the cause of the accident without insurance, he would have had his license and car back sooner. It was unfortunate that he didn't have insurance, and he had also been charged for reckless driving. They revoked his freedom.

We strolled through the silent streets, cherishing the serenity that came with it. It was a little less stressful to be able to go on a walk during the night without the fear of being raped or killed. Although, from my experience, school bathrooms were more terrifying when it came to being alone with a man who had an urge to take from a woman.

Of course, if someone did attempt it, Ayden would probably let it happen. I, however, was already dead. That took off half of the fear. The other half was just knowing that his presence beside me alone would ward off other men. He didn't realize it, but he made me feel safe. Just for that reason alone, it was a running start on my side of the field. My team had a point in the net.

We arrived at his rundown apartment. "I'm taking a shower. Do not even think about spying on me. I know your angel brain is curious," Ayden let out a little laugh.

I helped him into the bathroom, turning the knob to adjust the temperature and get his shower ready. He got caught in the tangles of his shirt. Booze restricted even the simplest of abilities. I pulled it over his head, tilting mine at his vulnerable physique. Ayden smiled but his eyes were half-closed. "I changed my mind. Feel free to join me. I would love to defile an angel." I shook my head, dismissing his perverted ideas.

I ended up in the closet where I slept, leaving him to shower and wash away all remnants of tonight's impression.

Taking some old blankets from the shelf in the back of the closet, I laid them down on the floor. I knew I didn't sleep, and I didn't need the energy that people gained from it to do so. This would just be my little haven for many months ahead until Mr. Dyer flipped his life upside down. This was my thinking spot, reminding me why I was doing this in the first place. Ayden was drowning in his echoes and he needed me to drag him out of the water.

PATRIARCH

Dreary described the mood throughout the day, spreading its disease to Ayden and everyone else nearby. Being dead, I was immune to those auras. Energy had no effect on me.

Ayden came out after his shower and used the towel to dry his hair, scrubbing it against his head. He looked at me and scowled, clearly dismayed by my presence. His attempt to destroy me at this moment and anything similar could never demolish my dreams.

The rag moved in circular motions on the surface and spread the disinfectant spray to kill all germs that made a living here. Someone had to keep up with cleaning this place.

He sat back on his small couch, his body sinking in about twenty percent of the way into the cushions. His eyes landed on me as if he were already over his negative emotions. "We know you've died recently. If I hold off just long enough on changing, which I'll have no problem with doing, I will get all of it out of you. What letter did your first name start with? An *A*, perhaps?" He studied my face for any reaction.

I kept it perfectly still. I wasn't going to let him take home the trophy. He went down the alphabet, carefully observing my face to see if I would crack. "*D*," he whispered as he leaned closer. I gave him a blank stare in return, knowing that my confidence was stronger than we both perceived. He wouldn't break me.

He rubbed his chin as thoughts ran amok in his head. "*E*."

As if on cue, my throat swallowed. I couldn't explain why. I no longer was human. My body was buried six feet under the grass while I was just a soul now. I had no muscle memory to throw off my game, but my soul knew. It had been the name I'd gone by my whole life. I had gotten accustomed to it. I couldn't overlook it with so much ease, even if it were useless now.

He narrowed his eyes in the slightest, sitting back. "*E*. Your name starts with an *E*. Eve? That would be ironic. Eva? Erika? I'll figure it out. Eventually, I will."

My gaze fixated on the counter I'd been wiping down. I had to direct his attention elsewhere. I would somehow fix this and try to get more baby steps walking across the carpet. A single question plagued my mind, where was his family?

As Ayden slept that night, I sat in my little nest in his closet, pondering on the people he would have grown up with. If I wanted to discover his secrets filled with hatred, I had to begin with those who may have caused it. Family came first, and they would be my next objective. Most charges I helped always had daddy or mommy issues. Was Ayden a mama's boy, or was he the target of his mother's neglect?

Over the next few days, I spent most of my time searching for those who shared his bloodline. It hadn't been too hard. They all shared the same last name and lived in the states. Birth records were easy to access when you could hide from the public eye and nobody would catch you snooping.

As his therapist, I left them a message to let them know about his accident. It wasn't a lie to get them here, so I wasn't obligated to feel guilty about it.

A soft but solid knock sounded through the door. I turned to face Ayden, but he didn't notice right away. His eyes were glued to his TV, and only when the knock repeated itself did, he look at me. "Are you going to get that?" He lifted his eyebrows in question.

I didn't want to answer it in case it was his family. I don't think he wanted them to know I existed, nor did I want them to know. However, if I answered it, he would notice that I had been in contact with them and they'd arrived because of me. For now, I was hoping to keep the reason as to why they came under the rug. Ayden held enough hatred for me. If I could strive to do this without being in the picture, we'd make more progress. "I can only do one thing at a time. I'll be your maid and you can answer the door, or I'll answer the door and you will live in a pigsty." The counter would never shine better than it was now.

To further my argument, I made him a plate of food. He was lousy at taking care of himself. It was his apartment and his responsibility to open his own door.

He groaned—annoyance plaguing his amygdala—and pushed himself off the comfort of the couch. He ripped the door open and his anger began to grow from who stood behind it. I inched my way towards the wall, keeping myself out of sight of the visitors. Ayden aimed to slam the door, but a foot got caught underneath it. "Not so fast, son."

He stepped inside and took a quick look around, disapproval

blanketing his eyes. "We were told you got into an accident. Why weren't we informed?" He had to be the original Mr. Dyer due to their striking resemblance. His voice was stern like a father's lecture.

A woman beside his father hurried to Ayden and grabbed his face as a mother would hold her baby's, checking his injuries. "My child almost died, and I had no idea! How do you think that makes me feel?"

From my view, his parents loved him and were not hostile towards one another, either. That begged the question—where did his animosity stem from?

Ayden glared at the woman who had birthed him, making sure she was aware he wasn't accepting of her affection. "I didn't tell you guys for exactly this reason. We agreed to go our separate ways." He spun on his heel, looking for some excuse to get rid of him. His apartment had nothing, so the idea failed in misery on his end.

His father stepped around his mother and stood in front of Ayden. "*You* agreed to go a separate way. We didn't agree to anything."

Mrs. Dyer nodded to what her husband had said, adding onto it, "We are your parents. No matter what happens, we will never agree to leave you alone and stop caring about you. You are going to have to learn to live with that."

Ayden still didn't buy into whatever they were selling. The genuine love and concern they held in their eyes were clear as day, but Ayden was blinded by his distrust based on his past.

"I didn't die so I think it's pointless for you guys to be visiting. Goodbye." He tried to push them out, but his father didn't budge from his spot, stronger than the man who lived the unhealthy lifestyle.

"We're not going anywhere. You scared us half to death. You owe your mother an apology for this mess." He pointed at Ayden, eyebrows raised high on his forehead.

Ayden hated being told what to do more than anything. He was an adult and refused to be treated less than such, even if it meant behaving towards his parents in a disrespectful manner. "No, I won't apologize. I did nothing wrong. Maybe my reasoning as to why I didn't tell you is because it would only worry you more. Why must you assume I only have ill intentions?" He crossed his arms, closing himself off to any counterarguments.

His father wasn't going to put up with his mockery, no matter Ayden's age. Ayden had no idea how *blessed* he was to be the son of parents who put him first. Not every parent gave their child the time of day. Some kids had to spend their Christmas alone.

Valuing your parents never stopped, no matter how old you got. They raised you, putting you above anything else if they did their job right. They were the only people who put up with their child's crap but still loved them, nonetheless. Parents deserved the credit. Ayden refused to believe that.

"You have ill intentions and that's not a lie. It's not wrong of us to assume such a thing when you've done nothing but put us through pain and heartbreak countless times. When have you not had bad intentions?" He mirrored his son's body language by folding his arms as well.

His mother said, "Where did we go wrong? We have tried so hard to give you everything. We have done everything to make you happy. Am I an awful mother?" Tears welled up in her eyes, the liquid threatening to spill over the rims of her bottom lids.

Her husband pulled her into his embrace, enveloping her in his solace. "Look at what you did to your mother. How can you live with yourself? What did we ever do to you?" He glanced at Ayden, waiting for an answer he would never get.

Ayden came into the kitchen, grabbing the plate of food I made for him. His eyes were fixed on me, going back and forth between the thought of saying something or not. He decided not to, letting my presence stay hidden in the *shadows*. He carried his plate back to the couch and sat down, digging in.

His father studied his lunch, gears turning in his head. A question was about to be released. "That meal looks pretty good. I hadn't expected you to make yourself such amazing food. Is there something we should know about? Did you get married in Vegas and keep your wife out of our life?"

Ayden chewed on his burger and shook his head. "Nope," he said with his mouth full.

"So, you made that food?" His chuckle lacked all humor.

Ayden stared at his dad, swallowing the bite. "Is that hard to believe?"

His mom nodded and turned her head up at her husband. "Even when he was seventeen, he still asked me to cook eggs for him."

Ayden rolled his eyes like a teenager would when their parents pried into their personal life. "They call that being lazy. I can cook. It's just a matter of wanting to. Why would I make my own food if I had a mother offering to do it for me?"

His father shook his head and rejected his excuse. Rather than making matters worse, he dropped the subject and went to a different topic. "Tell us about this accident you were in. You ended up in the hospital and your therapist told us that you were unconscious through it all. It seems pretty serious to me."

Ayden sighed in defeat and put his plate down on the nightstand next to the couch. He clarified he was not in the mood to talk but his parents would not take the hint, and he didn't take too well to them making it possible for his food to get cold before he finished it off. "I ran a red light and got hit by a truck. I'm fine. I just broke my arm."

"You could've died! Did we not teach you anything? Rules exist because they keep you safe! Was running a red light really worth it?"

his mother yelled at him, not expecting the next reply she received.

"No, it wasn't worth it. I admit that now. Is that what you want to hear? Can you leave me alone now that you have what you want? I'd like to eat sometime today." He gestured to his lunch.

His parents gave him a suspicious look as if he were about to spill some secret. Ayden would never do such an idiotic thing, at least not while he was sober. His father let out a sigh, rubbing his face. "Fine, we're going. This isn't over. You are still our son."

"Yeah, yeah." Ayden brushed them off as if they didn't matter. His cold shoulder was in full exposure to the people who made him. It wasn't unusual to see, though. It was unusual to see him end up as the person he was without more of an obvious family issue. His childhood had more exploration for me to do. Somewhere along the way, something in his life caused his downward spiral.

They finally exited the building, vacating the home of their only son. According to his family records, he had two sisters, but Ayden was the one boy they had. "You can come out now, Angel," he shouted.

I walked out from behind the kitchen wall. "You regret running the red light?" I couldn't ignore if his guilt were true. Admitting one was remorseful was a huge step in the process.

"Of course, because now I have some dead stalker who won't leave me alone. My life has gotten worse. You're a bad luck charm." He devoured his burger and potato salad, scraping the paper plate of all food.

It may have been an insult, but it was one that didn't bother me since it meant his regret was true. If I could now fix his family dynamics, we'd be miles closer to the finish line. "You're terrible to your parents. Why?"

"Because they only try to control me." He abandoned the plate on the side table and rested against the back of the cushions, arms spread wide.

"They love you. They just want to know what's going on in your life. They care." There was no sign of life in his eyes. It was a tragedy to see when a human with a beating heart was dead within their mental and emotional state.

"You must be fooled by their happy-go-lucky spirits," he joked.

I took a seat next to him. His face showed how disgusted he was by our proximity. I scooted away to give him as much space as I could, reminding myself he was already irritated with the surprise guests. If I could ask him what it was that made him who he was today, I would but he wouldn't answer that truthfully. He was very adamant about not changing himself.

"Thank you for keeping me a secret. I don't think it's right to tell your parents about who I truly am yet. Or at all if we can help it. Most people don't take well to the idea of a guardian angel. You would be surprised at how many people refuse to believe in what I do for their loved ones." I peeked at his expression, one that was calm and neutral.

As if trying to remove it, he wiped it off with the back of his hand and restored the hostility. "If people believe in you and what you do, that means they have to believe in an afterlife. They have to believe their actions have a cause and effect on their destination when they die, and most people don't want to change." He was spot on with his explanation. Ayden Dyer was intelligent even without alcohol running the show.

What still made zero sense was why he believed in Heaven and Hell, yet accepted his fate in the lake of fire. "You know I exist. You know that your destination is one of torture and *tribulation* if you don't change. Why do you stay the same?"

He downed some of the beer from the bottle that once stood beside the plate. What came as a surprise to me was the realization that this was his first beer of the day. He was not always drunk. "My fear of changing who I am is much greater than my fear of Hell for eternity. I don't want to end up in a place full of people better than I'll be. I don't deserve better than burning and suffering. Why should I change now?"

FORECAST

F og drifted throughout the streets, devouring everything within its path. Nobody would be out on a night like this—thick and heavy. It was impossible to see anything.

Ayden was not one of those people. He was strolling right through the stratus clouds while I lingered behind. I kept myself invisible to spy on whatever it was that he was doing. This was not a good way to gain his trust, but I knew it would help me somehow.

Despite what I was told, there was no way I would fall for Ayden. While he had some amazing thoughts from time to time, he was still an absolute jerk and that was never something I could be around for the rest of my eternity. I was here for one purpose, and that was to change his behavior and save his soul.

I glanced back, still wary of the life I'd once lived. I knew what lurked in the darkness. Humans couldn't hurt me now, but they were not the only ones who hid in the *shadows*.

Ayden ducked around a corner and paused at a door, picking the lock to the small library. He entered the building and I followed him right inside.

He took a seat in a chair in front of the computer. He turned the monitor on, waiting for the screen to allow him to use the internet. After logging in, he began typing in words. I swallowed my fear as a list of names popped up in recent deaths. He was attempting to find out who I was.

I stepped back, pushing my hair from my face. He could never know. If he knew, something dreadful would happen. The one wall standing between him and I would break. I'd be vulnerable to the feelings predicted to develop.

Ayden continued to search the list of names, looking up every name that began with *E*. My eyes landed on the name towards the bottom, the name that was my own. I was on this list and he would eventually see my face next to that name.

I quickened my pace as I approached the light switch and flipped it on. Ayden swiveled in his chair. "What the fuck? Angel, is that you? Are you spying on me?"

Keeping my back towards him, I unmasked myself. "You broke into a library. You have no access to the internet at home. You have no job. You're broke. You couldn't expect me to not keep an eye on you."

His presence appeared right behind me as he breathed against my neck. "You saw your name on that list, didn't you? You know I was about to figure out who you really are," he said in a low voice.

I turned to face him, now realizing how close he was. I was not comfortable with it. "You refuse to change, Mr. Dyer. You've made it clear that you are afraid to go to Heaven someday. Why does my identity matter that much to you if your hatred for me is plentiful? It isn't important at all."

"Have we not already had this talk?" He leaned in, giving me a hard look. "You know so much about me and I don't even know your name. It doesn't seem very fair."

"Only people I trust will learn my name. You are not one of them. You made that clear when you had sex with women in front of me. You make me out as the bad guy. It was not a pretty sight to see when I had to save your life from strange women because your judgment sucks. I can never trust you. You do not deserve to know my name." I was surprised by the lack of shakiness in my own voice. He was so close that his hot breath was fanning my face, and yet I would never show him that I was nervous in any way.

I moved out of this position and walked around him, putting much more space between us.

Ayden faced me and let out a chuckle. "I see. You think I deserve to be saved but I don't deserve to know your bloody name. Are you afraid of something, Angel? What is it that has your knees weakening? Is it me?"

Gulping, I shook my head. It was not the response I wanted to give him.

His lips formed into a smirk. "It is about me. I wonder what it could be. Could it be my charm? Is it because you've never been so close to a man?"

"You're hardly a man. A real man doesn't always need to be the alpha. A real man doesn't need sex to validate himself. He would never have sex in front of me. You are not a man. You're a coward, Ayden." I stepped forward. "You would be the last man I'd ever want."

And yet God had told me the opposite. I said the words out loud to make them ring truer as if I could erase the predictions that God made about Ayden and I. What worried me most was God was *never* wrong.

Something flashed in his eyes, almost as if he felt remorse for what he'd done. I knew better. Ayden would never blame himself. He blamed *me*.

Turning on my heel, I stopped when he said, "Angel, where are you going?"

Without turning around, I replied, "Anywhere but here. If I want to stay sane, I must get away from you and lift my own spirits. You won't drag me down with you." I vacated the library and made my way through the fog.

Someone was following me. I wanted to turn around and smack him, but I knew it was out of line. "Ayden, I already told you I don't want to be around you. Are you here to apologize?"

No response.

Looking back, I noticed the dark figure following me. This was not Ayden. This was far more disastrous than any human could manage. The temperature had dropped by ten degrees. "You can't do this. I have not failed or given up."

The shadow walked closer until I backed into someone else. I peered up at the fallen angel whose black wings stood out in the white clouds around us. "Hello." It was as if his pupils filled his irises—his eyes colored with nightmares. "Remember me?"

"You all look the same. It's hard to remember you. I do apologize." I kept my face neutral as I joked about forgetting his face. "Like I told your friend, I haven't failed or given up. You have no right to be here. He's not yours to torture."

He grabbed my arm, trying to inflict pain. This was earth. That wasn't possible to do to me. "He will be. He's made it very clear you can't change him. He said it himself. He doesn't belong in Heaven. He belongs in Hell."

I glanced at the shadow behind me, scowling. "We all deserve Hell, buddy. Even I deserved Hell but that never stopped me from trying to do better. I made a whole lot of mistakes, yet I'm a guardian angel."

His laugh didn't echo into the sky. It stayed within the fog, blending and evaporating. "You killed a man. That was never a mistake."

"What would you know? You can never prove how I truly felt during that moment. It was never intended to happen," I whispered.

"Angel," a familiar English accent yelled.

The shadow vanished into the clouds. "That's my cue, Angel," Levi teased as he tipped his nonexistent hat, flying off into the night.

Ayden caught up to me. "Who was that?"

"Nobody." I hugged myself.

"It doesn't sound like nobody. Was that Satan?"

I scoffed. "No, he is much worse. He knows he can't touch me here. I'm protected by the law."

"What is that law?" He tried to find them through the fog but had no luck.

"Unless I fail to change you, they cannot harm me—nor you. They can influence you but that's as far as it goes." I continued to walk back to his apartment.

Ayden sped up to block my path. "Harm you? Why would they harm you? Isn't it Satan who wants me dead?"

I stayed in my spot so I wouldn't run right into his chest and make contact. I could not be that close again. "He does because if you die now, you go to Hell and he wins. But that doesn't mean he doesn't want to see the good guys in pain, either. We are a threat. We change souls and that hurts his business. If they can break me down, they will have better access to influence humans." I let out a sigh. "I can't expect you to care about any of this." I semi-circled around him.

He said nothing else for the rest of the walk back to his place.

Ayden went straight for the kitchen and grabbed himself some bread. I took the food from his hands. "Let me make it. I know you suck at making your own meals." I dropped it in the toaster and waited for it to rear its head once more.

He planted himself on the couch, not saying a word.

I pulled the bread from the toaster as soon as it popped up. I spread some mayonnaise on before Ayden began asking questions again.

"How did you die? Was your soul at risk, too?"

I laid meat across the bread and scraped my teeth along my bottom lip. "You'd like to know but I won't say. I do care about you, Ayden. I want to see you happy in Heaven someday. I don't want to see you in Hell, screaming and begging for mercy. No one will ever be forgiven after they end up there. The decision is final." I finished his sandwich and handed it to him.

"Have you ever been to Hell? Can angels go?" He took a bite.

"Angels can, yes." I ignored his first question and went back to the kitchen to clean up my mess. "Did you know that flamingos are not actually pink? They turn pink from the algae they eat."

"Why is this important to me?"

I headed back to the living room. "Why isn't it a fun fact for you? I'm trying to spark conversation."

"One, I already know this fact. Two, you made it clear you didn't want to be around me earlier. Why change your mind now?" He lifted his eyebrows.

Rubbing my eyes, I turned away. "I won't talk to you if that's what you want. Enjoy your dinner."

I went to his room and made myself at home in the closet. I leaned my head back on the wall, closing my eyes. I had my arms wrapped around my knees to keep them against my chest. "Please, God, give me the strength to do this." I swallowed the lump in my throat as a tear rolled down the side of my face. I wiped it away as soon as it hit my hairline. I'd never let him have my failure.

We were not supposed to feel sorrow, but I could still empathize. I knew that Ayden felt something deep down and he was unsure of how to proceed forward. He wished to admit he wanted better, but he was afraid and it pained me to know he was just a scared man.

I had to teach Ayden how to love himself enough to believe he should change. He was not exempt from making Heaven someday and I had to show him that he had a right to be there if he tried to be a better human. He had to be himself. I could sense that who he was today was the forced result of fear.

Sex was good but he was never fulfilled by nameless women. Cigarettes didn't fill the hole in his heart. His rebellious personality was just a cover-up for the man beneath the mask and I was going to prove to him that he deserved so much more.

Ayden came into his room, leaving me to be alone in his closet. He wasn't a bad guy. He just made the wrong choices.

The fallen angels could try to stop me, but I was stronger than that. If I pulled Ayden's strength from him, he would have the right shield to turn away bad decisions brought to him by Lucifer and his army.

There were more angels in Heaven than in Hell. I had to remind myself that every day. We outnumbered the bad guys by two thirds. My only task was to convince Ayden to join the winning team. It was obvious that it had been my biggest challenge yet.

PRODIGAL

The knob twisted on the front door and swung wide open from the kick of a foot. It slammed against the wall, starting back towards closing but Ayden stepped in and smiled like a child who had just gotten a puppy. However, my money bet on Ayden not liking puppies.

In his arms was a stereo. "Look what I found, Angel! Someone just left this! I finally get to have loud music!" He carried the big box and set it on the floor next to the outlet off to the left of the wall.

"Did you steal that?" Disappointment settled on my face as he looked at me. Stealing a stereo wasn't exactly right, seeing as theft was one of the ten commandments. Change never happened that fast with a man like Ayden, though.

His eyes almost rolled back in his head as he showed me how annoyed he was. He would never understand my morals as it seemed. "No, someone left it outside. They were asking for someone to take it."

"Was it on the property?" I folded my arms. Teaching this boy about ownership and possessions was like trying to teach rocket science to a baby.

He scoffed as he began messing with the buttons. "You don't leave a stereo on your porch if you plan to keep it. It's just common sense." He shrugged.

"Ayden, I th—" The volume had been turned all the way up while the music boomed throughout the whole apartment building. I pressed my hands against my ears to block out most of the noise. While it may not have been able to bust my eardrums, I still valued my peace and quiet. Anything this loud would send me into a panic.

He turned it down and laughed it off as if the volume didn't even faze him. "We know it works." His eyes landed on me as the smile on his lips grew. The smile was genuine, proving that Ayden could be happy about something. It was unfortunate that his happiness came from taking something that didn't belong to him.

Shivers ran up my nonexistent spine. "Do you think this is good for you? You stole someone's property. How can you be smiling about that?" I could never begin to understand his logic, and it made matters worse because I had no idea what the cause was. With his family life being so perfect, I was back to square one on the root of his bitterness.

This was not to say I would forget about his parents. I'd do everything in my power to mend the broken relationships. His entire life meant something and he deserved to have a bond with them again. From what I heard during their visit, they never had problems with Ayden to this extent.

He stood up off the floor and faced me as he closed the distance between us, making it known how much taller he was. "I can do whatever I want. I am happy doing what I want."

"I thought you said you didn't do anything that was against the law. You keep showing me you do a lot of things against the law. I'm here because you broke a law and almost lost your life." I straightened my posture, showing him the confidence I held against his weak attempt to intimidate me.

"Oh, wow, I lied. I would have assumed you'd expect lies from a man who steals and enjoys making bad decisions." He lifted both eyebrows.

Clearing my throat, I dropped the subject instead of retorting back. There was no use arguing with him. Pointlessness would be written all over it and nobody won an aimless argument.

He walked back over to the stereo, switching it to a station he knew he would like. "This is what I'm talking about!" He turned it up louder and stopped caring about any of the neighbors in the apartment building he shared with them.

Complaints would be rolling in soon and if Ayden didn't comply, he would be on the streets. I was his guardian angel, but I could not get him things he needed. It was not my job to take care of him like he was my son. I was here to push him in the right direction until he did it on his own. I also did not have money on me to just buy him a place to live. Once he was out, it was over. Yet, he seemed to lack the ability to respect others.

The music was far from my taste. My style was more along the lines of calm oldies, songs that really gave away the era they came from. If Ayden didn't know any better, he'd definitely have thought I was from the fifties if he had heard the music I listened to. Due to my slip-ups as of lately, he knew I was not that old.

He bobbed his head to the music and my presence faded out into the background. I didn't mind too much. I could best learn more about his traits and habits by observing him in his natural state, one he showed when I wasn't interrogating him like a detective.

While Ayden was rocking out, I left the building and found a payphone. It played in my favor that I was an angel. I could press the buttons without putting in money and it would call that number. Being dead had to give me some benefits.

I held the phone to my ear, trying to remember the number. I would need to talk to his parents again and patch this bond even if it killed me. Although, I was already dead. That was my figurative way of saying it would be a task of mine for eternity until I succeeded and I would have to eventually, unless he died, too. Facing reality, Ayden would die someday but I was trying to prolong his life and give him something to live for. I had a duty to save him from ending up in Hell for the rest of his unlimited days.

The beauty of being an angel meant I was now immortal. I could spend as much time needed with my charges, never fading away. There would always be a new human for me to guide despite how long each one needed to change. My days were limited no more.

I pushed the right buttons in the correct order and waited for the line to begin ringing. Someone on the other end picked up after the second one. "Hello?"

Clearing my throat, I stepped into the role of the therapist again. Ayden labeled me as one anyway. "Yes, hello, is this Mr. and Mrs. Dyer?"

"Yes, who's this?" his father asked.

"I'm Elena Jones, Ayden Dyer's therapist. I had spoken on the phone with you the last time, informing you of his accident. I have been his therapist since the crash. Is there any way we all could meet up and have a discussion? It would really help him with his actions. Aside from helping him come back from the trauma, I wanted to help repair his relationship with you and your wife." I'd lied about my name. It was far too much of a risk to tell his parents my real name, knowing they had a connection to Ayden. Everyone here would be a victim of my secrets.

"Oh, yes. I do remember you and thank you for letting us know all of this. We want the best for Ayden, and you seem to ask the same of him. We've always wanted to fix our relationship. It'll help our son.

Thank you, again. We shall be there late this evening." He hung up.

When I came up with my name, I had to choose something that Ayden could believe if he asked his parents what I told them, and he knew my name started with an *E*. Jones was a common last name, so that meant it would most likely be a real person. I did expect Ayden to go and research the name at some point and come up empty-handed, but it would keep him occupied long enough to let me help him. If he thought he knew my name, he could be more lenient on receiving my help. I could then succeed on my task and move on before he'd find out the truth.

I dropped by the apartment to check up on Ayden, observing him as he enjoyed the *new* stereo.

It was time to get myself some clothes so I could dress the part of a human therapist. My best option was to borrow clothes from a store. Wearing manmade clothes would cause me to appear as a human.

Walking down to the store, I masked my form, now invisible to the naked eye. I was still learning how to hide myself in front of the public while staying visible to Ayden. My only two options were either total invisibility or none at all.

I ventured back to the far section of the store where I'd be given more of a chance to not get caught. That was also where the women's clothing happened to be. I gripped the bottom hem of my dress and formed a scoop shape to throw the clothes inside. It didn't bother me that I was lifting my dress this high since no soul could see me. Being hidden to the humans meant that anything covered within my special dress would disappear, too. I began throwing some clothes and a pair of heels into the bowl. I closed the sack made by my skirt of my gown and the clothes vanished into thin air.

I headed back to the apartment and removed the mask over myself, dropping the clothes onto the couch. I'd bring them back. I was just borrowing them for the time being. I could never steal them. I was required to look human when I met his parents for the first time, face to face.

Glancing back at my wings, I said a quick goodbye to them before they'd retreat into my soul, buried under the surface of the manmade fabric. I pulled my gown over my head and brushed my fingers across the feathers. It was not odd for an angel to miss her own wings. They made me who I was; they were a part of me.

The door opened to reveal Ayden behind it, his gaze glued to my naked form. I wrapped my wings around my soul as quickly as possible. My pale face turned red for the first time since I became a guardian angel. It'd never come easy for angels to feel embarrassed but having my lady bits exposed to Ayden Dyer sure did crack that egg.

His eyes never shifted from my body as he watched me with curiosity. "I love this look. You should go naked all the time," he suggested with no consideration for how it made me feel.

I was in complete discomfort with him here. "Please, leave. Please." I covered myself as much as I could.

He listened to my wishes and gave me back my privacy. I locked the door after his absence, confirming I was safe. I glanced at my wings one last time before giving them up for a few hours.

Just put on the human clothes.

I opened my eyes and complied with the voice's commands—my own voice. I got dressed, the heels soon following suit. My hair was twisted into a bun to keep it neat and tidy.

I wore a black pencil skirt with a white button-up tucked into them. On top of that blouse was a red blazer and it all was tied together with a pair of *crimson* heels—stilettos to be exact. Dark red seemed to be the choice of color for the evening, and not because my favorite color had been the shade of *blood* when I was alive or anything.

As I entered the living room, Ayden's attention was given to me. This was a first for us both. "What's the occasion?" he questioned.

"You'll see. I am simply borrowing these clothes. Wearing human fabrics disguises me as one of your own. Guardian angels can have costumes, too, by the way." I'd answered any more of his questions before he could ask them, knowing he would have.

"We should probably talk about that moment in the bathroom," he said as he faced the TV. He couldn't look at me for more than two seconds unless I was naked.

I let out a small sigh. "Ayden, I beg of you, please don't bring that up."

"Ooh, I like the thought of you begging." He shrugged and turned to look at me again. "I think it's interesting to discuss. What you offered me back there was pretty sexy. That's what I crave. It makes me wonder why you've ever been with a man."

I shook my head, dismissing all incoming comments. "That's inappropriate."

"You haven't, have you?" He pressed the situation further.

I heard a knock on the door, saving me from intense stares and awkward moments. Straightening my clothes, I gave Ayden a look. "Be good," I warned.

He scoffed, throwing his head back. "Of course, when do I ever rebel?"

I answered the door and met the gaze of his parents. They looked a lot more like Ayden when I could get a full view. "Hello, come in." I moved out of the way to let them in, closing the door afterwards. "Nice to meet you, I'm Elena Jones." I shook their hands. I could pull off this therapist act well. Maybe I could have become an actress instead of studying in college. I would have still been alive today.

Ayden was too peeved by his parent's presence to even notice the *fake* name they'd gotten out of me. "Bloody hell, you actually called my parents. You are unbelievable." That was ignorant on his part. He knew it was very well believable.

He walked with an ounce of fury in every footstep, returning to the main room with a beer in hand.

This caused his mother to frown, heartbroken to see her son willing to forget this night before it even started. "Ayden, can we handle this like adults, and I'm talking about sober adults?"

He rolled his eyes. "Oh sure, let's just have tea while we're at it." He popped the bottle cap off with a beer-opener and started to gulp down some alcohol to ease his pain.

I gave his parents a small smile, but sorrow coated my eyes. It hit too close to home to see a family so torn apart. "I apologize in advance. It's been a real work in progress with him, but I see a lot of potential in his heart and his brain."

His mother smiled in return. "You're an angel."

Ayden choked on his booze at the comment. "You have no idea," he said after he swallowed.

We all took our seats. This would be a long night with Ayden's attitude. I gestured to their son as I asked, "May I ask if you know why Ayden turned out like this? Please, I do not blame you at all. I just want to understand the root of the problem to better help cure his self-destructive behavior." This had to be kept professional but polite. Hellish was the real word I'd wished to use since it actually applied to his fate, but I could not say that in front of his parents.

His parents both turned to each other before looking at me again. "We have no clue. We did everything we could to make sure he grew up to be the man society would be proud of. We just wanted the best."

I nodded, tapping my chin. "Understandable. Sometimes there is not a real obvious reason as to why someone is the way he is." Not every well-raised child would grow up to be a role model. We fixed our eyes on Ayden who continued to alter his sobriety.

Within a half-hour, Ayden was drunk out of his mind after two and a half beers. My attempts to reel him back in had failed. Just like me, Ayden was not a quitter. Trying to get some good out of this, I used this moment of his vulnerability to ask a question he refused to answer when he was alert and aware of what it could lead to if he revealed it.

His parents deserved to know what made him into the man he was today.

"Ayden, why do you do this to yourself? Why do you make these bad choices?" I sat in front of him, resting my knees on the carpet. I studied his wasted demeanor as his green eyes scanned my face.

He reached out to touch my cheek, his skin rough but fingers gentle. "Because I'm weak, Angel. I can't love myself so I choose to make others miserable. You should *never* love me."

GLUTTONY

All the food had been cooked by me because Ayden was awful in the kitchen. I had no intention of insulting him but if this Thanksgiving feast was supposed to be a dinner for more than just him, I had to cook so nobody would get sick.

At the moment, the turkey was roasting in the oven. There was nothing special done to it since I was no master chef. My goal was to make food that was edible *and* tasted good. "Ayden, how are we going to host this dinner? There's no table." I gestured to his kitchen.

He looked over at me. "Just put it all on the counter. Simple." He shrugged without realizing I'd already used up the countertop to prepare the meal. It would take so much more work to clean it up and put food on it.

"But there are people coming," I said.

He narrowed his eyes. "People? Which people?"

"Your family...? Thanksgiving is about being thankful, and who better is there to be thankful for than the people you grew up with?" I gave him a smile. I continued to use the counter space I had left to mix the ingredients of the green bean casserole before putting it in the oven on the rack below the turkey.

"It's important that we make sure they have a proper place to eat." I glanced at the mess I created.

He pushed himself off the couch and came near me. "Well, I guess they just won't be able to come."

"Oh no, they're coming. I don't give up that easily." My grin grew as I began doing the dishes, drying them off. I used some disinfectant to clean off the counter, making way for our big dinner. Ayden's attempts to stop what was coming were poor. I'd solve everything if I had to. If everyone had to eat in the living room or on the floor, then that would be the plan. Nothing would deter me from mending what once was.

My outfit of the day was a red dress with black heels. I'd returned the other clothes, and now I'd be borrowing these for the day as well. I just had to be human for the rest of the day before I'd be back to my former self—wings exposed and my tongue free.

He groaned in defeat as he walked back into the living room. I finished up with cleaning and cooking, two things he believed only women should do. On the counter sat rolls, mashed potatoes, a sweet potato casserole, and a banana cream pie. Banana Cream Pie had always been my favorite. Food played no part in fueling me but that wasn't to say I could never enjoy it. I still had taste buds.

The doorbell rang through the whole apartment, causing me to squeal. "They're here!" I'd already met his parents but now I would have a chance to meet his sisters, women I could only hope to relate with. Ayden was the youngest child of three.

I rushed over and answered the door, inviting them all inside. "Hello, please come in. Nice to meet you all. I'm Elena Jones, Ayden's therapist."

They all greeted me in response, shaking my hands. I closed the door behind them and gestured to the counter. "I do apologize that we have to make do with what we have. The food has been cooked by yours truly, so I do hope you enjoy it. I wish to create good memories and healthy bonds for Ayden."

One of his sisters looked at him, not turning her entire body. "Yeah, because apparently he never had any good memories. Isn't that right, Ayden?"

He snickered as he came back into the kitchen. "Whatever you say, Arabella."

He started to dish up his plate, piling on the food. He was a big eater. His father had his eyes on him, too. "It sure is nice of Dr. Jones to be helping you with your behavior."

"She's fucking bossy," he simply stated.

His mother gasped. "Ayden, you need to watch your mouth. She is a wonderful woman who puts up with your issues when she doesn't even have to."

I smiled a bit, confident in the fact that his mother was sticking up for me. "It's okay, Mrs. Dyer. I'm used to it. Let us dish up and get this family feast started." We made our plates, finding spots around the living room to sit and eat it. It wasn't ideal but it would suffice for now. They were here and that mattered the most.

The other sister of his that I didn't know the name of turned to me, asking questions. "Is there anything you can tell us about yourself? I'd like to get to know the woman who is putting up with my brother day in and day out."

I smiled, remembering my training. On earth, most therapists never revealed their stories. At least I could say I was in character. "I can't say much. I'm his therapist, and some things about me would be easy to guess. I love reading and helping people. I'm determined to finish a job. I was in college." I chose to give out information that was vague and obvious. That was as far as I was willing to go.

"Do you have any siblings? Maybe a boyfriend? What is your

family like?" she pressed on.

I swallowed, cursing myself for being the center of attention. It was too much to ask for when I prayed for them to drop the subject. "Well, I don't have any partners as of right now. My family is probably trying to enjoy a meal as well, and no I don't have siblings. I'm an only child." It was hard to be vague when these were specific things about me. If Ayden researched my name, he had to eliminate anyone with siblings and women who'd been in a relationship.

"You mentioned partners. I'm just curious, and not at all judging you, but are you gay?" she asked.

I shrugged. "I said partners because it sounded more professional than a boyfriend or something." As far as Ayden knew, I could have been gay. I wasn't but that didn't stop me from not telling him my preferred type. He'd always assumed I was just a shy virgin, and I was, but I hated to be ridiculed for my decisions. It was easier than being an adult virgin. Well, maybe not here in Utah, the Mormon capital. But where I had come from, people were far more accepting of gays. I didn't understand why both couldn't be perfectly fine lives?

Ayden had proven with his porn that he was not against lesbians. However, he always got on my case about never having been with a man.

Ayden's gaze was fixated on me. "Are you into women?"

"Not in the sense that you'd jack off to. And fetishizing lesbians is harmful, by the way." Changing the subject, I asked his other sister, "What's your name?"

"Esme. This is my sister Arabella." She gestured to Arabella. Both looked very much alike, blonde and beautiful. All three siblings were confirmed to have received their good looks from the two people who created them.

"Nice to meet you." I continued to eat my food, glancing at Ayden who had his glare locked on me. Part of him was upset about my sexuality, and I suspected he was realizing I was never into girls, but the other part was infuriated with me for bringing his family into his home. He held some kind of hatred for them, and I had no idea why but now I had a chance to ask his sisters, hoping they had an answer for me. I faced Esme. "May I ask why Ayden doesn't like you guys?"

She rolled her eyes at the mention of his dislike towards them. Gaze now on me, she said, "Ayden is a very complicated one."

"You can say that again," I mumbled under my breath.

She cleared her throat. "He hates us because Dad wanted Ayden to go into the business with him, but Ayden just wanted to do whatever he wanted. Our parents started to judge him for everything and they favored Arabella and I over him. I guess you could say he's just mad at us because we made him feel outcast since he went his own way."

His gaze seared into their souls. If looks could kill... There was no way he could appear more enraged. He was in full power now.

Their parents must not have been aware of this based on our last conversation. I tilted my head as I observed Ayden's every muscle movement. "Huh, it was that simple. Thank you for letting me know. I have something to work with now."

"You're welcome." She smiled a little. "I think he's being a bloody baby about it all." Her eyes landed on Ayden, teasing him as siblings would do. I never understood what that felt like. I had longed for a sibling in secret for years before my death, and I wished for what they had now.

Ayden growled. "I am not a bloody baby. I just don't want to have my future forced on me. I want to choose my own career."

Arabella looked at him, folding her arms. "Yeah, and how is that working out for you? You're not doing a very good job. You call this dump your career. Who is paying for your medical bills and your therapist? You don't work, Ayden. You can't even hold a job. What makes you think you can get a career at this rate? You're already twenty-three and going nowhere with your life and you expect us to believe you have a magical plan stuck up your arse, waiting for the right time to pull it out. The time is now. You're not getting any younger."

The heat and tension at this get-together were fogging up the atmosphere. I guess family functions always seemed to be a rough event for everyone. Families found it hard to get along because there was an Ayden or two in every bunch.

His father decided to pipe in, "Ayden, it's not so much that we wanted to control your future and your life. We only wanted to see you get somewhere. This is not it. You never had a plan for your future and that was why we offered it to you. Yes, we are a little upset that you chose this over the family business. How is this lifestyle better than baking? What is so wrong with working at the bakery?"

Bakery? Whoa, they owned a bakery. That was a business I could respect. I had a bit of a sweet tooth. It was tiny, however. Selene would have argued otherwise.

He put the fork down and looked at his father. "Yes, a bakery is a bit strange for a man like me, don't you think? We wouldn't want the cursed son to taint the Dyer name. The business would be ruined if I had followed your dreams. You have two daughters already. They fit far better into the baking business than I ever will. They are both women, and they are your favorites." He slammed his hand down on the table.

It was a bit awkward for me to be present during the drama, but it was also my duty to study his life and I could never help him if I didn't understand the arguments. If he hadn't been so reckless with his actions and so careless with his choices, we wouldn't be in this position. His secrets would stay his and his privacy would not be breached. Although, that would not be the case here.

His father rubbed his face with one hand. "Ayden, I don't care if you go into another business, but you have no plan! I would much rather you go into our bakery and make sweets for a living rather than survive in this hole. This is not living, this is surviving; there is a difference. I'm your father. It's my job to worry about your future."

His wife rubbed his shoulder, trying to comfort him in some way. This meal had intensified beyond levels I'd expected. If this would calm down and stitch itself up in the end, I couldn't complain about it.

His mother gave him her attention, her voice much softer and more loving than his father's. "We care about you. Why can't you let us help you? If you want another career, fine, but let us at least bring you into the business to stand on your feet until you choose your career. Just let us give you a job and a stable income for a while. We know you best and we know how to work with you better than anyone else could. I don't want to see my baby live like this anymore." Liquid hit the brim of her bottom lid, tears forming as her eyes now portrayed a glassy look.

I could empathize with her pain, the pain of a mother seeing her child in suffering. Ayden had parents and a real family that cared for him and they didn't want to see him do this to himself any longer.

Silence enveloped everyone as nobody else knew what to say. Ayden was having trouble with how to respond.

He got up from the couch and disappeared into the bathroom. There were several reasons why he would go there instead of his own room, but I would never allow him to harm himself or take his own life. "Excuse me," I told the Dyers as I followed Ayden.

I came to a halt outside the door and knocked. "Ayden, it's me. Can I come in?"

"Whatever, you wouldn't listen if I said no." He grumbled from the other side.

It brought a small smile to my face because he knew me well. I couldn't decide if it was a good or a bad thing. I entered the little room and saw him sitting on the toilet with his head in his hands. He didn't bother to look up when I came in.

Standing still, I coughed to clear my throat. "Your family just wants to help. We all want to see you succeed. They love you. Why is it so hard to accept this?"

He lifted his head and his eyes drooped. He was void of all energy. I'd never expected to see him in this mental or physical state. I had seen him tired from working but now he was filled with sorrow as if he were giving up altogether. He let down his guard, exposing the hollowed-out shell of a man and the broken heart within.

"Angel, I do not deserve love. I deserve nothing. I hurt everyone. I've done very bad things nobody knows about. I could seriously ruin the family name if they trace these back to me." He rested his chin on his fists which were locked together into one.

I leaned my weight against the door to ease up my feet on the heels I wore. It had been a while since I'd walked around in heels this long and I was made aware of how much it wasn't a *cakewalk*. "Do you want to tell me about it?"

"No. Why the hell would I tell you? Do you think I'm going to suddenly open up everything and change? No. I won't," he warned me.

I pushed a strand of hair behind my ear. "What about your family? They are offering you a job. They only want to see you get out of this. It's temporary. Can you not do that for them? If this bad thing comes to bite you in the butt, you will still be connected to them whether you are working at the bakery or not. You have the same last names, after all."

"I—" He couldn't finish his sentence. He had nothing to refuse. Their last names were the same and anyone could pull the same stunt I did and search through his records. His family was not hard to find.

They weren't in the witness protection program. They resided within the same city and owned a bakery business with their name on it.

He stood and moved me out of his way, exiting the bathroom. I stayed close behind him as he stole the eyes of everyone in the room. With his arms crossed, he displayed his cautious trait and kept pieces of himself closed-off. "I will take the job for a short time."

His mother let out a gasp. "Oh, Ayden, that's great!" She jumped up and pulled him into her arms. He whined from the affection, but she hadn't let go. "We couldn't be happier at this moment. Thank you." She smiled beside his ear.

A smile made its way back onto my face. Beauty was subjective but nothing could top a family being sewn back together. Everyone continued to stuff themselves with food, tolerating one another and turning this dinner around for the better. This was the checkpoint we needed to remind me that I was not failing with Ayden Dyer. It kept me going strong with determination. I'd brought two parents, two sisters, and one son in unison but it hit me that I never had the ability to do the same with my own family.

LEAVEN

Glancing at Ayden, I watched him struggle with the pickle jar. His fingers were wrapped around the edge, twisting, but nothing would budge. I studied all of the ingredients laid out on the counter. "Are you putting pickles in a cake?"

He looked up at me and straightened his shoulders. "What—do pickles not belong in a cake?"

"Would you ever eat a sweet vanilla cake that had a pickle flavoring to it?" I lifted an eyebrow while flashing a small smile.

He huffed. "How do I make a cake then?"

I approached the counter and lowered my head to scan what he had. "Well, the items you will need are sugar, flour, eggs, milk, and some vanilla extract. Those are important." I got them ready to go on the counter. "It's important to get the right amounts in the cake mix, too. Too much flour makes for a very dry cake," I warned.

He crossed his arms and eyed the ingredients. "Well, are you going to show me?" He gestured to the counter.

As I rested my elbow on the surface, I gave him a look. "Why would I do it for you? That doesn't help you, now does it? Come now, young bad boy." I pushed off of the countertop, circling it and grabbing some bowls for mixing.

"I'm older than you," he said.

"Are you? My youthful appearance correlates to the age of when I died. For all you know, I could've died five years ago. I could be twenty-five figuratively speaking. You're only twenty-three." I threw him a playful smirk. Any progress at deterring his detective skills was a win in my book. What he would never know was that I was younger than him in the physical and spiritual sense. If he knew who I was, it would make it much more difficult to resist *falling* for him.

Lying was permitted when it served the purpose of helping Ayden. It wouldn't hurt him to hide my true identity so it couldn't be wrong.

He ignored my argument. "Are you going to teach me how to bake or not? I may come from a family business of bakers, but I couldn't bake to save my life."

I pulled the mixing bowl closer to us and set some ingredients beside it. "You do have to bake to save your own life. That's why I'm here, after all. Now, just pour in the ingredients I tell you to."

He measured out the contents of the cake and mixed them together as I instructed him. When the consistency of the cake batter was perfect, he sprayed the bottom of the pan to confirm it wouldn't stick. He poured in the mix and slid it into the oven. "All right, I didn't do too bad so far."

"You forgot to turn the oven on." I pointed to the dial.

He let out a groan and turned the oven to the correct temperature. "There, now I'm doing okay."

Until his cake had been baked unevenly because he never preheated it.

I nodded a bit and shifted my eyes towards the bowl. "Are you going to eat the leftover batter?"

"Do you want it?" he asked.

Sweet wasn't enough to describe his offer to me. Something in his brain was beginning to piece itself back together. I was starting to get through to him. "No, thanks."

He licked the entire whisk and switched to a spoon to scoop out the batter from the inside of the bowl. From there, he continued to eat it. "Wow, I did well."

"Thanks to me," I joked.

He shot me a glare. "I am taking the credit." He grabbed a handful of flour from the bag and threw it my way, coating me in powder.

Gasping, I widened my eyes. "Ayden! What was that for?" I shouted as I attempted to wipe it from my face.

He chuckled. "You're an angel and you guys are known for your white attire. I think it suits you."

I took out a fistful and returned the favor. It turned Ayden into a ghost as a laugh overtook me. "Your face is priceless!"

He swiped the whole bag of flour off the counter and dumped it on my head. "Ha, I win!" He laughed.

I shook my head in one swift movement, spraying the flour onto him instead. "Next time, don't stand too close." A big smile rose on my face as I walked towards the bathroom.

He followed and put his arm around me. "Mind if I join you? I need a good shower, too."

"I do mind. I need my privacy and that is inappropriate. You should also keep an eye on your cake." I closed the bathroom door and twisted the knob, pushing it in. I stripped down and took a quick shower before Ayden barged in to take yet another peek at what I looked like under the dress.

The level of appropriation started to plague my mind. Was what we did okay? Maybe it wasn't. My goal was to change him. I was never supposed to get attached and doing that could get me into major trouble in the end. However, wasn't there a saying in Heaven that we were to be like the people we helped? I couldn't remember it exactly but maybe I wasn't wrong about playing around. This was saving Ayden and that was the one thing that mattered to me.

The saying explained why angels could disguise themselves as humans. If we were to imitate those we aimed to help, appearing alive aided in relating to a person. Logic was written all over this and it was not questioned by me as to why it was promoted to us Virtues. People had the best chance at Heaven when they could connect with the guardian angels who'd influence their life the most.

To be on the safe side, I decided on finding him a friend. He could use a guy ally to rewire his brain and guide him down the right path even after I left. It was good for Ayden to bond with another male.

I stepped out of the shower and pulled my gown back onto my soul. My feet pattered against the floor as I ran into the kitchen, squeaking. "Ayden, the cake!" I rushed over to the oven.

He used an oven mitt to pull it out, inspecting the pan. "It's okay, I didn't burn anything." He set it on the stove.

Shaking my head, I released a sigh of relief. "That was close." I stared at the cake while Ayden cooled it off with the wave of his hand.

I took a seat on the stool and observed him as he studied his *masterpiece*. He had a strange personality, it seemed.

Steering back to my previous idea, I said, "I've been thinking about something."

He looked back at me and cocked an eyebrow. "Aren't you always thinking about something? That's your problem. You think too much."

"You should make some friends. I think it would be good for you to have a real friend. Everyone needs support. We need non-relatives who back us up. It validates us as people." I fixed my posture, displaying my confidence.

He rolled his eyes and turned to face me. "I don't want friends. I like being alone."

"So did I but it doesn't hurt to have someone to talk to. We need someone to be there for us. It's just reassuring when someone else is listening. Haven't you ever studied humans? One of our five basic needs includes the feeling of being loved. Without it, we are nothing." I set my chin on top of my hands which were propped up by my elbows on the counter.

He retrieved a container of frosting from the cabinets. "It sounds more like you want to set me up with a lover."

"I wouldn't do that. I don't meddle in people's love life. I wouldn't even know how to." I put my hands up to show him I was staying out of that area.

"Good. How do you call yourself a therapist if you don't like to meddle in people's love life?" He spread the frosting on the cake in a sloppy manner.

I put up one finger. "First of all, *you* call me a therapist. I never referred to myself as such before meeting you. The technical term is Virtue, which is a guardian angel." I lifted a second finger. "Second, I guide people in their lives as a whole. I have never focused on one area." What Ayden didn't know couldn't hurt him. When I was alive, I'd been focusing on getting a degree to help people as a career. My passion for this job was always within my heart.

"Whatever you say, Angel." He finished with his cake and put the butter knife down.

I had to refrain from laughing as I choked. It came across as awful, but I didn't want to discourage him from his new hobby. My eyes were fixed on the result of his baking attempt. I placed a hand over my mouth and swallowed. "Not bad at all."

He lifted an eyebrow at me. "Isn't it against angels to lie?"

"I would be lying if I said it was a good cake but if I say it's not a bad cake, that's not actually a lie. It's still edible." I gestured to his first time baking.

I pushed myself away from the counter and entered the living room. "You should shower so we can go show your parents."

Ayden sighed as he disappeared into the bathroom. I was shocked that he listened to me. I neared the cake and covered it up with aluminum foil.

Ayden washed himself up.

I changed into some backup clothes, some things I used when trying to blend in with humans. I was not stealing them because I always returned the clothes at the end of the day. They were for a good cause. Pathetic described me reminding myself that it wasn't a sin to borrow something for an adequate reason. I was unable to do anything sinful.

Ayden exited the bathroom with just a white towel wrapped around his waist, hair dripping wet. I turned my head the other way. "Like what you see?" he questioned.

"I don't see anything," I answered.

"Oh, well, I can show you if you want to look at the anatomy of a man." The smirk in his voice was prominent and I never thought it to be possible, but Ayden made it so.

"No, thank you. You should get dressed now."

"Suit yourself." He went into his room to put on a real outfit. He returned and picked up the cake pan from the stove. "All right, Angel, let's go to see my parents."

We walked down to his family's bakery. He went inside, setting the pan on the counter. "Here is my cake." The look he gave his father was bordering irritation.

His mother approached us with a smile on her lips, peeking underneath the foil. "Ayden, you can do better than this. We've seen you make masterpieces."

I twisted my head his way with my mouth hanging open. "You've baked before? I thought you just didn't like the idea so you never even tried it."

Ayden didn't acknowledge my words. "Mum, I would like it if you could not make me look like a freak and a liar in front of my therapist."

Her eyes landed on me, her expression filled with warmth. "Nice to see you again, Miss Jones. Ayden is not going to say it, so excuse me for saying it for him. Ayden has baked before, but he has never exposed his baking skills. This is his first time coming out as a male baker, as silly as that sounds. His father is very open about it, so I don't understand why Ayden is afraid of people knowing." She gave her son a stern look.

Ayden folded his arms over his chest. "Thanks for telling my therapist my secrets."

I shrugged, pushing out my bottom lip while lifting my eyebrows. "I think it's great that you've baked before. It sounds like you were good at it. What is it that you are afraid of when it comes to people knowing this about you?"

"That's not any of your business."

His mother said, "She's your therapist. Everything about you is her business."

He groaned, dropping his head onto the counter. "I don't want to talk about it."

The bell rang by the sound of someone entering the door. His mother smiled at the customer. "Welcome to Dyer's Bakery."

I moved out of the way as he approached the register.

His eyes were glued to the menu as he checked out prices and flavors. "I'm looking to get a custom cake for my sister. Her name is Sunny. I call her sunshine, so if something to do with the sun could be put on it, that would be fantastic. It's her twenty-first birthday this weekend."

She nodded with a slight tilt of her head. "Of course." She wrote down his order and glanced back up at him. "Can I get a name?"

"Mason."

She added his name to the order. "We will have this cake ready in a few days."

"Thank you, ma'am." His morals shined through based on his response to Ayden's mother.

Clearing my throat, I shifted my attention onto Mason. What was I going to say? I'd have to wing it. When I had a beating heart, I'd overthink everything that crossed my mind. I rehearsed every speech, sentence, and question before repeating it to the person it was directed at. This would be the one time I talked to a stranger without figuring out what to say and I hoped to not screw it up.

"Hello, Mason. Sorry for intruding here but may I introduce you to the newest crew member of the bakery?" I gestured to Ayden. "This is Ayden, and he is the son of the owners." That was by far the worst introduction I'd done but it was too late to do it over again.

Mason faced Ayden. "'Sup."

Ayden didn't seem pleased with my idea, but he knew I was going to go against his wishes anyway. "Hey, Mason, I apologize for my therapist. She's bloody nosy and always trying to build relationships that are not her own."

Mason nodded a little as he looked over at me. "That sounds normal for a therapist to do."

Ayden let out a small laugh. "Unfortunately, it is. I think therapists work on building our relationships because they are avoiding building their own."

I'd gotten Ayden to make a friend, but now that peer would just be one more person to make fun of me. Mason had better have been a good influence for Ayden. Ayden did not need any more peer pressure from the wrong kind of people.

The two shook hands like mature and civil adults. "Well, I'll be back in a few days to pick up my sister's cake. If you want to come to her birthday, you're invited. The more, the merrier." He said his goodbye and left the shop.

I squealed in delight as I clapped my hands. "Ayden is making friends! That is amazing. I am so proud of you."

He squinted his eyes at me. "You sound like my mother."

I shrugged off his poor excuse to insult me. "I sound like a lot of things to you but I'm sure friend will never be one of them." It didn't bother me if he didn't see me in *that* way. The last thing I wished to be placed in was the friend zone. I also wasn't here to make acquaintances anyhow. "Let's go back to your apartment. You're going to show me these amazing skills you're hiding." I gave him my best smile, causing him to sigh in defeat. That was one more point for team Heaven.

OVERLIVE

My eyes fluttered shut upon the first taste of pink frosting on my tongue. The creamy mixture combined with the crumbles of the vanilla cake was enough to send my mouth into sweet ecstasy.

"Are you having your first orgasm?" Ayden asked me.

I gazed at him underneath my lashes, swallowing the food. "It is a really good cupcake."

Ayden stood on the other side of the counter, facing me. His batch of cupcakes sat between us and he continued to decorate each individual one. When I had tried to make homemade frosting, I'd put too much butter in it, and it became runny. When Ayden did it, it was the perfect consistency of creamy and light.

"So, it seems that you do enjoy my baking. At least that is a plus." He placed the sprinkles in a specific pattern.

I finished off my cupcake before replying, "I never knew a man like you could hold so much talent dear to your heart."

He stopped what he was doing. "Tell anyone and I will have to—Bloody hell, you're already dead."

"That's the whole point. I'm dead. Who am I going to tell, Ayden? Everyone in Heaven already knows. We are angels after all."

"How do they already know?" He cocked an eyebrow.

I shrugged. "How do they not know? God knows everything. He knows what happened, happens, and will happen. And I'm sure Matthew knows because God tells him everything."

He pushed a sprinkle into the frosting. "Does He ever mention the future?"

"Sometimes, depending on the circumstances." I shrugged a little, remembering exactly what He'd told me before I arrived here. He'd told me something I refused to believe.

"Okay, so everyone up there with sky daddy knows. I just don't want the word getting out." He licked his finger after getting a bit of frosting on it.

I pushed a strand of hair behind my ear and smiled. "I'm not sure what you're afraid of. This is the twenty-first century. Most people are more accepting of a male baker. Believe me when I tell you this, but women find male bakers to be very attractive."

His lips formed a smirk, curved up in one corner. "You find me attractive, Angel? I'm flattered. I'm not surprised. Us English men have a way with words that American men do not."

"I find your sisters attractive, too, Mr. Dyer. I'm not blind. I can recognize beauty when I see it." I intertwined all ten of my fingers together as I laid my chin on top of them, my elbows supporting all the weight.

He choked as he screwed up a sprinkle pattern on one of the cupcakes. "Beauty? I'm a man, and I am not beautiful. I'm hot. I'm sexy. I'm handsome."

I kept the smile of mine plastered on my face as I continued to irritate Ayden in a playful manner. "You're very beautiful."

A sigh escaped his lips as he tried to fix his mistake. "I am not sure how to explain myself, Angel. I just know that I do not feel comfortable or happy with everyone knowing I'm good at baking. Explain to me why women like this anyway?"

I furrowed my brows. "I think it's because we like when a man knows how to cook. Seeing him with something that is portrayed as feminine is showing us his soft side. We like seeing that. It's the same as seeing a man with a puppy or a baby. It shows us that he's not afraid to be himself, to be soft and show some emotion. There is beauty and masculinity in a man that is not afraid of showing an interest for things."

Ayden's eyes landed on my wings and he got lost in his thoughts. I cleared my throat, wishing for him to say what was on his mind.

"What is it that you want now?" he asked.

I guess he didn't get the memo. "I want to know what you're thinking. It's about me and I can tell."

He finished decorating his cupcakes. "Can you read minds?"

"No, we are not vampires." I gestured.

"Are vampires real?"

"They're not. Angels, Heaven, and Hell are all real. Demons, shadows, and fallen angels do exist. God and Lucifer are both concrete beings. Vampires have never been real. Maybe there are people who choose to drink blood, but it has never been enough to make vampires immortal and superhuman." I licked the frosting off my lip.

Ayden walked around the counter and sat on the chair next to me. "Are you superhuman? I mean, what is it that angels can do exactly?"

I chewed on my lip, debating if I should explain this to him. What harm could it really do? He could be an angel one day if he changed his ways. He would find out eventually.

"Angels are superhuman in a way. Humans have souls. We all have them. Our bodies are temporary, but our souls are eternal. When our bodies give out, our soul needs a place to go. Heaven and Hell are the options. In Hell, you sit in a cell and burn. You are tortured. You are forever begging for mercy. In Heaven, you are an angel. You can fly. You get wings. You have a special white outfit made for you." I smoothed my white dress.

He sat back and folded his arms. "Are all outfits the same?"

"Not quite. Every outfit is unique to each soul, just as no two snowflakes are the same. Our outfits are the only clothing we wear that can turn invisible when we do. Angels have the option to be seen or not, and not all angels choose to be seen by humans. That is why you hear of stories where people are in accidents, but they see an angel. Those are guardian angels, protecting them and showing to those people they were saved from death. There are a lot more guardian angels walking this earth than you can imagine. You just can't see most of them because they keep themselves hidden for a reason. Or, they disguise themselves as a human," I said.

He continued to ask questions, "How do they appear human?"

I fixed the strand of hair that came loose from behind my ear. "We wear regular clothes made by humans like I did when I was around your parents. Human clothing will hide our wings and make us look like any other person so we fit right in. Only angels can recognize any other angels. We fly, turn invisible, but the best part of it all is we cannot feel physical pain on earth. We are not physical beings, therefore we do not feel pain. Unfortunately, if we deal with some serious trauma and never heal before we die, our souls split into fragments. Pieces, memories, and who we are is lost. Traumatized souls must spend the time after their death searching for themselves. That's why our job is so important to us. We want souls to feel the immediate joy that comes when entering Heaven."

He frowned. "That is tragic, and unheard of. You can't feel pleasure, either."

I laughed at him with no ill intentions. "False. We don't feel pain because pain is a result of sin. Angels made it to Heaven and there is no sin with heavenly beings, so we can't feel pain because of that. However, pleasure was always a part of life, even before pain became a thing."

"There is hope. You can still shag a man and feel that sweet gratification." He chuckled.

I shot him a smile in return. "There is hope for you, too, or else I wouldn't be here."

My mind kept replaying the words in my head. I had told Ayden that there was hope for his soul because I was his guardian angel.

Humans liked to believe we all had guardian angels or nobody did. Sometimes, they believed only the good people did. All those statements were false.

Humans like Ayden did get guardian angels. Not all good people had angels. It was all based on who needed them the most, and Ayden qualified for that.

If there was no chance that Ayden could change, I would never have been sent to save his soul. I wouldn't have been sent to waste my time, but God knew that I had a chance. I only wished He could tell me if I succeeded or not.

Of course, I could come to nothing and then what would be the point of me wasting my time? There was a point. Maybe I didn't change Ayden, but his path would cause me to run into another person who would change themselves. If I had never been sent to help Ayden, I would never have had the chance to go to that Halloween party where I talked some humans into taking care of themselves. I was not a total failure.

Justin. I fell short with him. He'd died before I had a chance to even try.

They knew I wouldn't save him but maybe I had rescued his wife's soul. I still made an impact and every person I attempted to bring to the light had a purpose to be on my list.

I glanced out of the apartment window. People passed by, rushing to get home or go somewhere else. In a city like so, nobody would have time to stop and smell the roses.

Rose. That was exactly what Ayden had compared me to.

Ayden saw me as a delicate rose with secrets to hide and emotions to release. I wish I could say he was wrong but that was not the case. I was the spiritual embodiment of a red and white rose, one colored in purity, admiration, and *blood.*

As I closed my eyes, the strangest scene played like a movie.

I twirled between the trees with my dress falling at my legs as soon as I stopped. Laughter echoed into the sky and I lost my balance from spinning like a ballerina.

A pair of arms caught me before my butt touched the grass. Pink lips whispered into my ear, something I didn't quite catch. Green eyes came into my view and the figure helped me regain my footing. By magic, a rose appeared out of thin air, the thorn-covered stem between his fingers. He held it out to me and I grasped it, noticing the blood dripping from his hand. He had cut himself.

In a flash, the scene pulled away and I landed in another movie. The rose wilted in the snow as it fell from my hand. Taking a quick look around the area, I recognized it all too well.

The trees were as dead as a corpse in its grave. The air could cut through a rock with the chilliness it bestowed upon the forest.

Before me, a brunette woman sat with a man on a picnic blanket. They shared laughs and smiles, the joy never faltering. Snowflakes made their way down from the sky, threatening to take away the couple's romantic moment. They would never allow it.

Within the blink of an eye, the man pulled out a knife and sliced her neck. She fell back into the snow and stained what was once so white. Her hand grabbed at her throat, attempting to stop the overflow of blood leaving her body. The gesture was of no avail as her brown eyes went blank. He put the food into the basket and pulled the blanket from underneath the bottom half of her body.

The world did not stop for her. It did not pause time or give a single moment for anyone to process this loss of life.

Winter continued to stretch its thin, bony fingers across the town, leaving frozen sorrows behind with everything it touched.

The man dragged her body back through the forest and ended at a building. He set up the picnic blanket and half-eaten food once more, to hide his own tracks.

The young woman's blood soaked through the thin layer of snow and into the depths of the earth. Hell would see that blood and know who was the cause. There was no way this man could end up in Heaven with his chosen path, attempting to escape his fate.

Continuing to set up the new murder scene to perfect his cover-up story, he wiped his crimson blade with a cloth and wadded it up in his pocket. He kept a lookout for any passerby, but nobody would be out in weather like this.

He rehearsed his act over again in his mind, getting the story straight. He would fool everyone with anything that involved the truth about her.

Opening my eyes and coming back to reality, I let out a little gasp. He was still out there, walking the streets and escaping justice by murder, and it was all *my* fault.

TEMPERANCE

While washing dishes, something came to mind. "Ayden, I have a particular question that relates to your baking. You're good at it, correct?" I glanced back at him.

He shrugged. "Yeah."

"Why do you make sexist comments about women being in the kitchen? When I make you food and clean, you say things like, *did you come from the fifties?*—that is offensive by the way—you contradict your interest in baking. Women cook and clean, too. You cannot judge why I'm good at taking care of you. It's not just my job but something I choose to do. You are good at baking and yet you're sexist." I took a break from the dishes, giving him my full attention.

He let out a deep chuckle. "In my defense, I never said you had to be in the kitchen. If you were a male guardian angel, I'd call you my maid as well. I'm lazy and it's nothing to do with thinking women should do all the work. Also, asking you which era you are from is just a guess. Women in that period offered to cook and clean because it was how they were raised. You offered to cook for me. I only said you'd make a good maid because I'm guilty of the deadly sin: sloth."

"I was raised to cook and clean but it's not for a reason you'd think." Shaking my head, I continued, "if this isn't true, why did you mention that your sisters would be a better fit for the business?"

"Because women are accepted as bakers. There is less judgment directed at them when they choose to bake for a living. Society sees it as a normal career choice. It's no different from a woman being skeptical to choose a more masculine career." He pointed to me.

His gesture had me dwelling in my worries. Did he know about me? Had he figured out who I was and what I wanted to do with my life? He couldn't have. My career choice had always been a unisex decision.

"Women are more keen to take a career that people expect men in because they want to show men that they can do what a male can. Males are mechanics. They do a lot of manual labor. They take on these lifestyles, and that's awesome but some females also enjoy working on cars or doing outside jobs in the wild weather. People tend to expect men to be doing these things and women just want to say they are capable of being passionate about cars and any career they choose." A shiver ran up my soul as I finished my words.

Something nagged inside my head. Women had wanted to prove that they could be good with cars, and men wanted to prove they could be good in the kitchen. Ayden was pushing away his skills due to a masculine mold he was told to fit into.

"That's fine. They can do what they want with their life and I won't judge. I'm just saying that there are people who do judge. Few and far between, they exist. My sisters never have to hear those comments." A sigh escaped his lips.

"No, they don't. But they will hear comments about how it was a fitting career choice because they are women. You can't please everybody and there will be judgment no matter who you are or what you do. If you were good with cars, people would think that's a good thing because you're a man and that's what fits you. I'm not too involved in gender issues, but when it comes to judgment, I'm not blind to the things people will say. If you're a woman breaking from the feminine mold, people will be upset because they want women to be all feminine. If you're a woman who stays within the mold because that is who you are and what you enjoy, someone will expose their sexism with something along the lines of, *that's where a woman belongs*. It's wrong, Ayden. I'm going to say this. If you want to bake, do it. You deserve to be happy. It may not be the most masculine decision, but it's yours and you are allowed to make those. It's not a sin to be a man and bake sweets. It never was and if you choose this, choose it with confidence," I said.

"Is this your way of telling me you wanted to be a mechanic?" He lifted an eyebrow and a smirk rose upon his face.

Clearing my throat, I suggested, "You should try to be more human."

Ayden gave me a strange look and sat back against the cushions to maximize his comfort. "Now what is that supposed to mean? I am a human in my blood. Even humans can be bad people. Bloody hell, we are the worst creatures to exist." He put the white stick to his lips, lighting the end of it.

I tilted my head to the side. "No, you don't have any humanity. I'm more human than you are, and I'm not even human." I'd keep repeating those words to prove to myself I was no longer part of the living. As much as I wished I still were, I wasn't. I had to bury these emotions deep below the surface, never allowing them to see the light of day. "You can never have a serious conversation. Everything becomes a joke to you. Here I am, trying to persuade you to do what you want that isn't harmful to you or anyone else, and you respond with a stupid comment about me being a mechanic."

"Oh, come on, I've done okay these past few weeks and that was one joke. I like to say silly things. Is that a crime?" He leaned forward, giving me a look that rendered me the bad guy in this situation. He inhaled some smoke and exhaled a few seconds later.

"You stole a stereo; you completely disrespected the people who gave you life. It's fair to say you need help. I know what we should work on next. What happened last night?" I questioned.

His eyes darted up to the ceiling while a smile sat upon his lips. "I had amazing sex."

"No, you did something with someone you'll never see again. You let your body speak for you when it should be your mind." I pointed my finger at my own head.

"My mind does speak. It says, *look at that fine woman; reward yourself with a good time.*"

"Ayden, I'm being serious." I folded my arms, starting to tap my foot. "This is what I'm referring to. You are never serious. You take things in a serious manner when you're mad or intoxicated and that in itself is not a good sign. I want to see genuine joy. I want to have a deep conversation with you and let it mean something. I wish to see proof that you see what I see when it comes to such big decisions about your own life."

"And when are you not being serious? In fact, when are you ever having fun? Do you expect me to be *boring*, too? We just aren't the same. You are too preoccupied to enjoy the small things in life. I'm not. There is no balance between us. We're two extreme sides." The burning cigarette bobbed between his lips.

An idea popped into my brain. "I want to challenge you."

"Challenge me? Sounds interesting. Go on." He gestured for me to continue with what I was going to say.

"I want to challenge you to see if you can go ten weeks without having sex with a single woman. Do you have that kind of control over yourself? Do you think maybe...you could win?"

"What do I get if I win? I want to propose an idea; I think you should admit defeat and leave me be if I win." He fixed his jacket and spread his arms out along the back of his couch.

"Well, if you win, technically I win. I want you to win. I wouldn't mind such a prize. You would be surprised at what you might discover in life when you direct the focus away from sex and somewhere else." A soft smile blessed my lips.

"All right, I have a better deal. If I win, you have to go to bed with me." His smirk developed into something more cunning.

It was absurd that I debated taking this deal. On one hand, it would help him show himself he didn't need sex to survive. On the other hand, I wasn't willing to bet my own dignity for his amusement. If he did win, he would get to taint me as a Virtue. Doing something romantic or sexual with a human was swimming in forbidden waters. That was far from doing the right thing. I'd refuse to bet on my virginity for a man like Ayden. "That's off the table. We need something better."

"You're scared I'll win if the prize is you." He stood up and crushed the rest of his cigarette in the ashtray. "You have to work with me, Angel. What do I get if I win?" He closed the space between us, green eyes locked on mine.

I couldn't come up with anything that was worth winning for him that also wouldn't be too harsh for me on my end. He still needed a prize to aim for or he was not going to take this challenge. Mr. Dyer was competitive and he needed a trophy.

"Angel, I'm waiting for an answer." Impatience blanketed his entire body as he tapped his foot to mock me in return.

"I don't know what else you could want," I whispered.

He lifted both eyebrows in surprise. "What? Did you just say you don't know? You must know everything about me, so how could you not?" I did not at all appreciate his condescending tone.

"Ayden," I warned.

"What? You won't do anything. You're an angel and you can't. It's your job to go easy on me and if you hurt me, you'll get into trouble with the big boss." He pointed up at the sky and moved his lips to one side of his face. "Tell you what, if I win, I get to kiss you."

I dropped my head to hide the embarrassment that hugged my face. That was most definitely not a good idea either. This prize offer wasn't supposed to give me butterflies, though.

"Oh, I see... Angel has never kissed a boy, has she? It's all starting to make sense as to why you are so against sex and romance." He lifted my chin with two fingers.

I pushed his hand away from me. "My past life is still none of your business but fine, you can kiss me if you win." I was determined to prove to him I was not the nerdy girl he painted me as. I'd never been against romance. I just did not support his sexual options.

He patted my head. "All right, I will accept this deal." He grabbed cancer from the cigarette box and lit it up between his lips.

"Ah, we haven't decided on what I get if I win." Both of my eyebrows arched higher upon my forehead.

"Angel, you're really pushing buttons." He exhaled the smoke into my pretty face. I was thankful it did not affect me, otherwise, I would have reacted in a *not-so-angelic* way.

"Good. If you cannot make the full ten weeks without sex, you must give up stealing, alcohol, and cigarettes forever."

"Deal." He put his hand out and we shook on it. He must've been confident enough that he'd come out on top to bet his addictions. "I only have to go without sex for ten weeks, then I get to kiss you and live how I want. It sounds more like a win." He continued to finish his last cigarette of the night.

"Ayden Dyer wants to kiss the dead therapist? You wouldn't truly wish for that."

"Why not? If I kiss you, I get to brag about it. I also get to say I have more control over you than you do me. Kisses are the open door to sex." Shrugging, he grabbed his sunglasses despite the lack of sunshine outside. He put out the embers of the stick in the ashtray.

I had to give him credit for his last statement. Kisses were the door to sex. A good kiss could be far too dangerous, leading to losing control of one's desires.

"Oh, I see. It's always about you." I let out a sigh.

"Of course it is. Don't you know that?" He chuckled. "Let's go to that stupid birthday party. The only reason I'm going is because it's her twenty-first birthday which means there's alcohol." He nodded as I shook my head.

Still without a car and his license, Ayden led us to the exact location where it would be taking place. It was my first time walking into a bar. Alcohol was not my scene. That and it hadn't been legal for me to even drink before I died.

Mason came over and slapped his hand against Ayden's, thumbs hugging and doing that guy handshake where they pulled for a quick embrace and a pat on each other's backs. Mason waved someone over. "Sunny, come meet the son of the people who baked your cake!"

A young woman approached us with a smile. "Heyo! I'm glad you could make it for my birthday. The cake was one of the best I'd had in a long time."

Ayden scanned her body and I nudged him. "Ten weeks, starting tonight," I whispered.

He groaned and gave me a look from a whiny child. "Now? That's just cruel. Look at her, the way her hair falls. I want that on my chest. Look at her cleavage and her curves. It's all perfect," he spoke in a quiet voice to keep Mason and Sunny out of it.

"Ayden," I warned him again.

He sighed in defeat. "Fine, okay, I won't do anything. I'll just go get drunk." He walked over to the bar, ordering a beer.

Mason watched Ayden with curiosity and looked back at me. "Well, thank you for coming. I'm going to go join Ayden and drink some beer." He turned and met Ayden at the bar.

I popped out like a sore thumb, wondering if I was attracting attention. My aim was to deflect it. Looking around, I joined the women at a table. It was a better option compared to having men observe my every move and attempt to touch me. I wasn't showing off anything special but that never stopped a man before.

Sunny's laugh mixed with those of her friends'. "Have you guys seen the man my brother invited? He's a real looker." She jabbed her thumb back at Ayden to point him out to the girls.

Ayden knew he couldn't do anything with her, but she didn't know that. Ayden really was an attractive man so it didn't shock me that the birthday girl was hitting on him.

One of her friends, the blonde one, wiggled her eyebrows in response. "He really is. You should introduce yourself."

Her eyes lingered on Ayden as she bit her lip. "Should I? Do you think he would go for me?"

"Girl, you are gorgeous. You got boobs. The guy will love you. Go on over there." Her friend shooed her.

Sunny stood from the table and pulled down the fitted, red skirt of her dress. "Wish me luck!" She departed the table to go see Ayden. I left them to their privacy because it wasn't any of my business.

A brunette girl turned to me. "What do they call you? How do you know Ayden?"

"Elena—I'm his dead therapist," I spit out in a hurry.

"What?" she asked.

I cleared my throat and racked my brain for excuses. "I mean, I'm his therapist. He calls me his dead therapist because my emotions are dead, or that's how he sees me." I let out a nervous laugh.

"Oh, cool. Is it romantic?"

"Oh, no, not at all. It is professional to the strictest extent." I nodded while furrowing my eyebrows and squinting just a little.

"Why does Ayden need a therapist? Is he mentally messed up?" She sipped her wine while her eyes stayed glued to me. It was respectful to pay attention while I spoke but something about her gaze caused nightmares to arise.

"No, no. He got into a serious car accident a few months back and I have been hired to help him with the trauma." I gave them some excuse to keep the full truth between Ayden and I. It wasn't a total lie but that was as far as I was willing to go with it.

I peeked over at Sunny and Ayden. The happy couple was laughing and bonding over Ayden's joking personality. I faced forward once again. Ayden made a deal with me. If he really cared about winning a bet and continuing to make bad choices down the road, he wouldn't have sex for the next ten weeks.

Alcohol stood in front of me, mocking me for my prude attitude. There was no way I was going to drink it, no matter how much judgment I received from this beverage.

After a half-hour of pointless conversation, Sunny returned and had a few more drinks with her friends. Everyone drank except for me, making me the outcast. All alcohol tasted like crap and I could not tolerate it enough to fit in with the cool kids. I only drank things my taste buds approved of on first impression.

The night came to an end eventually and I took Ayden home before he passed out on the floor. In fact, he was so drunk that I had to carry him home. That was why I had to stay sober. It had also been a sin to drink my mind into obliteration.

We arrived at the apartment and I led him to his bed, removing his jacket and shoes. I tucked him in and set a glass of water on his nightstand. He would want it in the morning.

I started to get up, but he grabbed my arm and pulled me closer. His breath made the inside of my nose shrivel. "What is it, Ayden?"

"I have a secret..." he slurred.

"Did you have sex with Sunny? Ayden, I told you no."

"No... I wanted to tell you that I like it when we argue..." His eyes were closed but his fingers were still wrapped around my bicep.

I laughed a bit, looking elsewhere before my eyes landed back on him. "I could've figured that much. You want to argue a lot."

Incoherent sounds came from his lips and his grip on my bicep loosened. I took my arm away and stood up to leave. "No, Angel... Don't go... I have a secret..." He struggled to get his words out.

I turned to face him. "It's okay, Ayden. You told me your secret."

"That wasn't my real secret..." He attempted to look my way.

"Then what is your real secret?" I asked.

"Come closer..." He gestured me over.

I walked over and kneeled beside his bed. He pulled me against his side to whisper, "I think you're actually very pretty and...more than Sunny..."

In one swift movement, I pulled back from him and swallowed my embarrassment. It got stuck in my throat and I choked until I coughed it up. "Goodnight, Ayden." I rushed out of the room before he could say more.

I may not have been a professional therapist, but I knew that drunk people expressed secrets they would never say while sober. Ayden told me something he thought in private and awkward described knowing about it.

Did he really think I was prettier? Of course, he did. He said so. He wouldn't lie. He couldn't tell a lie when his mind couldn't see straight. It was *not* a secret that Ayden became an honest man while he was under the influence. He was more of a sincere man than when he wasn't.

He was honest. Truthful.

And he thought I was pretty—prettier than Sunny.

Taking a seat on the couch, I pushed some hair behind my ear.

But why did that make me feel funny?

It couldn't be true. I did not want what God said to be true. If I gained any kind of feelings for Ayden, I'd be an abomination to the angel race.

Wrong was the word to describe the moment. I had no beating heart. He was my charge, I his guardian angel. It wasn't within my rights to feel giddy from his words of intimacy, words that ran deeper than vulnerability. What he had told me continued to confirm what had been predicted to become a reality. The possibility grew with ease and reminded me that Ayden and I would someday end up in an affair.

 ABJECT

I stepped into water in small puddles all over the tiles. "Ayden, what is this?" I yelled. I rushed out of the bathroom and shot him a stern look.

He looked over at me and lifted both brows in one slow movement. "What is what?"

"There is water all over the bathroom floor! You do not own this apartment. You pay them to let you live here and you are on the verge of getting kicked out." I rubbed my face due to all the stress. "If you are kicked out, what am I supposed to do? I can't get you a place to stay. I can't even stay with you if you have to move in with other people." I dropped my hands at my sides and let out a sigh.

Ayden chuckled in a low tone and stood from the couch. "You'll be gone? Sounds wonderful."

"Is it, Ayden? Is it really wonderful?" I crossed my arms. "I'm no expert but I know that you wouldn't want that. You need me in your life."

He choked on a laugh. "Whoa, Angel, you are being very egotistical today. Don't let that go to your head."

I let something slip, something he told me during a moment of vulnerability. "So, you won't miss our arguments? I recall you telling me that you love it when we argue. I doubt Sunny could argue as well as I can. In fact, I doubt Sunny will be as pretty as I am to you."

"Where did you hear that?" He narrowed his eyes at me and for once since our first meeting, I smirked. I had him in my grasp.

"A drunk little birdy told me. Maybe drinking isn't beneficial to you, but I can name one perk. You become an honest man, Ayden Dyer." I closed the gap between us. If I weren't so short, I'd be intimidating. That wasn't working very well in my favor.

"I do not think you're that pretty." He scoffed. He was a terrible liar when caught in the act.

I tilted my head and kept my gaze fixed on him. "No? Why would you be so keen on winning this challenge just to kiss me? If I'm not that pretty, why do you make all these crude jokes about us being sexual? These are questions you can only answer by admitting that you think I'm pretty."

There went my stomach again, doing flips and twisting in every direction. Why did it affect me so much when I thought about how Ayden saw me?

"Okay, so maybe you are pretty but that's because you're an angel. Angels are pretty people." He folded his arms in triumph.

I intended to crush his joy in an instant. "Angels look exactly as they did in their human life unless they had a deformity. I never had one, Mr. Dyer. I look exactly like my human body." A ping of pain hit my heart at that moment. I was being torn down by the longing desire of living a full life, given that I'd never had that chance.

What caught me off guard was the look of concern on Ayden's face. "Angel?"

I forced a smile, denying him access to any buried memories. "You can't lie to me, Ayden. I know the truth." I walked past him, entering his bedroom and disappearing into the closet. I closed the door behind me and put both of my hands to my face as the sobs broke out.

Using my hands, I did my best to silence them. When the worst of the hurt was released, I was left curled up in a fetal position with tears flowing in an endless waterfall down my cheeks. They resembled the waves on a beach, coming back for more.

There were so many dreams I'd had as a human. I never got to complete even a single one. My life had been cut short. I chose to be a guardian angel to help others never go through this kind of misery. There was no worse feeling than knowing your dreams were ripped away and you could never turn back the clock.

Ayden deserved a chance to live his life to the fullest. Nobody should die young.

I opened the closet door and stepped out, surprised by the person sitting against it. "Ayden?"

He was facing forward, not bothering to look my way. "What did I say?"

"Pardon?" I shivered, not sure where that came from.

"What did I say to make you cry?" He turned to give me his attention.

I wasn't even sure how I was supposed to respond to him. He had heard me which wasn't even intended to happen. I was his guardian angel. *I* was supposed to be the rock. "Nothing. It wasn't anything you said. It was something stupid." I cleared my throat. I was not about to burden him with my problems.

He wanted to press for more questions, but he didn't. I wasn't sure if it was because he didn't want to worsen the situation by pestering me, or if he realized he wasn't supposed to care about my feelings.

The spot beside him was calling my name. I listened to it and took a seat on the floor as I leaned against the closet door. "Demons are the bad guys..." I looked at him, now believing Ayden chose not to ask more about me due to him wanting to be the villain of his story.

"Why are you telling me this?" He turned away from me again, focusing his eyes on the bed in front of us.

"Why not? They're our enemies. Demons are the enemies of humans and heavenly creatures alike. The only friends they have are fallen angels and shadows. Yet here you are, making friends with demons. I can't battle and win if you listen to them over me. Who do you think it is that tells you to steal and make bad decisions? There are so many demons and fallen angels, and they influence humans to screw up their life." I had an urge to lie my head on his shoulder but that was far from appropriate. I was his protector and I had to remind myself of that.

"What can you offer me that they can't?" he asked.

I answered with a simple, "Joy. Eternal joy."

He laughed but his laugh had not even a drop of humor in it. "Joy? Do angels get to have sex? Do angels get to drink?"

He really knew nothing about Heaven and Hell. "Jesus turned water into wine, so it's not against Heaven to drink. It's against Heaven to get drunk the way you do. We're supposed to be sober and alert in case of anything. Angels can have sex, yes. If they're married, sex is not wrong. And before you ask, yes, angels can have sex however they wish. If they want to do it in front of a mirror, they can. Sex doesn't have to be the same boring routine. Spicing it up is encouraged." I shrugged a bit. "But I guess that doesn't work for you because you enjoy being drunk and you'd never settle for a woman."

"What is the point of marriage, really?" He gave me a look. "Why settle for just one person, one woman to shag for the rest of my life?"

"Well, this may be hard to explain because it takes maturity to understand the point of marriage." I pushed some hair from my face. "We were originally made to have one person and one companion. Adam's rib was used to make Eve, who became his companion because he deserved to love. There's a rib for everyone out there. I believe that. It's our innate desire to crave love. Not everyone finds love, which is depressing to me. Marriage may seem crazy because you see it as a contract but it's not a contract. It's a covenant. It's a promise two people make to one another, vowing to spend forever together. It's beautiful. I can't begin to explain the desire of wanting to spend your life with one person. If you don't have it, you can't be taught it," I said.

"It seems crazy to me. I like being able to explore different women." He gave me a nod.

"You don't date. You have sex. You explore vaginas. If you explored women, you would be dating them rather than humping and dumping. You're in it for yourself. Both of you always are. Sex between two strangers holds no meaning because the emotional connection is absent. When you fall in love and have sex, you are connected in every way. It enhances the sexual experience. When you love someone, you want to please them. Your focus is redirected to satisfy them rather than yourself and there's something wonderful in being able to please the one you love. You can never replicate that feeling with a stranger." I shook my head and glanced down at my dress.

He nudged me. "How would you know this, Angel? Have you had sex? Were you in love?"

I lifted my eyes to meet his. "I know because I'm dead. God created sex. I know what His intended purpose was. I've heard from others who've experienced this on how it feels. I've met angels who were in your shoes once. They found love. They are the ones who tell me. There's something different about being with a stranger and being with someone where love is true. That is common sense. Without those other connections before having sex, it will feel different."

Ayden ran his fingers through his hair. "I'm not looking for emotional connections. Demons are my friends because they don't judge me or tell me who to be."

Scooting away, I almost rolled my eyes, but I controlled myself. "Demons judge you, too. If you choose good, they judge you. They possess you and control you to be the bad guy, Ayden. Demons are the exact opposite of us. They are here to hurt you. You do not seem to understand the seriousness of this situation. It isn't a joke like humans make it out to be. You humans always talk about how cool it is to be friends with demons as if it's this edgy thing to do but it's not cool. It's real and they will destroy you. They are not your friends. They are the friends that pretend to care and then turn around and backstab you. They tear you apart."

"How would you know what that's like?" His stare was intense but filled with curiosity.

I swallowed, remembering *his* face as he watched me bleed out. He was the demon who had deceived me from the start. He misled everyone. "I just know." My gaze focused on the walls.

Ayden got up from the floor and pulled a shirt over his head. "I'm going out."

"Where are you going?" I watched him put his boots on.

"Out. I'm meeting up with Sunny. She said she wanted to hang out. Who am I to turn a beautiful girl down?" He tied his laces and shoved his arms through the sleeves of a heavy winter jacket. This coat was made of all cloth, not water-resistant in any way.

"You turn me down every time I try to help," I said to him.

He chuckled and pulled a beanie over his head. "Don't flatter yourself, Angel. There goes that ego of yours again." He winked at me and exited the room. I flinched at the sound of the front door closing behind him.

Why did it bother me that he was hanging out with her? I wanted him to be serious with a woman. Sunny was the perfect opportunity. She was gorgeous and he couldn't have sex with her which meant he could only be a boyfriend or a friend rather than her one-night-stand. Ayden could have a real chance to discover his need to love just one woman.

Sunny was a stunning woman, and I'd be an idiot to deny it. She had the perfect body and she was out of his league in a good way. Her hazel eyes matched well with her red hair while the freckles on her skin complimented her complexion.

I had no right to be mad at Ayden for recognizing beauty when he saw it. He was hanging out with a girl for more than sex. It was a good start and he deserved to change no matter how he did it.

I was in the wrong for thinking this could be a bad thing for him to do. Maybe she was that special woman who had Ayden realizing that he wished for more. *Maybe* she could get the bad boy to love again—something I couldn't seem to do.

So, why did I feel a ping of spite for their sprouting relationship? *Because she was a threat to me.*

TESTIMONY

The home of the Dyers was filled with joyous melodies and cheerful tunes that sang for the spirit of the holiday. "We wish you a merry Christmas," the family carefully caroled.

Ayden rolled his green eyes at the cheery faces of his relatives. His mother called everyone into the kitchen for the holiday feast. Everyone rushed over to the table.

The dinner was organized to perfection—blending into the air before meeting our noses. Every seasoning that coated the turkey had it screaming with flavor.

I took a seat with everyone else and we began dishing up our plates. As they shoveled food into their mouths, I took note that they weren't the type of family to say grace before a big meal.

As I ate my food, I savored every bite. The level of taste was exceptional compared to my Thanksgiving meal. The spices added to every portion in just the right mixture.

Ayden watched Arabella until she said something to catch him off guard. "Any girlfriends?"

He moved his food around with his fork, not mentioning Sunny.

Clearing my throat, I said, "Sunny. He's been hanging out with Sunny, a girl we met at the bar."

Arabella's eyes shot up in surprise. "Sunny? This is the first I've heard about you even hanging out with a female for more than sex."

Their mother gave them both looks. "This is the dinner table."

"Sunny is just a nice girl. Nothing has even happened between us." Ayden shoved some Yorkshire pudding into his mouth, a common English dessert served with their roast turkey.

"Nothing?" My interest piqued.

Ayden's eyes darted over to me and a small smirk appeared on his lips. "Does that surprise you? I told you I can control myself."

Arabella choked on her food before wiping away at her mouth using a napkin. "You can? I've never seen this side of you. This is shocking, and in a good way. Sunny sure can turn around a rainy day over here," she joked while playing with Sunny's name.

I finished eating and smiled at his mother. "Thank you, Mrs. Dyer. That was an amazing meal."

"Thank you for being here." She gave me a smile and gathered up the dishes.

Decorations were strung about throughout the home. Some sat atop counters and others made the entertainment center pop. One was a red embossed platter topped with a Santa surrounded by cinnamon-scented pinecones. A few holiday-spirited plaques hung on the walls and the railing of the stairwell was wrapped in silver and gold tinsel.

The tree stood tall in the living room, in front of the big window for all neighbors to admire. At seven feet, the tree was dressed in navy blue and gold bulbs with different patterns and designs, even spacing between each one. Warm, white lights were built into the fake tree to make everyone's life easier. Blue and gold ribbon were wrapped around with elegance that only someone with attention to detail could manage. A metallic gold skirt circled the bottom while dozens of presents kept the trunk of the tree warm. A pure white angel stood at the top with a bright light illuminating the darkness, inviting everyone to watch.

The angel was fitting for the occasion, but I was the one angel that never glowed on Christmas. Too many monstrous memories plagued my thoughts on what was meant to be the happiest season of all.

Presents were wrapped in paper and ribbon that fit the color scheme of the entire tree, tying it all together with one coherent theme. Like a puzzle piece, it all created the ideal mood for the exquisite evening pictured before us.

I watched the Dyers as they all interacted with each other. Arabella was talking to Ayden. It filled me with bliss to know they were bonding like siblings were supposed to. Ayden was not exempt from being annoyed at certain times, but they were having a conversation and I couldn't ask for anything better.

Getting off the couch, I exited the house and stood on the balcony to get some fresh air for the evening, overlooking the winter wonderland. Snow fell from the sky, creating a white blanket amongst the earth. The scene was mesmerizing but even more evoking than anything. I reminisced on this date today, Christmas Day. Something happened a year ago that changed my entire life.

In one swift motion, he sliced across my neck with a clean cut and the skin opened to let the dark red fluid spill onto everything in its path.

My body collapsed without warning, my muscles giving out on me. He squatted down, pushing hair away from my face. "You were too smart for this. I had to get rid of the enemy before you got rid of me."

I choked, unable to breathe or stop the blood as my hands flew up to try to keep it from leaving my body. The thick liquid spilled through my fingers, unfaltering, and within seconds, I dropped to the floor as the twilight swept me away. Now I would know if life ended here or if there was more waiting on the other side.

It had been one whole year since my death, and it never failed to slap me in the face and make me wish I'd just seen it coming.

The more time passed, the more reality set in, dread deep within the pits of my stomach. Losing the battle with that man displayed the level of catastrophe I had found myself ensnared in.

Christmas was a rough time of year due to two deaths. It would be difficult for the rest of my angel days, but I was going to push through like I always had. My struggles may have come every now and then, but I was always stronger than what tried to tear me down.

"Aren't you cold?" Ayden asked me out of the blue.

I'd been so lost in my own head to notice he had come outside at all, yet here he was, smoking a cigarette and blowing some of it into my face. "I guess you could say that."

"What does that mean? Are you women ever direct with your words?" He shifted his gaze towards me and lifted his eyebrows in question.

"Sometimes we are direct and sometimes we aren't. Either way, I'm also an angel and I am not obligated to tell you what I mean." I never turned his way but instead, I studied the snowflakes as they grew in size.

"I thought we'd become friends enough for you to tell me your story," he joked.

"I thought you didn't consider us friends. I guess we both were wrong. Why are you out here?" I twisted my whole body his way, giving him my undivided attention.

"I'm not a very joyful person in general and Christmas is not my thing. The music and decorations become too much for me. I guess I'm Scrooge." He snickered. He waved his cigarette in my face as well, showing me he needed the nicotine.

I smiled a little. "I never pictured you as anyone else. Then again, so am I," I said the last sentence in my quietest voice.

"How are you grumpy during this holiday? You're an angel and you're very hard to bring down from cloud nine." He gave me a small nod.

"There are many things you don't know about me, Ayden Dyer." I leaned my right side against the railing of the balcony. "This is your first Christmas with me and you haven't seen me as overly cheerful like your family, now have you? Rather, I've been here admiring the snow for its sparkling beauty, just thinking about the past."

"You think about the past? I guess I didn't suspect that Angel thought about it at all. Speaking of which, I know your name isn't really Elena Jones." His smile faded as his face turned serious.

I straightened my posture, stepping away from the rail. "Who's to say I'm not?"

"I researched your name. It's ironic because Elena Jones is really a doctor in some form like you claim to be, but she is not you," he stated.

"Why not?"

"Because there are pictures of her to go with her name and you're white. She's not." He lifted his eyebrows in the slightest form. He caught me in my lie.

I faced the backyard and crossed my arms. "I'm not Elena Jones. You still don't know my real name and you never will."

"Why is that? You don't really think I can't investigate, can you?"

I stiffened at the word investigation. The events flooded my mind, taking over what attempt I made to forget about them. Being dead never erased my old life from corrupting my pure thoughts, and it would never do so either.

Ayden took notice of my body language and he came closer, his breath fanning the back of my neck. "What is it that makes you react that way? You don't really think I can't put the pieces together. You forget that you also don't know very much about me, and I am very capable of figuring out a mystery."

Goosebumps covered my skin and I tried to hide the reactions my body gave away without a second thought.

"Soon enough I will know your real name and I will know everything about you. You're not very good at keeping secrets, Angel." He disappeared back into the house after smashing the cancer stick under his shoe. The cold air rushed at my backside to pull me in its embrace.

I faced the empty space he left behind without any effort. Ayden was right and we both knew he would have no problem discovering my real identity. That was what I feared the most, the outcome of my entire plan.

Heading back inside, everyone passed around gifts and opened as if they'd been children to this day. I planted myself down in a chair and watched it all as if they were in a movie, wading in the feeling of a family being together again.

My eyes lingered on Ayden's for a little too long but neither of us seemed to care. We zoned out during our staring contest and it wasn't until a hand waved in front of my face that I came back to earth.

"Sorry," I said as I glanced at Esme.

She sat back in her spot, eyes fixed on me. "I got worried for a moment. You looked brain dead or something." She returned her attention back to her family.

I looked up at the ceiling and wondered if something was going to happen soon. My figurative heart screamed that something was off and I needed to be cautious. I couldn't quite guess what it was. I decided to let it go for now—allow it to float off in my brain into another corner.

The rest of the night was filled with the spirits of the Christmas season. Laughter, jokes, and childhood stories bounced between each person. Ayden pitched in from time to time, but I never uttered a word.

Being his dead therapist meant I was nothing more to them than just that. I didn't have anything to contribute to this family gathering anyhow. I observed Ayden and his actions, confirming my own eyes that he was saving his soul. I was witnessing his change in a slow but sure time-lapse.

My mind wandered back to the incident from the previous year, turning this night more sour than it should have been. Today marked the one-year anniversary of my murder and I was never going to move on from it as long as I worked with human beings. Nothing else could be more foreboding than the recollection of my own demise.

ABASE

Someone knocked on the door, causing me to wonder who it could be. His family wouldn't visit this late, would they? I never knew. Families were an interesting bunch of people.

Ayden answered the door while I put on human clothes to blend in once again.

"Come on in. You don't have to knock, you know. You can just come in." Ayden's words echoed throughout the apartment, laced in that thick, English accent of his.

I peeked out of the bathroom, my curiosity getting the best of me as if I were still alive. "Who's at the door?" I asked him.

He began to approach me, but another person popped in front of me, blocking my view of Ayden. However, he was taller than she was and his entire face was still exposed.

"Hello, you must be his therapist. You were at my party, right? I didn't know he lived with his therapist. Live-in therapists—are those a thing?" She looked at Ayden, questioning his intentions.

I scowled within my head. He'd brought another girl home again. He invited Sunny to his apartment of all people, and I could only imagine where this was going to end up.

Ayden noticed the anger mixed with annoyance on my face, flashing me a small smirk in return. "Is something wrong, therapist?"

"Nope." I straightened my posture and put my hands behind my back. "I could only imagine how this is going to go." I eyed Ayden, not careful to keep my words vague.

Sunny looked between us and cleared her throat, butting into the conversation, "Of course, I can't deny this man is a handsome one, but Ayden told me he's a virgin and he's trying to save that. I respect it. I think it's more attractive." She gave him a cute smile and he responded with a fake one.

I choked on my own saliva, picturing Ayden as a man who'd never had sex. "Oh, he's a virgin." I nodded, shrugging a bit. I knew that was the biggest load of bull. I indeed found abstinent men attractive, but Ayden was nothing but a liar. He was the farthest from a virgin. My best guess to explain this was that he didn't want to expose the truth that he'd made a deal with his dead therapist about it. He chose to give up sex for ten weeks. He just had around six more weeks to go if he could control himself for that long.

"I suppose I shall leave you two kids alone then." I disappeared into his room and made myself cozy in his closet. This situation would backfire on him, strengthening my side of the bet. Ayden could never be alone with a woman like that and not make a move towards sex. He was not that strong, and I knew so from watching him talk to women. Lust won the battle every time.

Hours passed by as I kept to myself, afraid that they would soon end up here. I made the decision to leave the room before I got stuck listening to them go at it.

Upon entering the living room, I was surprised to find the two of them watching a movie. This was quite unusual for Ayden. It appeared to me that he had more self-control than he chose to show.

His arm was draped around her shoulders while she rested her head against his chest. The sight bothered me in a way, and not just because I was trying to change him. Something about it didn't sit right with me.

Sunny turned her head to Ayden and asked a question that almost made my soul shrivel up. "Are you sleeping with your therapist?"

He looked over at her, making the wrong joke, "I wish." Ayden wasn't good at any kind of real romance and it was only a matter of time before Sunny realized this.

"What does that mean? You live together." She took her head off his chest.

He let out a small sigh. "I'm sorry. No, we aren't sleeping together. I promise. She's a virgin anyway."

"So are you," she replied.

He cleared his throat, trying to cover up the lies slipping through his teeth. "Yes, I am. Both of us are abstinent so we aren't going to be into that kind of thing."

It baffled me that Sunny believed this guy. She couldn't possibly think he was a virgin. Ayden was an attractive man that loved to smoke and drink all the time. The trinity of sin wouldn't be complete without sex and she had to be a real airhead to ignore that. I was supposed to be the blonde here but Sunny outshined me in that department.

I let go of my absence, walking out in full view and facing both of them. "What are you guys talking about?" I sat down beside them, interrupting their little date. It was all done with a purpose—to keep these two under my watch. As his therapist, it was my business to know, right?

"It's none of your business," Ayden answered.

I got comfortable on the couch, giving up my innocent game. "Well, if it's any consolation, we aren't sleeping together. I would never do such a thing. He's my patient. I don't get involved with my patients like that." I shook my head with a lot of confidence.

I'd lose my job if Ayden and I ever had a thing and I was not going to risk my entire future based on one boy who had one too many issues.

Sunny nodded, feeling better with my confirmation to back up his claim.

Boredom settled in within seconds after I folded my hands in my lap. Being here with them grew awkward, like I was their chaperone. I became the parent nobody wanted around.

I tried to zone out, to leave them to their conversation. They wouldn't have sex whether I was here or not. Ayden was apparently a virgin. I was more curious than anything to see how long that lie would last. He'd have to break at some point. Nobody could keep going forever and I knew because I'd seen it many times before. This wasn't my first lesson.

"Well, I should get going to bed." I left for his room again, sitting back down on the little nest I made within his closet.

One may have thought life would be dull in this small space, but I begged to differ. I had my thoughts to keep me occupied.

An hour had gone by when the door squeaked open and someone entered the room. My body tensed up, expecting multiple footsteps and the sounds of buckles coming off the pants. I peeked out when I hadn't heard a single sound.

The buckles did come off, but it was just Ayden. It was a shock to see him alone, getting into his bed. He looked in my direction and noticed my eyes glued on him. "Is there a reason you're going to watch me get undressed?" He gave me that stupid smirk.

I cleared my throat as I tried to remove the shakiness from my voice. "I'm sorry. I was just surprised that you didn't bring Sunny with you."

"She went home. A deal is a deal, and I plan to win. I have motivation rooting for me." He pumped his fist in the air.

Fear clouded my mind as I swallowed my own lump. Ayden couldn't do this; he just couldn't. Could he actually go a whole ten weeks without any sex...?

He fell asleep for the rest of the night while I spent mine wondering if I'd made a losing bet. The terrifying scenes that played in my head were of Ayden kissing me, and me craving more. I could lose my job over this. I refused to be just an angel because of him. I wanted him to win and prove he was bettering himself, but I didn't want that at the expense of my own position.

Ayden was up after ten in the morning, and I made a savory and sweet breakfast to wake him up. If I hadn't, he would have slept in until noon. He'd done it plenty of times before.

One of his arms was across his face like most guys would do when they slept. He slowly pulled it off as he opened his eyes up to the sight of food, drooling over the morning meal. The scent of French toast and bacon floated through the air, teasing his nose with a hint of cinnamon.

He got out of the bed and came over to me, to the plate of food I held for him. I certainly never made it for myself. "Good morning," I said to him.

His lips curved upward. "Good morning, Angel." He took the food and began to devour it as if he weren't going to make it until tomorrow.

Taking a seat on his bed, I studied his face while he shoveled the meal into his mouth. "Are you dating Sunny now?" It was a genuine question and I had to ask.

He lifted his eyes to meet mine, chewing food as he spoke, "No."

I asked another question, "Do you plan on more dates?"

"Why do you care?" He lowered his plate for a minute and swallowed his food.

I shrugged as I stood. "I just want to know."

"I don't know. I would like to go on more dates. I think she's cute. Her brother and I get along. I've never had much of a serious relationship but there's a first time for everything." He started to eat again.

I let him eat in peace while backing into the corner, processing this new information. He wanted a serious relationship with Sunny? Why? I was trying to understand the reasoning, but I just couldn't. Whichever way he went, I was still prettier. He'd said so.

He exited the room and left me alone. I didn't bother to follow him because I needed that time to myself. It seemed I would have a lot of time to be with myself. If he were going to have his first girlfriend, I would have to fill my time without his help.

He came back into the room and interrupted my thoughts. "Do you want to help me make a cake? I have to go to the shop and make one. Mum and Dad think I should be more involved so they want me to go in and deliver the special order."

"Why can't Sunny go with you?" It came out faster than I could catch it. It sounded rude and I hadn't tried to come off that way, but it happened.

"Whoa, you sound crabby. Did she do something to you?" He put his hands on his hips to mock me, acting as if he was a girl engrossed in the gossip.

I shook my head, my face heating up from the embarrassment. I didn't want to elaborate on what I meant with that question because

I couldn't. I couldn't decipher my words as to why I said it the way I did.

"Let's go bake a cake," I said as I fixed my clothes.

We walked a few streets over before coming to his parents' shop. Based on location, the shop would open at 11:00 at the earliest. On Saturdays, they opened just an hour before that. He unlocked the door and I followed him to the kitchen where the supplies waited for us.

He put an apron on, first and foremost. Once he was settled in, he grabbed a bag of flour and set it down on the table. "All right, what is about to happen next is not supposed to be seen by anyone," he warned me.

I chose not to start any arguments, nodding instead.

He gathered more ingredients, stirring them together in different measurements. He mixed the wet with the dry and poured the completed batter into the baking pan and put it into the oven at a set temperature.

While we waited for his cake, he carried the bag of flour over to me and dumped it on my head. I gasped as I straightened my arms out in front of me. "Ayden! What did you do that for?"

"We need to add some entertainment to the job." He gave me a genuine smile.

I wiped off as much as I could, but the flour clung to my skin. Anything he did never made sense to me. He was just as bad as a girl on her period. One minute he despised me but the next minute he wanted to play games as if we were best friends for life.

I let out a sigh, observing the mess he made on the floor and the one he made me into. "You're cleaning this up."

He grabbed a bowl and put it beside my head, pushing as much as he could out of my hair and into it. Being an angel meant I could not produce human flaws such as sweat and dandruff. I would always be as clean as a whistle. My hair stuck out everywhere, betraying me in its imperfect glory. "There, all fixed. Let me teach you how to bake a cake."

"I know how to bake. I had to teach you when you pretended that you couldn't." I crossed my arms with my eyes narrowed at him.

He picked up an egg and cracked it on my head, smearing it into my hair. "You're the cake."

"What does that mean?" I shot him a glare, my irritation rising with every second he ruined my appearance.

He grabbed another egg, getting ready to break it. Before he could, I ran around the counter to the other side, palms splayed on the edge. "No, you are not going to mess it up anymore! You are going to stop this right now!"

He held a mischievous smile as he began to chase me around the island. I was determined to not get turned into a fluffy sweet treat, and he was just as *hellbent* on making me into a cake, whatever that truly meant.

I gripped the wooden counter, watching his moves. He came around and I ran again. The flour that powdered the floor stripped that ability from me as I slipped and fell right into it.

Before Ayden could stop and save himself, he tripped over my foot and came down on top. My hair was splayed out around me, my arms beside my head. Ayden's elbows kept him hovering above me but the gap between us was too small for this to be considered family-friendly.

Our eyes were glued together while I swallowed, my face burning a bright red. Our faces were inches apart, the heat of his breath hitting my lips. Everything about this was wrong, and yet neither of us did anything to prevent it.

No muscles moved except for Ayden leaning his face closer to mine.

The timer beeped, bringing us both back to earth.

I whispered, "You should probably get off now."

Ayden didn't smirk or make any inappropriate comments. He got off of me in a hurry, helping me up. He rubbed the back of his neck due to the awkward energy hanging in the room. He pulled the cake from the oven, distracting himself from the events that just took place between us.

I attempted to scrub away the redness, but it wouldn't work. I couldn't describe any of this because I didn't know what was going on. Everything was new to me when it came to romance or anything lingering in that vicinity. My whole body was reeling the effects of what had happened and I was unable to find the off switch. Ayden and I had come a second away from kissing and that was going to haunt us both until I moved onto someone else.

ANATHEMA

H er presence carried throughout the building. She was airborne, enough to saturate every place nearby where she was. "Ayden, stop!" Sunny screamed between laughs. No, he wasn't killing her or raping her. He was *tickling* her.

I was sitting in the kitchen, listening to the two of them have the weirdest date I had ever witnessed, and I'd observed some strange dates in my days on earth.

Ayden stopped tickling Sunny and chuckled as the two of them fell onto the couch. Sunny was exhausted from all the laughing, and it was clear that she was far more ticklish than I was. She could have also been faking it just for show. It was her way of flirting, and it was pathetic.

However, she had his attention. I may have been prettier, but she was the one being tickled. If he threw flour on her at some point...

"Let me get us some water," he said as he came into the kitchen. He gave me a small smirk and poured a glass. "Are you having fun?"

I shrugged and leaned in as I whispered, "Are you?" I knew he was still struggling to enjoy the presence of a woman without taking her clothes off. "Can you imagine the sex?" I had ripped a paper plate apart at the thought of them.

His eyes zoomed in on the torn plate. "I can imagine it, but my question is, why can you?" He faked a gasp. "Is Angel jealous?"

I scoffed. "Jealous? I do not get jealous. You're attractive but I do not have a thing for you." Although, I feared he could be right. He could never find out about any of this. It was foretold I would fall for him and it was beginning to come true. That terrified me.

He finished with his drink of water. "Mhm, sure." He leaned onto the counter. "But every woman has a thing for me." He reached out, brushing his knuckle under my chin and leaving the kitchen.

Shivers ran through my soul and I took a deep breath to keep myself calm. This wasn't true. It couldn't be real.

Sunny came into the kitchen and noticed the nervousness written all over my face. "What's wrong?"

I fixed my expression and shook my head to tell her I was fine. I was the therapist. It was my job to ask that question and not be on the receiving end.

She leaned over the counter. "Did Ayden say something? Do I need to smack him for you? I'm not a therapist. Just say the magic words and I'll do your bidding."

Shame washed over me and flushed out any lies I used to tell myself to feel better. Sunny was not a bad girl at all. She drank on her birthday like most adults would do to celebrate. It didn't make her a bad person. She found Ayden attractive and wanted a relationship, which I couldn't fault her for. I couldn't fault Ayden, either, for trying to start a real relationship with a beautiful woman to counteract his craving for sex.

Nobody was to blame but I. It was I who felt off about seeing them together and yet it never made sense. I knew Ayden and everything he'd done since I met him. There was no way I could love a man who found himself through law-breaking and stupidity.

"Ayden didn't say something. It's not your concern. Go—have fun and cuddle with him," I said those words to her and punched myself in the gut for even suggesting it. I was battling *myself.*

A smile brightened her face. "Thank you. I promise we won't do anything too inappropriate." Sunny left the room and joined Ayden on the couch.

I turned around on my stool and peeked at them, closing my eyes. Before something unholy came into my head, I walked into another room—the bathroom. Seeing my reflection wasn't an option but that didn't stop me from looking into the mirror. What was I searching for? I couldn't be sure.

I needed to be anywhere but here. Being around these two would drive me crazy and yet I also had to know what was happening.

A knock bounced off the walls as someone's knuckles met the other side of the bathroom door. "Yes?" I asked.

Sunny's voice came through, "I just wanted to use the bathroom. I kind of have a girl emergency. You understand. I forgot a tampon. Do you happen to have any?"

I widened my eyes and swallowed. This was not supposed to happen. If I lived here, it only made sense for me to have feminine products, and yet I didn't because periods were not a thing in my life anymore.

"Uh, sorry, I actually came in here to find one myself, but I guess it totally spaced my mind and I ran out before I bought more. I can go to the store and get a box for us both." I opened the door, meeting her eyes.

She laughed and walked into the bathroom. "Well, I guess I can use toilet paper until you get back. It's always funny how a lot of girls sync up like that."

I didn't feel awkward about leaving these two alone, knowing

Ayden and Sunny would not have sex while breaking promises and rules during a bloody time. Well, I could hope... I knew almost next to nothing about Ayden at this point in our charge-guardian angel relationship. It was possible that he could still do the dirty while she was menstruating. Sunny? I mean, maybe she was in pain and sex would help. Either way, I was hoping they were not those kinds of people.

I vacated the apartment to go get tampons. Sunny had no idea that Ayden and I couldn't pay for these tampons. Did I feel wrong for stealing tampons? A little, only because it would mess up store inventory. But most of me felt it was a right and not a luxury. Girls deserved to have feminine products for something they had no control over.

I shoved the tampons into the scoop of my dress, hiding it until it disappeared with the rest of me. I exited the store and returned to the apartment, changing into human clothes before walking back inside.

As I entered the bathroom, I didn't see her red hair in sight. I checked the bedroom, but she wouldn't be there if Ayden was in the living room. "Where did Sunny go?"

"She left. She went home." He shrugged.

I looked at the box of tampons. "I stole tampons for her. That is so unappreciative."

He chuckled. "Tampons? You stole from a store? You get worse every month. You can return used clothes, but you can't return used tampons."

Sighing and shaking my head, I dropped the box onto the counter and sat down on a stool. "Tampons are a need—a necessity. Do not even get me started on this."

"Condoms are, too." Ayden nodded and sat forward.

I sat with my back against the counter and spread my arms across the surface. "Condoms? This is what's wrong with society. Condoms are free at clinics, yet you must pay for tampons. It's complete bullcrap. Condoms are for people who can't keep their pants on. Tampons are for women whose pants get ruined by something they cannot control. Eve had one job, Ayden. She had one job and she didn't listen. If she had just stayed away from the tree of knowledge, women would never have periods!" I groaned in frustration. I didn't have one anymore, but I never forgot the feeling of my uterus contracting.

Ayden rubbed his neck. "You seem pretty angry about it."

"I'm a girl. I got the worst end of the stick. Of course I'm angry. Did you ever happen to wonder why women get periods, why sex hurts and why giving birth tears apart your vagina?" I swiveled on the stool, leaning over and giving him more of my attention.

He clasped his hands together as he went into deep thought. "I figured sex hurt because it's a new experience for women, having a baby hurt because you're pushing a watermelon out of a ten-inch hole, and periods are there to get rid of old eggs." It took me by surprise that Ayden knew the size of a woman's cervix when she was ready to give birth.

"Valid reasons, yes, but I know the truth. I'm an angel and I have direct access to God. The truth is women are cursed because Eve ate the apple first. It was she who disobeyed first, then talked Adam into it." I got off the stool, pacing around the room. "And of course, Adam did choose to eat the apple as well. But Eve screwed us all over. Your actions and choices don't just affect you. They affect more people than you think. Maybe when you decide to steal, someone loses their job over it. Someone breaks down because it was special, or maybe they were going to sell it to help pay bills they can't afford. I know why you do it, though."

He leaned back, relaxing into the cushions and spreading out. "Is that so? And why do I steal, Angel? You know me so well, of course.

Go on." He gestured for me to continue.

"You're the alpha." I pushed some of my hair behind my ear.

He choked on his laugh. "I'm a werewolf? Bloody hell, that's a new one."

"No, Ayden, you're trying to live up to this alpha image. It's a mold that society has created for males and you're afraid of not fitting it. I know how this works. You're the bad guy because you want to be seen as someone who is tough and takes what he wants. You want to be strong and in charge, and not the baker's son. You are afraid to show people you are a human with passions and emotions." I stopped pacing and faced him, taking a step forward.

"You believe I'm afraid?" He cocked an eyebrow.

"I don't believe it. I know it. You shouldn't be. You do not have to be the bad boy to be accepted into society. Girls like fixing bad boys but nobody really likes one. They enjoy the idea of who they can help you become." I chewed my lip, concern etched in my eyes.

Ayden rubbed his face with one hand. "I see what you're doing. You want me to embrace my baking dream and expose it to the world."

I got closer, getting onto my knees. "I want you to be happy with what you do. You're a baker and you deserve to share it."

On cue, Ayden ruined the moment with, "You're a bit low there, Angel. Is it my turn to get a blowjob?"

"Oh, gosh, Ayden, no. What is wrong with you? That's so disgusting and inappropriate." I scooted away from him, putting more space between us. "Did you hear me? Do you even care?"

"Do I care?" He leaned down, resting his elbows on his knees. "You're the only one who wants me to embrace it. I'm content with where I'm at."

I crisscrossed my legs. "You're not, Ayden. You were never content with any of this. You don't take care of your apartment. You sleep around to get validation for the love you think you didn't get from your family. You got into a car accident because you ran a red light. You keep telling me not to tell anyone about your baking and it proves you are afraid of it all. You are squeezing yourself into a little mold of a man that was never made to fit any human being on this earth. Smoke doesn't belong in your lungs. Alcohol doesn't belong in your liver. STD's don't belong in your body. These basic facts prove that you are scared and you are not content. No living person would destroy themselves the way you continue to do so if they were so happy with their journey in life."

Silence settled and grew thicker with every passing minute. Ayden was at a loss for words for which I was taken back by. He knew I was right. No human was made to live this way, and I knew that was enough to say he was far from being filled with tranquility.

My eyes shifted to the carpet, staring at the cigarette burns he caused every now and then. "You don't believe your own worth. You don't love yourself and it's tragic to witness it day in and day out. I'm here to help you love who you really are, who you are supposed to be. I'm going to show you how much you mean to this world and your family. You're with Sunny, but she doesn't know that you're with her because of our sex deal. She cares about you. Don't hurt her, Ayden." I brought my gaze back up to him. Something inside me ignited when I caught a glimpse of the resentment he directed towards his own flesh. "Don't hurt *yourself.*"

HONEST

The sound of the knife hitting the counter got louder every time I cut into the carrot. My anger rose while I watched as my clean surface was being tainted with makeout sessions.

Sunny sat on the counter with Ayden between her legs. No, they were not having sex, but their kisses were sloppy at best.

They both pulled away after losing their breath during the battle of the tongues. I was about to lose my cool. In fact, I did.

"Do you two mind if I make dinner here? I'd rather not eat saliva and hair. I don't want to eat this soup and picture you two eating each other." I put my knife down, refusing to touch it until they gave me my space.

Sunny got off the counter. "I'm sorry." She went to the living room. Ayden followed her but only after giving me a death glare. There, they continued to put their tongues down each other's throats.

Something about all of this just made me want to scream and pull my hair out. I never knew Ayden and his girlfriend could drive me crazy.

Sunny giggled. "Ayden, that tickles." I did not want to picture what exactly it was that made her tickle.

Her giggles turned into moans and I cleared my throat to end it all. "Ayden, do not forget about your virginity. Is this how you want to lose it? I'm sure you want it to be special, with rose petals and candles, and not with your therapist five feet away."

Rose petals and candles—they were cheesy but romantic. If I had been alive this whole time and had a chance to find my soulmate, that would be my way to lose it.

Right on time, Ayden came into the kitchen and grabbed the edge of the counter. "Must you ruin everything?"

"Must you always let your second head think before your first?" I gave him one of my cocked eyebrows.

Ayden laughed, running fingers through his hair. "Okay, that was clever. I can admit you got me there."

"All I ask is that you don't make me listen to it again. You did that a few times before and I can't handle it. Those sounds don't go away. It's destroying my pure mind." I cut into a carrot, slicing through my finger. Nothing happened except for my finger becoming transparent enough for the knife to go through and come out unstained of blood.

His Adam's apple bobbed. "I won't. I promise."

"Whoa, careful as not to make promises you can't keep." I pointed the knife in his direction.

"This one I will keep." He looked at Sunny who sat on the couch and waited for his return.

"How can you be so sure?"

His voice deepened as he said, "I'm sure. Stop pestering me about it." He left the kitchen with bubbling frustration trailing behind him.

I wasn't so sure what had gotten into him. Why did he seem to get so mad when I suggested how he would keep his promise? He was the one who told lies.

I finished with dinner and called everyone into the kitchen.

Tonight, the silence blended with awkward tension.

The soup was the only good part of this. I had added just the right number of carrots and celery to give it the flavor it needed, aside from the broth, noodles, and other flavoring.

When my bowl was empty, I stood from the table. "I'm going for a walk."

Sunny gave me a look, and I knew what it was for. "This late?"

Ayden nudged her and nodded towards me. "She'll be fine. Trust me. This girl can kick arse."

"Is it something I said? We can stop making out." She continued to talk me into staying. It was no use.

"No, don't worry about it. You should cuddle and watch a movie or something." I dressed in warmer clothes to hide that I wasn't cold just for being dead. Pretending to be human was crucial.

Leaving the house, I took in the fresh air, admiring the sparkle of the snow. The color of snow brightened up the night. It just never illuminated my path through the darkness.

It reminded me too much of the tragedy that took place in my human life. Winter was a numbing season. Disdainful. Even a little aloof, but most definitely empathetic. More than people would tend to give it credit for.

The buildings towered over me as the moonlight cast a shadow. Being dead, I didn't have a shadow. Humans did.

Turning on my heel, I faced the man in the hood who'd been following me for a block. "Don't think I didn't see you. You do not want to do this."

"Why is that? Because God said so?" his words echoed inside my head. He pulled down his hood and I scowled at the sight. "We know, Angel. We always know your darkest secrets. What do we enjoy more than anything? We enjoy scaring and torturing you. It is just too easy." He closed the gap between us.

He deserved none of my fear. "How do you suppose you will scare me when I know who you are? You can't touch me. You have no right to touch me unless I fail my mission. I fail when Ayden is in Hell or I give up, and neither has happened."

He leaned forward, attempting to intimidate me. "It wouldn't be the first time you sent a man to Hell." A shadow stood by his side, acting as *his* to portray him as a human. It was bogus.

"Seeing as I made it into Heaven, God doesn't seem too upset. Sam had it coming when he tried to do unspeakable things." I waved my hand back and forward, against the air. "And use a breath mint."

He stepped back. "Do you know the future?"

"None of us know unless God tells us. He is the only one who knows. Not even your precious Lucifer knows the future. He likes to pretend he's God, but he isn't. He needs to face the facts. He was the created, not the creator." I folded my arms across my chest, dismissing the nerves of mine hanging from the edge of the cliff in my mind.

"Ah, but did He not mention that you would fall for our sweet Ayden? What happens when you realize you're falling in love? What happens when Ayden tells you that he has a girlfriend and you're just his therapist?" His eyes smiled with the impure thoughts that ran rampant in his mind.

"I'm not falling for Ayden." Why did I find it hard to believe my own words?

With a chuckle, he turned away. "No? What do you call it when his girlfriend and him kiss in front of you?"

I shrugged, averting my eyes. "I call it being sick of PDA. I'm still an angel."

"Exactly. You're an angel. Your reaction was far from called for. You were ready to cut out their tongues." He turned his head to look at me.

"What's your point? Get to it." I rolled my eyes as he spun his whole body in my direction.

He came, not daring to touch me this time. "My point is you will fail sometime in this task. You can't win a war with someone you love. Your love cannot save Ayden."

I clicked my tongue. "I never used my love to save him. I'm still capable of doing my job. Do you not see? He has a girlfriend and I could never get between that."

"Ah, but you already have." He snapped his fingers for the shadow to follow him and together they abandoned me in the dark.

I wasn't sure what he even meant by that. How had I already gotten between them?

Images, voices, and scenes flashed in my head. Ayden had called me pretty. We had come close to kissing as he chased me around the counter and we slipped. There were times in which he confided in me and asked if he made me cry. These were the very things that I thought of when I wondered if I was becoming smitten. Was I *falling*?

He had tried to deny calling me pretty, but he knew it was true. If he were here now, he would be trying to tell me he said petty instead of pretty, but I knew better.

I closed my eyes, looking into the green windows of his soul. I asked myself if I ever had a chance with him had I loved him, but I knew the answer. I did once, and I was the one who told him to make friends. It was I who sent him to Sunny. He was with her because of *me*.

He didn't react well to pain and sorrow. If Ayden were here and he saw me dwelling over everything, he would make some joke to try and turn it around.

I had to fill in for him because he was taken now. I'd use what he had taught me to turn my sorrow into giggles.

Keeping my eyes shut, I imagined a scene, one that made me happy.

The stones were scorching and the fire was blazing. Aside from the crackling sounds, a harmonica whistled through the caves.

I followed this music and stopped at a sight before me, chuckling to myself. The Lord of the Flies sat in his chair, blowing into his instrument. He furrowed his brows and shrugged. "What? Everyone found a loophole out of Hell and now I have nobody to torture."

Coming out of my little mindless video, I scanned my surroundings. A smile was plastered to my face as I kept imagining the image of Lucifer playing the harmonica because the souls were in Heaven. A defeated Lucifer was a spectacular idea.

My mood was dampened by the thought of Ayden and Sunny curled up next to one another.

My whole life I had grown up knowing right from wrong. I was taught morals from a young age and I kept them. Fear of the darkness was something most children and adults were told. There was just a single flaw in this kind of lesson.

They never told us what happened in the *light*.

I knew things I was not supposed to know, things that have made it much harder for me to do my job at all. In the light, I was in misery. They were cozy on the sofa and I was standing in the black of the night.

Heaven was a place of joy and wonder. Angels would laugh and love and help humans below. I was lacking every ounce of heaven tonight. I was filled with the emotions and experiences of humanity. It was far from pleasant, and I knew I had never missed this part. I dreaded the future and what was to come.

My walk back to the apartment was slower than ever. I took my time to let the voiceless words inside my head make themselves at home.

Days had once been simple. Everything was easier when I was a child and I didn't have to worry about being the bigger person. Before Ayden came along, everything still made sense. Now, I wasn't sure of myself. Complex barely began to describe what my afterlife had become since he was assigned to me.

My eyes landed on the empty parking space in front of the apartment building. Her beat-up green car was gone which meant he was alone. With all these mixed feelings swirling inside, I wasn't ready to face him. I couldn't walk in there and see Ayden in the flesh.

Instead, I sat on the curb. I would wait until I knew he was asleep before going into the closet. I wanted no interaction tonight. All I wished for was to forget anything related to how I felt for Mr. Dyer. I would let go of those thoughts.

As I pondered over my choices on the curb, I named a perk to being an angel. When I was alive, I'd been taught not to venture out at night. Bad men existed. Evil lurked around every corner and the darkness waited for me to make that mistake. However, nothing could harm me now that I had no beating heart. I was free to enjoy the serenity of a winter night and nobody was able to teach me about rape or murder. I had the upper hand. I was safe from harm, yet my heart could not be guarded from the warmth of *love*—a love only Ayden Dyer could provoke.

Crickets chirped and not a single cloud floated in the sky. The snow on the ground had been from previous days but tonight, stars shined for the whole world to see. What was it that they wanted to say? It was not anything I desired to utter. I couldn't even figure out what was really going on.

I had one question that kept wandering around and curiosity struck as if it would one day be answered. Why had God told me all of this in the first place?

EXECRATION

I tugged the beanie over my ears and blinked away the snowflakes on my eyelashes. Humans passed by as if I was one of them. People came and went from the building, pushing and pulling the door as they entered or exited the college.

Here I stood, reminiscing of the events that all led up to this moment.

I tried to deny the truth, but I couldn't any longer. I had to face the facts, or I would drive myself crazy trying to believe it wasn't so.

I was *in love* with Ayden Dyer.

We could never control who we fell in love with and I never knew it to be so true until it happened to me.

When he and Sunny would laugh while kissing one another, my heart stung. It was wrong for me to act upon it, but it didn't change that I had feelings for him.

Days passed since I last spoke to Ayden. We would have passing words, but nothing went further than a minute of talking. It was a constant war with me, Heaven, and Sunny.

I was not supposed to be the type of woman who continued to be involved with a man who was taken, and yet I was still his guardian angel. I couldn't just cut him out of my life if I wanted to save his soul. It didn't lessen how morally wrong it was to hang around Ayden so much when he was with another woman while knowing I loved him in a romantic kind of way.

At night, I would imagine his green eyes lost in my own. They would be filled with nothing but joy and admiration. There was no hatred or resentment.

When his lips met with hers, I would switch places with her in my mind. I imagined him kissing me instead.

I knew better. When the day ended, it was always Sunny. It would never be me.

Sunny was the beautiful woman who captured Ayden's interest enough to keep him around for more than sex. I never knew Ayden had a thing for redheads, but I wasn't surprised. I'd envied the fiery hair and freckles. The way they could pull off any eye color, or even all shades of fashion.

When Ayden got in a car crash, I was there. When Ayden ended up drunk, I was present to take him home. When Ayden had issues with his family, I was the one to bring them together and fix it. I was always the one who stood by and aided him to better himself. I helped him realize his talent for baking and it was me, the only woman getting inside his head and who always encouraged him to be himself.

Sunny was never there when he almost died. She wasn't there when Ayden was too impaired to drive himself. She was never there for Ayden the way I was, but he chose *her*. I knew why.

Sunny was alive. Sunny was a fresh start.

I was the person who hid everything from him. I never told him my name. I tried to keep secrets out of his reach. I wasn't even human anymore. Ayden and I had too much history and too many little fights to get past.

I promised I would protect him, but I couldn't continue to keep those vows if he changed. Once he became a saved man, it was my turn to move on.

The hardest part of this was knowing it would never go away. I could never fall out of love with him. It was far too late for that option. He had me wrapped around his finger for the rest of eternity. When he'd find a wife someday, I would assist someone else to change while he and Mrs. Dyer stole kisses throughout their day.

And she would never be *me*.

Ayden was a wonderful man when he tried to be. He could be sweet, funny, and respectful. Sunny didn't know as much as I did but it was not for me to decide. It was Ayden's decision, and he picked her.

Being a guardian angel, it was against the rules to even be with a human. Humans and angels were never supposed to love one another. We were from two different worlds. It was like loving a demon. The act itself was forbidden and unnatural. It was never *meant* to happen. So why did it? Why was it allowed to fester and build? Why couldn't I stop the inevitable from tearing my heart out?

Interspecies romance was frowned upon. We were not the same species the moment *my* heart had stopped beating.

The snow landed on yesterday's sheet beneath it with not a single sound as if careful not to make a sound that would set me off.

As I watched students go about their day, chills ran down my back when his face came into view. He didn't see me, for which I was thankful for. I never got over the way he betrayed me, or how he turned his back on Selene before they had ever met.

His smile sickened me to the core. My hand ached to slap it right off his face and take it for myself. I wanted to steal two things in this world, and one of those things was the joy of my killer.

A woman walked beside him, linking her arm with his. He was always a deceitful man, just as Lucifer was. This man could be Lucifer himself. He fooled every human on earth. Unfortunately for him, he could never fool Heaven or Hell. His soul was damned to the depths of the burning lake under the earth. It pleased me to know his fate to this day. Without repentance and remorse, he would never make it to Heaven.

The two of them made it to his car. I snickered when he opened the door for her. He once did that for Selene, but it was all just a game to him. He circled his car and got in the driver's seat. Together, they left the campus and I feared her fate. My muscles begged me to move and go after them. I wanted to save her from making the same mistake Selene and I made, yet I couldn't do it. It was not my place.

I was Ayden's guardian angel and not hers.

Ayden. The second thing I wanted to steal was his heart. I wanted his heart to be mine, but it was not reality. It was wrong for me to think this way because of how sinful our love could become, but it was my fault. I was the angel in love with the human. Ayden felt nothing for me if it wasn't annoyance.

I'd spent many months with Ayden, about four if I were being accurate. Over four months, I learned things about him that nobody else but his family knew. No other woman he slept with could ever know, and that somehow made me feel important to him. My purpose in his life revealed things even Ayden could never have known about himself. Between all the time with Ayden and knowing his deepest fears and desires, I had fallen in love with the English bad boy. I loved him because he had begun to *let me in.*

My lips formed a smile as the scene replayed inside my head. Ayden throwing flour at me and chasing me around the counter. He was filled with genuine elation that day. His green eyes were the brightest I had ever seen them and there was no pain or self-loathing buried there. It likened to seeing a memory from his past.

I wanted to get that back. He deserved to return to that day again and again until forever ceased to exist. Every person should have been that blissful. If every human could be that way with their interests, this world would be a much better place. The demons would never have a chance to get a hold of their souls.

Ayden was not the only man to fall into this hole. Humans all over were plummeting into the cracks of Hell, damning themselves to the blazing eternity that needed them to thrive.

He was just one of the millions of people who made bad decisions and needed guidance getting his life in order. That was where guardian angels came in. I was not the only one. Millions of guardian angels chose this job to give back and serve the people. Souls were that important to Heaven. The fate of a soul was everything to both Heaven and Hell alike.

A gentle wind breezed by me, moving my hair in one direction.

One thing I missed about being alive was going to college. University was the one place where I felt welcomed and at ease. Maybe I wasn't surrounded by friends, but I wasn't judged because we paid to get there and start our future.

Learning, reading, talking to teachers were all things I enjoyed doing during my days spent in classes. Ayden had a small interest in baking, but my dream was to help others. I would offer to tutor anyone who needed it.

Those days were far behind me now. I never got my degree. I never finished the school year. Nothing but the debt was left to my name. Life ended just as fast as it began, and I missed out on my hopes. I never had a chance to love.

Another pain added to my never-ending list was due to the fact that I had fallen for a man in my afterlife and he wasn't even mine to hold. Another woman had his attention. I never had a chance to achieve any fantasies—even after my neck had been sliced open.

Turning on my heel, I headed away from the college. My hands were shoved in my pockets for comfort and warmth. The ice within my soul didn't come from the temperature of the weather but rather the feeling of loss inside my heart.

Times like these were when I wished I weren't a guardian angel. I could leave Ayden but only for a short time before I had to return and check on him again. I desired to run away, far from this place. I wasn't picky about where I went but I wanted to be anywhere except for here. Any place that could put a smile on my face would be good enough for me. Maybe Mexico, or San Jose. I wasn't sure where but wherever the sun would shine and wash away the hurt and the grief was my fantasy destination.

Winter reminded me of the many bad memories while the gloomy weather sucked out the glee. Sunshine made it much more difficult for me to comprehend what desolation was.

Swimming in the ocean, riding the Ferris Wheel, or eating ice cream were all activities done under the burning star in the sky. Memories of the good times were where my heart wished to be to cope with the lack of Ayden's excitement in my presence.

My toes could be in the sand, waves rolling over my feet and running away. The sun would warm up my cold skin and give it the golden tan it needed to be socially acceptable to my family. The water would be freezing but I would get used to it within a matter of minutes.

Enjoy the little things, is what Selene said to me. So, I did. I savored the little things that kept me strolling through life as if I had it by the reins when I was struggling to start each day.

Selene was my encouragement and voice. She was the part of me that had always needed the push to find happiness in life. I controlled my own paradise. It had never been Ayden or Selene, or anyone else. It was always up to me what I was. I chose to be elated when Selene came into my life and taught me the importance of making lemonade with the lemons that life gave me.

Not a single human could rule everything. Nobody would be in total domination over their life in its entirety, but we could control how we dealt with it and I had chosen to handle it with class.

That was the solution to this predicament with Ayden. I was going to make lemonade and move on. I would never take away any joy he had with Sunny just for myself. If that was who he wanted, he could have her. I would save his soul and go elsewhere after that. He never had to worry about me getting in the way of anything.

He would never even know how I felt about him. My love for him was my secret and solely mine to keep. He had no right to know if he was with somebody else. With my head held high, I was going to be the best actress I'd ever known when I was around him. I was stronger now. I was more powerful than any negativity that hung heavy in the crevices where Mr. Dyer sat within my thoughts.

FIRMAMENT

A yden's back was facing me as he cooked some kind of stir-fry on the stove. Sunny wasn't here today due to work, but it was fine by me. Ayden turned around and looked at me, dipping one of his eyebrows. "You doing all right, Angel? You've been very distant."

"I'm doing fine." *Lies.* Women were never fine when they said so.

He shrugged and scooped the food into a bowl.

"I'll be around if you need me." I slid off the stool and left the apartment. I turned my invisibility on and flew up to Heaven, leaving earth behind me.

Ayden had been right. I was distant and it was because of the truth he could never bear to hear.

Landing on the fluffy clouds, I headed towards the gates and walked inside. Everyone was busy doing what they were assigned to or entertaining themselves with, whether they were keeping up with angels or humans.

Heaven was an interesting place compared to earth. Earth was the middle ground, the place that directed the journey to the end.

Heaven was much different. It was a location of pure euphoria never to be let down. Animals were wild and full of love. Angels were part of a community in which we all played a part. Here, there could be no sorrow or pain. There was no negativity. On earth, I would sit and remember all the agony of being alive. I would feel the ping in my heart at the thought of Ayden and Sunny.

However, I was not on earth. I was in Heaven right now and I was unable to feel that way. I was carefree and happy just being me.

Hell was another story. There, I'd feel nothing *but* suffering. I'd only be able to watch Ayden and Sunny over and over, a never-ending misery. I would always question why I was never enough for him.

Earth was a place of hurt and joy, a mixture of both. On earth, anything was possible. It was the all-access pass to Heaven and Hell, but one had to go through earth first to get to the other. Earth was a stunning place, but it could also be so ugly. It was the best and worst of both worlds. There was a saying that earth was the closest to hell anyone going to Heaven would experience, but earth was also heaven for people like Ayden when they were damned to the lake of fire waiting beneath the surface.

In Heaven, the temperature was always perfect. The wind ceased to exist, and it was just right the way it was. The clouds were fluffy and ranged between sloping whichever way they pleased or laying flat.

Underneath the earth, flames engulfed souls. Heat was everlasting but the souls left to their sins were cold and empty within. When the temperature dropped just enough below freezing, limbs eventually became numb which played in favor of the vessel. However, the fire could never numb the body, nor the soul. Blisters would fester on the surface and torment would forever be bonded to the soul in prison.

There were no cities or countries here. It was just one whole community filled with millions, and probably even billions of angels. Nature was here, and it was unable to die. Not a single flower could wither away, nor could a leaf fall from its branch.

There was no winter and no summer. It could never be too

extreme. Everything was always just right, exactly like Goldilocks wanted it to be.

Angels could fly because gravity did not exist up here. We had large wings to help us get around, but those wings didn't get in the way of anything else. They were versatile to our needs.

On earth, this was not the case. Nature could rot. Gravity was real. There were continents and countries and everything else you could imagine. It was a whole world mixed with pleasure and pain.

There were opposites. Hot, cold; nice, mean, etc. It all could dwell here. It all connected like a Venn diagram.

There were night and day, darkness and light.

Hell was the opposite of Heaven, holding all the power of evil. There was no ecstasy. There was no purity and no pleasure. It was wicked and gruesome, filled with bleeding souls and screaming misery due to the endless torture that took place.

There were caves and stone paths surrounded by lava and fire. It was far too hot for anyone to not burn up within a matter of milliseconds. Yet any creature that was eternal would boil yet never turn to ash. It would be a constant state of pain as they begged for mercy. It was dark, only illuminated by the heat sources dwelling within. It was Papa Bear's kingdom. It was the hottest summer ever, a summer that would never end and where no thirst would be quenched.

I took a seat within the gardens, the original gardens replicated to match that on earth called Eden.

Bushes, trees, and plants grew with ease, decorating the once-good memory before Adam and Eve tainted it all. In the middle stood a tree of knowledge, not one that could affect us now that we contained all there was to know about right and wrong. Humans did not know everything, but they knew good from evil. The Tree of Knowledge granted Eve and Adam the right to what God had known all along.

Animals didn't have the ability to be jealous. They had no idea that killing for sport was wrong. Rape was not seen as a sin, and none of it was their fault. That was how they had been made. They were made to not know what they did, and so they just followed their instincts.

We would have been in the same boat had the first man and woman never ate that forbidden fruit. Now we knew what was a sin and what wasn't. This is what determined why we were all sinners on earth. We knew what we did wrong and for that, we couldn't escape it.

We knew the harmful effects of murder. We recognized that stealing was against moral code. We understood all of these things and yet we chose to do them anyway, to please ourselves and nobody else. Selfishness was just another effect of knowledge, comprehension we were never supposed to have in the beginning.

The forbidden fruits that hung above my head were named apples, the things that men had on their throats.

Women bled red once a month after Eve ate the red fruit first, but men earned the Adam's apple after Adam nearly choked on the apple he was never meant to eat in the first place.

The same way dogs would eat food they knew they weren't supposed to. When you told a creature no, they desired to do it even more.

They had all the berries and fruits they could dream of, but they chose the apple. I couldn't name the reason why. Apples were not even that delicious.

Bushes of berries were scattered about in the garden. My favorite bush to eat from was the raspberry bush. It was the one berry that was always sweet when ripe. Blackberries were a whole other issue.

Maybe it seemed typical, but rose bushes were one of my favorite creations. Beauty had thorns beneath, waiting to cut and draw blood. It was a lesson to teach humans not to be deceived by beauty as any seductress was only the surface of their games and danger could lurk beneath.

Ayden's cute little comparison of me and a rose was not going to be forgotten, and I had to give him credit for it but roses, first and foremost, represented the deception humans fell into when they sinned. Pleasure was on the outside, but the pain was hidden in the vines.

Other flowers were there to complement one another and build an array of colors. Each one stood out on its own, but they also brought out the elegance of others around it.

The world needed more grace and artistry which nature provided. When the mountains stood tall behind a wall of trees on a clear, blue day, it was a wonderful sight. Nothing could replicate such an allure that God could create with the realm we called earth.

The good parts of it were only a clone of what Heaven had to offer. Nature began in Heaven, but God wanted to design it down there as well. No naked eye could see Heaven because it was not for humans to see. Much like angels, Heaven was invisible when it needed to be. Humans had to walk by faith now.

God tried sight once, but those people killed the only human who never committed a sin so now we did it solely by faith.

It reminded me of Ayden in a way. He never believed in any of this until I came along and proved it. He was easy to convince of the afterlife, which showed me that a part of him had always believed even if he didn't know or show it. However, even with sight, he had no faith.

Sight could only change some minds, but the true want for better things came from believing and having faith. It could never be as true and pure if the belief were based on sight.

The Garden of Eden still held beauty and bliss even if it had been the birth of all sin and misery. In Heaven, it showcased the hardships and learning curve of humanity. All things could be used for good, even if something bad came of it.

I fell in love with Ayden. It was bad on my end, but I had to use it for good. I would use it as a teaching moment to remind myself why I had to keep a distance. I could get close to them but not close enough to spend forever with. I was only a temporary guardian. I was the push that Selene once gave me.

Leaving the garden, I walked down to the ocean, chuckling to myself. Of course, if all animals went to Heaven, we needed our own ocean for any sea creatures to live in.

I flew over to a rock that created a little sitting area in the middle of the water so I could interact with animals passing by.

Sticking my hand out, I smiled at the black and white face that popped up. Dolphins were intelligent, and nobody doubted that. But one dolphin that was always misunderstood was the Killer Whale. They were seen as whales when they were not even whales to begin with.

Killer whales could not be whales because they had teeth, and those teeth are exactly what made them dolphins.

They would kill sharks on earth, which is all they really killed, but they were one of the sweetest animals to people. They deserved all the love.

I ran my hand over the skin of his head. He nudged my hand some more and knocked me into the water. I came back to the surface and listened to the echo of my own laughter.

Playful things, they were.

A few more killer whales came over to play and this was a moment in which I was void of all sorrow. What could I ask for? I had animals to keep me company and entire sceneries to fulfill my visual needs. There was nothing to complain about above the clouds.

The dolphins surrounded me and splashed me with more water. I began to splash back and give them what they were asking for.

Since this was the perfect place, our wings could not get wet. It was another perk to their flexibility.

My hair stayed dry despite being in the water. Every part of my soul could not be touched since everything in the part of the supernatural world was all spiritual. I could interact but I was not affected.

Something swam by my feet and I gasped as an octopus showed its face. This octopus was a deep purple, a color I found so fitting and delightful.

His tentacles came out of the water and threw water in my direction. He just wanted to join in on the fun and how could I deny him such a thing?

After the weeks I spent denying my feelings for Ayden, then wallowing in the guilt, I deserved this. I needed a moment like this to redirect my focus on what truly mattered. I may have been dead, but I did not get this kind of bliss on earth. Animals made it so easy to smile.

Love was complicated, and Ayden was, too. One thing that wasn't was how Heaven functioned. When I needed to get away and find happiness, I would come back here and let the animals tell me how much they loved me. Animals came before humans because they were better than we ever could have been.

Animals were loyal and loving. They just needed acceptance in their lives. They were appreciative and appealing to be around. They didn't know how to hurt the way humans did. That was exactly why I loved animals. I did not love animals more than humans, since it was about equal, but I could say that I had always been an animal lover. They were the puppies who would kiss you when they were locked in a trunk. Humans would only slap you and steal the car.

Ayden was that human. And yet, I was still pulled into *his* trance.

CREED

The Dyers were decorating for Valentine's Day in their shop while I sat at a table, watching them. It was my least favorite event of the year, the most pointless day to ever exist.

On a regular basis, the color scheme was baby blue and light brown. Gold trims lined the area to vibe with the aesthetic bakery glow. The wooden counters kept the shop light and friendly to anyone who walked through the door.

Their register was not made of fancy technology because that wasn't how they rolled. They wanted it to be more local than corporate, and it made the bakery feel much homier that way.

The new decorations were more subtle to go with their simplicity, not taking away any pleasure from the eyes. The front windows were big and open, to let in all the natural sunlight that showcased the store's beauty.

Deep red Valentine's decor complimented the existing colors that made this shop what it was. Red and white balloons floated in one corner, and some transparent balloons with gold spots drifted around the room. A chalkboard stood next to the counter, advertising their new special on wedding cakes to empathize on the special day of celebrating love.

"All right, my parents have let me go free," Ayden said, getting my attention. Nodding a little, I got up from my seat and followed him out.

It had been quieter between us. It made it far more awkward that both of us ignored our almost-kiss and he went out with Sunny as if it never happened.

We arrived at his apartment and I figured it was time to talk about the moment we shared.

Looking at him and sighing, I broke my silence, "Okay, we need to talk about that thing." Talking about it would help me feel better after I realized how I truly felt about Ayden.

"What thing?" He headed into the kitchen for food, playing dumb.

I went in after him and grabbed his arm, spinning him around and pulling us closer together. "This thing." I noticed the extent of my actions and stepped back. "Sorry, I probably shouldn't have done that. We should just clear the air now, and make it go away."

"It has gone away for me." He shrugged. He was lying through his teeth.

"It hasn't for me." I huffed.

He let out a low chuckle. "It's probably because you've never been so close to kissing a boy before. In a week, my ten weeks are up. I get to kiss you." He pointed at me.

I knew he was right. It turned my stomach into knots because being near Ayden like this was against the rules, and yet I wanted to test them for myself. I always made everything more complicated than it needed to be.

"Sunny won't like that," I stated.

He scoffed. "She's not going to know. It's just a silly bet. In a week, I will win. I'll get to kiss you and still have her." He gestured around us.

I played with my fingers, trying to redirect us back on topic again. "I just want to make the awkwardness go away. It turns out I'm the only one feeling weird about it, though. No, that's incorrect. I can't be. You've been quieter, too, and that means we both are still dancing around us almost kissing."

"Yes, that does seem to be the case." He gave me a genuine smile which only confused my already puzzled feelings. He would never be straightforward with his answers and trying to get it out of him would be too much work. I gave up on trying to talk about that moment.

I moved in front of the sink and began doing the dishes. Ayden came over and grabbed something from the cabinet, trapping me against the counter. My mind came up with other thoughts, impure ones that took over. I froze in my place as he wrapped his arms around me, pouring water from the tap into his cup.

He noticed my reaction and began to laugh. "You were in my way. And it's fun to tease you." He walked off, drinking his water along the way. I swallowed whatever was happening to me and fumbled with the plates in the sink. This was a game to Ayden. He knew what he could do, and he was messing with my emotions.

Over the next week, I watched Ayden and Sunny begin the boyfriend/girlfriend phase. It wasn't the idea I had in mind when I told him to give up sex but now, I had to hear him talk about another woman, and more than just her body. I lived inside his apartment so I couldn't escape his words.

He had still said *I* was prettier.

I'd have to move out soon and get assigned to a new charge because he was changing himself for the better. He didn't want to admit it, but he was.

Entering the room, he smiled to himself. He turned towards me and saw my face, asking, "What's wrong?"

"I'm just wondering why—never mind." I brushed away the idea, wondering if I should even tell him what was on my mind.

"Tell me." He didn't say it so much as a command, but more as if he was trying to be understanding.

I sighed a bit. "Don't take this the wrong way but why haven't you kissed me? You won the challenge."

"I did, sure. I just thought about what you said, and I honestly think you're right. It wouldn't be right to kiss you when I'm with Sunny." He shrugged. I almost gasped at what he said. He was being serious.

As I nodded, a small ping of disappointment vibrated in my chest. It might have been because I'd never kissed a boy and I wondered what it was like to do so, or maybe it was because I thought about what it would be like to kiss *Ayden.*

No, that was absurd. I mentally laughed at my own silliness, pushing away the ideas. I could never crave that.

I went into the kitchen to cook him some food. Making him dinner was entertainment for me. I never had anything else going on. I was dead, after all.

He followed me in. "Why do you want to kiss me now? Oh, I see. You want me because I'm in a real relationship. You want what *you* can't have." His intense gaze burned through the back of my head as he chuckled amongst himself, as if it were his inside joke.

I struggled to not give him a real reaction. Instead, I managed a fake one. "Or I have curiosities like anyone else. I was human once. That hasn't gone away." I mixed the ingredients until it became dough, and I started to knead out bubbles.

"Ah, yes, speaking of humanity, what else can we learn about you?" He came around the counter and hovered behind me, trying to help me knead.

I stopped and turned around too quickly, regretting doing that in the first place. We were close again and I didn't have control over my emotions like this. "Why do you keep doing this to me? You have a girlfriend."

He gave me a big smile, eyebrows wiggling. "It's fun to mess with you. You keep making these arguments about yourself, yet I can use actions to prove them wrong. You pretend you don't want me, but you do. You wonder what it might be like to be in a romantic relationship." He laughed and backed away. I couldn't tell if he was trying to joke about it or not. He confused every piece of me. I couldn't seem to make sense of any part of myself.

He took notice of my neutral expression and left me to make the pizza alone.

I decided to use the rest of this time to think about other things, distracting myself from whatever it was that kept happening between us. It couldn't be real; it couldn't be romantic. That wasn't allowed and I wasn't going to break the rules for some boy. I had never gone against my boundaries. I would always wonder about breaking them instead.

But what did a kiss feel like? There was no amount of research or movies that could teach me the touch of a man's lips against mine. It was an experience I had to learn for myself, but Ayden could never be my teacher. One kiss wasn't worth the risk of my entire guardian angel career.

I shook my head as I sprinkled on the cheese, placing the pepperoni around the pizza in even sections. I added some green peppers to it and put it in the oven to bake. The doorbell rang, causing my shoulders to slump on command.

Sunny was back.

Ayden answered the door and invited her inside and she gave him a sugary kiss as a gift. I looked down at my hands, observing the lines that crossed my palms. She came over to me with a smile and I gave her my attention.

"Hey, Sunny." I waved a bit, keeping my lack of joy about her presence to a subtle level.

"Elena, hello. Ayden and I are going to watch a movie in his room. Let us know when the pizza is done." I clenched my jaw. She has some nerve to assume the pizza was for her and Ayden. She joined their hands and took him to his room.

I sighed and twisted around to face the oven. I wanted to be the one watching movies. I didn't want to be stuck in the kitchen, making a pizza for the couple. I desired to *be* the couple.

It was hard to keep hiding it, to pretend everything was all okay. It wasn't. I wished for what they had. I missed being alive because I lost my chance at true love. I craved that. I was the oddball angel for wanting romantic love, but I was the oddball human when I didn't think about boyfriends.

Pulling the pizza from the oven, I set it on the stove and used the cutter to create eight slices. I pulled a stool over to the stove and planted my butt on it. The first slice ended up in my hands and after a few bites, I continued to eat away my pain.

I finished off the pizza by myself, not bothering to call them out. Food wasn't useful to me, but it sure did *feed* my sorrow.

Maybe they would get mad, or suspicions would arise as to why I ate it all. It didn't matter to me what they assumed. I was just going to eat myself into oblivion until I left Ayden and found a new charge.

They exited the room, laughing in unison until they saw me. Sunny looked at the empty pan. "Did you eat all the pizza?" Her eyes displayed her shock.

I straightened my back, eyeing the dish. "I guess I did." I shrugged it off because I decided not to worry about it. Too many problems in my afterlife bothered me and I refused to let this one add itself to the list. They could deal with it and make their own food. They would enjoy it together and Ayden could dump flour on her, too.

I left the kitchen and retreated into his closet, contemplating my whole existence. Why did this have to happen to me? I was supposed to be the good girl. I was supposed to be an angel who didn't gain feelings for her charge. I was never meant to wish for a kiss from the man I was saving the soul of.

The question nagged at me, making me realize I had been the one to push the two together. I was the one who wanted him to make friends with Mason. My own pain was the cause and effect of something I told Ayden to do.

I closed my eyes, wandering from the reality that was. I never wanted to return. I'd stay in this void forever, forgetting my worries before they ate me whole.

In that void where I went, Ayden was there. Like a film, I watched us do stupid things like what he and Sunny would do. We would watch movies and laugh, trying to feed each other at the same time.

As I opened my eyes, I abandoned the hole. I couldn't go down that path. I denied it any control over me. I would need to devise a plan to get rid of these feelings I had growing for Ayden. I'd spent months with this man, seeing the worst and best of him. I had seen his darkest days and I still stuck by his side to keep him protected from Lucifer. I never gave up on him and yet she was the one who got to have him.

What did they call this? *Jealousy.*

My thoughts rendered me speechless, but I was in love for the first time ever with someone I wasn't supposed to be with. It was wrong of me to ever desire anyone like that. I wished to return to the easy path, one that didn't involve heartbreak and loss.

I hadn't realized what time it was when Ayden opened the closet door. "I know you're awake. You don't sleep." He chuckled. I lifted my eyes to meet his, admiring his joyful aura. She made him so happy, but I could never do that.

That was a lie. I was the one who opened up Ayden to the possibility of being in such a blissful state. It was because of me that he was able to grin to begin with. That had to count for something.

His smile faded away. I wished my desolation would be taken along with it. "Okay, well, I'm going to go to bed now. If you need me, please don't wake me up." He pulled the door closed.

In the blink of an eye, an idea popped into my head. I had to tell him. If I didn't, I'd never know how this would go. I could never feel at peace. He *deserved* to know how I felt about him.

I jumped onto my feet and slid the door open, facing him. "I have to tell you something."

He turned his attention to me. "What is it?"

My stomach did flips, nausea growing within. I swallowed my own fears before I changed my mind and made things worse for myself. "I'm falling in love with you." I managed to get the words out, but the air fell silent when they'd been spoken.

Staring at him, I waited for an answer or a reaction. I needed anything, anything but the quiet enveloping us. Reticence scared me.

He crossed his arms over his chest, defining the muscles in his biceps. "Explain to me, Angel, why on earth you would tell me this. Do you think I'm going to say it back? I don't love you. There is no love anywhere near where I stand. You couldn't possibly be in love with a man like me. It seems you're begging for misery."

I straightened up my shoulders and cleared my throat to show off my confidence in what I said. He was a head taller than me, but it wasn't intimidating. He could never intimidate me. "We can't help who we fall in love with. I may be dead, but I never lost my ability to fall into it. Love was never exclusive to humans. Everyone can accept it. You just have to let people in."

Disappointment swirled within his eyes as he shook his head. "I will never love you. I will never let you in. You're nothing more than my guardian angel, and don't you *ever* forget that."

OMNIPRESENT

The stinging tears rushed to my eyes, falling over the bottom lids. It was never my intention to expose my vulnerability, but my emotions were very much present whether I had a beating heart or not.

Ayden began to realize how the words came out, but it was too late to apologize. I sprinted out of the apartment. He tried to stop me by calling me but much to his disappointment, he failed.

Ignoring him, I kept at a steady speed through the city and ended up at the edge of the forest. I picked up my feet again, running into the pitch-black cluttered with tall trees.

I came to a stop when I was far enough inside the depths of green that nobody could find me. I fell to my knees, hugging myself. I took a deep breath to regain my sanity, but I knew buried inside me was nothing but irrationality. I should have seen it coming. He hadn't changed. How could he turn around with so much ease?

My insides were cold and hollow. I had never felt like this as an angel. My brain was a jumbled mess that I couldn't put back together. My eyes landed on the tree to my right and I let out a small sigh. It was no use crying over him. He made his choice and it was the best choice for us. I couldn't be with him anyway, at least not without losing my job.

Why was Ayden so terrified to love?

As I scanned the forest, an eerie mood settled in the every inch of nature. How far had I ended up inside the woods? I stood back on my feet and spun around, watching the fog creep in and envelop me.

It had come out of nowhere which led to one conclusion. Goosebumps covered every inch of my skin when a deep voice came from behind me, "Well, it looks like we found ourselves an angel."

I turned towards the voice, facing Levi as he stood, dressed in dark attire. A few more emerged from the trees and surrounded me. I didn't stand a chance against all these fallen angels. "You're just mad because you chose Hell over Heaven." I narrowed my eyes. "That's on you."

"You've only been an angel for a short time. Don't pretend to know our story," Levi, the leader, said as he stepped closer.

I put my hands behind my back, joining them together. "Then why do you care about me now? What have I done to you?"

"Sweetheart, we've had a feud since the beginning. Good and evil have always been against each other. That's the beauty of evil. You don't have to do something to make us act upon our sinful actions. We just do it anyway." His cunning smile danced on his face.

"What do you want with me? I'm already dead and I failed my mission. Ayden is going to be all yours. Let a girl pity herself in peace, please." I had said *please* to the bad guys, but that was just my lame attempt at getting out of this.

He came over to me, closing the space between us until it became nonexistent. "Because an angel in sorrow is the best kind of target. This is exactly what we *live* for. Well, you know what I mean." He chuckled and glanced at the others.

"You saw what happened. He's already going to be yours. I failed. Go to him. Don't come to me." I realized what I had said, guilt washing over my entire soul. Selfish was an understatement of what I was.

"That's not very nice of you to save your own soul over his. I thought you said you loved him." He towered over me.

I backed away, bumping into another angel. "I—"

"We may be wicked, but we knew love once. Love is true. It never ends. Love is selfless. It is patient. It is kind," he quoted. "If you truly loved him, you wouldn't be here. You would be worried about his safety."

"I can't think. My heart is in pain. I'm suffering from his rejection and it's difficult to think." I rubbed my head.

"Love doesn't require thinking. It just is." He shrugged before grabbing my arm. "What you're experiencing is hurt, and that is what causes you to act the way you do. Even evil knows true love is too pure to cause bad things."

I struggled within his grasp. "Get your filthy hands off me!" I yelled.

Laughing, he pushed me to start walking. "Not with that attitude."

With firm grips on my biceps, they led me through the forest and stopped before an odd tree. Levi waved his hand in front of it and the ground opened up while smoke flowed out.

They dragged me underground to an area that burned too hot, threatening to melt my skin. An orange glow illuminated the path for us. I hated every inch of it. Stone stood out everywhere, broken and jagged as if destroying a structure.

I cursed myself for being such an easy target. They wanted to torture me as vulnerable as I was. They were *almost* like demons. Fallen angels inflicted pain on the good guys for the sake of their pleasure. Sadists described them to a T.

He took me over to a wall and pulled out a chain, locking it around my ankle. "This will keep you under control." He stepped back as I tugged at the links. I grunted, losing my balance and giving up.

He bent down to my level. "You won't be able to get out of this one, Angel," he teased.

I'd warned Ayden that they wanted him. They had been watching us and I was his shield, keeping him safe from their darkness. Now with me chained up in Hell, Ayden was in danger. I'd been stupid enough to let my feelings get the best of me. Feelings had never been safe to follow because they led us to make the wrong choices.

He waved over one of the angels. "I want you to go get Lucifer. I would love to see his reaction to this."

The other angel nodded and went to get their lord. I knew I was in trouble now, but I couldn't do anything about it. I had to stick to my instincts and escape the underworld somehow.

A man came back, pure corruption dwelling inside him. The power radiated from him. "You must be Angel. I was informed that you have failed your mission. You fell in love with a human. Welcome to the dark side, my dear." Keeping my identity hidden from Ayden didn't work. I fell for him anyway, and I fell *hard*.

I spit on the rocks. "Don't call me that. I am not on the dark side. Nothing happened between us. He rejected me and I ran. That's all. I never acted upon it. I am still in the guardian angel business."

"We'll see how long that lasts," he threatened.

I swallowed. "What are you planning to do with me?"

"Everything and anything you can imagine. I love hurting *His* angels. It pleases me." He came closer. "What is it that makes you shrivel up and beg for mercy?"

I wasn't sure what my weakness could be. I had a determined soul from day one and not even the Lord of the Flies himself could ruin that.

He looked back at Levi. "You said she'd fallen in love with a human? Which human would this be?"

It was a struggle to keep my cool but inside I was going nuts. I couldn't even begin to imagine the horror they could inflict on Ayden. This would be the first time that Ayden would begin to beg for mercy. He would change his whole mind about going to Hell if he truly felt the pain.

He turned to me again with a *devilish* smile. "It looks like you did. I can see it in your eyes."

I had to remember that he couldn't predict the future and he couldn't read minds. He was only the Lord of the Flies and not God Himself.

Pulling my knees to my chest, I wrapped my arms around them. This would not end well for Ayden or I. I'd never forgive myself for letting my emotions take over and cause me to expose his soul to Lucifer.

Levi approached me, holding my gaze captive. "She loves the ridiculous human man. I think it's fair to say that it does sound like our best bet is to hurt him to make her scream."

They all abandoned me down here, in the pits of the fiery lake. I thirsted for water for the first time since my death, but it wasn't an option. Taking a deep breath, I tried not to burn up. My skin was boiling. I was similar to a turkey roasting in the oven.

I pushed away the hair from my face as it began to cling to my moist skin.

An image popped into my head, causing me to choke on what little air I had and taking all control. I attempted to make it disappear, but it wasn't within my grasp. I saw things I never wanted to see. Ayden was being damaged before my eyes. This would be the eternity waiting for him.

"You can give me your worst. I can handle it," Ayden said with

venom lacing his voice.

Lucifer let out a dark chuckle while staring Ayden down. "You can't. You're just a human." He stepped closer, gripping his hair to pull his head up. "You are absolutely nothing. You are exactly what you told her. That's why you said it, right? You lied to her face and insulted her to redirect how you felt about yourself."

"I'm not capable of love." Ayden spat in his face, daring to challenge the Lord of the Flies.

"Oh, aren't you? Whatever you do say, goes." He flashed Ayden a smile, but a wicked glint peeked from his eyes. "It's a shame that these things go the way they do, for you of course. I enjoy every second." He nodded towards an angel who whipped the leather rope against his back.

Ayden cried out and seethed, trying to hold in his abuse. "I can still take it."

"Fair enough. If you wish." He gave the green light to the dark angel, leading to the angel ripping into his skin. His back gained a new stripe of blood with every whip that tore through the air.

It became too unbearable to watch but it wasn't my choice to look away. I witnessed as they made him bleed with no end in sight. His soul would never wither away.

Heavy breaths left my lips as I wrestled to get it managed, drenched in sweat. Watching like a movie broke my every being. I wished to be elsewhere. I wanted to be back home in Heaven, or even helping someone else. I needed to be somewhere familiar.

I laid my head against the hot rocks, wondering if Ayden was okay. I couldn't endure the thought of him suffering because I'd put myself first. My biggest regret was telling him I loved him.

It all had started when I let Selene go with the bad guy. Everything happening now could have been avoided if I'd seen the signs.

She sat up as her phone pinged. Reading the message, her smile grew wide. "He wants to hang out. I'll see you soon!" She rushed out of the room as I laughed to myself. Nothing could compare to the feeling of being alone.

I suppressed that emotion. I wasn't going to allow jealousy to eat me alive. I wanted to be everything she was, but I couldn't be. I desired her presence to keep me company, but that void would never be sewn back together. There was nothing interesting about me according to the human population.

I sat on my bed, the ache growing in my chest.

A knock echoed throughout the dorm hours later. I answered the door, but I would regret opening it to hear the news. I'd had no idea that she was already gone from my life forever. "Yes?" It was her boyfriend, the very man she left me to go hang with instead.

Returning to reality, my sobs were filled with dry heaving. My fluids had evaporated but I couldn't keep the cries contained. It was all my fault. Everyone I loved was stolen by death and I made the mistake to continue to love them.

The guilt and remorse were attempting to devour me, and they were doing a great job. I couldn't live with this kind of agony. I didn't deserve to be an angel. I wasn't worthy of Ayden's love. I didn't earn helping others and relishing in the joy. I warranted nothing because I was far beneath that level.

Ayden was in the right to reject me, but I wasn't ethical to run away as I had. I hoped to get back to him. I needed to protect him and make sure he didn't experience what they had in store for him. Unfortunately, I failed Ayden. I couldn't save him.

APOSTLE
AYDEN

I punched the wall, letting out my anger. I let her get away because I had to hurt her to save her from myself. I didn't understand how else I was supposed to do that other than crush her heart.

There was only one thing left that I could do now. I had to find out what Angel's real story was. If I was going to find her, I needed to find out what made her who she was.

I went to the cemetery to see if I could get any clue. I was curious to know if I could possibly get close to finding her tombstone.

The stars were hidden by the clouds and fog covered every inch of the cemetery. I searched the graveyard, despite the darkness, wondering if she would come to her own grave. I used a flashlight to show me the names of each tombstone. I passed any tombstone that didn't have a female name or a female's name with an *E* at the beginning.

Wickedness settled in the black of the night. As daunting as it was, I was focused on finding her grave—and hers alone.

One of them had a strange symbol in the corner, catching my eyes. I stopped and took a picture of it with my camera. I used an image search option to figure out the context of it, and after reading the meaning, it was impossible not to pat myself on the back.

I read the name on the tombstone, associating it with Angel. *Eliana Wilson.* Her name must have been Eliana, but what was her story?

The birth and death dates stuck in my mind, coming in handy when I researched more about Angel.

I stood up but something among the grave popped out of place. I faced the blooming rose in February while the rest had all wilted. This rose was white, but the tips were dyed in red. It seemed odd to me.

The library wasn't open when I arrived but that had never stopped me before. I picked the lock and made myself comfortable in front of the computer. I cracked my knuckles and typed in her name, only following articles that confirmed the birthday and death that were on her grave.

Angel was twenty when she died, putting her right around college age. It had barely been over a year since her death. I noticed the specific date of her death, one that matched right up with Christmas. I hadn't even thought about it until now, but it started to make sense as to why she was outside by herself during the Christmas dinner.

The girl had hit her one-year death anniversary.

With some more digging, I found pictures of the girl named Eliana Wilson and there was no way to deny it was Angel. The symbol on her tombstone was that of a virgin. I knew for a fact that she was a virgin and it made much more sense.

She'd stepped out of her comfort zone to confess her love and I turned her away. She had never done anything that difficult before.

I found articles about her death, but the school found no evidence of someone breaking in. She lived the perfect life as far as I could tell, and I doubted she would've killed herself on Christmas.

Her roommate was murdered just a week before, but I couldn't picture Angel slicing her own throat open. Would she do that to herself? These were questions even the internet couldn't answer.

I skimmed more of it, seeing a picture of her land in my view again. It was a school picture of her this time, one of her smiling. She wore a flannel shirt and a light sweater. I never pictured Angel as the type who wore glasses but now it would be hard to picture her without them.

As I rubbed my face, I scanned the library to see if anyone was watching me. The coast was clear.

Sitting back in my chair, I couldn't believe my own eyes. "Wow, Angel. You had a juicy life," I mumbled. I printed out multiple articles on her death and her life beforehand. I would dig up more about her later now that I had known who she was. However, it was time to go find out where she ran off to.

After leaving the library, I got back to my apartment and put the papers on the counter. Some noises came from the other room as if someone were shuffling with my things. "Who's here?" I yelled out.

I walked around the counter and pulled out a knife just in case. I doubt Angel would have come back so soon. I wished she would, but I knew better.

"That's not going to work on me. It's going to be a lot harder than that," a man's voice came from behind me.

I spun around, narrowing my eyes. "State your name and business."

"Hello, Ayden. I work for Lucifer and we have been waiting for you. Seeing as Angel has given up, we will be taking you with us now." He gave me a vile smirk, his eyes turning to slits like that of a reptile about to pounce.

"What are you talking about? Where is she?" I raised my weapon. I would love to kick some arse right now.

"Where she is, is none of your concern. You should be worried

about yourself. You're the one who's going to be in real trouble here."
He came closer.

"Don't you dare come near me, you wanker!" I yelled at him, taking a swing.

He rolled his eyes. "That's not up to you." He snapped his fingers and more of his minions came out of hiding. They grabbed my arms and pinned them back, holding me.

I yanked my arm from one of them and elbowed the other guy. The blow only took him by surprise, but the pain didn't register. Pulling his arm back, he sent his fist toward my face. The hit did some damage. It drew blood from my nose, enough for me to wipe away with the side of my hand.

"You have to kill me before I give up this fight." I balled my hands into fists, but I knew my moves wouldn't affect these guys in the slightest.

The leader's eyes narrowed but his lips formed a wicked grin. "That can be arranged."

With the green light on, the other angels grabbed hold of me once again, and this time their grip couldn't be shaken off.

I still struggled, refusing to go down like a coward. "Let me go. All I did was reject her. I didn't know falling in love with an angel was required to get to Heaven." She kept more secrets from me, and it was beginning to become clear at this point.

He chuckled and came closer, grabbing my chin to make me look at him. "It's not. She gave you to us."

I stopped struggling, my strength weakened by those words. The truth shot me right in the chest, causing my muscles to freeze involuntarily. She couldn't possibly have given me to them. She wouldn't do that. Would they lie?

"Your friend gave you to us because you rejected her. You insulted her, and therefore, she believes you haven't changed. Guardian angels are the ones who report back to us on the status of their mission. Unable to lie, they admit if they failed or succeeded. She failed with you and we now get to take you down with us." He shrugged, weighing his options using gestures.

He continued, "She warned you when you first met that someone wanted you. She said Lucifer wanted you. We are evil; we are death. Lucifer has been waiting, and we mustn't keep him." He beckoned his minions with his fingers, and they led me down to Hell through some portal in the ground.

They took me to a room that burned hotter than the fire itself. They forced me down on my knees, chaining my wrists to two walls on either side of me. A man came into the room, looking amused by my presence. "You must be Ayden. It's nice to meet you; thank you for choosing us. I'm Lucifer."

I growled. "I didn't choose this. I was trying to change but she messed it up with her bloody confession. I didn't know she would report to you that I wasn't changing."

"You had your chance. There is no going back. You knew the consequences were going to put you in Hell. Well, here we are." He turned around, gesturing to the whole place as if it were his proud achievement.

I looked over at the other guys. "Then who are these twats?"

"This is my army. They are what I like to call fallen angels. They are the ones who *chose* me. Is there anything else I can help you answer before we get started on this exciting event?" He folded his hands like a businessman.

"No, I have nothing to say to you. I will take what you give me. I'm not a weak human and I will prove it to her. That will be the last thing she sees from me." I would not show him any fear. He deserved none of that.

Satan nodded toward one of the angels. He grabbed a whip from the wall. The rope looked to be made of thick leather material.

I wrapped my fingers around the chains just above my cuffs, giving them my best poker face. I refused to look weak. I had to show Angel, wherever she was, that I could take it. I was going to prove I was still willing to save my own soul.

The angel began to whip me, not getting a single scream. He stopped as Satan gestured for him to pause. "How are you feeling?" He bent down to my level.

"You can give me your worst. I can handle it," I told them. The alpha mould wasn't the reason I took pride in this pain. There was more to it.

Satan chuckled darkly and stood up, walking around as he watched me. "You can't. You're just a human." He stepped closer, pulling up my head by my hair. "You are absolutely nothing. You are exactly what you told her. That's why you said it, right? You lied to her face and insulted her to redirect how you felt about yourself."

"I'm not capable of love." I spat in his face, testing the boundaries. I rebelled against society and today I'd rebel against the Devil himself.

"Oh, aren't you? Whatever you do say, goes." He smiled at me with an evil prominent in his eyes. "It's a shame that these things go the way they do, for you of course. I enjoy every second." He then nodded toward an angel who then whipped the leather rope against my back again.

I cried out, seething through the pain and trying to hold in my anger. "I can still take it." I knew she would see this. Somehow, I knew Angel would watch this and I had to tell her that I didn't want her to save me this way.

I had to save myself.

If this was what taught my family that I had a goal in mind for my future, this would do the trick. I wouldn't leave this world and let them hear that there'd been no signs of a struggle. They deserved to know they meant something to me, and I still had to tell them that in person.

"Fair enough. If you wish." He nodded again, causing the angel to whip me nonstop. Blood seeped from my wounds.

My grip loosened on the metal links of the chains, wanting to give up everything I had. I couldn't. I refused to be like that.

Eyes on me, he nodded toward the angels. "You can stop. We should try something else."

He smiled at me, but nothing about it permeated purity. "I think it would please all of us to see both of you hurt." He turned to look at his angels. "Bring her in." It didn't shock me that they had her in captivity, too.

I gained any strength I could to look up as they brought Angel into the room. Her eyes were apologetic, and it made me feel awful for everything I had said. It wasn't her fault. She was just in pain because of me.

I could never ask her to bury her feelings for my comfort, nor could I wish harm on her for turning me in.

I deserved this after all.

She was pushed down on her knees, looking me in the eyes. "I'm so sorry, Ayden. I swear I would take it back if I could. I didn't mean for this to happen. I can't excuse or justify it."

I smiled a bit, trying to reassure her that it was okay. I didn't want her to hate herself for this, yet I couldn't say the words. I was far too exhausted to get anything off my tongue.

With a sigh, she looked up at Satan. "Tell me why I'm here. You already got what you want."

"We are killing two birds with one stone." He looked at his angels. "Is that what the humans say?"

"I think so," the leader spoke.

I looked at Angel, wanting to tell her so much. I wanted to explain that I knew what had happened to her, but the words didn't come out. My brain was beginning to shut down.

She turned her head toward me and sat on her legs. "All right, go. Hurt me. This is my fault anyway. He's just a human. He can't handle anymore abuse. I'll take the pain for him because that was my duty in the first place."

They looked at me, observing my bruised appearance. "Take off her dress," Satan told his minions.

They grabbed her dress and quickly ripped it over her head. Now naked, she looked down at the ground, sitting on her legs as she gave herself up to them for my sake. I wanted to say something. I needed to stop this. I just couldn't do so.

He grabbed the whip and pulled his arm back and let it fly forward, making a whipping sound as it hit her back.

She let out a cry and took the abuse for me, something I wish I could stop. They continued, watching her lower to the ground until she lay against the hot cement. She wouldn't fight back like I did. She would take the pain to spare my soul and it shook my bones. I wish she would stop caring so much about me.

I glanced up at the cruel men and choked on my words.

The toughest of the angels came to me, cupping his ear. "What's that? You say she can handle it?" He laughed.

The Devil shook his head. "All right. These two need some time to themselves before we continue the torture. I can't be all bad." He let out a little chuckle.

All of them abandoned Angel and I here.

I dropped my head, watching my skin boil and burn against the rock. I lifted it to look at Angel, wondering if she was even conscious anymore. I coughed, clearing my throat. In a raspy response, I said, "I'm sorry."

EXODUS

Lucifer walked in and grabbed my hair to hold my head up. "Do you give up yet?"

I shook my head with the little strength I had, fighting to keep my sanity. "I refuse to."

He snickered. "Wrong move, kid. You are just as sick as he is." He threw his arm out, pointing to Ayden.

Ayden lifted his head to look at us, eyes half-closed. Sweat and blood dripped down my soul and his body, coating us in thick fluids. Lucifer dropped my head and I fell back onto the cement. My worn wings laid out on either side of me, covering the nudity.

"We need new ways to torture you. What is it that girls can't handle?" He bent down and invaded my personal bubble.

A stabbing pain ripped through the area where my uterus was before I lost my physical form. My arm stretched out while I clawed the hot stones. I cried out, not having missed the feeling of a period.

The horror came to a sudden stop. He picked me up by my hair once again, pulling my head up. "You know what satisfies me? Misery. I like making people suffer."

I scoffed a bit, not surprised in the slightest. He was Lucifer after all.

"What would make you suffer? You're a virgin in love with the whore. He's a human and you're an angel. If you act upon this, you're kicked out of Heaven. All I need to do is make it happen." His gaze met Ayden's.

It was not out of the ordinary for Lucifer to force sex. Demons would possess virgins all the time, forcing them to lose their virginity to someone they never chose.

Rape. That was what it was called, and it caused so much trauma to the victims involved. That was exactly what Lucifer wanted from us. Trauma was the worst kind of suffering. You could *never* forget it.

Ayden struggled a bit and grunted. He was weaker than I was from the torture and nothing shattered my heart more than this sight. Lucifer grabbed his chains and tore them off, letting him drop to the stone. He kicked him. "Come on. Flip over. We both know you've been wanting this for a long time now."

Ayden managed to say, "No."

Lucifer choked on his words. "Excuse me? You want to pretend you have morals now?"

Ayden didn't say anything. He was trying to keep the pain at a minimum. He didn't need to tell Lucifer because it wasn't important enough for him to know but I knew. I knew Ayden enough to know why he wouldn't go through with Lucifer's scheme. Ayden had never forced himself on a woman. He only enjoyed sex when it was a willing act between both parties.

Lucifer kicked him, rolling him over, and Ayden groaned as his injured back hit the hot cement that burned into his open wounds.

The Lord of the Flies approached me and wrapped his fingers around the back of my neck, dragging me over to where Ayden lay. "I will ruin you." He dropped me and left to get something.

Lifting my head, I placed my fingers in Ayden's that were sprawled on his chest. "It's not your fault. It was never your fault," I whispered.

He wished to respond but his mouth wouldn't listen to him. Instead, his eyes spoke in place of his words. He would never stop believing this was his doing.

A growl echoed throughout the pits of Hell.

I turned my head a bit to look back, but a bright light appeared, blinding Ayden. It didn't affect me as I recognized who was behind it. He was an angel below me but much more important—a warrior angel.

He moved his hand, causing Lucifer to fly against the wall. Lucifer pretended to have so much power, but his abilities were controlled by God Himself, therefore, angels could be much more.

He came over to us, inspecting our state. "I've come to save you. We got word that one of our own was being held hostage in Hell."

My limbs shook involuntarily as I sat up. "Ayden. Please." I pointed to him, falling back to the ground. I had no strength to keep myself upright.

He closed the space between him and Ayden, helping him up. "My name is Matthew. I was sent down to get you out so let's not waste time," he said to my charge.

He didn't notice my weak soul and Mr. Dyer's weak body. He also lacked the ability to see when Lucifer came from behind. He swept Matthew off his feet, snatching a silver blade. "You angels just don't give up."

"It would be pathetic of you to assume we did, *angel.*" Matthew pushed him back, sending him in the air. He stood up and met Lucifer's gaze as Lucifer came running at him. He swung a punch at Matthew, but Matthew dodged it.

He grabbed Lucifer's arm and flipped him onto his back, slamming him down on the ground. He attempted to kick him, but Lucifer grasped his foot, tugging him from his standing position. Matthew lost balance and fell to the floor.

Lucifer grabbed Matthew's hair, slamming his head onto the stone. It would take more force than that to truly harm a supernatural being. Matthew kicked Lucifer's chest, causing him to stumble.

Matthew got up from the rocks and took a swing. His fist made contact with Lucifer's jaw, but Lucifer chuckled in response. "You'll have to do better." He forced a blow to the side of Matthew's head.

Matthew staggered but caught himself and walked towards Lucifer, throwing him back with his power. Matthew put his foot against his cheek before he got up, keeping him against the melting rocks. "I am doing better. Try to keep up." He grabbed Lucifer by the collar and punched him. He started smashing his knuckles against Lucifer's face with all his force. Matthew pulled back in a hurry while Lucifer was down.

He rushed over to us. "He won't be stunned for long. We should be quick." He helped us up with each arm underneath ours. He walked at a fast pace, being our aid as we walked up the stairs and exited through the portal. We ended up in the forest, right where I had first been kidnapped by the fallen angels.

Matthew set me down for a moment while he gave me a jacket to hide my naked form. He guided me back to my feet and took us both back to Ayden's apartment. "You guys will need to heal. I would recommend not getting into a lot of trouble. Lucifer will be held back by God. Don't worry about him coming after you again," he assured us.

He left us in peace, and for that I was thankful.

I glanced over at Ayden who lay on his stomach, letting the scorched whips heal. Closing my eyes, I let the darkness take over my mind. It was void here. I saw nothing but an empty soul begging for a purpose.

When I came out of the pitch-black, it had been days. I acknowledged that Ayden's sister was here, taking care of us both. She had cleaned our wounds and let us heal in with proper treatment.

"I see you're awake," she said. I wasn't awake. I was just opening my eyes. I had been awake the whole time but in another state. It was similar to a blank daydream.

Esme looked between us. "Sunny tried to come over, but I've been holding her off since you two have been in serious pain." She looked at Ayden who then nodded in return.

Sunny. I had forgotten she existed. She was Ayden's girlfriend, the one he wanted instead of me.

Esme sighed. "You poor things. What happened to you?"

I knew we would have to explain this somehow, so I had to come out with the truth. I couldn't lie anymore.

Ayden beat me to it, doing what I couldn't. "Someone wanted to hurt us. He thought that it would be funny to hurt a therapist and her patient."

She nodded and grabbed the cold towel. "People are sick and cruel." She laid the wet towel across his back. Ayden tensed up, adjusting to the feeling of a cool cloth against his skin. The blisters turning into scars were what hinted at the weapon of fire. Esme knew how to take care of us because our wounds had been so obvious and source specific.

Esme went to go get some food for us, not that I needed it.

Ayden directed his statement at me. "I know who you are, Eliana."

I twitched at the sound of my former name, forgetting it had once been mine. I didn't know how he knew but he was right. Eliana was *my* name. "How did you find out?" I asked him.

"Turns out I had enough information to search the graveyard for your headstone. There was a virgin symbol engraved in the stone and your name started with an *E*. Oddly enough, there was one live rose just sticking out while the rest had died." He scrunched his face in a cute way, puzzled.

I smiled a bit, not focusing on the stinging pain that hugged my back. "I guess it's because a part of me lives."

"How so?" He'd asked the question I didn't want to answer.

"Because I love you," I whispered. My love was the only thing keeping that rose alive on my grave. I somehow just knew this bit of information.

"I wanted to ask you about your murder." He changed the subject for which I was glad. It was awkward enough that we were in the same room after he rejected me.

"What about it?" I shrugged the best I could without causing more pain to my wounds.

"Do you know who did this?" He slowly moved his arms into a new position, under his head.

"I do. I trusted him but I hadn't realized that he was the one who did it. Liam was his name. He killed my best friend who was his girlfriend at the time. He told me a different profile from the real man we were investigating to hide himself from being suspect. He gained our trust and *ripped* us apart. I never saw it coming, and for that reason alone, I feel foolish. I let her down." I looked off in a different direction, lost in the memories.

"How did you let your friend down? You didn't know. It's not your fault that you were murdered," he argued.

"I guess that's true. I just wanted to honor her good name. I wanted justice for her. I didn't do that. I got myself killed in the process. The whole time, the killer was in my room. He was the one I trusted." I fixed my eyes on the floor, studying the little imperfections of the carpet.

Every time I closed my eyes, I saw his face. Ayden would be staring at me, begging for mercy through his eyes as Lucifer embedded each sin into Ayden's soul. I choked back a sob. I would not give anyone else my weakness.

Before Ayden could respond to the pure heartache pushing against my chest, he sneezed.

"Bless you," I said.

He cleared his throat. "Is that story true? Does your soul fly out when you sneeze, and you have to say that before the Devil takes my soul?"

I laughed but my laugh held no humor. I could never forgive myself for what I'd put him through. "No, Ayden. If that were true, you would've lost your soul long ago and I wouldn't be here. It would be pointless to try and save you if your soul was Lucifer's." I shook my head against the cushion.

"Who was your friend? Tell me about her." He gestured to me to talk about what made her so wonderful.

A small smile formed at the thought of her warm brown eyes. "She was the best. She taught me a lot of things. She made me feel like I mattered to this world. Selene made me believe that someone could love me. She was wrong, of course, but it's the thought that counts." I tried to sit up, slowly, wincing at the searing pain. I grabbed my back, widening my eyes. "Ayden, Esme saw my wings."

I looked towards the kitchen where she was. She could be telling everyone right now. She knew my secret. There was no possible way for her not to have seen them without healing my back. I knew I was in danger.

Ayden sat up, taking his sweet time and putting his hand out to calm me. "Hey, it's okay. We might have a hard time getting along but I don't think she's the type to hurt someone. You've been helping me. You brought my family back together. She must understand what you've done. You're an angel—*not* a demon. She can trust you."

I swallowed a bit of my paranoia, unsure if I should've believed him or not. "How am I supposed to be okay with this? She knows. Nobody is supposed to know about me except me and the people I change. Half the time, the people I change don't even have to know. I'm in danger," I tried to explain to him.

Esme came out of the kitchen and moved her eyes between us. "Why are you guys looking at me like that?"

Ayden attempted to talk to her first. "Is there something you want to say?" He tried to ease it out of her, seeing if she would confess first.

Her eyes darted back and forth from Ayden to me, holding the plates of food. "I don't know what you mean. I didn't see anything."

He shot me a look. "She always was a terrible liar."

Esme let out the loudest sigh I'd heard. "Okay! Fine, I know that you're an angel." She set the food down. "I guess I just didn't expect it. It makes a lot of sense, but I didn't see it coming."

Eyeballing the food, my mouth watered. "Okay, so then I suppose that's useless. Yes, I'm an angel. I'm his dead therapist. I was sent for the same reason I told you. I'm his guardian angel. We were in Hell, getting tortured by Lucifer. Matthew, another angel, saved us. I just didn't tell anyone because my mission is to save someone and get out. It has been the same task every time since I died."

"When did you die?" She sat down, intrigued by my story.

"A little over a year ago, on Christmas. I was killed because I was involved in a case of solving my friend's murder and the guy I worked with was the culprit. He took me out, too, before I would suspect him. I was dense. I didn't seem to think that it would be the one person who inserted himself into the crime scene but of course, it was. It made so much sense. He wanted to investigate. He wanted to get closer to me and gain my trust. He was loved by everybody, including us victims." My fingers turned white from my tight grip on the cushions, rage boiling within.

She put her hand on top of mine. "It's not your fault."

Ayden shrugged, butting into the conversation. "I tried to tell her that."

I let go of Esme's grasp, sighing to myself. "He was the perfect suspect in plain sight, but I ignored the signs." I had let Selene down and after what Ayden endured due to my confession, I had fallen short of my mission. Ayden would now wither as his days continued to go on. Together, we would be the wilted roses amongst the tombstones.

INCONTINENT

Water boiled in the kettle pot as Esme kept her eye on it. Her intentions were innocent while she attempted to make us tea. It was taking a while and I couldn't confirm nor deny whether the hot drink would warm my insides. If I were traumatized just enough, the heat from it would trigger memories from Hell that I did not wish to relive.

With my knees to my chest, I was sitting on the couch and Ayden was beside me, glancing at me every now and then. "Are you all right?"

"Define all right. Am I still here? Yes." I couldn't answer anything else. Mentally, emotionally, and physically, I was not okay. I was present but that was all I was. Ayden knew I loved him and yet nothing changed. He was still with Sunny. His new scars were the result of my negligence.

"We should talk about...everything that conspired the past week," Ayden said.

I put my legs down, pulling a blanket over myself. "What is there to talk about? You made it clear I'm nothing to you. It's fine. I could never expect you to feel the same. It was wrong of me to run away and let them torture you."

"Me? Angel, I wasn't the only one tortured. I'd seen you cry but seeing you so weak and vulnerable, that was the worst. You have scars from that." He gestured to my back.

I winced upon hearing him mention it. "It's fine. I deserve it for giving you to them. I am not a very good guardian angel."

He rubbed his neck. "I'm the one who sent you running. Nobody deserves to be tortured to the point of breaking. All you did was confess your feelings and I said terrible things. You were hurt when you told them you failed."

I folded my hands on my lap. "Ayden, being hurt doesn't excuse getting you into that situation. If I were hurt after my friend betrayed me, would it be okay if I left her behind to drive herself home while drunk? No. Feelings get us into a lot of trouble, and mine happened to do just that."

"Were you lying? You told them I can't change. I don't think it was a lie." He looked over at me.

I swallowed, not wanting to hear the truth. I wanted him to turn himself around more than anything, but he admitted he hadn't done that at all.

Esme exited the kitchen and set our cups of tea down on the side table. "I wish I could help speed up this healing process." She gave Ayden a look.

He stood from the couch. "You can't do anything. Nobody can save me."

Every muscle in my body cringed at the sight of Ayden's back. It was bandaged in every area, not a single spot uncovered. I'd done that to him.

His sister let out a small sigh. "How did this all begin? Angel said some things, you said some things and you both ended up in Hell? Why did you end up in Hell Ayden?"

"Because I told them he would never change," I said.

Esme put her hand up. "I'm asking Ayden."

He rubbed his face, not wincing at the pain as if moving his shoulders didn't cause him trouble. "Because the angels came and took me. I was trying to figure out who she was in her life so I could find out where she went. I wanted to make it right."

Esme looked at me, but I didn't give anyone my attention. My mind was trapped within the depths of sorrow and remorse. If I had just told Ayden that his words were cruel and I hadn't let my emotions get to me, I would never have put him through hell as I did.

"Esme, can you leave us for a moment?" Ayden asked.

She nodded and went to the bathroom to freshen up or something of that sort.

"Angel, look at me." When I didn't do as he said, he spoke louder, "Eliana, look at me." That got my attention.

The sound of Ayden saying my real name made my stomach uneasy. I didn't like it when he called me Eliana. I liked the nickname *Angel*.

Ayden sat beside me, keeping a little gap between us. "You'll never believe it wasn't your fault, will you? Why don't we agree it was both of us? I said bad things; you let your pain control your words. We both could have handled it in a different way than we did."

I still said nothing in response, afraid of my own words.

He leaned in. "What you did was stupid. Taking the torture for me like that—*that* was stupid."

I turned my head to face him. "You never said anything against it when it was happening. I did it because I love you. You may not like it, but I can't control how I feel. When you love someone, you take the pain away from them and inflict it upon yourself."

Ayden seemed unsure of what to say to that. He was at a loss for words because he knew it was true. I did it because I was in love with him. If that made me a moron, then I would accept it. *Love* made me idiotic.

His hand landed on my forearm and he pulled me closer. My heart began to race, and I thought maybe this was my moment. Love did make me stupid because I forgot he was with Sunny. I chose to let go of the thoughts from the moment he told me I was nothing to him. Yet, I didn't stop him from leaning in.

His chin rested on my head and his arms wrapped around me. For a moment, I was confused by what this was. It wasn't a kiss; that was obvious.

I didn't pull away. I allowed his warmth to sew me back together. Closing my eyes, I inhaled his scent. Maybe he did smell of burnt skin and sweat but he still managed to keep his musky cologne on through it all.

"You're a fighter, are you not? How did fallen angels manage to control you?" Ayden whispered.

I took a deep breath and looked at him. "I didn't fight back all that much. There was no use in it. I tried to..." I shut my eyes, realizing what I said. "I told them to go after you since you were the one they really wanted."

He coughed a bit. "And I tried to stop them, but when they told me that you gave my soul to them, I lost all my strength. I was in shock that the Angel I knew would do that. I guess it was true. You did."

Instead of pulling away and hiding my face, I buried it into his chest. Quiet tears escaped my eyes as the memory resurfaced. It was all my fault.

Ayden must have felt the tears against his skin, leading to him petting my hair. "But I deserved it for the things I said to you. Telling you that you're nothing is not okay. I'm sorry for that and sorry for getting you into that situation to begin with. My mum taught me better."

Pulling away from him, I wiped away my wet stains. "I'm sorry, too." I looked at the time and stood. "It's time to change our bandages. It's not as if I need it but I want it to soothe the pain. I do not miss this part of being human."

I walked into the bathroom to find Esme sitting on the toilet, fully dressed. She looked at me and got up. "What happened?"

I reached under the sink and grabbed the first aid kit. She was smart to bring one for us. "We both admit we are at fault for it all. We're sorry for putting each other in the position we're in. It's time to change out our bandages. Since we can't reach our backs, I'll change out Ayden's for him. It's the least I can do after causing the marks. I'll call you when I need to change mine."

Taking the first aid kit with me, I sat on the couch. "We can't have the gauze getting all gross and filling with gunk. I was never a *doctor*, but I knew enough about these things to know the importance of taking care of wounds."

Ayden turned his back towards me, rubbing away the dark circles under his eyes. "Why are you doing this?"

I was careful as I peeled off the old ones. My stomach twisted and turned at the sight of his injuries. "Why am I helping you? Because that's what you do when you love someone."

I laid out strips of gauze, planning where they would go. I dabbed some of his cuts to remove any gunk or excess blood. Ayden winced at my touch and I wanted to take this misery, too. If I had that ability as his guardian angel, I would use it at full force.

Taking my time, I laid the pieces over the cuts, making sure to use medical tape to adhere it to his skin.

His voice had been stolen. His dignity was waved in his face, just out of reach. He had too much pride to admit his mind was a field of corpses yet to be buried.

Changing his bandages was tempting me to kiss him myself and see what it was like. I wanted to run my finger down his bare arm, kissing the part of his shoulder that wasn't touched by darkness. *Self-control.* I had too much of it to make the mistake of kissing Ayden when he didn't see me that way. He was into Sunny. He wanted to kiss her—not me.

"I'm done." I got on my feet once again, heading to the bathroom.

Ayden's question stopped me in my tracks, "Where are you going?"

I twisted my body to look at him. "To get my bandages changed."

"Why don't I just do it myself? Since we're here. It can be part of my apology." He patted the cushion.

I decided to accept his offer, sitting down and facing him. I was an angel and being naked wasn't a very appropriate choice around Ayden. If I were a man, maybe. But I had boobs and those boobs were not for display.

My white dress had a scoop on the back of it, giving plenty of room for my wings to breathe. It still covered areas that did need to be rebandaged, so I had to pull the straps off my shoulders and hold my dress against my chest. As many would say, I was blessed in the breast department.

"Do these leave scars?" Ayden asked as he removed my bandages.

"They will. Hell is the one place that can physically hurt angels, and it will leave scars." I turned my head to the side, glancing back at him.

He seemed focused on changing my bandages. I had to wonder if he wanted to kiss me, but I knew that was a lie.

He was careful not to put too much pressure, but I swear my wings twitched when he touched them to move them out of the way. He finished taping and gazed at me. "All done."

I fixed the straps of my dress, releasing out a small sigh. Already, I missed the feeling of his fingers brushing against my back.

I asked, "Why are you being so nice to me? You're claiming to not have changed but you're being the good guy."

He gave me a smirk, and I was surprised by how much I missed it. "That's what friends do, Angel."

Friends... He considered us *friends*. He knew I loved him and yet I was just a friend. That's exactly how he saw me. I was in the friend-zone for good.

"Thank you. Thank you for this. I know we didn't get along well in the beginning and you don't necessarily like my presence here but I'm grateful for this small glimpse of hope. Maybe you really can change, Ayden. I see the potential." I faced him. "Hell is not a good place to be and you see the reality now. Maybe that was your rock bottom and there's a future for you, a good one."

Ayden leaned his side against the back of the couch with his eyes fixed on me the entire time. It was a charming trait coming from him. "You believe this? I saw what that held and all I could think about was the way you looked defeated. I never once thought about myself or how I would end up in that fate for the rest of my time. My mind only suffered from the way you were beaten. Humiliated and shamed. It was focused on *you* the entire time."

AFORE

Ayden connected his phone to the stereo he stole and his playlist vibrated through it. "It's a whole other musical experience."

I folded my arms and tilted my head as I listened to the lyrics. "What an intriguing song." The artist sang about a man who'd screwed up and promised to finally be good. This was not quite what I expected Ayden to be interested in.

Esme came with Ayden's sandwich. "Do you still not buy yourself food? You have a job now. You can afford it."

Ayden shrugged. "Why should I waste my time shopping when I like sandwiches?"

Esme leaned in close. "Why does a baker have so many tools and ingredients for multiple kinds of sweets?"

He choked on his air. "Well, I see your point." He huffed and grabbed his food from her, shoving the first bite into his mouth.

She laughed and patted his head. "You are so disgusting. I can't see why Angel likes you. But it is a shame you don't feel the same." She looked at me, causing my cheeks to turn red.

The glassy look in my eye appeared and I turned before anyone could see it. I didn't want to cry at a time like this. "I don't think I should stay for long." I blinked away the tears before facing them again. "Heaven needs me. Other humans need me. Ayden made it clear he won't change, and I can't continue to save someone who won't—" I couldn't finish the sentence.

Ayden snickered. "It's about time you realize I don't want to change. You can't save someone who doesn't want to change." He had no clue how serious I was being this time around. I was planning to leave him permanently.

"It's not easy to watch you destroy your own life. I can't watch the man I love ruin himself day by day. It's time to move on, Ayden. When my wounds turn to scars, I'm leaving for good." I swallowed the sorrow.

Esme looked back and forth between us both. "Bloody hell, she's serious. Ayden, she is trying to help. She's been making progress. Accept it. You even have a girlfriend for more than just shagging."

Closing my eyes, I pictured Sunny. He was still with *her*. The hazel-eyed beauty had his heart and not I. "And I imagine you have had sex with her." I had already seen a peak of Ayden with women in bed and I could easily place Sunny on his lap or in front of the mirror. It was not difficult to taint my heart some more.

Ayden put his sandwich on the plate, looking at Esme. "What do you want me to say? I can't love Angel like she wants me to. I can't control my feelings, either."

"I was never asking you to love me back, Ayden. I was only asking you to give a crap about yourself. I care about you, and you should, too. That was all I was ever here for. Your parents care. Your sisters care. I am trying to show you that you have people trying to be there while you push them away. You should be so thankful you have a family that loves you," I said, drawing a deep breath.

His sister grabbed my hand and gave it a light squeeze. "She's right.

You know she is. We all know, and you have to accept that we aren't going away. Accept her help and change. That is all she wanted to begin with and that's all we ask."

"This war between Heaven and Hell will never end. Lucifer will always want your soul and if you give up, he will have it for himself. You will never get to see your family. You'll never get to be happy. You'll be stuck in a cell in Hell. I know it's cool to steal and you don't like sex when it means something, but that stuff is ruining you as a person. You are living a life of reckless behavior, headed down the highway to Hell. You have a choice. Please, make the right one," I begged.

"How did this all begin? Is it exactly like the Bible says?" Ayden gestured. "Heaven and Hell, how did it begin?" He avoided the topic of change like the plague. That made it clear he wasn't keen on the idea, and soon I'd leave him to be whoever it was he attempted to become.

I was careful as I took a seat on the couch. "It's not a pretty story but...it's one that is important."

Esme and Ayden took a seat as well and Ayden continued to eat his sandwich as he paid attention to my history lesson.

It all began thousands of years ago when God created Adam and Eve. That much was true. They were real people and they did screw up the rest of humanity by eating the forbidden fruit. It showed how we just couldn't listen when we were told no.

Once Adam and Eve were evicted and banned from the garden, a whole different world was rolling into place. If they had just been fine with what they had and had not wanted more, this would never be the world it is today.

There were stories, and most of those stories were true. Moses freed the Egyptian slaves. The red seas parted. David did defeat Goliath. Giants walked the earth as a result of humans and angels having children. These were all once part of our world. Crazy things had evolved since then.

But before humans, there was just a supernatural world. There were God and His angels. Lucifer was His best angel, His beta.

Everything had been fine and dandy. It was going well until Lucifer decided he wished for more. Just like Adam and Eve, he wasn't satisfied with his position. He wasn't appreciative. His goal was to rise to the top and be God Himself. God was betrayed by His favorite, and Lucifer chose to get cast out of Heaven after that point.

This was at the time that a third of the angels chose to follow Lucifer and together they went to Hell, a place created just for Lucifer and his angels. That was the end of that, as far as everyone knew.

However, humans were created. At this time, Lucifer used his ability to create shadows and demons. He was nowhere near as powerful as God, but he had enough to form the evil that lurked in the darkness.

He was angry with God for what He had done to him, and his plan was to destroy His creation. Lucifer took the form of a serpent that convinced Eve to eat the forbidden apple that gave all humans the ability to knowingly do wrong. From there on out, humans were screwed.

Over time, Lucifer used his demons to possess people and destroy them from the inside out. His shadows terrified us until we killed ourselves to make it stop.

There were four tiers of angels in Heaven, all formed since the fall of humanity in the beginning.

Thrones, Virtues, Archangels, and angels. The simple explanation of these positions went in the same order from top to bottom. Justice Angels, Guardian Angels, Warrior Angels, and regular angels.

I was considered a Virtue, only chosen by me and God when I desired to help others.

It wasn't until humans finally had access to Heaven that Virtues and angels became a thing. Guardian angels are there to protect and change people so their soul has a chance to go to a better place in the end. Angels are just those who have died and made it to Heaven and forever enjoy their days in paradise.

"There's much more to it but I could never explain it all tonight." I lay on my stomach and kept my eyes on the wall as if it were about to run away from us.

Esme rubbed her eyes. "It seems so wild that this is all happening in front of us and we have no idea."

"The battle is constant, but it is worse than what we see. Well, I should say what you see. I notice it all the time. I recognize the shadows that hide. I identify the demons that take over bodies. I spot it all, honestly, and it is scary, but I know that even if it seems terrifying now, it doesn't end that way. We always win because they will never be as powerful." I curled my toes as a way to distract myself from the wall.

Ayden was quiet the whole time and I was dying to know what was inside his head. Pun was intended.

Esme stood from the floor. "Okay, so this is no big deal. Ayden, we just have to get you to change. Please. I could never bear the thought of seeing you in Hell. Angel saw it, and I know she can confirm it was horrible."

My eyes met his and I nodded. "Seeing Selene's lifeless body in the snow was tough. Spending Christmas alone was tiring. It was burdensome to experience those things but watching you get tortured was like watching my heart get shredded. It was far worse than you telling me I meant nothing to you. I'd take the pain all over again if it meant I could take it away from you."

She bent down. "Listen to her. We want you to be with us when we all die. Never seeing you again will crush me. Mum, Dad, Arabella, and I all love you. Family is forever."

If only *my* parents believed that.

He shot up from the chair and pulled at his hair. "Stop pressuring me. I need to take a cold shower." He disappeared into the bathroom and the water started.

She turned to face me and planted her butt on the carpet in front of the couch I lay on. "I am so sorry for his behavior. I wish I could say he was happy. I wish I could say we were a real family again like in my childhood. It's such a shame that he doesn't feel the same way. I can't begin to imagine the pain of being rejected like that and then watching him make the same mistakes. It was hard on us when he got expelled from schools and chose the alcohol over us but now knowing that he will end up in Hell forever... I don't even know where to start. He's not a bad guy. He just makes the wrong choices."

I smiled a little. "Esme, it's all right. I never thought he was the bad guy. I understand and I don't hate him. I could never. I just hate that I love him because it will never make me feel better. He will always push me to the curb like trash. That's why I must go. I must leave what can't be fixed. It's only going to bring me down if I keep doing this to myself."

She placed her hand on my arm. "You don't have to explain yourself. I don't blame you, nor judge you. I understand Ayden is a bit much and you must do what's best for you. You can't pour from an empty cup."

It was never the route I wanted to take but it was the one that had to be walked. Giving up on Ayden hurt me more than it did him, but I had to do this for myself now. He made it clear he was done with me and Heaven.

Many people believed that what I was doing was a sin. They would see this as abandoning Ayden and giving up on him. It was anything but. I was accepting his decisions and leaving him with choices. Being an angel did not mean I was obligated to be stepped on or mistreated the way Ayden treated me. He'd made it clear I was nothing more than his guardian. Virtues had every right to walk away from someone who continued to make the same mistakes. We could only get so far with a charge before our welcome was overstayed. That time had come for me. It was time for me to leave the nest and let Ayden attempt to fly with his own wings if he wanted to use them.

Others needed me. Other people were in danger and they mattered just as much. I had to straighten up my priorities now. If Ayden wanted to turn his life around, he had a good start and the resources to do it on his own, but I would no longer be a part of it.

Whether or not he would continue to date Sunny was up to him. He won the bet. He could dump her and go back to his one-night-stands and leave her in the dust. It was his decision and I had proven he could at least put sex out of his mind. I showed him his own strength—his self-control.

It was up to Ayden Dyer to take what I taught him and turn his life around for the sake of his soul's eternity. I feared the worst if he chose Lucifer over God. I trembled at the cursed thoughts plaguing my mind with images of Ayden's soul burning as he begged for mercy. Now was the time for him to accept mercy before he lost his *soul.*

FALLIBLE

E sme and Ayden sat on the couch, taking bites of food at different paces. My eyes focused on Ayden and his eating habits. He might have rejected me, but I couldn't give up loving him. It didn't work that way. He looked at me and I immediately turned my head in another direction.

He swallowed his food before he asked, "Can you tell me more about yourself now? I know your name. I know how you died. It's useless to keep hiding it."

He knew that much but he would never know the darkest part of me. *Sam* was the memory I could never relive. Nobody else knew except the one person I despised the most. It would stay my dirty little secret.

I glanced at my feet and moved my toes. "Well, I guess it's only fair." I lifted my gaze to meet theirs. "I was born on June 22nd, 1998. I was born—"

"We didn't mean start at the beginning," Ayden interrupted.

My face burned red, showcasing my embarrassment. "Well, I'm fine. I'm new to this. I don't know what you want to know."

Ayden lifted an eyebrow and looked over at his sister who stared back at me. Ayden faced me again with a sigh. "We meant for you to tell us about your hobbies, interests, your family life, and your recent life before you died. You don't have to mention the murder again, though."

Again, my eyes landed on my feet as I curled my toes. "I come from a rich family with no siblings. I'm an only child. My parents always put their work and careers above me. They would leave for weeks at a time, doing business wherever they went. It was always the same." I gave a slight shrug.

Ayden gestured for me to go on while he continued to eat his food.

"I don't have many hobbies. I like to read and help people. I liked school because it was easy, but I hated the social part of it. I was never good at making friends."

Ayden's gears turned as a question popped into his head. "What about that Halloween party? Everyone loved you." He took a bite of his fry.

"Yeah, because I'm an angel now. I'm a literal angel and I help them. I wasn't very good at helping people when I was alive. Selene is a famous example. I didn't save her. I couldn't save myself. I can't save you. It's time for me to face the reality that love doesn't equal saving. I can't save the people I love; I can't protect them." On cue, shivers slithered down the spine that no longer existed.

Esme choked a bit, coughing to clear her throat. "Love doesn't equal saving? How many have you saved because you love them enough to care about their soul? Ayden is just the exception." She pointed to her diabolical brother.

I nodded a bit. "You've got a point, but loving Ayden was a mistake. It wasn't very smart of me, I admit. An angel falling for the one she protects is against the law. He likes Sunny anyway. I'll get over it someday." I grabbed a blanket from the side of the couch and pulled it over my icy soul.

Neither of them spoke another word, implying that we change the subject. It was a smart move considering I did not want to relive the rejection. I'd been turned down one too many times in my life.

Continuing, I said, "I remember it like it was yesterday. Every morning I would walk downstairs, and there would be another note on the fridge. It was always from them, telling me they had left me essentials and would be back later. I didn't know why they had a child if they didn't want to be in my life. Why do parents even do that?" I focused my eyes on Esme and Ayden.

She stopped chewing and looked over at him, unsure of how to reply.

"Sorry, I don't mean to make you guys uncomfortable. I should probably drop it now." The blanket snuggled me as I wrapped it tighter. I gazed up at the ceiling, releasing the small breath I'd been holding. "That's just how it goes. This world needs good. Evil keeps ruining everything. It wasn't supposed to be this way, but things changed. We were supposed to be good and always have compassion. Darkness came in and ripped humanity apart. Look where we have gotten ourselves with murder, racism, rape, and hatred. It's all wicked. We could've had more."

Ayden didn't finish swallowing before he said, "Humans can be the best and the worst. I'm not saying evil doesn't suck but at least we can choose good. Some humans choose that—like you. You chose to help others. That means a lot because it wasn't just something you had in you. You made an effort to be a good person."

"We aren't good people. We are just people making good choices. I may be good now because I'm an angel, but I was never a good person. I still had negative emotions. I had bad thoughts. I made the wrong choices, too, because humans aren't perfect. We will somehow screw up, and I was no different. I'm only different now because I'm dead and purified by light." I chewed on my lip, the thought of Sam plaguing my mind. There was no way around it. What I'd done was out of defense, and yet it was still immoral.

They let me go on, listening to my every word.

"I'm an angel now but I was human once. I was murdered in cold blood. I made those bad choices that ultimately led to so much bloodshed, Selene and I included. I'm the soul stained in crimson," I finished, whispering the last sentence.

A knock sounded on the door. "Hello? Ayden?" The voice was that of Sunny—his girlfriend.

She reminded me of what I never had. I was being corrupted by my love for a human man. I was failing as a Virtue.

Esme left her seat to tell her to go away but Ayden stepped in. He winced due to every movement in his back, making his way to the door and answering it. "Sunny, we should probably talk."

She hugged him in a hurry, and he yelled out in pain. She pulled back, scared of what she had done. "What did I do?" She covered her mouth with both hands.

Ayden grabbed the frame of the doorway, his knuckles beginning to whiten. "My back is not in any shape to be touched."

"I'm so sorry; I didn't know." She apologized over and over, hoping this would keep them on a good note.

Ayden grabbed her wrists and withdrew a deep breath. "I really do apologize for this, but we should break up."

"Why? I said I didn't know about your back. Ayden, please. What is it about me?" She gripped his hands, desperate to keep her hold on him. "Please tell me what I did wrong. I will fix it."

"You can't," he told her.

She shouted, "Why not?" She had to have been desperate to fight for him. Yet, I couldn't blame her.

She went in to kiss him, but he moved his face out of her way. "I'm sorry, Sunny, but I don't love you."

"That's okay. You don't have to love me. We can just wait until that happens." She nodded a lot and believed that she had a chance to salvage what they had left.

He let go of her hands. "I can't. I shouldn't rope you into a loveless relationship. You deserve better." He closed the door before she could argue the opposite.

No banging followed, nor did any yelling. Silence pursued and Sunny was left in doubt with herself as a woman.

Esme's lips pressed in a thin line to keep herself from saying something to make the situation worse. The awkwardness hung in the air around us, as loud as a trumpet. Ayden looked between us both. "That has been taken care of."

Wrapping my arms around my knees, I was unsure of what to say to that. He liked Sunny. Why was he suddenly saying no to her because of love? Ayden wouldn't change for anyone, including the cute redhead he met at the bar on her twenty-first.

I shook my head to dismiss the tension. "That wasn't awkward at all." My eyes landed on Ayden. He was off in another world inside his head, gaze locked on the window.

I'd never been in love before, and I'd never had such a big crush on any man.

Admiration settled on my face, taking in the structure of his jaw and the way he slouched his shoulders. His eyebrows furrowed a bit in a mesmerizing way, making me wonder what went on his brain. His green eyes stored so much emotion and mystery all at once, and I wanted to explore his every nook and cranny. I wished to know exactly who he was, understanding his nature. At this moment, I only knew the surface of Ayden Dyer.

He held so much more beneath the exterior. There was a depth to his personality. I *craved* to know more. I begged that he would let me in, but he would only allow me to see so much. If only men told us how they felt instead of burying it inside forever...

He rested his elbows on his thighs, his arms out, hands clasped together. He didn't move due to the wounds.

Esme cleared her throat, bringing me back to reality.

Ayden wasn't mine to love.

I glanced at his sister and the heat rose to my cheeks. She had seen the way I looked at him and it wasn't something I could be proud of. I stood up from my spot. "I should probably get going. Ayden doesn't need me and it's pointless to stay. I need to get a new dress anyway." I folded the blanket and laid it on the back of the couch.

Esme shot to her feet to stop me. "Please, just stay a bit longer. I don't want to see you go yet. You still need to heal."

"If I go back to Heaven, they will heal me there. I belong there. I shouldn't be here when I'm not in the middle of a mission," I explained.

She nodded as her eyes darted to the carpet. "I understand that, I do. I'm asking for one more week."

I let out a sigh. "One more week. After that, I must leave. I can't stay any longer." I sat back down, squeezing my eyes shut from the pain of my injured back. Once it had subsided, I opened my eyes.

A small smile formed. "Thank you."

Chills scurried up and down my legs. I pulled the blanket back over them and shivered some more.

Esme approached the stereo and turned it on to uplift some spirits. I wasn't sure how well it would work but it was ironic when a song began singing about things getting better. It was as if music could read our thoughts. It played the perfect songs at the times they were most needed.

She came and sat between Ayden and I. "Things are going to get better real soon. Have hope and be faithful." She assured us. "What have you got to lose?"

My eyes stayed glued to the blanket as my fingers messed with the fabric. "Everything. I will lose my spot in Heaven. I won't be able to help anyone else."

"Why?" She crossed her arms, challenging me and Heaven.

"I love a human." I hugged myself to keep myself warm.

"And why is that bad? You were a human. You're just dead now." She gestured to me.

"Exactly. I'm dead. We're a different species now. We're in different parts of our life. He's alive. I'm not. That's just how it works. I'm a soul. I'm an angel. I'm supposed to help people; I'm not supposed to fall in love with them." A sting sprung on my back, causing me to groan.

She was about to speak but I stopped her. "Besides, why would I stay and get myself kicked out of Heaven for a man who doesn't love me back? Even if I weren't in trouble with God, I would still have to face Ayden every day, knowing he didn't return the feelings."

She faced Ayden and shook her head in disappointment. "He's just a stubborn one."

Ayden didn't turn to look at us as he said, "I can hear you."

"That's the point. It's true." Esme smiled but dropped it soon after.

"What are we supposed to do for another week? We're both weak and I know there's nothing else I can do. Ayden needs rest. I need rest." I could compare this injury to a sunburn because the two were similar in pain levels with burning, stinging, and *Hell's Itch*.

"You both can rest and maybe just talk. I'll be here to help you guys." Her lips curved upward but it never reached her eyes. Even in her subconscious mind, she doubted we would ever be a thing.

My eyes averted to Ayden. "He doesn't look like he's in the mood to talk anymore. There's nothing to even talk about." I pointed my thumb in his direction.

Esme looked at him and he turned to face us both. Proving me wrong, he said, "You can tell me more about yourself. You have more going on than meets the eye."

"Why should I have to reveal myself? That's your job. I'm the guardian angel. My identity is supposed to stay secret," I argued. "Yours is the one I'm supposed to know to help you."

"I know your identity. If you want to know mine, you will tell me yours. It's a fair trade, *Elli*," he mocked.

I froze up, that name haunting my mind as it did after her death. Selene had called me that. That was the name she'd given me. He didn't have the right to call me by that nickname. He couldn't have known but he would be taught that it wasn't his name to speak.

"What's wrong?" Ayden's face filled with concern. He walked over to me, forgetting about his own injuries.

Shaking my head, I whispered, "She used to call me that... Selene called me Elli to make me feel more like she was my friend." I wiped the first tear before it could reach my cheekbone.

He nodded, understanding. "I'm so sorry. I didn't mean to make you upset. I'll just call you Angel instead."

As much as it hurt to hear that name, I couldn't control him and he knew that. Telling him no would be like telling a dog to avoid human food. They just never obeyed.

Our eyes met as I swallowed my sorrow and said, "I'll be gone next week. What you call me isn't an issue." Ayden would move on with his life and I'd become yet another voiceless echo.

 MALIGNITY

I set the four cups in a line, biggest to smallest. I tapped the tallest cup. "This is where the Thrones stand. They are Justice Angels. They are the ones who deal with heavenly justice situations. It's not often when they are used but they're important. They make sure everything runs smoothly and according to the system."

Esme nodded. "Okay, so they're like the judges and court system of the heavens?"

"*Heaven*," I corrected, "and yes. They are not judges as much as they are there to solve a case and get information. Everything they gather will end up going to God who is the ultimate judge, and these judges will then just relay the message He sent." I gestured.

Her head tilted to the left. "So, who's the second-highest in Heaven?"

My lips curved upward. "Virtues. Guardian angels. We are important to Heaven because we take on a task that helps get Heaven more souls. That is the ultimate goal, to get souls to the good side. Humans screw up all the time and trust me, Ayden is not the worst. However, there's hope for everyone. Everyone has a chance and that is why we do our part. We change people and protect them from Lucifer's influence which is very deceptive. After all, he was once an angel of light."

She choked on her laugh and grabbed the counter. "Hold on just a moment. Ayden is not your worst? Bloody hell, who is?"

I glanced at him as he devoured his cake. He didn't give me any attention, which did sting but I was sure the cake beat me by far.

"People who don't realize they're wrong and continue to think they're perfect. They can be frustrating because they don't see the error of their ways and that's the first step to change. They must see a problem. Ayden realizes he's making bad decisions and he doesn't say he's getting into Heaven because he's a good guy. He knows why he's headed for Hell." I coughed a bit. "Better to be hot or cold than lukewarm."

With my back almost healed, I'd be leaving by the end of the week.

Esme pointed to the third cup. "All right, now this. Which is this again?"

It bubbled within my stomach, making me giddy. I hadn't had a friend in so long. It felt good to be this close to another girl. Esme was sweet, too.

"This is for Archangels. Archangels are lower than guardian angels, and it seems odd, but they are. Archangels are the only tier that other angels can't get into. They are the warriors, and when Archangels were created, they were made to fight all battles, and it became set in stone. No one gets in or out, basically. Well, unless you betray God and go to Hell with the fallen angels." I snickered.

Lifting her chin, she grabbed the cup. "Archangels. That seems so interesting. They're warriors you say?"

I gave her a small nod. "Yes, they fight all the wars and battles. When Matthew came to save Ayden and I, he was an Archangel. He is the warrior who was saving us from Lucifer's wrath. This is what they do. They're a good legion."

"And the bottom is just all other angels, people who go to Heaven and choose to enjoy their afterlife and not serve a higher purpose?" She put the cup down, looking at the last one.

"Correct. God knows the hardships of being human. So, He doesn't blame any human for just wanting to sit back and relax in their afterlife. Angels like me still exist. We choose to be guardian angels or serve justice. It works out in the end." I gave her the reassurance that if she wanted to relax, it was her choice. Nobody was being judged for what position they chose. Even garbage men were important on earth.

Esme circled around the counter and opened a cabinet, getting some snacks to munch on. "All right, what about Hell? What is the order of these bad guys?"

I twisted myself until my back was against the counter, elbows resting on it while my hands hung off the edge. "Fallen angels are actually the first. This is all because they were the first to rebel. Shadows and demons are just holograms in a sense. But fallen angels were the first of the angels to rebel with Lucifer so they get top priority. That's why they are the ones who torture souls, the ones who come to consult about the status of a person. They are the ones waiting for us guardian angels to fail our mission. Demons and shadows are the ones who tend to get the most flack, though. Nobody remembers the fallen angels because they don't show themselves on earth. They work from underground.

"I consider them like holograms because they're more like a projection of evil. Lucifer can't actually create anything. He merely takes what's already there and twists it for his gain. Fallen angels, for example. Shadows are used from the shadows created by the light when it shines down on people. Demons? They're like a mix between broken technology and shadows. They're a little more powerful. They can possess. Get inside heads. Destroy the mind. A glitch in the darkness."

Her eyes fell to the floor. "But if they're like broken technology and you say he can't create but only use what's already there, how did demons come to play? Technology didn't exist when they came to be."

"No. But they knew it would. They all knew what was coming. And they knew how this ends, yet Lucifer still fights. Shameful. Foolish. There's no other word to describe it." With the shake of my head, I released a little sigh.

Esme put her hand on the counter and shifted her weight to the other side of her body. "Wow. It's crazy that all this is happening in front of us and we can't even see it."

"It really is." I laughed to help let everyone in the room there was really nothing to fear. Even if Ayden wasn't keen on listening. "But yes, demons and shadows are the ones that people actually see a presence of on earth. That is why people end up fearing them the most when it's really fallen angels they should be afraid of. Those are the ones who actually torture them."

"And you say they possess people? Demons?" she asked.

"Yes. They influence them to do bad things. They are second in line and they are the evil equivalent to guardian angels, only we don't possess people." I nodded. "Not only that, but demons are not dead people. All souls that end up in Hell are in jail cells. Nobody goes to Hell and ends up as a shadow, demon, or fallen angel. Those are positions that cannot be added to, just like Archangels." I leaned to one side.

"And shadows?"

I took a deep breath. "They scare people. They scare people because they feed on fear. Hell is basically fueled by the fear of human souls."

Esme looked over at Ayden and leaned in. "What's next once you leave?"

I sat on the stool to ease the pressure on my back. "I'll keep going. I'll save more souls because that's my purpose in Heaven. It brings me joy to see people turn themselves around." Subconsciously, I began to rub the hem of my dress between my fingers.

"He's an arse, Angel. Please know that my brother does not always mean well but I want him to change. We will try even after you leave. How he picked Sunny over you is beyond me. She's beautiful but she's still not you. You should have been the one he chose to date." She attempted to mask the sorrow in her eyes with a smile.

I put my hand on top of hers and patted it. "You're kind, and I love you for being accepting of me and all of this. It's not anyone's fault. Feelings cannot be controlled. If he doesn't love me, he doesn't. I would never force him to, and I can't blame him for not loving me back. It's not mine, either. I also did my best and now it's time to move on. Others need me just as much."

Esme walked around the counter and pulled me into a gentle hug. "I'll miss you. You didn't just impact him, but you also imprinted on our lives. You're such a good person for taking on such a job in the afterlife. We will always love and appreciate what you do."

With that, the waterworks began.

"Oh, did I say something wrong?" She stepped back. "Why are you crying?"

I swallowed and shook my head. "It's nothing bad, Esme. You just... It means so much to me that you say that. I didn't have very many people say that to me my entire life and hearing you say it *now* means I had a reason to be here. Ayden didn't change but I had a chance to meet you and make friends. That is what makes this so worth it in the end. Thank you."

Esme turned me around and checked the bandages. "Your back is healing up very well. I'm happy I got to be a part of this journey with you." She fixed the gauze.

I folded my hands together on the counter. "We both are."

Ayden walked into the kitchen, stopping in his tracks to eye us both. "What is this?"

"This is what two people do when they care about each other. They talk like normal people," Esme said in a sarcastic tone.

His nose scrunched up. "You're bonding. It's weird."

Clearing my throat, I shrugged. "I had a friend once and she was killed, and I've been alone since. Esme is just nice enough to quiet the voice in my heart that calls for one in need." I couldn't decipher whether or not it was wrong of me to like reminding Ayden of how alone I always was. It was wrong to enjoy guilt-tripping him, right?

Ayden pulled a shirt over his head, fixing it. "Esme is the one you picked? Arabella is much closer to your age."

"Why should age matter? I happen to connect with your sister. Our mentalities are on the same level. There's no law that says I can't be friends with..." I trailed off, not sure how to finish. "How old are you, Esme? Don't answer if you don't want to."

She shrugged. "It's not a big deal. I'm thirty-five."

"Okay, so she's thirty-five. That's not a big deal. I was friends with my professors and teachers when I was alive, and they were way older than me. My maturity just matched up with theirs and I didn't get along with other kids my age." I averted my eyes to the floor.

"And that is your first problem with why you never had friends." Ayden patted my head and left the room.

Esme put her arm around me and pulled me closer. "Don't mind him. He doesn't understand how some people can't play with kids who pick their boogers and think girls have cooties. You matured faster and that's okay. When did you mature?"

"Probably when I was like ten. I mean, I was still a kid. I would do stupid things. I ate dirt. I slid down the stairs on a mattress. I stole rings from a store when I was five. I just never found it easy to make friends. I was the quiet girl in school." I spun on the stool.

Esme watched me spin around. "What is your most embarrassing childhood memory?"

I choked a bit. "Oh, well, I guess that has to come back up. When I was in third grade, I made the mistake of walking into the wrong bathroom. I thought they renovated the girl's bathroom and added urinals, which I had no idea what those were at the time. I sat in the stall and did my business and two boys came in. They saw my girly shoes and laughed at the fact that a girl was in the boy's bathroom and I never felt so mortified in my life. On a lighter note, they never found out who I was so at least my poor reputation was intact."

Esme's laugh lit up the apartment. "I had peed my pants in school once and had to change them. A kid accused me of peeing my pants since I wore these ugly red track pants as back-up. I denied it but we both knew deep down I had a weak bladder."

Giggling, I rubbed her shoulder. "It's all right now. It's an old memory and nobody remembers but you. At least that's what I tell myself to feel better." It was the same situation when I made up the excuse that I was still *prettier* than Sunny.

ATONEMENT

I gazed out the window, studying the world as it continued on. I planned to leave today and there was nothing stopping me. I couldn't leave without Ayden, but I had to. It was better for both of us.

Spinning around, I scanned the apartment. Ayden exited the bathroom with just a white towel wrapped around his waist. His body glistened through the warm drops of water, wet hair pushed back. His eyes landed on me. "You're leaving already?"

I'd be a liar if I denied how wonderful he looked at this moment. The dip of his V-line was visible to the eye, but his towel covered the rest of what he had to offer to women. It was all kinds of wrong for me to even see him this exposed.

Coming back to reality, I answered, "I said I was staying for one more week, then leaving. That usually means I'm leaving when I say I am." I laughed a bit, trying to lighten the mood. It was a lame attempt since nothing could lift our spirits. This was the end of an era, and it was not an ending I'd ever hoped for.

The smile on his face was laced with desolation. "I don't want you to go."

"I should. I must go because I can't stay here and make matters worse. That's not my job." I walked over to where he stood, patting his damp shoulder. "I wish you well in your life." My fingers were so close to ripping his towel off, but I controlled myself before I made such an idiotic decision.

I said my goodbye to Esme, hugging her one last time before moving onto my next task.

I ventured out to the forest, asking for some help from Heaven. My back was still in the process of healing and my wings wouldn't be of any use to fly me up.

They sent Matthew down to guide me back. They repaired my dress to make me feel a little better about what happened. Our clothing was made with care up here so that they didn't cover our wings and hide them as human clothes did. My white dress flowed with ease, matching my large, white, feathery wings.

The special angels healed my back so that I could use flight if needed, and not suffer from Hell's fury.

I stood from my hospital bed and bowed my head out of respect for my fellow nurses.

Now wandering, my eyes landed on Matthew. "I'm sorry. I failed my mission. Ayden Dyer did not change his ways. He refuses to love."

Does he refuse to love, or does he refuse to love you?

I planted my butt on the clouds, mind focused on my next charge. There was a high chance I'd not get another for a good while. "I understand if I don't get sent on another task."

He kneeled in front of me and reassured me that I was not the failure. "We don't disappoint Heaven because we try. We let everyone down if we refuse to accept a charge in the first place. You planted that seed. You got the ball rolling. You can only do so much, but you cannot control his life for him. He must make those choices. You've already made great progress with him, and that alone is enough to say you have done well, kid." He gave me a small smile.

I returned the gesture with a little smile. "Thank you." I got up, my feet standing on the softness of the puffy cloud as I curled my toes against the voluminous path before me.

Heaven was always illuminated by the light. It'd never be dark, but it wasn't blinding to us. Angels had better eyesight to withstand sensitivity to brightness.

Clouds floated everywhere, right beneath our feet. Rooms spread out, rooms that led to different places. Inside them were libraries, churches, and anything else we could ever want.

A large building stood at the end of it all, a kingdom created by the One and Only. It was where God stayed until He was ready to come out when needed.

I entered a room full of animals.

I kneeled and put my hand out, an apple slice in my palm. A small horse came over and lowered his neck, eating right out of my hand. With a smile, I pet the space between his eyes. "There, you are happier than you were. You still like apples. Somebody has to." I climbed back on my feet and began to smooth my hand down his neck. "Your fur is soft. I wonder what it's like to have fur. Do you ever wonder what it's like to be naked and bare-skinned?" I tilted my head.

The horse neighed in response.

"I don't think animals would care. You guys can be pretty open about things." I let out a small laugh. "No knowledge that being naked can lead to lust or humiliation. What a freeing thought."

I spent some more time in the room until I made my way to the library. This building was a whole other world of wonder. I found a book to occupy my empty thoughts, sitting down and opening it up. I pulled back my head, widening my eyes when a scene took place in my mind. Inside my head played a movie I couldn't control.

Ayden and I approached the door while I knocked. A deep breath escaped my lips to ease my nerves. Nothing could come close to explaining the level of anxiety that was flooding within me now.

Love had always been forbidden between an angel and a human and it hadn't changed since the dawn of time. The question was, was it wrong between two angels? Angels were not supposed to be able to love in a romantic way, yet I could. I proved what was possible beyond all belief.

The big, golden doors opened to reveal a bright light, setting forth a room filled with clouds of Heaven. They were delicate and fluffy to the touch, yet still too transparent to feel between my fingers.

I walked in, watching the doors shut behind me. They echoed throughout as if we were in closed walls, but we weren't. I clasped my hands together in front of me, bowing out of respect.

The room stayed silent for a moment while He gathered His thoughts, figuring out what to say. We had loved but now that we were the same species, our love could not be wrong.

Like fornication, a couple could marry and the sin would stop. It stopped by his hand.

I broke the silence, afraid that it would lead down a negative road. "You called for me?"

I came back to reality and moved my eyes around the library to check for any odd looks. It was difficult to believe what I saw. That wasn't true. That had to be a mind game. Why was I shown that kind of scene?

Matthew set foot in the library. "We have a new charge for you."

He gestured for me to follow him.

Going to see my new charge was an immediate curiosity but I was still unable to process the scene I had witnessed moments ago. I was desperate to distract myself and this would help me do so. I needed some way to forget about Ayden and move on from my troubles.

I halted as we neared the same doors I'd seen in my *vision*. Matthew knocked and we waited for them to open, revealing the grand room inside. We went inside as the doors closed behind us.

An angel hurried over, handing me a piece of paper. "What's this?" I asked her.

She smiled and pointed to God who sat in the chair. I glanced at the paper, seeing the name that was written on it. *Sunny Smith.* "You have to be kidding me."

"Pardon?" God asked.

I shook my head with a smile. "Thank you, Father. I'll go now." I left the room and sighed to myself now that I was alone. "Sunny. Of all people, I must deal with her. What has she done this time?"

I fixed my hair and smoothed out my dress. "Here we go."

I entered the apartment. Her place was a mess. Tissues littered the floor and I saw bottles of wine all over the kitchen counter. She'd lost it after Ayden left.

"Elena? What are you doing here?" She stopped as soon as she spotted me. I'd forgotten about the fake name I gave myself when Sunny knew me.

I looked at her, clearing my throat. Her face was red and puffed while she smelled of wine. The drunkenness radiated from her and clogged my nostrils. She came closer, stumbling along the way. She reached out and touched my wings. "You're an angel." She laughed, not sure of what she was really saying. She seemed so out of it.

My eyes darted to the gun in her hand. I put my hands up to keep them on display for her to see. She couldn't feel threatened or things would end in a terrible spot. "Sunny, what are you doing with that?"

Her lips formed a frown as she lifted the gun without a care in the world. "Elena, it's..." her words trailed off.

She didn't need to answer my question. I knew. Sunny planned to take her own life today. Something deeper was going on inside her head, something that was far bigger than being dumped by Ayden.

When she looked away, I took my time approaching her and pulling the gun out of her hand. I set it out of her reach and led her to the sofa. I helped her sit, sighing. "I get it. You were dumped. It sucks. We all don't want to be dumped but it happens. I promise you are the one who's not at fault. Ayden has things he has to work out on his own." I pulled a blanket over her. I entered her kitchen and poured her a glass of water. I brought it back, giving it to her.

She sighed as she lowered her eyes. "I love him."

I almost laughed at her words. She didn't *love* him. "Sunny, you are a beautiful woman. You are going to find an amazing man someday. You need to focus on yourself and be happy with who you are. Do you have any hobbies? How about those? You should probably work on some of your hobbies. That always helps. Ayden is just a complicated man. He sucks at romance. It's nothing personal."

I helped her drink water, holding it to her lips. I set it on the coffee table afterwards. She looked at the ceiling and released another sigh, not saying anything.

She drank more water after asking for it again.

"Better?"

She nodded a bit and closed her eyes, rubbing her head. "Do

you think if we stayed together, Ayden could've learned to love me? Would it be possible?"

I didn't know how to help her with this. It wasn't the type of question I wanted to answer. I loved him, too. "I think it would've been tough. If two people aren't meant to be, it's just not going to work. You two might've gotten into a lot of fights. There would be cheating, possibly. You guys wouldn't be able to work because it wasn't for you. You both want different things." I put a pillow under her head.

She nodded a bit and put her head on my shoulder instead. "Do you think I'm crazy for doing this? I want him to love me and it's hard to accept that he doesn't."

"I don't think you're crazy. I think you're just lonely and you don't know how to handle rejection after your first confession of love." I realized it was easy to say these words because they applied to me as well.

She turned her head to face me, waiting for me to go on.

I continued, "Sometimes it's very hard to love someone who doesn't feel the same way. It hurts. It absolutely blows. You make stupid decisions because you feel so heartbroken, and you later regret them. We must learn from our mistakes and become better people. You can be a better person. You'll do amazing. I promise. You will find someone to love you." I smiled at her.

She gave me a pitiful look. "Did you love someone? Did he not return the feelings?"

A sad smile appeared on my face as I dropped my head. "I did. I do. I love him but I must move on because it's no good for me to pine after a man who doesn't feel the same way. It damages me to stay on this path. It hurts him if he were to be forced into a relationship he isn't invested in. We both must do what's best and go our separate ways. It aches but if you love them, you let them go." I lifted my head and stared out of her window.

She hugged me. "Thank you. You are the best therapist anyone could ask for."

I didn't hate Sunny. I never did to begin with. In fact, I couldn't even dislike her. She was just a girl who liked the wrong guy, just as I was unfortunate to fall into the same position. It was never her fault. She had no clue how I felt about Ayden Dyer.

"Promise me you'll get help. I know it seems shameful, but it shouldn't be. There's nothing wrong with admitting you need people to help heal your mind. I know Ayden is not the only reason why you would even consider killing yourself." My eyes stayed fixed on the view outside. "It is far better if you get some counseling and maybe even see a psychiatrist. I'd be pained to see you take your own life. You deserve so much more and there are humans willing to help you achieve the life you were meant to enjoy." I twisted my head towards her.

As if taking my advice, she texted Mason to come over and help her with finding guidance. If her mental health wasn't intact, it was best for her to take care of herself first before she used love to repair it. Love could put pieces back together, but it was not romantic love that could achieve this. It was self-love and focusing on her own condition that would heal her through time, and with the right kind of treatment.

She fell asleep before he could arrive, but I knew he would have a better chance talking to her than I could. I lay her down on the couch, tucking her in the blanket. I left the water for her and cleaned up her apartment to leave her feeling refreshed when she woke up.

I removed the gun from her home, taking it with me when I returned to Heaven. I locked it up in a safe, away from all humans. Guns couldn't be returned to stores and trying to hide it or throw it away was too risky. The one place humans could never reach was

Heaven. They couldn't see such a glorious location.

Having made progress with my task, I took a stroll through the park outside the library. I'd done well because I was experienced enough to empathize with her. I knew what it was like to love and not be loved in return. I'd wanted to be a psychologist in college, and I understood the importance of mental health more than some people. Sunny needed the help that I could never give her at this rate. I'd never finished my degree and I wasn't a professional.

I reported to the angels and God, letting them know that Sunny was going to change for the better and she would have help from her brother to find her the assistance she required. I'd return to her when she needed me most, after she'd discussed with Mason the kind of guidance she'd accept. If she got care in a hospital, I would promise her to be there. I was her guardian angel now and it was my duty to watch over her, protecting her from herself and the distress poisoning her mind.

The library was nearby, and I decided to read some books, occupying my time the only way I could. I had the option to also play with the animals but that wasn't my job at the moment. I was studying the ways of being a guardian angel. I had to brush up on how to be a better Virtue and not get myself or my charges into any trouble. I desired to do good. I wished to continue to change lives and save souls.

When the time came to leave, I vacated the library and observed the flowers outside. I hummed a gentle tune from a song I had heard during my days on earth. It was a beautiful melody and I couldn't keep the lyrics from playing inside my mind.

A bell sound echoed and I turned my head in every direction, wondering where it had come from. I'd never heard anything like it before.

Gasping, I heard Ayden's voice resonating in the air around me,

"Angel, if you can hear me wherever you are, listen to me. I need you. Come back because I need you to change me. I'm ready to turn my life around."

COMELINESS
AYDEN

I stepped outside the door and huffed. It was way too warm out here today, and it was only seventy degrees.

After praying to Angel last week, there was a soft pain in my chest. She never came back. I called out to her and she left me in the dust. There had been a day once where she said I could call out to her and she would listen. I guess that was a lie.

I went to the bakery and clocked in for my shift. It was a good distraction from the rest of the world right now.

As I headed to the back, I heard the bell ring. I turned to greet the customers, but I recognized his face. It looked just like *Sunny's*.

"We should talk about Sunny," he said. What was his name again? Mark?

"Oh, sure." I cleared my throat and sat at a table in the corner. "What is it? Is this about our relationship? Manny, I swear I did not mean to hurt her. I really did like her but something serious hit me and I realised it was wrong to string her along for the ride. I didn't mean to lead her on the way I did."

"My name is Mason," he corrected me. "I'm going to cut to the chase here and tell you she tried to take her own life. She's currently admitted to a private facility so she can get some help."

My Adam's apple bobbed as I blinked away the surprise. "I'm sorry. Do you happen to know why she would do something so horrible?" I knew Sunny was clingy, but never did it occur she would try to harm herself.

He sighed as he ran his fingers through his ginger hair. "I have some theories. I also wanted to ask about what happened between you two. Maybe knowing how it ended could better clarify part of the source and confirm my theory."

"She seemed fine." They always did. "We met at her party and hit it off. I invited her to my apartment and we would hang out sometimes. We never even had sex." I stroked my beard as my forehead creased. What is it that brought her to this decision?

Michael rubbed his face. "I know she's her own person now, but I still look out for her. Let's just say Sunny is not the most secure girl around. She's had a lot of insecurities in the past and I should have told you that she gets very attached to boys. She wants love more than anything. My best theory is about our dad. Our dad died last year at the end of the summer and she hasn't been the same since. It's like she searches for his love in other men—in you."

When she had begged me to stay with her, she asked what it was she could fix. When I told her she couldn't fix this part of herself, she asked *why not*. The answer had been so simple, but it was only now that it came to me. *Sunny would never be Angel.*

I nodded a bit. "I'm sorry to hear that. I hope she gets better in that place." I meant every word. The last thing I wished on anyone was for them to kill themselves.

"Me too." He stood up. "Thanks for talking to me. I'll leave you to get back to work." He exited the shop and the bell dinged behind him.

It was tragic to hear that Sunny would do that to herself, but I believed it. People hid how they really felt all the time. I guess a part of me just wished she was the exception.

I stood from my chair and walked to the back of the shop. I put a black apron on and grabbed some ingredients.

"Angel, where are you? I know I screwed up but bloody hell, I didn't realise you hated me now." I leaned both hands onto the counter as I peered up at the ceiling.

I spent my day baking sweets and treats. Mum came in at one point even to remind me of the order we had to fulfil. It was a set of cupcakes put together to create one piece of art.

By the end of the project, I was covered in lots of flour. That stuff got everywhere.

I licked the frosting from my finger and washed my hands following it. I moved my head to the beat of the drums from the song playing through my phone speaker. It kept my mind off the one woman who chose to ignore me.

"Is this appropriate, Ayden?" Mum asked as she gestured to the device.

"Is listening to music on the job a bad thing? I figured it was okay because my mum is my boss. This is our own business. We aren't run by a big corporation." I shrugged. "Did the music not help me make beautiful cupcake cakes?"

"I'm not talking about the music. Well, I am but not because it's on. Do the lyrics sound appropriate?" She turned it down.

"They are appropriate for a man like me. She's singing what I'm thinking. Heaven knows I do belong down below. Let's face the truth and stop hiding from it." I looked up at her.

She leaned over the edge of the counter, admiring my work. "Why do you do this to yourself?"

I was ready to change but I heard no word back from Angel, so nobody had to know that I wanted to turn around. I wouldn't get their hopes up for no good reason. "Do you mean to ask why I do this to you? I love you, and I mean that, but change does not happen overnight."

She straightened her posture. "Change? Does this mean you are trying?" She fanned her face as her eyes watered. She walked around the counter and pulled me into a hug. I'd made the wrong word choice.

"Oh, bloody hell, Mum, you are way too emotional for your own good." I groaned.

"You're my baby boy!" she yelled. "The only might I add."

"I'm also a grown man." I pulled away from her hug. "I'm far from a baby."

"Yeah, you like to think you're not a baby." She grabbed my hand and kissed my knuckles. "But you're my baby and you always will be no matter what." She lowered my hand. "Your father wants us to go on a date tonight. If you need help, you can call Arabella. She's been asking about you. I love you." She kissed my cheek and left the shop.

I sat on the stool and released all tension from my shoulders. I placed my elbows on the counter and locked my fingers together as I rested my chin on them. "Angel, I know you're up there. I know you can hear me." I let out a shaky breath.

I got no response.

"I need you. I do. I can't do this on my own. That's what your job is. You are supposed to help us when we struggle. I'm just a human and I can't do it all on my own. Save me, Eliana," I finished my prayer.

I was not at all surprised by the empty room. She wasn't coming back. I had scared her away. It was my fault for treating her the way I had.

The plastic covering was better to use than saran wrap for covering up any kind of sweets, so that's what I did. I learned long ago when my father freaked out because I had ruined the frosted design.

I put it into the fridge and closed the bakery before going home. I sat down on the couch and closed my eyes. She would never come back to *me*. I had to give up on believing she kept her word. Could I blame her? Hardly. Nobody wanted to face the rejection of being loved.

I checked the messages on my phone and tossed it beside me. For the past few weeks, Sunny had been leaving messages and voicemails but there wasn't a single one today and now I knew why. She couldn't have her phone if she were in a recovery hospital.

I didn't mean for any of this to happen to her, but it wasn't something I could reverse. It would destroy her more if I continued to rope her into a relationship that had no future.

A knock sounded from the other side of my front door and I couldn't gather strength to answer it. "Come in."

Arabella closed the door behind her and smiled at me. "Mum told me you wanted to talk."

"She must be mistaken because I never once said I wanted to talk. I want to be alone."

"How does that work for you? You're always alone, Ayden. If you're left to wallow inside your own head for too long, you're bound to think about how life sucks and you'll fall into this hole." She came over and moved my phone before sitting down beside me. "I know that we aren't as close as you and Esme but I'm here for you."

I turned to look at her. "How so? You can't fix me. Elena was supposed to, but she left, and she refuses to come back." I had to remember to call her by the name Arabella knew her as. Only Esme knew who Angel was and why she was really in my life.

"Does she refuse to come back, or do you refuse to change? Are you serious about turning your life around? We've also been trying but you keep shutting us out. Your therapist was just trying to help you. You got into a serious car accident because of a decision you made. We could've lost you. Do you understand what that's like? I was there when you were born. It was so painful to see you grow up and destroy yourself like this." She wiped some tears from her cheeks. "You're my little brother and I want to see you succeed."

I sat back against the cushions. "I'm aware. She was just the one person who was helping me make any progress and I told her I was done with it all and she said okay. Now, I can't find her and she won't answer my calls." She sent me straight to voicemail.

"Give her some space. She had a lot of stuff to put up with when it came to you. She needs some time to process this. You can drive someone crazy with your justifications. She needs to regather herself." She put her head on my shoulder. "I hope you understand her decisions and I'm sure with time, she'll come back."

"How do you know she'll come back to me?" I folded my arms.

Arabella laughed. "Because she's already such a good person for trying to help you."

Good person. Angel used to tell me that good people didn't exist. They just made good choices, but they still made many mistakes. I was the type of person to make bad choices.

Arabella and I stayed in silence for a few minutes. I enjoyed the peace and quiet. My sisters were always wanting to talk. What was it with wanting to talk? I hated talking. Why couldn't anyone respect that?

"What's on your mind?" Arabella turned her cheek on my shoulder to look up at me.

I shook my head. "Well, I'm wondering why the bloody hell you all want to constantly know what I'm thinking about. I'm not that interesting."

She laughed a little and patted my arm. "You'd be surprised but we think you are. You're so confusing so we just wonder what a man like you thinks about all the time. You have to have much more going on to keep yourself occupied when you shut us out."

"Nothing much goes on in my brain. I'm not a poet like Elena." I crossed my arms and looked up at the ceiling.

I had one regret and it was how I talked to Angel when she told me she loved me. If I had just let her down in a gentle way, we would not be where we were now. She would be here, helping me. Instead, she was probably replaying my prayers as if it were satisfying to hear me begging for help. She wanted to be worshipped—as much as she wouldn't admit it. I had even done so, and she used her power to do me dirty and reject me in return.

I could see her sitting on a cloud and laughing at my words. She found pleasure in leaving me out to dry as I had done the same to her. I ripped her heart out and stomped on it and she was only returning the favour. Did I deserve it? I had a solid belief that I earned every bit of rejection she threw my way.

A vibration went off and I grabbed my phone. I checked the message from Sunny, confused as to how she had access to her phone.

What had me even more puzzled were the two emojis she sent, one with a halo and one with the sun. What the fuck could this mean? An angel of light was my best guess, but I didn't want to believe Sunny was sending me a suicide note.

 SINCERE

Tick tock—the hand landed on twelve, and the doctor came into the room. My invisibility mask was on the entire time, keeping me hidden from everyone here. Well, it wasn't the whole time because I would show myself to Sunny when nobody was around. A girl nicknamed Sunshine would try to end her own life. Ironic, but also tragic.

Sunny had taken some of her pills to distract herself from the thoughts taking over the corners of her mind. *Antidepressants* were what humans called them, and they were used to treat mental illnesses. However, there were times that those who were prescribed them were under the assumption that taking more would be beneficial to their mental state. Other times, they knew the consequences but needed the escape. When she took more than the recommended amount, all Sunny knew was that she wanted to close her eyes and get away for a brief moment of time.

When the doctor left, I reappeared. "So, Sunny, what is it that you like about this place? I know it's not ideal but they're just trying to help you. That's what I want, too."

She shrugged. "It's hard to say. I guess I like that I can go to group therapy and relate to others about my problems. I was never the most secure person in myself."

I sat beside her. Every time the employees entered the room, I had to stand in the corner so I couldn't make any dips in the soft furniture to give myself away or raise suspicion.

Rubbing her back, I said, "It's okay. It's okay to admit you have insecurities. Humans aren't perfect and there's a lot of crap to deal with. Tell me about it. I'm here to listen. I don't judge."

She nodded a bit, keeping her gaze fixed on the bed sheets.

They were a yellow shade, which was her favorite color. And I agreed that yellow was a pretty color.

The room wasn't too big and there weren't any kinds of objects she could use to hurt herself. Sharp objects had been confiscated and she was checked up on every now and then. She wasn't locked in this room, either. The door was open, but she chose to spend her solitude in a smaller space. I was also here to help her through this.

"When Ayden came to my party, I thought maybe it was my chance at love. You read all these romance books about girls dating their brother's best friend and Ayden showed up like that. I know Ayden and Mason had just met but just maybe I could make a romance novel come true in a way... I wanted those to come true for me. He was perfect, ya know. British, green eyes, tall... He could do without the beard because it looks ridiculous on him, but he was so attractive," she said with a small smile.

I disagreed. The beard was a great look on him. I loved that he looked so masculine. It was also cute to see him get frosting in his beard while baking. It really showed me what kind of man he was—a baker. A baking man was the best a woman like me wanted.

She continued, "When he came to talk to me, I was happy. I thought it was my chance to have happiness. I went for it. We hung out, and eventually, we cuddled and made out every now and then. He is such a wonderful kisser. All my past boyfriends are nothing compared to him. He knows his stuff, which is surprising because he's a virgin, but they never said virgins can't know how to kiss."

I swallowed and tried to push away the thought of kissing Ayden. I could never think that way. Now that she had mentioned his lips, I couldn't stop imagining them on mine.

She zipped up her sweater and shoved her hands into the pockets. "When he broke up with me, it was like my world crumbled before me. I didn't know what I did wrong. What could I do to make him stay? We weren't sleeping together so I knew it wasn't the sex. We never made it that far," she paused for a moment. "Is Ayden possibly asexual? He never even tried to go that far. He just seemed so...composed." She looked at me.

I almost choked on my tongue. Asexual? Ayden? Not even close. That boy was as sexual as they came. But why didn't he have sex with Sunny? I was certain they had done it by now. He'd won the bet. He could have sex and yet he chose not to.

"Asexual?" I asked. I wanted to lie and tell her he was but if I would gain her trust and help her, lying was not the way. "I would never notice. Ayden very much liked to look at women. He once looked at a picture of a woman in a bikini and had to adjust his pants because the boner was so noticeable." It wasn't a lie. I had seen it before. The man was very much into women and he wanted sex more than anything else. "I had also caught him masturbating." The memory danced like an uncoordinated man, obliterating all comfort within my thoughts. "It's safe to say he's not asexual."

"I guess I was never one of the girls to turn him on." She frowned. "So many times, I tried to wear low-cut shirts and he never noticed. Imagine being a woman and not being able to turn on the man you're with. That would make our sex life nonexistent. I was afraid he wasn't attracted to me."

"Sunny, I'm going to be honest with you. You already know I'm not just his therapist but an actual angel. I was his guardian angel, too. Right before you. When Ayden came to your party, it was because I told him to make friends with your brother. Ayden was never a virgin. That was a lie he told just so he wouldn't have to tell you he promised me he wouldn't have sex for a few months," I said to her.

She furrowed her brows. "What? He *isn't* a virgin?"

"The whole time he was with you, he was definitely not a virgin. I've had to be the unfortunate one to witness him having sex multiple times with multiple women. I know it's not what you want to hear but it's the truth. When he first saw you, he asked me if we could hold off on the bet so he could sleep with you. He did notice your cleavage. As for why he never offered sex after the bet was over, that I can't say. Only Ayden knows why he did that. We'd have to ask him." Yeah, that wouldn't happen. However, maybe it *could*. If I remembered, I could ask him why he never had sex with Sunny. He said he did want to change. I was hoping he got the text from Sunny that I sent. I was trying to let him know I was with Sunny right now and I'd be back as soon as possible. It wasn't exactly his business who I was with, and I couldn't legally say anything about it according to Heaven, but I did my best to hint at it.

Sunny swallowed. "I'm so sorry, Angel."

"What is there to be sorry about?" I asked.

"What isn't to be sorry about? You are just doing your job. You were trying to get Ayden to be a better person and I'm complaining because he wouldn't have sex with me. It's your fault he wouldn't and that's good that you could help him see that... What can I say? I wanted to rip his pants off. I wanted to see him naked." She looked up at the ceiling, leaning her head back against the wall. She was very open about her sexuality.

I'd be lying if I said I didn't want the same. I was sure Ayden had a great body under all the clothes. I'd seen him in just boxer briefs before and he had a really nice butt.

A shiver racked her body. "He looked so good without a shirt and I could only imagine how good he looked without pants. Am I a bad person for wanting sex with him? It's been a while since I had sex and I remember how good it's felt in the past. If Ayden was that good of a kisser, I could assume he was even better in bed."

"You're not a bad person. Nobody is bad or good. We just make poor choices." If that was true, I was making bad choices. I, too, wanted to see how he was in bed. Lust was an ugly color on every unmarried person. Unless Ayden was my husband, I wasn't supposed to picture him in bed. *Husband*—what a funny word. Ayden would never become a husband at this rate.

Sunny stood from the bed and went to the dresser filled with her clothes. "I spent my whole life being insecure. I tried to fill the void with Ayden and now he's gone. I want him back and I know I shouldn't because that is only going to make it worse, but I do. I want him back." She turned to face me.

I wasn't sure what I was supposed to tell her. It wasn't ideal for me to listen to her go on about wanting him. I wanted the same and every time she told me her desires, it reminded me that Ayden was not mine to have. He turned me down. I meant *nothing* to him.

"Sunny, I know you do. It's normal. But you're here now. You need to focus on yourself. You matter and you must come first. Your mental health is much more important than Ayden being here." I smiled a bit. "I'm here. I will help you through this."

Sunny scratched her head and leaned against her dresser. "What can you help with? What about you?" She glanced out the window. "You were human once. Were you insecure? Did you want to end your own life?" She stopped to look at me and when I didn't respond right away, she asked again, "did you?"

"I'm a girl, of course I was insecure. I never had a boyfriend. I never kissed a boy. I didn't spend an hour making myself look pretty. Instead, I threw my hair into a bun and forgot about my looks. I couldn't focus on them because it would drive me crazy. There were days in which I did want to end it all. You'd be surprised to know I didn't have a perfect life. I didn't have people to love me. Did I end my own life? No. My position now is based on another death, and not suicide." I shook my head. "Your brother cares. I want to help you see that. You matter and it can get better. Your validation in yourself should not come from what other men think of you. You're beautiful and strong. You should own it."

She sat down on the mattress. "I should but it's hard."

I put my hand on her arm. "I know. And I will help you. We will make progress. Trust me, there was a point in time where I was as insecure as you are now. I hated myself so much and I only felt good when others told me I was pretty. It takes a lot of work to change that mindset, but we can do it. When you feel confident, never let anyone tear you down. After spending so much time hating yourself, you deserve to show yourself some love, and you sure as heck earned being happy about it." I rubbed her arm a bit. "A man will see that and you will find love someday but for now, let's focus on helping you love yourself and knowing your worth."

Sunny got up from the bed again—like she had ants in her pants. "I'm going to take a shower. I'll be back." She left the room. The showers here were communal and open so that she would not be able to harm herself in private. The happiness she warranted was justified. She deserved *sunny* days.

I masked myself from the human eye and walked around the facility. It was open—bright—but the big windows were also locked tight to make sure nobody jumped out of them. It would be a lot harder to help someone out of their own hole if this place was dim and dingy all the time. Seasonal depression was real, and many suffered from it.

It was part of the reason why I hated Christmas, too. It meant darkened days and snowfalls. I hated anything that wasn't sunshine. The sun brightened my spirits. Maybe a lot of this was meant to happen for a reason to teach me and Sunny both a lesson. I needed the sun to see the light at the end of the tunnel.

It was peculiar that an angel needed a human to see something they should have already been able to. With Ayden's rejection and my love for him, the brightness within me had been cut off. Now Sunny could help bring it back out and show me that there was still more to life than Ayden Dyer. We would get through this together.

I loved Ayden and that was true but none of this had ever been her fault. I couldn't blame her for dating Ayden. I had nobody to blame because nobody knew I loved him, and I hadn't at the time the two of them got together. Even involved, she'd still been a bystander. We all were simply just spectators in the complex life of the man I'd had the unfortunate events of falling in love with.

REMISSION

S unny sat in a circle with the rest of the patients. She didn't say much today and I assumed she wasn't up for speaking, but I couldn't exactly guess why. When the therapy ended, she walked back to her room and looked at me after I turned off the invisible button.

"May I ask what happened?" I sent her a frown.

She shrugged and sat on the bed. "What was I supposed to say? I mean, I just feel like it's a large crowd. They're all staring at me. It's too much pressure."

"You don't need to talk if you don't want to." I dropped beside her. "Tell me whatever you feel comfortable saying."

Her eyes met mine, her red hair falling over the front of her shoulder. "I was a daddy's girl, ya know? I love my father so much."

"Oh, I am so sorry..." I shook my head. Losing a parent could never be easy. It wasn't supposed to be. It was a dreadful experience.

"He was so great to me. He was wonderful. He *is* wonderful. Why did God give him cancer? Can you tell me? My mom was devastated. We all were lost without him after he died. He was in stage four and he was gone so soon." She leaned back.

I swallowed, mind wandering to *Justin Smith*. He was the same man, was he? Her name was Sunny Smith. It would fit perfectly if the two had been related. Did I also watch her dad lose his life?

"Angel, are you okay?" she asked.

She was asking me and yet she was the one in a hospital. "I'm doing fine. I just wish people didn't die. You were really close to your dad, huh?"

She nodded. "We were before he began screwing up. After being diagnosed with cancer, it was like regret washed over him. He didn't want to be our dad. Mom found him at bars and strip clubs. He was spending his money on things he wanted to live out before he died. When a ticking clock was placed on him, he changed for the worst."

I closed my eyes, an overwhelming feeling of guilt filling me up like a glass of water. Her dad was the one I couldn't save before he died of cancer. This had been such a small world. How pitiful for me.

"What is it?" she asked again.

I wasn't quite sure if it was my place to tell Sunny about her father being one of my charges. It was a tough decision that could make or break it all. "It's nothing. I was just thinking about how sad it is that your dad regretted his life he built after getting diagnosed. I'm truly sorry about that."

Sunny nodded a bit, lowering her gaze to the white stone floor. "Thank you. Without my father, I felt incomplete. I was missing half of myself, and that was when I began fulfilling that hole with men. I wasn't sleeping around but I was desperate to get into relationships and fix what I lost. Is that weird? I searched for romantic love after losing my own father."

"No, it's not weird. It's very normal. I know a lot of people who will do that. Boys and girls alike will try to fulfill that broken heart through romance. I've seen boys have sex with other boys because their father neglected and abused them. I've seen boys search for prostitutes when their mother wouldn't be their mom. I've seen many cases, and it's always upsetting. Parents need to be there for their kids and it's painful when something happens and they aren't." I pulled her in for a hug. "You deserve better."

Sunny wrapped her arms around me. "My world feels so empty without my dad here. It was hard to move on. I don't think I ever did."

I said, "Then it's time to confront your grief and deal with it. You can't move on by burying your feelings."

I stood by the tree as Sunny sat beneath it. The sun was high and bright in the sky today, and the temperature was just perfect.

I was keeping an eye on other doctors who were making sure she was not going to do anything she shouldn't.

She was here to deal with her feelings in a healthy way. She had to express how she really felt so she could heal from losing her father. To make sure she didn't take her own life again, we had to get to the root of the problem. Her insecurities stemmed from trying to fill the void in her heart somehow.

The birds chirped while flowers bloomed from the trees. Nature was so lovely and I could see why God created nature before anything else. It was stunning. It brought a smile to my face when I stopped to smell the roses and I did mean that in a literal way.

The wind was almost nonexistent today which meant my hair was not blowing all over the place. That was nice. Ever since I died, I stopped putting it into a bun and since, it'd be in my eyes or stuck between my lips.

It was still too cold for swimming but warm enough to walk outside in shorts and no jacket. Perfect weather for her to confront her problems.

"It looks like it's snowing but they're just flower petals falling from the trees." I twirled around in the falling petals.

Sunny didn't hear me because I'd turned on the invisibility. Too many doctors were around.

I danced in the flowers and grabbed a tree before I got dizzy and toppled over. "It's just so beautiful."

My mind went to Ayden and what he was doing. Was he okay without me? I had tried to tell him I was with Sunny on that emoji text, but I didn't know if he understood.

I would give nothing more than to move my feet to the beat of nature under the sun and with the petals while he was beside me. I wanted to be around him, but I knew it was better for Sunny and I to be together right now. She needed me and I needed time away from Ayden.

He had to understand what kind of pain it put me in when I saw his face. It was hard to be around him when he didn't love me back.

I walked down to the small stream and dipped my feet in. The water was cool but nothing like an icebox.

Sun rays shimmered on the surface and reminded me of the summer days on their way. The best time of the year for many reasons.

Growing up, I'd always wanted to move to Hawaii and that was because I wanted to swim every day. I wanted to be somewhere where the sunshine was out all year round. I couldn't get that here. Here, it snowed about three or four months out of the year.

However, I could thank my parents for never moving to Alaska. I couldn't live somewhere where the sun didn't exist. That would have been far too distressing for my taste.

I looked back at Sunny and saw her walking away from the tree.

Standing up, I followed her back to the room and unmasked myself. "How was that?"

She nodded. "Good. It was painful but it felt good to release feelings and face my demons. It's going to get harder before it gets easier, but I know it will come. I guess that's why people have to grieve. It helps us get to the healing stage of things."

"It's true." I twirled again. "Sorry, being outside in the sun makes me happy. How's Mason?"

"As far as I know, fine. I hope he doesn't hate me for what I did. He was there to help me through it but when you warned him about what I'd almost done, his demeanor changed." She hugged herself.

My spins came to a stop and I grabbed her arms, forcing her to look into my eyes. "No, he doesn't. He could never. He was more hurt than anything that you would do that to yourself and he's probably just worried and hoping you come out alive. He cares about you and I can tell. I first met him when he came into Ayden's family's bakery and he talked about you the whole time. He's a good brother."

She let out a small sigh. "You think so? You think he really cares?"

"I don't think so. I know he does. He loves you. He will be there for you when you get out of this place and he will greet you with a big hug. You're very lucky to have such an amazing brother." Smiling softly, I pulled her in for one more hug. "I think you're doing a wonderful job here. It's okay to be afraid and upset. Emotions are never wrong. Just don't react to them in the wrong way. These people are here to help you and care about *you*."

"Why are you telling me this? Are you leaving?" She pulled away and looked at me.

I took a deep breath and kept my gaze on her. If I looked away, it would make her feel worse. "I'm not needed here. You're making progress and changing. But Ayden does need me. He's in trouble again."

"What kind of trouble?" She seemed more worried about Ayden than herself.

Laughing a bit, I patted her shoulder. "It's nothing serious. He just needs me."

"Come on, you'll be okay. I promise. Just continue to heal—grieve, and you'll be home soon. Mason will be there to welcome you back. If you ever want to, you can come around and say hi to me. I'm not going far. We're friends, after all." I smiled at the sound of that. We were *friends*. I never pictured myself becoming friends with Ayden's ex-girlfriend, but it happened. She was sweet, and easy to get along with.

The reality was, I helped people change but I wasn't always there until the end. I helped them see where they wanted to get better and I was there for part of it, but I had too many humans waiting for me to allow me to see their entire journey. I could be with someone for years if I stayed until they turned their lives a full one-eighty.

"I love getting to know you. I love being your friend, and your company is refreshing. I hope you'll visit Ayden when you leave this hospital and come see me." I waved at her.

Sunny said her goodbye and I flew off into the sky. I landed on the clouds and reported back to God about how it went. He was pleased with the results. Sunny was getting better and I was proud of her for taking the step.

As I plopped onto a cloud, I swung my feet over the edge. The temperature began to cool as the sun set. It was the one thing I hated about spring. It was warm in the daytime but cold at night. The constant temperature changes like these were what bothered me the most. Spring was gorgeous with all the new flowers and leaves, but it was still a transitioning season into summer, and transitioning seasons were annoying with the extremes.

Summer would not be too far now, and it would soon be June

twenty-second, the day I was born. I was no longer alive or aging so it didn't matter anymore but it was weird to pass it and realize it was because I was no longer breathing. I didn't have a birthday as an angel. Instead, I had a *deathday*.

.

REDEMPTION

Waiting in his room, he finally made his measly appearance. I stood up from his bed in a hurry—too much of a hurry—and cleared my throat to gain his attention. "I heard you needed me."

The surprised look on his face told me he didn't expect me to come back. He rushed over, pulling me into a warm hug. It was something that certainly caught me off guard. We had never been so close before. He let go when my body tensed up at the awkwardness. How else was I supposed to react? Ayden and I had barely ever had any contact.

He said desperately, "I can't believe you heard my prayers. You came back for me."

"Yes, because you said you're willing to save your soul. I can't abandon someone who asks for my help. We all deserve to change for the better." I nodded, a smile plastered on my face.

He rubbed the back of his neck. "Yeah, about that..."

My smile faltered. "What are you talking about?"

His nervous chuckle worried me. This couldn't be good. "I just said that because I wanted you down here."

"Ayden, that's not allowed. You said you were going to change. There are no take-backs." I gestured for him to sit down on the bed and he complied. "We are going to start with your hobbies." I planted myself next to him. "What are your hobbies and interests? What do you like to do?"

He lifted his eyes to meet mine. "Nothing. I like to do bad things."

"That's not nothing." I cocked an eyebrow while letting go of a laugh. "And no, I mean in a serious sense. You can be open with me. I'd told you all about my life. I won't make fun of you or laugh. Tell me." I attempted to give him my sternest possible look, but it was difficult in a moment that he was turning around to be silly.

I took notice of his eyebrow twitch. "Fine, I enjoy baking." He crossed his arms like a stubborn child.

I lifted both of my eyebrows in surprise, as high as they could go. "Really? I know you're good at it because you're in your family's business, but you actually enjoy it?"

"You said you wouldn't make fun of me," he warned.

"I'm not." I put my hands up in defense. I had asked the question to confirm my suspicions, but a giggle never escaped my lips.

He glared at me, which I assumed was playful. "Yes. I enjoy baking. It's not enough that I'm good at it but I also love doing it." He got off his bed.

I nodded while my eyes wandered on the carpet before landing on him. "Can you bake for me?"

"And waste a perfectly good cake? Why? You don't even eat." He pointed to me.

"I can eat food. I just don't need it to fuel me. It's like sex. It's great to have in your life but you don't need it to survive. That's how it is for me. Although, I've never actually had sex—not that it's any of your business." I cleared my throat, hoping to change the subject. "I want to see you bake. I wish to see you bake without any worries that someone might see you having fun with it. It's just me and now I know your dirty secret."

He hesitated. "I don't know."

"I'm an angel. If I were to go out and get people to make fun of you for it, I would be a terrible Virtue. I enjoyed things people didn't. They thought I was weird, too. We can relate in that aspect." I shrugged it off. I left the bedroom and ventured into the kitchen, grabbing the ingredients for him. "It's ready for you!"

He entered the room. "Keep it quiet. I can hear you." He eyed the items laid out on the counter. "You're not going to let me say no."

"Nope. I didn't let you say no when I helped you and I won't let you say no now." A grin took over my expression.

He groaned. "Great, you control my life now." He approached the counter and grabbed a bowl. He picked up the measuring cups and used them to pour the flour, vanilla, and other ingredients. He began mixing them in different bowls, dry separate from wet.

I stood back and studied, admiring how concentrated he was. "It's kind of cute that you like baking."

He didn't turn to look at me as he asked, "Why is that?"

"Because you're supposed to be this tough, bad boy type of man but you have a soft spot for something." I smiled a bit. My heart melted at the sight of Ayden Dyer's passion for something so *sweet*.

He blended all the ingredients together in a new dish and poured that batter into a nonstick pan. He preheated the oven to 350 degrees and slid it in to bake. "There we go." He set the timer for thirty-five minutes. "Now we have to wait." He grabbed more items around the kitchen, mixing those together as well. "We need some frosting, fondant, and some other things for the design I'm attempting."

I stopped walking when I reached his side. "Maybe you want to teach me these things? I don't know everything."

"And she admits it," he joked. He grabbed a clean bowl and set it near me. He pushed some of the food over. "Mix those together, then knead it like dough. Then we want to flatten it out, but make sure you put flour down so that it doesn't stick to the counter or the rolling pin." He was already blending new ingredients. It appeared to be food coloring and some kind of jam.

I nodded, following his instructions. I mixed them into a bowl, beginning to see the dough form as they stuck together. I grabbed it with one hand and pulled it out. I sprinkled some flour on the counter and began kneading with the heels of my hands, getting rid of bubbles that might've formed. When I was sure it was good to go, I used the rolling pin to flatten it until Ayden said it was thin enough. "What is this?"

"Fondant," he replied.

"Oh. What is it again? Is it sugary dough?" I looked at him.

"Yes. It's basically just sugar that makes a cake look neater. It's like solid frosting in a way but still soft to chew." He finished the jelly-like filling. "I think that's the right color and consistency." He showed me.

A smile crept up on my face and every metaphorical muscle in me relaxed. "It looks yummy."

He told me his plan for the cake and what kind of decor he was going for. We were creating a cake filled with jam and covered with donut toppings. I approved as it sounded like the most delicious treat I could ever imagine. I knew I'd underestimated him all this time. I never could have guessed that he would've been the type of man to be so artistic when it came to baked goods.

"You have to put a bit more pressure while rolling it out." He came behind me and put his hands over mine.

I widened my eyes, unsure of what was happening. The old Ayden would've never done anything this out of the blue before with such a serious expression on his face. I kept my cool on high, trying not to overreact. I didn't want to be *that* person.

He started flattening out the fondant, using my hands to do so. "You have to do it like this and apply this much pressure. Does that make sense?"

"Yes..." I was in genuine shock at myself for having said that without stuttering. He let go and pulled away. I turned around in a hurry, ready to go to the bathroom to catch my sanity but I ran into his chest. He was still here. "I'm sorry..."

He gave me a playful smirk while crossing his arms. His muscles were enhanced by this action, stealing my attention. "Well, hello there."

I swallowed and tried to change the subject to get us off the topic of awkward. "So, your back wounds are healing I see." I averted my gaze from his intense stare, unable to look into those beautiful, green eyes.

"Mhm, they sure are." His muscles flexed. Without a shirt on, he was much more appealing to me. Guys were topless more times than not, but he also had the excuse of whip injuries to keep his shirt off for.

I moved around his figure, going towards the oven to check the cake. He turned as I walked from in front of him, causing me to stumble over his foot. He caught me in time, and I wrapped my arms around his neck from reflex, my fingers brushing over his wounds.

I pulled my hand back. "I'm so sorry." I didn't want to be reminded of what pain he went through. He went through the torture because of me. If I had just not overreacted when he rejected me, he wouldn't be in this mess.

The sound of the leather slapping against his back filled my ears. Cringing at the memory, I squeezed my eyes shut for a second.

He shook his head to dismiss my thoughts, making me question if he could read them. "Don't worry about it."

His gashes had dried up, but scabs took their place. Scars would soon form to remind him of the pain that he endured, forever leaving that story on his skin. I reached out to touch them again, begging for the power to heal. I wanted to make them go away. I hoped he would have flawless skin again. It was the least he deserved for having gone through hell with me. He had never even blamed me once.

How did someone do that? How did they not boil with rage at another for causing them so much trauma? His self-control was stronger than I'd ever took him for. I supposed he could teach me things, too.

I lifted my eyes to meet his, freezing in my position. My soul was unable to react or move. His lips were so inches from mine. I waited for him to kiss me, but an alarm went off. It was the timer buzzing to let us know the cake was done.

He let go once he made sure I had a footing on the tiled floor. He put on an oven mitt and pulled out the cake, checking it with a toothpick. Before he could turn in my direction, I vacated the kitchen and entered the bathroom. I locked the door behind me and attempted to calm my racing mind.

My thoughts were speeding up a mile a minute. I couldn't quite grasp them as they passed me by. I just knew they were full of chaotic emotions, whipping around in my brain. I held my head to see if it helped with the spinning. We hadn't even kissed and yet I was losing myself to the turmoil that broke me down.

I couldn't quite wrap my head around the thought, but I focused on the lingering touch of his body. He had been so close. He was going to kiss me, and I could confirm that. It wasn't the first time we'd almost done such a thing, either. Why? Why would Ayden try to kiss me? They were questions only he could answer but I wondered if he ever would.

I asked myself for a moment if he felt the same. Why else would he keep leaning in whenever we got close? He called me back here. He wanted to change. He'd dumped Sunny. Had I been stupid to not notice that a small chance for Ayden returning the feeling was possible? How was I going to confirm that?

A piece of me was bothered by the thought that he wanted to play with my heart. He had always been the type to string women along for the ride and I prayed that I was not going to be one of them. I desired his kiss to be real.

I took a few deep breaths to calm the raging storm within my mind. The waves of serenity begin to wash over me after hope replaced what was once anxiety. I had to hold onto aspiration.

After a moment of silence, I arrived in the kitchen again. Ayden was already in the mood to pretend it hadn't happened. How could men just brush it off so easily? Over here, I was having a near anxiety attack.

Ayden saw me and not an ounce of embarrassment showed on his face. "I wanted to show you the cake." He lifted the pan in the slightest to give me a view. I nodded at him as he set it back down on top of the hot pads. He retrieved a cutting board and dumped the cake onto it, upside down.

I observed him, keeping an eye on his body language. I wish men would just tell us how they felt. They played so many puzzling games with us.

Ayden filled the cake with some jam filling. He cut out a section of the fondant and smoothed it over the whole cake. He poured the chocolate glaze over the top, letting it drip down in all its glory. M&Ms were sprinkled on top with cinnamon, bringing the whole creation together.

It appeared to be the sweetest cake I had ever seen. Cavities were waiting to happen with one bite. I walked over to him, glancing at his current masterpiece. "That is so adorable. I want to eat it now."

Ayden choked on a laugh. "You think it looks adorable? The correct term is delicious. If I'd made a puppy cake, that would be adorable," he paused, shaking his head, "that came out wrong. We don't eat things because they are cute."

I lifted my index finger. "Actually, a fun theory about humans is we want to eat or squish cute things, so we can kill it to make it go away. The cuteness is too much that your mind can't handle it, therefore we want to get rid of it so we aren't overwhelmed by the cuteness. However, that's just a theory. It's not a fact." I wiggled my finger at him, warning him not to go out and tell people this as if it were true.

He chuckled, his eyes glued to me. "I would say I want to kill you then but you're already dead. You can't kill something adorable if it has no beating heart." That last sentence stung but also made my heart flutter—all at once. Ayden Dyer was a force to be reckoned with.

REPENTANCE

Ayden sat on his couch, stuffing his mouth full of his leftover cake with jam filling. "This is the best cake I've ever made."

"It's the only good cake you've ever made," I said. I'd let it slip before it was too late to hold it inside.

He choked on his food while his eyes met mine. "Bloody hell, Angel, tell me how you really feel."

My face burned with crimson. "I'm so sorry; I didn't mean to say that."

He chuckled, shaking his head. "No, it's good. You're learning the ways of humanity."

"That's not a good thing. I'm basically learning how to be a bad person. I don't want to make bad choices." I pressed my lips into a thin line while lowering my head. "Humans have flaws and angels are not supposed to."

Leaning back, he got comfortable as the cushions hugged his body. "Welcome to the family, Angel. We sure love new members." He winked.

Something about his words grasped my heart. "I've never had a real family."

"Now you do. You are always welcome here. My family accepts you anyway." He shoved the last bite of his treat into his mouth.

I could have kissed him. I could have slipped my tongue in to taste the sweetness before he swallowed it for good. But those thoughts were dangerously fatal.

I took a seat down on the other end of the couch, afraid to move any closer. After almost kissing twice, I think it was awkward for both of us to be near each other again. "Can you tell me more about your childhood? I would like to know." I pictured him as the bully or the outcast-bad boy type like he had been when I first met him.

Ayden turned his head towards me and for a moment, gathered his thoughts. "I want to say it was okay, but I'd be lying, and you hate that. I mean, I wasn't exactly a very likable kid. High school was definitely the worst."

"Why is that?" I liked high school more than junior high, but everyone had a different experience. High school had been less judging of who I was and there was no popularity spectrum to fit into. Nobody thought twice about me and I preferred that over being made fun of.

"We had a lot more options for our classes. I decided to join a baking class to get an easy A. Well, you can imagine how that went over well with some of the other guys. They thought it was strange that my cakes and other sweets were always perfect. They would tease me about it. I was the outcast but not in a good way." He shrugged it off like it wasn't a big deal anymore.

It didn't stop my heart from cracking. Ayden enjoyed something that harmed not a single soul and other boys had made him feel ashamed for it. Judgment was the downfall of humanity.

My lips curved downwards.. "That sounds awful. I didn't realize we had so much in common."

"Yeah, you could say we relate to each other on some level. We would make good siblings." He grinned wide. The smile was mesmerizing and there was no way it'd ever be forgotten by me.

"Ayden, that's disgusting. I confessed my love for you." I scrunched up my nose in repugnance, refusing to imagine us as brother and sister.

"Ah, yes." He clicked his tongue.

I thought for a moment, wondering if he thought of us in a sibling way. Did I get sister-zoned? *Mind games.* Men always played these confusing mind games with us.

He straightened his arm across the back of the couch. It looked cold without my shoulders wrapped in it, but I held back from scooting closer. Why was I here again? He needed me but I didn't think I could stay much longer if he was going to do this. It was difficult enough being around him when he didn't feel the same way.

My eyes landed on the wall. "So, this is nice." It wasn't, but I needed to make up a lie and not give away how miserable I was.

"What is? How so?" He faced me.

"I don't have to be with a man who thinks only about himself." I shrugged in response. If I loved him and had to hurt, he would hurt as well. Maybe it was wrong of me to do it, but I wanted him to know what he would miss out on now. It was my turn to convince him I dodged a bullet when he rejected me.

"What does that mean?" He leaned in, listening to what I had to say about the great Ayden Dyer.

I followed along and leaned closer, whispering, "I witnessed you with your previous partners. You have no clue how to please someone who isn't yourself." I could play mind games in return. I would prove to him I was better off. He didn't need to know that was a white lie.

He pulled back with a frown. It was adorable to watch him realize what was true. Maybe that was why he never had sex with Sunny. He knew he was terrible at pleasing a woman and he didn't want to ruin a good thing with something he wanted to believe he was a pro at.

Words rolled from my mouth before I could stop them. "You smell nice." A tiny piece of me must have been plagued with guilt for taking a blow to his ego and it was my job to bring it back up.

He gave me a look as if pretending I'd never hurt his feelings in the first place. "I took a shower. I also have cologne on. It's this thing that men wear, like perfume but for boys."

I turned red and began picking at the fabric of my dress. "I know what cologne is," I mumbled.

"Wait, why are you even smelling me?" He furrowed his brows as I lifted my head to look at him.

I said, avoiding the truth, "I was just trying to start a conversation. Was that not clear?"

"No, you are confusing." He folded his arms as if I were the one in the wrong. He rejected me. How was that my fault?

Cocking my eyebrows high, I asked, "Really, I'm confusing? Do you want to go down that road? Ayden, what do you think of me?"

"I just said what I think of you. You're confusing. Keep up." He moved his hand in a circle, gesturing.

"And you aren't? You just compared us to being siblings. You've tried to kiss me twice now. I have no idea what you think about me. Did you throw me in the sister-zone?" I crossed my arms, swimming to get to the bottom of this pile of puzzle pieces.

"Wait, what? Angel, no. I like you. I was just joking about us being siblings. You of all people should know how much I love to make jokes." He leaned away from the back of the couch.

"Wait, what? You like me?" I swallowed. Did I hear that right? This couldn't be what he meant. "You mean as a friend, correct? Are we friends now?"

He put his elbows on his thighs, using them to hold his face up with his hands. "Bloody hell, did I not make myself clear? I thought that was obvious." He began to gesture at me in a strange motion. What was he doing?

The only thing he'd ensured was that he'd hated me and he'd never change.

"No, asshat, you did not make that clear." I noticed what I had said, wondering how that came out. Everything was rolling off my tongue these days.

Ayden's eyes almost popped out of his eye sockets. "Whoa, did I hear Angel say a curse word?"

My face was hotter than a stove and redder than a tomato. "No. That was a...creative word."

"That was a curse word." He chuckled. "You really are becoming part of the family." He sat back again, amused. He spread his arm along the back of the couch while the other arm rested on the arm of the couch. He lifted his leg up, resting the side of his calf against his other knee.

I stood up in one swift movement. "No, I'm not a part of the family. I'm just a girl who is making mistakes. That is all."

"Angels don't make mistakes." He gave me a look.

"Ayden, let's talk about you. You like me. What does that mean? Is this a friendship now?" I tried to change the subject, all while getting the answers I needed at the same time. The expression we used in Heaven was *killing two giants with one stone*. Angels didn't believe in slaughtering birds.

"It means I like you." He pointed to me.

"No, I'm serious. What does that mean? Do you like me as a friend, or do you see me as a romantic partner?" I didn't know what his answer could be or how I would respond to either of them. I wished for either one, yet I didn't.

"I see you as both." He had said it so casually as if this wasn't the biggest deal in the world. It was. He returned the feelings I'd been hanging onto for so long. Our relationship would be forbidden, but he had now confirmed he liked me. How would I even go about this? I could have him and lose my job, or I could help him and move on someday.

"Angel?" He waved his hand, trying to get my attention.

I blinked and focused my gaze on him. "I'm sorry. I'm just trying to understand."

His smile fell in an instant. "What bloody confused you this time?"

"Everything," I answered.

He got off the couch. "I am not trained to explain everything. I can't help you if you need that much help. You are supposed to be helping me, or did you forget? Let's face it, Angel. You are very new to this romance thing and so am I." He didn't finish his words in the way I suspected.

I spoke before he could say something, "Let's just be friends. It's the best solution for us both. We're a bunch of losers with no real experience. We don't know what we're doing. Besides, I'm going to get into trouble if we decide to pursue any relationship. It's a good idea to just stay in the friend-zone." I couldn't believe that had come from my mouth, but I knew deep within me that it was the right decision.

All this time, I'd wished he would somehow have feelings for me. I had longed for this moment. Now that it was here, I couldn't go through with it. It was not a good idea for us to be together. We needed to change him and help him find *true* love.

I wasn't it.

Ayden nodded a bit, a small glint of disappointment in his green eyes. "I understand. We shall remain friends then." He put his hand out for me to shake.

I shook it, solidifying the consensus. "Deal." We would never be anything more.

"What are we supposed to do until then?" I asked him.

He shrugged, scanning the apartment. "I have no idea. I will probably eat more cake."

"How are you not fat? You eat so much food." I looked him up and down.

He looked at his own body. "I guess I just don't gain much weight." His eyes glued themselves to mine and the gears in his head could be heard from a mile away. "You know something?"

"I know a lot, depending on what you ask me. Shoot." I gestured for him to go on.

"I won the challenge. I had taken the time to listen to you and not have sex. Now that I'm single, do I get a kiss?" He pointed to his lips with pride.

"No. We agreed to remain friends. You also said you changed your mind, so the deal was killed when that happened. You can't just revive some old contract and demand to get your reward again. It doesn't work like that." I tilted my head. It would be much harder for him to accept our friendship if he was asking for my lips.

"Why not? I want that kiss." He pouted like a grown man child. "You can't just rip up the contract without my permission. I earned my prize fair and square."

"It's not fair for the reasons I just stated. For Heaven's sake, just open your ears and listen to me for once. You asked for change. This is what you're going to get. It is you who ripped up the contract. That is the end of it. Do you want to talk about anything else? We can discuss why you're so stubborn for a kiss." I took a seat on the couch again with my legs crossed.

"You're the one who's stubborn. It's just a kiss." He scoffed.

I narrowed my eyes at him, refusing to put up with his crap. "Don't start, Ayden. It's a lot more than that. I could lose my job and it serves no purpose. If it's just a kiss, you'll leave it alone, won't you?" I let the smirk take control of my expression while I leaned back with a boastful look in my eyes. I had stumped him.

He groaned with a hint of whining. "I just wanted a kiss for my hard work. I deserve a bit of encouragement. It's like a little treat, pushing me to continue with my change. Right?"

"My gosh, can you not just leave it alone already? It's just a kiss!" I yelled out. The frustration was climbing up the walls inside, beginning to push against the gates.

He planted himself next to me. "It's just a kiss, Angel. I just want a simple peck."

"And I want to be left alone, but we both lose in this situation." I snickered at him.

He sighed in defeat, rubbing his hand over his face. "Fine, I won't kiss you." He turned away and mumbled something.

"What?" I asked, suspicious thoughts arising inside my mind.

"Nothing." He sat back against the cushions. He gave me the fakest innocent smile I had ever seen in my life. *What a bullshit smile.*

Nobody heard me say that, no? Of course not. It was only in my head. I cursed Ayden for bringing out this side of me. Oh, shit, had I just said that, too? Damnit, Eliana!

I cleared my throat to distract myself from the words raining inside my brain. Ayden was influencing me in a major way, and I knew it was a bad road to travel. "So," I dragged out the word.

Ayden put his hands behind his head, relaxing. "I'm not talking to you until I get my kiss. That's final."

"Would you quit being a baby? You're a grown man for crying out loud." I squinted my eyes at him.

He struggled to not ask me what I was squinting my eyes for. He almost looked like someone trying to hold in a fart, and we all knew how that ended. I would make him talk one way or another. If his romantic infatuation with me was true, he couldn't ignore me forever.

REVELATION

I knew his deepest, most concealed thoughts and yet I didn't know if he preferred one food over the other. "Do you want burgers or hot dogs?" I peeked my head around the corner of the kitchen wall, eyes on Ayden.

He ignored me as he listened to the music from his stereo.

Scoffing, I shook my head. "Fine, hot dogs then." I pulled myself back in and threw some hot dogs in the pot. I put it on medium and poured in the water, just enough to drown them.

An idea popped into my head and I hoped to execute it just right. I grabbed my side and cried out, acting as if I was in pain. I slid to the ground and made some ugly noises. I glanced around the counter to see if he was right there, but he wasn't. I narrowed my eyes and cried out louder.

Ayden came to my rescue, staring down at my soul curled on the floor. "Get up. You're faking it." He tapped the bottom of my foot with the toe of his boot.

"No, it really hurts." I groaned.

He bent down to inspect my injury. "Really?" He poked my side, right underneath my hand. "Does that hurt?"

I nodded.

"Angel, you are a bigger liar than I am." He stood up. "I know you can't feel pain on earth. Did you think I forgot about that? I'm not stupid like you assume I am."

I frowned and got off the floor and onto my own two feet. "Fine, I was faking it but only because you won't talk to me!" I waved my finger in his face.

He crossed his arms. "Yeah, exactly." He left the kitchen and went back to the couch as if she were his long-lost lover.

I glared at the spot where I last saw him standing, irritated by the silence. He pushed my buttons farther than they could go.

The hot dogs cooked all the way through and I exited the room, leaving them alone. If he wasn't going to talk to me, then I wouldn't speak to him. He could take care of himself.

I grabbed one of his sweaters, putting it on to hide my wings. He gave me the attention I wanted before it was too late. He cleared his throat, confusion emerging. "Where are you going?"

"Oh, you want to talk to me now?" I twisted my soul to face him. "Yeah, that isn't going to happen. You seem to be fine by yourself so I'm going for a walk to clear my head."

"Not with my sweater." He stood from the couch, pointing to his clothing that kept my torso warm.

"Why not?" I crossed my arms, reflecting the stubbornness he rubbed off onto me.

He let out a low chuckle. "Because it's mine. Stealing is wrong, Love."

"Who taught you that one?" We both knew it was me. He also knew I always returned the clothes I used to hide my true form. "It's called borrowing. I at least plan on bringing it back."

"Actually, borrowing would require permission, which I did not give," he argued in opposition.

"Fine, you can have your stupid sweater." I started to remove it, but he stopped me.

"No, you can leave it on. It looks better on you." He laughed as he watched me struggle with his hoodie.

"For Heaven's sake, make up your mind!" I pulled it back down over me in a rough manner.

"I have made up my mind. You get to wear my sweater if I get something in return." Mischievous suggestions entered his smile.

"Oh, I see where this is going. I'm not going to kiss you. I already told you no." I shook my head and took the hoodie off.

He rolled his eyes, annoyed by my resolute attitude. He was just as persistent. "You've already worn it and that deserves me at least one peck."

"You deserve nothing!" I threw it at him and he caught it in both arms. "You deserve—" I didn't continue my sentence because I wasn't going to go down that path over an argument about a kiss.

"I deserve what?" He tempted me to say it.

"You deserve—" I didn't want to say he belonged in Hell. I couldn't say it because I didn't mean it. It was purely something I thought about out of spite.

"Mhm, go on." He gestured for me to continue.

I had to lie if I was going to keep us as friends or save his soul. "You deserve to change and this is the only way to help you. You're making such good progress. Please, don't ruin it now."

"Ruin it with a kiss?" he asked.

"Yes. If we kiss, I will be kicked off the job," I said.

"Not if we hide it." He came closer.

I backed up, putting space between us. "We can't hide it. Trust me."

A sigh escaped his lips. "Fine." He turned away and let me go free. I didn't leave, considering my wings were in full view and he wouldn't let me wear his clothes to make them go away.

I walked to his room and stopped at the closet, huffing. "Why are boys so bull-headed? I just wanted to go for a walk." Yelling out, I smashed my fist against his pillow, pretending it was his face. I realized my mistake and fluffed his pillow back up. "It's not your fault. It's his."

I smoothed out his comforter as I heard a voice behind me, "Oh, I see your game." That damned English was thicker than it had been moments ago. I begged for the American accent to run and hide when Ayden was around. My heart would break if he lost his own to the northwestern attitude that I owned.

I spun around with my hands placed on my hips. "There is no game or whatever you seem to think. There is just me, and this bed." My eyes opened wide, cheeks beginning to burn like fire. "I didn't—"

Ayden chuckled as he cut me off, "I know what you meant. It's okay. You can admit it. You already love me and you're curious." He shrugged as he took a step forward.

I straightened my posture, attempting to show off my confidence. I was anything but assured at this moment. "I may love you, Ayden, but I have control over my desires. I'm an angel after all." I gestured to myself.

"An angel who is already rebelling," he joked.

"No!" I shouted at him.

"Calm down. You have too much anger for a little angel." He grabbed my shoulders to keep me poised. His cologne carried over, filling my nostrils. He smelled like Heaven and I had every right to say that as someone who was from that very place. It smelled of musk oil, which somehow enhanced the masculinity he wished to show to the world. For me, it caused some dirty thoughts to form within my mind. Those thoughts stemmed from one of the seven deadly sins called *lust*.

I slapped his arms away. "Don't you dare patronize me, Ayden Dyer. I am scary. I put you through hell, and that is in a literal sense."

He gave me a smile. "I know, Love, and I'm not scared. Is it supposed to make me curl up and cry because you used my whole name?" He tilted his head. This gesture of his was adorable. If he were a teddy bear, he'd be in my arms for eternity.

"All I have to do is tell them I failed and they will take your soul." I squeezed my fingers shut, creating fists. If I could feel pain, the nails would be cutting into my skin and causing my nerves to panic.

"But you won't do that over a silly argument because you love me too much," he said in a nonchalant tone. While his face was neutral, his eyes revealed his buried emotions. The joy radiating from him was genuine. He was having real fun while messing with me, and that sent me into a fit.

I screamed, reaching my peak. He just infuriated me to my core, and I was ready to give up on saving him. My insides were boiling like heated water on a stove. His smartass remarks made me want to pull my hair out. I wanted to cry from the mountains until I had no more energy. He drove me wild with his ridiculous teasing.

I could never catch a break with him. To counteract the murderous scenes playing inside my head involving Ayden, I pinched my arm.

"Careful there. You might strain a feather with that rage." He winked at me as he took another step forward.

Blinded by my rage, I could barely register the gap shrinking between us as distance soon ceased to exist. "Ayden, for the last time," I started, "I want you—"

His pink lips cut me off as they brushed against mine. On those lips of his, a little smile formed, knowing he had taken control of the situation. My mind had gone blank and the anger was sucked from me in an instant.

His lips were soft but firm as he deepened the kiss, hands gripping me by my waist. He nibbled on my bottom lip, which sent me into a slight frenzy. I wanted to return the favor, to forget all of my problems and just enjoy this moment but I didn't know if I could do that.

After having just eaten sweet desserts not long ago, Ayden's lips tasted of *white chocolate and raspberries*, the most delightful combination in the baking universe. The addiction for his kiss grew with every passing second.

He slowly pulled away, lingering a bit and releasing the hold he had over me. I opened my eyes and witnessed him smiling like a boy who just got candy. "I wanted to see what it felt like to kiss an angel. I also wanted my reward. Now, we're even."

"We're even?" I choked. "What the hell does that mean?"

"It means you can wear my sweater now." He left the room with a smirk plastered on his face. My mind was all over the place as those words swirled inside my head.

I wasn't sure where I stood. On one hand, I wished for that kiss to be more than a way to get even. It was something I had needed since the day I met Ayden. Only real men could kiss a woman with that much *fire*.

On the other hand, we could never be together and that kiss had just been a way to even the playing field. I was in love with Ayden but if he felt the same way, I would struggle with saying no to him.

I followed his lead into the living room. "I gave you that sweater back."

"And now you can have it." He stopped in his tracks and turned to face me. "I know you want it. Tell me, Angel. How was it? I know that was your first kiss. I'd like to hear some feedback." He waved for me to talk.

I swallowed, not sure where I was going to go next with my words. I folded my hands together in front of me. "It was nice," I said, answering him and nodding in just the slightest.

"Nice? You can do better. You read books. Be poetic." He folded his arms, gripping his forearms.

"Are you serious?" I lifted an eyebrow.

"Yes. Do you know how many girls I've kissed?" He raised an eyebrow in question.

I cleared my throat, lifting my head up a bit more. "I don't want to know."

"I've been with about too many to count. None of these girls were anything like you. They weren't good girls. They weren't angels. They weren't even the girls who were into education the way you are. I genuinely want to hear the thoughts of a girl who is like that." He waited for me to respond.

I nodded and looked down at the floor. "I guess I can try." He gestured for me to go on, growing impatient. "It was beautiful. I've never kissed someone. This was my first impression, and I can't lie and say it wasn't anything magical. You did it for some silly reason, but I could feel the passion. I don't know if it was because of my love for you or because you feel something for me, but it was there. The kiss was heavenly and yes, the pun was intended. Your lips tasted like the last thing you ate and it was the perfect blend of Ayden and sweets. It is the kind of flame burning within our romantic moment that makes me crave more," I said. I focused on him, seeing if he would say something. "Are you going to respond? Those are my honest thoughts."

He shook his head and glanced at the ground. "I don't know what to say." His gaze met mine once more.

I smoothed out my dress to do anything but stand there in the awkwardness. "You kissed me to get even but I still want to do it again." Something had to be wrong with me for wanting to put myself in pain.

"I also like you. Remember when I had to make that clear?" His eyes cut through me with a disappointed glance. The look was a silent warning telling me he wasn't in the mood for any drama.

I was going to crush his wish. I was nothing but irrational. We would create chaos when we were in the same room. "Why do you like me? You can have any woman you want but you want to be with the one who won't give you sex right away."

He ran his fingers through his hair while the answers sat on the tip of his tongue. "Those women give me sex, yes, but you said we don't need it to survive. Those women didn't want to get to know me. They don't care about my soul. There was never a point in which they loved me for who I was. The one thing they wanted from me was my dick. You've accepted me and you've proved your patience. There may be a day in which we do have sex, but today, I'm content with just being the man who loves to bake. I know you're just as content as I am with that." His pupils widened just a bit when his eyes met mine. I knew what they entailed but I didn't dare say it to his face.

He didn't need to say he loved me. I already knew.

"Have you ever let any others in? Do they know your story?" he asked.

Shaking my head, I replied with, "Nobody else knows besides Selene." Not even my parents knew. Everything immersed in the depths of my isolated secrets was just that—a secret.

He took a step closer, the smell of white chocolate and raspberries drifting over me again. "You let me in. We've experienced Hell together. Hell can bring people closer, and I'd like to believe that's us. I know things that nobody else knows and I think that means something to us both. You trust me. You love me and we both know that's never going to end."

"But we can't be together," I whispered while closing my eyes.

He grabbed my hand and spun me around. As someone who became clumsy due to sudden coordination, I lost balance and he had to catch me. "We can be together if you let us. I can't do it alone."

I didn't know if I could. I knew it wasn't permitted and I would have to forfeit my status. I wasn't ready to give that up, but I'd also never been in love either, and I wished to see this to the end. My mind was in a battle that was losing either way it went.

My back pressed against his chest as his arms embraced me, wrapped around my abdomen. I peered up at him and let out a big sigh. "Fine, we can try to make this work. I can't promise it will end well. It probably won't."

He let go after confirming I had a footing. He turned me to face him. "That's great! I've never been in a relationship like this before. How does it go?"

"I don't know. I haven't been in one either." I shrugged a bit.

He tapped his chin, the tip of his finger touching the stubble where his beard once was. He'd shaved recently to start a new beard as the old one became a mess. "I guess we're just two rebels in love, going at it blindly." He gave me a small smile.

I grabbed his sweater. "Why do you keep it cold in here?"

"Because it's too hot." He chuckled at my nonsensical question.

Against his wishes, I wore his hoodie and rubbed my shivering arms. "It's freezing if you ask me."

"Nobody asked you," he said with a small head shake.

I cleared my throat as I pointed my finger at him. "I knew you'd say that. I fricking knew that was in your list of phrases."

"Did you just say fricking?" A cute smile appeared on his lips, the same ones that held mine hostage earlier.

"Shut up," I grumbled.

He faked a gasp. "You just told me to shut up. An angel actually told me to shut up. How rude."

"Ayden, don't act so surprised. I'm dating you, aren't I?" I smiled with a hint of delinquent behavior.

He lifted both eyebrows high on his forehead. "Bloody hell, Angel, I will need some ice for that burn." He gently patted the area over his heart.

I hit his arm with a soft blow. "You will. There will be much more to come." I laughed.

He poked my side, leaning in. "You look so adorable. You make me say the word adorable, Angel. You broke me."

"I didn't break you. I just merely built you into a better human, a man who wants to be with me in return. That's all I did. It's harmless." I patted my hand against his cheek.

He tickled my sides but halted as soon as he noticed it didn't affect me. "Why aren't you laughing?"

"Because I'm a soul, not a body. I do not tickle easily," I stated.

"If you can't be tickled easily, it'll be harder for me to even touch your skin and make you feel things." He frowned at the thought of not being able to do that.

My face heated up, causing me to laugh in a nervous tone. This was an awkward topic for me. "We feel pleasure but not pain here. I've told you this before. That has to do with not being able to sin. Pain is a result of sin, not pleasure. Pleasure was always available to every creature." I took a deep breath, relieved. I got that conversation out of the way in as little time as possible.

Ayden's fingers intertwined with mine between our figures. I had to warn him about the consequences of messing with my heart. "I know that we're both new to this and I feel required to tell you to be gentle with me. I still hurt within seconds and I'm fragile. If you cause me any pain, you will *never* be coming back from Hell," I threatened.

 PRIVY

W alking out of the theater, I shook my head. "No, it was all wrong. That is not how it goes. Have they never watched a crime show? It was obvious." I pushed my hair back to keep it from falling in my eyes.

Esme had given me some of her clothes since we both happened to be very similar in body size. This way I blended right in with the crowds.

Ayden bumped his side against mine and chuckled. "You would know. You were involved in a big crime investigation." His arm snaked around my waist as he pulled me against him. I realized then it wasn't a romantic gesture. He was just trying to move me out of the way from walking into someone else.

My heart swelled as I reminded myself that I was dating Ayden Dyer. After all this time, it happened. Nothing made me happier at this moment than reliving the fact that the man I loved was mine to hold.

"Tell me again how we are hiding our relationship if we are in public?" he asked me.

My grin widened. "Nobody here knows I'm actually an angel. I look human."

"You told me that angels can recognize other angels. Are you not worried about them seeing you with me?"

I hit him playfully, and with a sarcastic tone, I said, "Damn, why didn't you tell me?" I sighed a bit. "Listen, I won't kiss you out in the open, but we can hang out in public. As far as they know, I'm your guardian angel. That means this cannot happen." I removed his arm from my waist. "Out here, we *are* friends."

He smirked. "And behind closed doors, we are not."

"Time to go watch a good movie. This time, you pick," he said as he pointed to me. I laughed a bit while we walked back to his apartment.

I was careful not to let things go too far and Ayden respected that. I did love him, but I was not in any state to give him all of me just yet. I knew most people thought it was absurd, but I wanted to seal our relationship with marriage before making that step. It was clear Ayden was already good in bed. As for me? We wouldn't know until our wedding night, but I could learn like everyone else.

Once inside, he grabbed my hand and spun me to face him and before I could say a word, I was deep within a trance from his kiss.

When he pulled away, he said, "I wanted to do that for a while but apparently we aren't allowed to be affectionate in public."

I patted his chest. "No, we are not." I turned away and picked a movie. "We should watch a documentary. I like watching documentaries on killers so I can study the behavior of criminals."

We played the movie and I was already engrossed within five minutes. Ayden, on the other hand, was bored. Letting out a laugh, I turned my head towards him. "Wow, you could have told me you don't like documentaries."

"It's not that. I just had something else in mind." His infamous smirk returned. Although, I supposed it had grown on me and I came to crave it.

With the shake of my head, my smile stuck. "You and I both know that will not happen for a long time."

"And why is that? Is making out a crime?" he whispered against my hair.

Sitting up, I gained enough balance to keep myself upright. "Making out? Like you and Sunny used to do?"

His Adam's apple moved as he swallowed. "This will be better because the feeling is mutual and much stronger."

"I'm not sure." I was more worried about it going too far. I wanted boundaries to be clear.

Ayden leaned in. "What are you not sure about?"

I pushed the hair on both sides of my face behind my ears. "This. I love you but at the same time, I'm not ready to take a big step and have sex. You know that." Ayden returned my feelings and I hadn't expected him to. I was trying to be patient and let it grow.

He grabbed my hand, intertwining our fingers. "I do know. I won't push you. Sunny and I were together for a few months and we never had sex. I can control myself. It'll be harder with you because you, Angel, do look very good naked. But I've never been a man who has pushed a woman to do something she didn't want to do. You can tell me which lines not to cross and I will respect them."

I nodded a bit. I had forgotten that Ayden saw me naked once, but he just had to remind me. It wasn't on purpose that he saw me naked. At least, it wasn't on purpose on my part. "Okay. No sex. Clothes stay on. Your hands stay off my butt, boobs, and away from my vagina. That stuff is off-limits. Capiche?"

He leaned in, planting a small kiss on my lips. "Understood."

I took a deep breath. It was relaxing for me to know that he would respect my wishes. Either way, I was still nervous. Ayden was the first boy I'd ever kissed. Now we were going to be making out. This would be a big step for me.

He kissed me again but this time it wasn't quick. I had to agree with Sunny that this man knew what he was doing. He poured more into the kiss and I lay back against the couch arm. Was it smarter if I were on his lap or under him? Well, there was no time to decide now.

I was impressed with his listening skills as one of his hands grabbed my neck and jaw while the other stayed at my waist.

Something wet pressed against my lips until I recognized his tongue. Of course, *this* was making out. My lips parted on their own and his tongue entered my mouth, colliding with mine. A moan left my throat and he pulled away from our little session. He had to catch his breath for a moment. Me? I could make out until forever ended and never run out of air.

The next time his lips met mine, he kept it simple—kissing me with sugar lacing every promise he ever made to me. His lips moved to my cheek, then my jaw and down my neck. A part of me squirmed beneath his touch, worrying that he would go farther than I told him to.

And if he did, I wouldn't want to say no.

He used two fingers to grab my chin and pull it down towards him. "Hey, I can see you getting nervous. Don't worry. I promised not to go too far, and I won't break that."

Taking yet another deep breath that I didn't need, I closed my eyes. "I just get very nervous around you."

Lifting it, he exposed the gulp stuck in my throat, placing a few kisses along my throat. "Remember, Angel, I like to steal objects, not virginities."

It was the simple line that ruined the mood. Those seven words caused me to choke on my own laughter until it erupted into a whole fit of hysterics.

Ayden sat up. "What? What did I say?"

I wiped a few tears and grabbed his shirt as I pulled him back down.

"You always make me laugh." I brought our lips back together and used my free hand to grab the space behind his neck. This was the moment I realized he had hair that I was finally allowed to touch. Taking full advantage, I threaded my fingers through, tugging at tufts.

A groan slipped him as we shifted our bodies, but just seconds later, he had found his way back down my jaw. His lips hovered over what had once been my pulse only for them to press against the soft spot before I had time to react.

At first, it'd been sweet. Gentle.

But within a minute, his kisses turned tenacious. Dragging along my throat, nipping at the vulnerable parts. Something buried inside had awakened, and with a moan, I wrapped my fingers around his and slid them along my stomach. I made it as far as my inner thigh, under the skirt, before Ayden slipped his hand from mine to ensure he wasn't going that far yet.

I still wanted to know what his touch felt like.

"Bloody hell, I did not know this was going on," a female said.

Ayden looked up while I bent my head over the couch arm—view upside down—observing whoever was bold enough to interrupt.

Esme closed the door behind her and smiled. "So, I imagine Ayden realized he does like you? It's beautiful. I was really hoping this would happen and my prayers were answered."

He sat up and pulled me with him. "Mine were, too."

Glancing at him, a small smile formed. "I heard every prayer. I just couldn't come back at that time. I had other business to attend to and I'm sorry I left you for so long but by the time you asked for me, I already had another human to watch over and I couldn't leave them. I had to make sure they were good to go on their own before I reported back to God and came back to you. But I'm here now and everything is okay with the world."

Esme took a seat between us. "You guys will be so happy together. I know you mentioned it was against the heavenly law to date a human so how is that working out?"

I began chewing on my lip. "We're trying to hide it."

"Hide? You realize you can't hide from them, right?" She pulled a snack from her bag and ate it.

I nodded a little. "Yeah, I'm aware." I was probably going to lose my job.

Ayden reached over Esme and grabbed my hand. "Hey, don't listen to my sister. Let's not think about that right now."

She took another bite of her granola bar. "He's right, you shouldn't listen to me."

I got off the couch and walked to the kitchen. "Just because we don't kiss in public doesn't mean they don't know about what we do in secret. They know. They must know. We just made out on the couch and I'm positive they saw that. Angels are not oblivious to things, and God is not blind to anything happening in this world."

He followed me into the kitchen. "I know you're worried. Why don't you go to Heaven and talk about it if it makes you feel better? I don't want you to be unhappy or miserable this whole time. You deserve comfort or clarification."

I turned my attention to him. "Go to Heaven? That sounds risky. What if they tell me I can't come back? Are you prepared to never see me again?"

He leaned his weight against the counter. "I'm only suggesting this to help ease your fears. This relationship won't be any good if we are not completely in it together."

Esme appeared beside us. "I'm sorry for bringing it up. I just worry because I really do think you two are so good together, but it scares me that it's going to end in the blink of an eye."

I swallowed my worries and agreed. "If I don't come back, you know what happened."

He moved around his sister, grabbing my hand and kissing my knuckles. "Should we say goodbye here or...?"

I gasped. "Ayden, don't joke like that!"

He chuckled. "You said it first."

Squeezing his hand, I glanced at Esme. "You can wait here or do what it is you do. I'm not sure how long it will take me. It could be days or weeks. Can you handle that time without me?"

Ayden leaned in, whispering, "I'll try."

Esme choked, but a smile still danced on her face as hard as she tried to get rid of it. "Okay, you two are beginning to get on my nerves. I was happy for you but now you're way too into one another and that's just weird to see coming from my brother."

He pulled back and looked over at her. "Sunny was the practice I needed to make it work with Angel for real."

My jaw dropped just a little. "What?"

When his green eyes met mine, my knees almost buckled. "I mean, I didn't have feelings for you at that time, but I realized that Sunny gave me the relationship practice I needed to be a good boyfriend. Now I can make sure I don't screw it up with you. Although I should probably mention that I also never planned to be with Sunny forever."

"What on earth does that mean?" My invisible heart was pounding against my chest.

Esme slapped the counter, squealing. "It means that he sees a future with you and you could get married someday! You got Ayden to consider marriage!"

He turned to look at his sister. "Now we just need to get you to consider it, too," he joked.

She smacked him on the arm.

The thought of spending eternity with Ayden made my stomach

do flips while my insides fluttered. Some people didn't like the idea of being tied down to one person, but I never thought twice about it. I wanted to spend my life with one man and Ayden filled that position. There was no question that I'd be happy and the romance would never grow to be dull. He'd always been unpredictable and that made me bubble with excitement.

I hoped it'd work out, but I couldn't get my hopes up too high. I could lose everything over my love for Ayden. "Just to keep me going." I kissed him with every overwhelming emotion inside of me. He returned the kiss within seconds and rested his hand against my cheek. "I'll try to make it back," I said in a quiet tone against his lips.

He lifted his head before pressing his lips to my temple. "I don't doubt you'll do your best. You've always been so stubborn. Love makes one very *persistent.*"

PARAMOURS

My knock echoed throughout the large room, bouncing off the golden door and white walls. I stepped inside as soon as I was told to come in.

God wore the sharpest of white suits around, with a white button-up made of soft material. The jacket worn had silk lining the edges. The one thing off was the lack of shoes. We never wore those in Heaven.

"I wanted to talk about something." I looked up at God Himself. He gestured for me to continue, so I did. "We were trying to be secretive about it but hiding our relationship from Heaven is impossible. Ayden and I are...together."

He sat back and smiled. "I already know, Eliana. I know all these things. I knew long before you ever met him."

I was aware of that, too. But why was He smiling?

I fiddled with my fingers. "Am I losing my job? Do I have to stop seeing Ayden?" my voice cracked on the last word.

"Did I say you were no longer a guardian angel?" He leaned forward, keeping His eyes fixed on me. "Remember what we told you when you first got assigned to Mr. Dyer," He said, His tone more affirmative than curious.

Nodding, I lifted my eyes to meet His, showing more of my own confidence. "Yes, I do recall what you told me. I thought maybe it was a test to see how I would react, or if I would be able to stop it from happening. Well, I did try. I can't stop the future." Chills ran down my arms as I swallowed any fear daring to reveal itself.

He chuckled and tilted His head a bit. "Precisely."

"Am I okay to go back then?" I was a bit surprised by His reaction to all of this. He knew and yet it wasn't like I'd just killed someone. Maybe it wasn't as bad because I *had* taken a human life once before.

"You're okay to go back." He swooped his arm forward.

I turned around and started heading out when Matthew came in. He shifted his eyes between God and I, giving me a look. I shrugged and made it to the door.

"What's stopping you, Eliana?" Matthew asked me.

I glanced back at him. "I'm confused as to why God is letting me date Ayden when we're two different species."

We were so different in many ways. My fingers twitched at the mere thought. A part of me worried that there was something darker behind why God would allow this, but I had to dismiss it. God was good and He would not be doing this for such a reason, right? *Right?*

God answered with, "I have my reasons. You'll figure it out soon." The tone sounded more ominous than I'd hoped for.

I paced back and forth. "And then He said I would figure it out soon. What does that mean? What reasons are He referring to? Ayden, are you bad for me? You're going to break my heart and I'm going to learn my lesson. That must be it. This is all a warning for me. Every person I help has a purpose in my life and we're not in trouble because it's going to teach me a message and any future guardian angels why we don't date humans." I covered my mouth, coming to a halt. I squeezed my eyes shut as I realized I would be the example used to make a point to other angels. I would be the fool who hung her head in shame.

Ayden laughed. "Angel, no. I am not going to break your heart. I'm in this. He said it was okay, so you have permission to be with me. Why are you questioning it?"

"Because I'm worried, Ayden. Something bad is going to happen. I sense it, and I just have no idea what it is." I let out a small sigh as my eyes lingered on the cake he just baked. "We have spent so much time together. My love for you is real. I've seen all these raw parts about you, and I know your deepest fears and desires. It is so hard not to think about how it could be ripped away. I can't imagine life without you. I spent my whole human life trying to figure out myself. I was always alone. I never had a family; I barely had one friend and then it was taken from me and I'm terrified to lose what I have now. I don't want to suffer the loss of your family. I don't want to be deprived of your sisters. I do not want to stop having you in my afterlife. You're the first man I've been with. I'm dead and I finally have a chance at love. My life was cut too short and yet now I'm in love and happy and I can't lose that. I have to fight for what we have." Despite what threatened us, I would confront whatever or whoever.

He grabbed my hands and warmed them. "You will. I know you. You always fight for what you want. You're strong and that's what I love about you. You don't give up. Even after you did, you *didn't*. You wanted to take the pain away from me when we were tortured."

"I can't shake this feeling that something big is about to go wrong."

Our eyes met and I almost lost myself in his bright luscious eyes again. I knew better this time. "We have to be prepared. We have to prepare for whatever is coming."

He pulled me closer, our chests touching. "How do you suppose we prepare for what we don't know?"

I let go of one of his hands to tap my chin. "I'm not sure. We need to make one promise, right now. We stick together no matter what."

He leaned in, brushing his lips against mine. "What do you mean?"

It was hard not to kiss him. He wasn't taking this seriously and that was what I had to say to reject him. "I've read plenty of romance books. There's always some ex or someone who tries to make up lies about the other to tear the two apart. We must promise not to believe any crazy exes or crushes. Trust each other."

"I always trust you." His lips curved upward. Getting confirmation that he was on board, I accepted his kiss and molded into his arms. He moved his lips along my cheek and groaned when someone walked into the apartment. "Fuck, Esme, why do you always ruin good moments?"

She shrugged him off. "Lock your door if you don't want me walking in. I got you guys some clothes. You spend too much time cooped up in the apartment and it's beautiful outside. It's almost summer. Get some bloody sunshine, will you?"

Sunshine. I wondered how Sunny was doing and if she was making more progress. I wanted to see her again soon, but the time was uncertain on when she would heal and be released from the facility. I prayed for the best outcome for her.

She laid out a dress on the couch. "I brought a cute dress for Angel to wear, and Ayden, I got you a nice shirt because your shirts are all black and black is last year's style."

He pulled away from me and looked at the shirt before he crossed his arms. "Black is never out of style. We've been over this."

She grabbed the dress and held it up to me. "Listen, now that you guys can be out in public together, I want you to spend some romantic time outside. Ayden, if you want to keep a woman, you have to do more than kiss her neck. Taking her on nice walks helps. Just because you have the girl, doesn't mean you get to stop being romantic."

Ayden put his finger up. "In my defense, I was never romantic."

She threw the shirt at him. "Now is your chance to learn. Angel deserves to know that you're trying to keep her. I was there when she told us her story. If you are her first boyfriend, I guarantee it will take a lot more to make her happy than making out. Making out is more of your thing. Right now, she's trying to make you happy. You should return the favor. Relationships are a two-way street."

He turned to his attention to me and I smiled in return. "I think a walk would be wonderful."

His sister patted his shoulder. "See? I know what a girl wants."

Ayden went to his room and changed into lighter clothes. The shirt Esme bought for him was a light gray. It was still considered a close shade to black, but it was progress towards a *brighter* future.

She took me to the bathroom and looked at the dress. "I thought maybe this color would look really pretty on you."

"My favorite color is red."

"Well, today you and Ayden are both trying new styles. Nothing harmful about that." She pulled my blonde waves back. "Is it okay if I do your hair?"

"What do you want to do?" I asked, looking at her through the mirror.

She split my hair into two sides. "I want to do two French braids." She started with one side. It didn't take her very long to do the style. Yes, my hair was long but French braids were not as time-consuming as fishtail braids were.

Selene had liked to do both, too.

Once she finished, she left the bathroom so I could get changed into the dress. It was a mustard yellow color, which wasn't ugly, but it wasn't my favorite, either.

I removed the current clothes on my body and fixed the bra straps to make sure they wouldn't keep falling off. I pulled the yellow dress over my head. The skirt was of a flowy material while the top fit me just a bit too small. The straps were thin, and the neckline shaped a V down my chest. My cleavage was showing but that was the price I paid for my size.

Before I left the bathroom, I called Esme in. "I don't know. I'm trying to do it, but I am not used to showing my chest at all."

She adjusted the straps of the dress. "It's okay. You're not showing a lot. It's a tiny bit of cleavage. Are they going to send you to Hell now?"

"It's not even about that. It's about the fact that I don't want anyone else to see. Ayden is the only one, and I only want him to get a good look when we have said *I do*." I played with the end of one braid.

"He's barely getting a view of your cleavage. These are not your nipples. If you are worried, I'll get you another dress. It'll be hard because you do have big breasts. You can't deny it."

I looked at my own chest. "Big? You make it sound like I'm huge."

"What's your cup size?" she asked.

I blushed as I said, "F."

"Which correlates to triple D. You're blessed. God blessed you very well." She finished with the adjustments.

"So I've been told," I mumbled to myself.

It had been something I struggled with for a while. Finding shirts to cover my cleavage had been difficult. When I wore plaid, I had to get shirts in men sizes just so the buttons wouldn't pop open. However,

I could be thankful I never had any problems with my chest other than that. I knew some women would get chest pain and they'd fix it with reductions. I didn't blame them for it. Large breasts had their pros and plenty of cons to go with it.

She pulled me out of the bathroom and Ayden waited, tapping his foot. "It took you two long enough." He faced me and let out a laugh. "Aw, Angel, you look so cute."

"Cute? I look cute?" I never expected that word to come from his mouth like this.

Esme pushed me forward. "Go on, you two. You should go enjoy the beautiful weather."

He slipped his hand into mine and we left the apartment. Instead of taking his beat-up car—because his license had still been suspended for not having insurance and reckless driving—we went for a walk. I scanned the city, admiring how blissful everyone seemed. It was a good day.

"Where should we go?" I nudged him.

Instead of answering my question, he pulled me through the streets of people until we ended up at a park. "I've lived here for about ten or so years now. This is where I used to hang out during the day when I wanted to be alone. I would sit in that little booth beneath the playground slide and pretend I was a manager at a fast-food restaurant. It was always so much fun."

I smiled at this little bit of information. Finding out more about Ayden made me flutter with excitement. He was such an interesting man and there were so many little secrets behind him. Even if nobody else agreed.

"I'd pretend the bark was the food. Other days, I'd pretend we were on a pirate ship, or even that the ground was lava. My version of *The Floor is Lava* was a thing before the new version existed. Those were my childhood days before I grew up and realized how much worse life could get." His gaze honed on the equipment.

I rested my cheek against his shoulder and rubbed his back. The scars were just that now, and all pain had fled.

Hearing about the memories that made Ayden smile caused me to do the same. It showed a side of him I'd been dying to see since the day we first met. He was more than the cold exterior he had everyone perceive. He was a human. He had a childhood and memories—good and bad alike. There was something soothing about being allowed inside his head. He'd lowered his walls just for me.

I no longer had to remind myself I was prettier than Sunny. I no longer had to be the bearer of bad news—news that Ayden would never return the feelings. I knew better now. Someday, I could be Mrs. Dyer. There was a real chance and I would seize it the moment he asked me to marry him.

"Then I met you." He twisted his head to look at me. "You turned my world upside down. I begged you to leave me alone, but I'm thankful you're so stubborn that you refused to abandon me. I hated you yet, I never wanted you to leave. It's like eating the last cookie. You know you can't resist it, and it'll bring you so much trouble. You were trouble, Angel, but I would *never* take any of it back."

RIGHTEOUS

The sound surrounded us as explosions blasted in our ears and gun shots blared. "You have spent way too much time around me, Angel." Ayden didn't take his eyes off the massive movie screen as he spoke.

"How?" I tilted my head, eating a handful of popcorn.

Everyone around us shushed me into silence. Ayden looked at me and smirked as he whispered, "That's how."

My cheeks heated for being quieted in a movie theater. I cursed Ayden for having made me do such a thing. I despised being the bad guy.

Our movie finished and I hit his arm as soft as I could once we left the theater. "Was that necessary?"

"Yes, because it was funny. That is what we do in this relationship." He flashed me a smile.

I narrowed my eyes, flipping my fingers in his hand and squeezing tight. "It'll be really funny soon, won't it?" I had some ideas in mind on how I could embarrass him in public.

A confused expression appeared on his face while his eyebrows tilted inward and his nose scrunched up. I gave him an innocent smile of mine and walked along the edge of the curb.

The day was beginning to bloom in all its glory. White and pink flowers filled the trees with their beauty, falling to the ground as if they were snow. The breeze was gentle, sending my hair every which way.

I balanced myself along the curb of the sidewalk, still holding Ayden's hand if anything happened. "I used to wear heels all the time. You think I would have balance by now." I laughed a little and glanced at him. "But I've been barefoot for over a year, so it's bound to happen." I pushed hair from my face, pulling strands out of my mouth.

Puffy, white clouds floated through the sky like ducks on the water. The sky was a lighter shade of blue compared to the oceans. They said the ocean was blue due to the reflection of the blue sky that hung above it. I didn't know how true that could be, but the ocean did change with the weather. However, blue was still a dominant color in its depths.

I lost my step and stumbled off the curb. An arm wrapped around my waist, pulling me away from the street. "I always have to catch you. I thought you were supposed to be saving me?" Ayden chuckled in a low tone beside my ear.

A deep breath escaped my lips and I patted his arms that were still enveloped around my torso. "I am but it's also an equal team effort. You're a man. Act like it."

He pretended to be offended. "Angel, this is a new age. We don't do gender roles." He scoffed in a playful manner.

I let out a laugh as I regained my balance. "I died a year ago and I'm also still involved with humans, so I know." I pecked him on the cheek, testing out the PDA.

"That was the wrong spot." He pointed to his lips.

A smile formed on my face. "You have to come down here. I'm no ballerina in pointe shoes." I gestured for him to lower himself to my height.

He bent his knees a little and I kissed him on the lips. "Much better." It was a delicious kiss, one filled with candy and chocolate. That's what I saw in my mind every time our lips connected.

He gripped my wrist and pulled me back to him when I tried to walk away. He continued to plant kisses on every inch of my lips, the very being of who I was.

"Eliana?" my name echoed in the tone of a man's voice behind me.

Ayden and I ended our kiss early and turned our eyes on the man, a lump forming in my throat. My heart began to beat at a rapid speed, threatening to burst from my chest. My stomach tried to claw its way up my esophagus. As I breathed out his name, my voice became shaky and hoarse, "Liam."

He was taken back by the fact that I stood here without a scar on my neck. What he didn't know was that I had died and I had no heartbeat to this day. I just happened to be an angel.

Ayden wrapped his arms around me in one quick movement at the mention of Liam's name. He knew. "What do you want from us?" I'd spent so much of my time protecting him from evil. He was now returning the favor. We both knew I had no energy or confidence to go against Liam. The shock overpowered me, dragging me down into the pit of anguish.

He put his hands up in defense as if we threatened to cut off his family bits. "Can we talk somewhere privately?"

"No," Ayden answered in a cold tone.

Grabbing my hand, he led me down the street, away from the scariest monster of my past. We arrived back at his apartment and locked the door just in case Liam had followed us. I could never trust him.

We both knew this required a talk now that Ayden knew Liam was confirmed a free murderer.

I began pacing as my eyes scanned the room. "He knows I'm here. He's the very person who slit my throat and now I must face him again. How do I explain coming back from the dead?" I stopped, shooting Ayden a worried look.

He snickered. "You don't. You don't owe this wanker a single explanation. He murdered you and your best friend. Avoid him. He's nothing but a demon." I'd never seen Ayden look this enraged before. It'd been so long since I saw the red rush to his ears. His green eyes darkened, releasing the secrets of what he was capable of.

As I sat down on the couch, I struggled to hold back the tears. I refused to let him have my sorrow. "I just can't believe he's still walking. He killed us. Is he ever going to get put away? Does the justice system even care about Selene?" I knew the answer. The justice system didn't give a shit about any of us.

He pulled me into his chest, stroking my gold hair as he whispered sweet things to calm me down. "It's okay. You're happy now and that's what matters. Selene is happy wherever she is. You both are free from his power." He started to rock me like a baby.

I swallowed, a hatred icing over the inside of my stomach. "Nobody will ever put him away at this rate. He needs to pay. He has to go to prison." I lifted my head. "Ayden, we have to expose Liam for who he really is. It's up to us now."

"Whoa, Angel, we can't do that. Where would we even begin? We wouldn't know how to solve a crime." He shook his head to dismiss my idea a little too quickly.

I grasped his hands, using them to warm up the coolness within my body. "You have to do it because I have a death certificate. I'll guide you through it. I will teach you every step of the way. I need you to put him behind bars. He killed Selene." That wasn't enough to get

Ayden into crime-solving. There would be one person he'd do it for. "He killed *me*."

Ayden's eyes conjured up emotions of fury and desolation. He squeezed my hands, shaking his head from the thoughts running rampant inside. "I'm in. He must go away, no matter the cost. Breaking into someone's place is not the worst thing I've ever done." He placed a kiss blanketed with heartache, reeling us back in from the intense decision we'd just agreed upon.

I rested against his shoulder while the horrifying scene of Selene's murder played inside my head. "We need to find the murder weapon. That'll be our best shot. It'll have his fingerprints and be linked with our deaths, leading the police right to him without any denial. I can go into his apartment and retrieve it. He'd never be able to see me because I can disappear from the human eye."

"How will it be evidence after a year?" he asked.

"Because police know this stuff. I don't know all the technicalities of it, but they'll figure it out. It's been a whole year since he killed us. I can't begin to think about it but there won't be much left behind by our murders. This will be difficult to find after such a long time but I'm going to do anything to bring him down." I wrapped my arms around his neck, holding onto him for comfort.

He placed a small kiss on my forehead. "We will figure this out. If he's a serial killer, he can't stop. He must have trophies of some sort or even a signature they can trace back to him."

I slid my arms from his neck and down his chest, gripping the fabric of his shirt. "That's a good idea. It's a start."

He helped me off the couch and guided me to his room. "Okay, so here's what we are going to do. You search his apartment. After this, we see where we are with any evidence. If we have it, we will go to the police. If we don't, we will have to check on any other recent killings similar to yours."

He attempted to help me get his clothes off my body.

I pushed his hands away before the shirt and shorts came off. "I need you to turn around."

"Angel," he whined.

"Ayden, turn around." I narrowed my eyes at him until he followed my orders.

I removed everything on me until not a single article of clothing was left. I picked up my angel dress and pulled it over my head. I glanced back at him and widened my eyes. "Were you watching me?"

He rubbed his neck. "Maybe. You can't change with me right here. It's too tempting not to look at you."

"Oh my gosh, I'm dating a pervert," I muttered, shaking my head in annoyance.

"You knew that when you started dating me." He smiled with pride. "And yes, Angel, your body is very stunning to eyes like mine." My cheeks flushed and I didn't dare say a word. He came closer and put his hands on my shoulders, brushing away the silly moments. "Let's do this."

He leaned in as he pulled my waist closer to his, connecting our lips as one. We both relished this moment, taking our time to share another kiss. I grabbed onto his neck, surprised that this hadn't cost me my job. Maybe *Liam* was behind the reason.

Ayden put an inch of space between us, whispering, "A kiss for good luck."

He stayed behind in the car while I approached the building. The vehicle was parked far out so that Liam wouldn't be able to suspect a thing.

I closed my eyes, a tingling sensation coursing through my veins as my body disguised itself from the world. I became the air, blending in with everything around me in an instant.

I walked up the cold cement steps, getting closer to the front door. I stopped in front of it, staring at the navy-blue. It was dark and ominous. It was icy and vicious, just like the man who lived here.

As I stepped through the door, a force passed through me like the strong wind against my bones. I scanned the apartment, looking around for anything that could present itself as evidence. I started with the laundry, then moved to the drawers, and tried everything else I could think of.

Nothing stood out. I hadn't carried much with me at the time except the glasses on my face.

I kept searching for anything, checking hiding places that Liam never thought I knew of. I spotted something in the back corner of his closet. Closets held so many secrets, and his could become his downfall. I grabbed them from the top shelf, admiring the black rims and one missing lens. They had still been in his possession and now I had something against him to lock him away.

Hurrying to the door, I made a bowl with the skirt of my dress and dropped the glasses inside. This was the one method that could make them vanish into thin air, enough to pass through the door with me. I left the building and rushed down the steps.

I ran back to the car, turning off the invisible switch within my soul. I waved the glasses in the air, attracting Ayden's attention. "I got something!" I shouted.

I got inside the car with a giant smile plastered on my face. "I have something against him." As my eyes landed on Ayden, my metaphorical heart stopped beating. Time slowed to a near stop. My mind was having a difficult time functioning at all.

"Have something against me?" Liam chuckled as he held the silver blade against Ayden's throat.

"Liam, you don't have to do this." I twisted my body in his direction.

He glanced at Ayden and back at me. "I do." He looked at the wings behind me. "You're going to mess up everything if I don't do this." He sighed as if he were the victim and not the monster.

"Liam, if you do this, we will make sure you pay and it's going to be so much worse than prison and death row." Tears filled at the brim of my lid but didn't dare spill over.

I averted my eyes from Liam and got lost in the forest ones before me. I was slow to reach over and squeeze his hand. "Ayden, look at me. Don't let him get to you. That's his game." His Adam's apple bobbed up and down and I couldn't deny the fear that was swirling inside his head.

Intertwining our fingers, I said in a quiet voice, "I love you, Ayden Dyer."

His eyes spoke for him, and I knew without a doubt in my mind that he loved me just the same. Nothing could tear that apart.

Liam chuckled but nothing humorous or joyful laced his tone. "How cute, you think this will work? *Wrong.*" He sliced the blade across Ayden's skin, opening it up for blood to spill down his chest.

"No!" I buried my head into Ayden's shoulder, allowing the tears to pour out. "Come back to me, Ayden." I locked his fingers tightly in mine as the choking sounds slowed until silence filled the air.

While Liam was distracted by my pain, I ripped the blade from his hand, shoving the knife into his stomach as the rage controlled every piece of my soul. "This is for killing Selene!" I pushed him back against the back seat as he coughed up his own blood. "This is for killing me." I climbed into the back and pulled it out of his stomach. The blood poured out like a glass of milk. I lifted it above him and drove it into his chest. "This is for killing the only man I've ever loved."

The door to my right opened. I covered my eyes a bit, slowly climbing out of the car. I noticed the blood that now stained my hands and dress, tainting the purity I assumed I once was. "He deserved it. I swear he did." I gazed up, ready to explain everything to the police officer or witness.

My curiosity piqued as I looked back at the body of Liam, studying my own chaotic doing. His finger twitched, releasing the last of his movements as his life drained from him.

The English accent caught my attention, causing me to forget about Liam's entire existence. "He did, Angel. He deserved every bit of it." Ayden's white wings were larger than mine as they spread out behind him. Then he pulled me into his chest, embracing my dread and agony as he placed his lips against my hair. "He deserved to die for every heart he broke and *every* life he stole."

Here's a sneak peek at
Beauty of a Burning Flame
by *Monica Shantel*

COVENANT

The blood seeping out of Ayden's neck haunted my mind, keeping me locked in a place of agony. The apologetic look in his eyes stuck with me forever, even long after he made it into Heaven. We were together, but I could never move past the sensitivities I was forever tied to after watching the man I love die right in front of me. That kind of feeling could never be replicated.

"Angel?" Ayden whispered in my ear not to disturb anyone around us.

I gave him my best smile, easing his fears. "I'm doing great." I needed to focus my pain on the pleasures of today. I would not let suffering burn away the commitment I made to Ayden when I told him *I do.*

Flowers littered the clouds as gentle music drifted through the air to the beat of joy. What set the mood was the lightness of the atmosphere and the openness of every angel present. Not an ounce of sorrow would be able to ruin this event. The moment was soft and romantic but also blissful and forgiving.

I had been so worried about falling in love and losing my job, yet not a single soul here judged us for our promise to one another.

Ayden placed a small kiss on my forehead while we danced to the sound of a harp playing, careful not to move fast. "Never did I imagine I would be here." He chuckled as he scanned the area, examining everyone who was studying us.

I rested my head against his chest, letting out a small sigh of content. "But aren't you so glad you are? We get to spend forever together now." As cheesy as it sounded, it was also a dream come true.

His arms had been wrapped around my waist as we swayed to the rhythm of the melody. "I wouldn't trade it for a second chance at life." He lifted my chin with his finger and placed his sweet lips on mine. He pulled away, spinning me around and pulling me back to his chest all in one slow motion. This moment couldn't be ruined by a single *worry*. I was in love and our relationship had been welcomed now.

He grabbed my hand and kissed my fingers as he stared at them with curiosity. "We finally get to do the dirty."

"Ayden." I laughed as I shook my head. It didn't surprise me that he was looking forward to getting naked and doing sexual things.

"What? It's not wrong to talk about it. We are married and wedded couples can want to have sex with each other. I will proudly admit I am so ready to do that tonight." He pushed some hair behind my ear.

"Me too. I've never had it, but I can say I'm ecstatic to physically connect with you. There is no guilt or shame in those words." I released a giggle, gazing into his mesmerizing eyes. "I love you, Ayden."

A smile formed as he kissed my nose. "I love you, too, Angel."

"Elli?" I heard a female's voice echo behind me.

I turned back and gasped at the face that belonged to the one person who called me by that name. My eyes didn't seem to deceive me, and I prayed it was true. Where had she been since I'd died? In one breath, I whispered, "*Selene*."

I hadn't spoken to her since the day she died and seeing her before me now evoked emotions I could never conjure up on my own. There had been a hole in my heart when I heard about her death, and that missing piece was now being repaired as we spoke through our eyes. She was calling me over.

Ayden gave me a reassuring nod.

I followed Selene over to a table. "I can't believe you're here. I haven't seen you all this time," my words cracked as they rolled off my tongue.

"I'm sorry. I guess I just got caught up in things after realizing Liam killed me. It's not exactly the best feeling in the world when your boyfriend murders you." She lowered her head down to see the clouds beneath our feet.

I pulled her into my arms, offering her my comfort. "I'm so sorry. I wish I could've done something. I missed you so much after seeing what happened. You were my only friend and I was just lost without you. After your death, I barely found my way back."

She pulled away from our hug and smiled a bit. "It's okay now, Elli. I'm here. I want you to know that."

I wiped a tear from my cheek and nodded. "Of course."

"I heard what happened. Liam killed you, too, huh?"

"He did. He killed you. He killed me. He killed Ayden. It's horrendous. Justice will never be served."

"Tell me more about Ayden, please. I want to know about this boy who captured your heart." She replaced the sorrow on her face with a smile.

I looked back at my husband, our hearts connecting as one even without beating with life. "He's amazing." I turned to Selene again. "This man was a tough one. I worked hard to change him and save his soul, but he refused. I learned so much about him. I've seen his darkest parts and I've seen what makes his face light up with joy. He even looks adorable when he's baking."

"Baking, huh?"

"A bad boy who loves to bake. Who's ever heard of such a thing? I guess you don't normally expect a man like him to be good at something like that. He reunited with his family. He wasn't a good guy, but he has become a better person. He never gave up smoking but now that we're dead, he doesn't have to smoke. No smoking, drinking... He gave up sex before dating Sunny. That is a big deal for a man." I chuckled.

She grinned. "Wow, Elli, you've really made an impact on him. He really loves you, doesn't he?"

"I sure hope so. He begged for me to come back when I left. He apologized for everything he's done, and he hasn't done it since. He really changed. He returned what he stole. He's waiting until our honeymoon, for me."

"You mean..."

"Yes."

"That is attractive. A man who has self-control is perfect. I mean, he's no virgin and that's unfortunate but the fact that he has given up sex until your honeymoon... That takes some self-control. I know you were the type of girl who wanted to wait. I'm glad you found someone who makes you feel complete." She stood as Ayden came over.

He faced her. "Selene, I'm guessing? Angel has talked a lot about you. She's said some bad things," he joked.

I playfully hit him. "I did not." I got up but never matched their heights. "Selene, this is Ayden, my newly wedded husband. As you can tell, this is our wedding."

"Yes, congratulations. I'm glad someone loves Elli the way she deserves to be loved." Selene eyed him.

He wasn't at all intimidated. "Yes, I do. It was a bumpy road. We went to Hell and back but now we've reached Heaven. I don't mean any of this metaphorically either." He lifted both eyebrows with a tiny smirk displayed on his lips.

She shot us both a surprised look. "You went to Hell? What was that like?"

"Awful. Endless torture. Pain. Trust me, you never want to go there. I thought I was going to die, and I'm already six feet under and thousands of feet above," I said.

Eyes darting between us, she showed us pitiful expressions. "I'm so sorry."

"Never mind that. Why are you showing up now?" I asked.

Selene went silent for a moment and looked down at the clouds stuffed under her feet. Then she lifted her gaze to meet ours. With a smile, she shook her head. "Don't worry about that. I'll tell you guys soon. Enjoy your wedding. You deserve this."

Her eyes admired the decor surrounding us all. Lights were strung about throughout the tree branches while flowers attracted the eye to the center of every table. The cloths on each one were white but the chairs circling were black to represent Ayden and I coming together. The centerpieces were made up of red roses to symbolize our love.

A white dress flowed from my shoulders to my bare feet. My hair was loose as it always had been, waves free to be themselves. Nothing else enhanced my appearance and I didn't need it to.

Ayden's clothes were just as casual as mine. He wore brown shorts with a black shirt that suited his figure in a complimentary way. His hair had been left ruffled and his beard kept neat. Everything about his appearance turned me on in ways that made me blush.

I peered at him and grabbed his hand, intertwining our fingers. "You should try some of the desserts. Ayden baked them himself."

He puffed out his chest, wearing a proud look. "I did. I'm going to make a great husband."

Selene glanced at the desserts table and nodded a bit. "I was told that you baked."

Ayden walked over to the table, taking me with him as our fingers stayed locked together. He grabbed a cupcake and held it up. "It's something I enjoy." His mischievous eyes met my lips.

Selene came over and picked up a cupcake, a bright smile on her face. "I'll be the judge of that." She took a big bite. "Wow, this is good," she said with her mouth full.

"Well, you must try the fruitcake," Ayden said as he gave Selene a look.

Her eyebrows creased downward as she tilted her head. "Fruitcake? No cake?"

I chewed on my lip. "Ayden's from England and it was important to me that a tradition from his country was incorporated. In England, they have fruitcakes at the wedding. Besides, we have cupcakes in place of a cake. I think it suffices just fine." I glanced at Ayden as my heart *fluttered*.

My thoughts turned sour in an instant as a realization hit me. I lost him as I did Justin. I was beginning to question if I was losing my ability to be a good guardian angel.

"Time for the bouquet toss! The bride carried it, now the groom gets to pass it on," one of the female angels told everyone.

Ayden looked over at me. "Wait, males toss the bouquet? What did I sign up for?"

I admired the disapproval on his face with the approval on my own. "You signed up to toss the bouquet. Go on." I pushed him over and he grumbled in response.

He grabbed the bouquet from the angel's hand and peeked at the male angels. They gathered into a crowd and Ayden turned his back to them. He threw the bouquet back, but the men ran.

I chuckled, watching Ayden's expression. He was thoroughly confused by the reaction to the bouquet and came over to me, pointing in their direction with his thumb. "They really don't want to be tied down, do they?"

"Angel weddings are different from human weddings." I slipped my hand in his. "And up here, we really do have forever."

He pulled me into his chest and kissed me. It was as short and sweet as I was. He rested his chin on top of my head, taking my attention away from everything that threatened our happiness. "I cannot wait until the honeymoon."

I laid my head against his chest and laughed. "We've got that by now. You want sex."

"You're my wife now. I'm allowed to want it."

"You guys look so adorable together," Selene said beside us.

We pulled away and looked at her.

"I'm glad that you guys are happy, despite Liam trying to ruin that when he killed both of you." A hint of regret had laced her words.

"We are. Isn't that right, Ayden?" I looked up at him, patting his chest.

He chuckled and shook his head. "I'm not happy."

"You don't mean that." He had to be joking. He wouldn't have married me if he wasn't happy. He was not shy of expressing his negativity towards anything.

He placed his free hand on my cheek and kissed my forehead. "Nope." He peered over at Selene.

My eyes lingered on the roses and one word flashed through my mind—*crimson*. Our lives had consisted of so much blood. Now the color stained our flowers—meant to inspire peace and devotion. Again, images entered my brain and refused to let go. Its hold was firm and triple-knotted. I could never unsee the moment I witnessed Ayden's life get severed. But Liam was dead, wasn't he?

Selene decided to try a piece of the fruit cake, using her fingers to shove it into her mouth. "This is a fantastic cake."

Ayden's lips curved upwards. "I know." He held my hand tightly and the three of us ventured over to a table and sat down.

I leaned against Ayden and looked at my best friend. "I never thought I'd see you again and now you're at my wedding. I'm glad. It makes my life feel complete. Well, I'm not actually alive but it makes me feel complete either way. I know I died young, but I still got my happy ending. That's what matters."

He rubbed my arm, his warmth sticking for years to come. "The journey was rough, but it was worth it."

I lifted my eyes to meet his, smiling to hide my fears. "Of course. I got you in the end."

Her eyes followed our every move. "Elli found love. This is quite a sight to see. I never imagined it'd be this joyful but I'm glad it is. Who thought it was going to happen this way? I don't think anyone could've guessed."

Ayden moved some hair from my face, pushing it behind my ear. "Well, every love story is different. Ours just happened to involve Heaven and Hell. That's got to be some kind of normal."

"Who wants normal? Normal is boring," I said, sitting up.

Ayden started to get out of his chair. "I'm going to get more cupcakes."

I grabbed his shoulder, pushing him back onto his seat. I stood up and smiled. "Let me get us both cupcakes. I want to try them." I walked over to the table and picked up some. I put them on a plate so I could get more than just two. When it came to his baking, I made it a habit to indulge in the delicacy of his passion.

I glanced back at the table where the two I loved most had been sitting. My heart almost started beating again at the sight of Ayden laughing. It made my day when he was the definition of euphoria.

He deserved to be nothing but gleeful.

Turning my head slightly to the right, I saw Selene and noticed she was laughing, too. My best friend and husband were getting along so well. Could I not ask for more? I never imagined this day would come and yet I was wrong. My mood was beyond fulfilled. This was my wedding day, and my best friend had returned to me.

I headed back and took a seat between them both, placing the plate of cupcakes between Ayden and I. "What are you two laughing about?"

Selene took a cupcake from the plate and took off the wrapper, biting into it. She chewed and swallowed, her laughter echoing into the sky once more. "Your husband is hilarious. He was telling me about the time you two were throwing flour at each other."

Ayden nodded as he faced her. "Her face was priceless."

"I don't know if Elli has ever had fun before you came along." She continued to let out uncontrolled giggles.

His eyes landed on me before he kissed my cheek. "I think I'm the one who introduced her to what the word fun even means."

My cheeks flushed as I tried to hide my embarrassment. I didn't want them talking about my silly moments. "Let's talk about something else, shall we?"

Ayden brought up a subject I wanted to bury in Hell. "Selene, you didn't want to tell us why you came here but I think it's time we know what's going on. Don't sugarcoat it." The tone in his voice was enough to make anyone obey his commands. As much as I dreaded the news she bore, I knew my husband was right. We could walk on eggshells for the rest of eternity if given the chance.

Her smile fell. What she carried with her wasn't easy to throw around. She was uncertain—hesitant about what would come next. Despite how she felt, she eyed us both, waiting for our reactions. "About that happy ending you guys thought you earned, I'm here to tell you that it's not coming just yet. Liam has other plans.

"Other plans?" I glanced at Ayden before my eyes returned to her. What did that mean? He had plans from beyond the grave? Impossible.

She hesitated, stuttering. "He's... He's s-still alive."

Looking for a twisted what-if version?
Here's a sneak peek at **Grave of a Fiery Poison**
by *Monica Shantel*

(Grave of a Fiery Poison can be read after the trilogy, or in place of
books two and three. Choose your ending.)

ALPHA

S creams pierced the sky, burning every inch of the forest surrounding me. I pushed my feet harder—faster. My skirt was bunched up in my fists as I followed the fallen angel to the highway of Hell.

Levi.

"Ayden!" I screamed again, getting caught by a branch and tumbling to my knees. "Let him go!"

That damned smirk on Levi's face grew as he held Ayden by the throat. "There are no happy endings around here." He jumped down the stairs that had opened up in the ground, dragging Ayden behind him.

"No!" I hurried to my feet and ran over as the opening disappeared.

My entire world shattered at that moment. The moment Ayden disappeared from my arms. The moment he'd been taken by a fallen angel. The moment the only man I loved had been dragged to Hell.

After his brutal demise, his apartment had been cleared out and put up for rent as if his memory hadn't tainted the walls of that structure. Anyone who had been bold enough to consider living where a man's life spiraled downward would still be haunted by such nightmares to come.

Not of my doing—no—but of *his*.

His taste still lingered on my lips as his scent began to fall away from my form the way they'd torn him from my soul. What had my soul been without his? Nothing but yellow police tape that reminded the public to keep their distance. I became caution.

As hard as I tried to keep my mind from wandering, I conjured up all the terrifying things they'd inflict down below the earth. The scorching heat that forever blended with a stinging nobody could shake.

I had to do something. I had to save him.

Again.

Nowhere to turn to. That had been my fate. Not his family, nor mine. Nor Selene. Not a single soul was available for me to confide in all my darkest fears.

What would become of Ayden? All alone, begging for me to save him the way he did months ago. Only this time I could not come to his rescue. I could not take on his pain the way I had when I first fled.

How could I get down there and pull him out without getting caught?

Sure, angels could not be killed for we were already deceased. However, we were at great risk of harm when we were at the mercy of Lucifer himself. It was not a place any angel, or sane human wished to be. My boyfriend was being chained up and tortured endlessly until he bled out on the stones, sizzling like a strip of bacon in the morning sun. Reliving that kind of pain was a far worse fate than death.

"Don't look so glum, Elli."

I whipped around to face the man who brought my world to the ground. "Don't you dare call me that, Liam."

He tilted his head. "Why, is that not your name?"

Eliana Bree Wilson.

A name I kept hidden from Ayden for months. A select few still knew it, and Liam had been no different. I did not wish to hear my name leave his lips at all. He made it *poisonous*.

But the next words made me want to murder him all over again. "I think I could help you, Elli."

My eyes narrowed as every last buried emotion slithered from the cracks of the graveyard in my bones. "What makes you think you could be of help to me?" As he opened his mouth to respond, I cut him off with, "no, actually, what makes you think I'd even accept your help? You murdered my best friend. You murdered me. You murdered the man I love and now that he's been kidnapped by your friends, you think you can waltz around with an offer? In what delusional world do you think I'm going to ever team up with someone as vile as you?"

Stepping forward, his gaze focused, unwavering, he said, "Because it's simple. Ayden is trapped in Hell, and I'm the one person who has an in with Lucifer himself."

I admitted I wished to stab him all over again. I would have loved to have had the chance to make him feel the way he made me feel just thirty minutes ago.

Terrified. Feeble. Fraught.

"Why?" it came out in a whisper.

His eye gleamed. "Why what?"

To prove to him I wasn't afraid, nor did I allow him to have the power, I closed the distance until our faces waited inches apart. "Why do you want to help me save the very man you just ripped away from me only a half hour before?"

"I don't have much time." He glanced at the sky, his form flickering.

I'd been reminded that his body was lying in Ayden's car, bleeding out. He was supposed to be dead, yet here his soul stood. Blood poured from his abdomen, but not a drop truly stained the earth below our feet.

Was he dying? If he did, would I watch him be sucked down to Hell?

"Your lack of time and piss-poor decisions are not my burdens to bear, Liam. The day you slit Selene's throat, you lost all of my respect."

His lip curved upward to one side. "Did I? Don't be so sure about that. You were all over me. I could see it in your eyes." He reached up, his fingers brushing my chin. "You're just upset that you weren't smart enough to catch on before I tore you from your body."

I opened my mouth to curse him out, but before I had the opportunity, his soul disappeared. Wherever he went, I couldn't be entirely sure. Regardless, I yelled out to release all pent-up rage inside me.

I remembered that week leading up to my death so vividly, and I had never once saw Liam as a potential date. I'd never been attracted to him.

Falling to my knees, I clawed at the grass, pulling out clumps as I laid my soul to the forest floor in hopes I'd be able to hear him from under the earth's crust. "Ayden, I'm coming for you."

In what universe had it been fair that I found love only to lose him to Hell? To Liam? To Levi?

None.

Not an ounce of it made sense.

Slowly rising to my feet, my wings fanned out behind me as I screamed to the skies. Every tragedy that painted my name would go down in history, and I'd be the one to set the world on fire if it meant I'd finally have him back in my arms.

If I had to unleash the monsters of Hell, so be it.

It wasn't going to end like this, and I'd be damned to ever accept a fate where the man I loved suffered at my hands. All because he'd had the bitter pleasure of meeting the very beast who'd taken everyone I've ever cared about.

No more nice girl. No more Eliana Wilson, or Angel.

For him, I'd do whatever it took.

I wandered the clearing, but the portal never opened. I inspected every rock and branch for some secretive opening, yet nothing came about. Fire spread through my veins every second that passed in which Ayden suffered their wrath.

If someone had asked me to take their life, I wouldn't have hesitated. Not for a second, in fact.

The venom that traveled my soul spilled out through the crevices of promises once kept—now shattered. I'd beg for forgiveness once I was certain he was safe in my arms.

I hadn't spent the last nine months fighting for his soul just to succeed and lose it all in the span of thirty minutes.

Despicable. That's exactly what the fallen angels were.

Nothing about me felt the same, but it still felt pure. Pure of hatred.

We'd been told never to hold that amount of fury within us, but I could certainly spare enough of it for the very creatures who'd done nothing but leave my afterlife in shambles.

My petal torn from my stem.

A piece of me gone.

The only soulmate ever made for me just stolen.

Eliana didn't get second chances. Finding him even in my death had been a miracle all in itself. To get that all to lose it? Unspeakable. I'd never find another Ayden, nor would I want to.

Once upon a time I swore never to fall for him. He'd been nothing but trouble.

It turned out I reveled in disorder. I was a guardian angel, and I'd be nothing without it.

Breaking promises seemed to be something I'd been a pro at. It'd be a lie if I didn't admit that, and now that the truth became crystal clear, I'd wear that like a badge.

It'd be what fueled me to bring him back.

The fallen angels hadn't been careful enough, and because of their carelessness, they'd feel whatever I'd been bottling the past nine months while dealing with Ayden's incessant insults.

I would hate to be them.

But more importantly, I'd hate to be Ayden. I had been him when we had been tortured in Hell. When the flames licked our souls and left permanent trauma. The sorrow written in his eyes as he saw the destruction he caused by walking the path he had. The bloody strikes against his back as he cried out, trying as hard as he might to bite back the cries. He had wanted nothing more than to be strong. To prove to me who he was. Not weak, but rather in charge. He believed he deserved such torment. He took it like a man should have, and that had been the moment in which I truly hated him and admired him all in one breath. He proved not only his strength, but how much I loved him and ached without him by my side. Choosing to walk away after our injuries healed was the hardest decision I had to make.

But for us, I made it.

Because without me, he realized how deeply rooted his cravings for me latched on.

I'd grown on him the way he'd fused to my soul.

So this time around, I'd save him again. I'd take great pride in being his guardian once again.

Nothing was sweeter than revenge, best served with the scorching of a female's rage.

Ayden had taught me well.

My downfall.

Also my mentor.

And Liam? The asshat truly believed that I'd team up with him. Never. Not in a million years, nor if everyone vanished and he were the only human left.

Human—if he stayed that way.

Given his current state, everything had been on the line.

I'd never lose sight of Ayden, either. Being immortal gave me all eternity to fight for him. Nothing to truly hold me back except the monstrous beings Lucifer called his pets.

His bright green eyes stuck in my mind, begging me to save him. He could argue that he didn't need rescuing because it wasn't his role to be the damsel. Once he'd become vulnerable to me, he proved that to be a façade. He'd always put on that front so nobody saw the broken man shouting for someone to hold him tight. To kiss his head and promise everything would be okay.

Now he didn't believe it ever would be.

I'd let them take him. I'd allowed him to go.

As the vexation towards them grew, so did the resentment of my own failures.

Ayden Dyer was *mine*.

They couldn't have him. They couldn't have his laughter, nor his smiles. They couldn't taste his sweets, nor steal the beating of his heart. Everything he did had been made for me. I'd go down there and when they witnessed a glimpse of what I was capable of, I'd tear them apart and relish their pleas. I'd never show them any mercy.

They gave me all the permission in the world when they took the other half of me.

I'd run my fingers through his hair again. Stroke his beard, even. Savor the taste of white chocolate raspberries lingering in every kiss.

I'd marry him and give him all of me if he'd allow that.

One thing was always certain, despite how hard he tried to deny it and how hard he fought.

Ayden Dyer belonged to me and nobody else.

Not Sunny. Not Liam. Not the fallen angels.

Having everyone believe he was never mine had been the biggest mirage we put on for the world, but we all knew down in the dark corner of his heart, he had never been anyone else's.

Like honey, I'd be *dripping* from his teeth.

Even in Hell.

They couldn't take what was mine and live to see the nightfall.

I'd never allow it.

And for that reason alone, the world would burn in their wake.

Acknowledgements

Thanks to my mom for always supporting my writing, even as a valid career. Thanks to my brother who's asked questions and made me think about my plots, and to the other family members who have picked up my books just to say they were proud of me.

To Ashly for always supporting me.

And thank you to Cass for pointing out the rights and wrongs of this book to help me make it the best it would be. This book needed all your help. You brought this trilogy to life.

ABOUT THE AUTHOR

Monica Shantel has always had an interest in artistic and creative hobbies of sorts, including but not limited to: drawing, crafting, graphic design, and painting. Although all she has is a high school diploma under her belt, she is not new to the writing community. At the age of twelve, she began building stories to escape reality and find hope in life once again. Her debut novel is Beauty of a Crimson Soul. Along the same genre, she writes dark tales of mythical romance which only add more to the growing fantasy worlds inside her head.

9 781960 696106